P9-CDE-730

A HOLE
IN THE
UNIVERSE

ALSO BY
MARY
McGARRY
MORRIS

Vanished

A Dangerous Woman

Songs in Ordinary Time

Fiona Range

MARY
McGARRY
MORRIS

A HOLE
IN THE
UNIVERSE

VIKING

VIKING
Published by the Penguin Group
Penguin Group (USA) Inc., 375 Hudson Street, New York, New York 10014, U.S.A.
Penguin Books Ltd, 80 Strand, London WC2R 0RL, England
Penguin Books Australia Ltd, 250 Camberwell Road, Camberwell, Victoria 3124, Australia
Penguin Books Canada Ltd, 10 Alcorn Avenue, Toronto, Ontario, Canada M4V 3B2
Penguin Books India (P) Ltd, 11 Community Centre, Panchsheel Park, New Delhi—110 017, India
Penguin Books (N.Z.) Ltd, Cnr Rosedale and Airborne Roads, Albany, Auckland, New Zealand
Penguin Books (South Africa) (Pty) Ltd, 24 Sturdee Avenue, Rosebank, Johannesburg 2196, South Africa

Penguin Books Ltd, Registered Offices: 80 Strand, London WC2R 0RL, England

First published in 2004 by Viking Penguin, a member of Penguin Group (USA) Inc.

10   9   8   7   6   5   4   3   2   1

PUBLISHER'S NOTE: This is a work of fiction. Names, characters, places, and incidents either are the product of the author's imagination or are used fictitiously, and any resemblance to actual persons, living or dead, business establishments, events, or locales is entirely coincidental.

LIBRARY OF CONGRESS CATALOGING-IN-PUBLICATION DATA
Morris, Mary McGarry.
    A hole in the universe / Mary McGarry Morris.
      p.   cm.
    ISBN 0-670-03288-3 (alk. paper)
    1. Ex-convicts—Fiction.   2. Self-actualization (Psychology)—Fiction.
    I. Title.
    PS3563.O874454H65   2004
    813'.54—dc21   2003053761

This book is printed on acid-free paper. ∞

Printed in the United States of America
Designed by Nancy Resnick

To Michael,
with whom all things are possible:
goodness, friendship, and such long love as this.
Thank you for your brilliance, your strength,
and the joy of your wit.

A HOLE
IN THE
UNIVERSE

CHAPTER 1

"The way to look at it is, that was somebody else, some eighteen-year-old kid with the same name. It wasn't you." His brother, Dennis, sat at the foot of the bed, watching him in the mirror.

"Who was it, then?" Gordon Loomis squinted through the blur of sweat. The jug-eared face was the same, bland, the deep chin cleft its only discernible feature. He dragged his starched sleeve across his forehead. He still wasn't used to the heat of a proper room. The closeness of his brother's voice seemed the only air to breathe.

"You know what I mean!" Dennis said. "And besides, people forget. I mean, twenty-five years! That's like what? A lifetime ago when you think of it. Nobody's the same person they were then, just like you're not."

"But I am. I'm still the same," Gordon said. His thick fingers struggled with the tiny collar button. Three hundred and fifty pounds, six and a half feet tall. Just as big then—"Loomer," because he took up so much space. Because of the way he leaned so close to hear. Because he never knew quite what to do with himself or where he belonged.

"No, you're not! For one thing, you used to be a complete slob, and now look." Dennis laughed, pointing at Gordon's hairbrush, the comb placed in the exact center row of bristles. "What do you call this? Obsessive-compulsive? Anal retentive?" He meant the rows of coins stacked heads up, the sleek black flashlight, and still in its box the blue tie Dennis had bought for him to wear today. Gordon had laid it all out last night. Some things he could control. Most he could not, like this job interview.

He took deep breaths to block out the nasally thrum of Dennis's voice. "I don't get it. Lisa and I had you all set up in Mom and Dad's room. So why'd you go and move your stuff in here? It's the smallest room in the house."

"It's my bedroom," Gordon grunted, chin raised and straining, the button almost fastened.

"*Was* your bedroom. Was—twenty-five years ago. But life moves on, Gordon! Right? It does, doesn't it?" His brother's pained smile rose like a welt on his lean, boyish face.

Gordon knew better than to answer. His younger brother was as thin-skinned and mercurial as he was generous. It couldn't have been easy all these years with his greatest desire, Gordon's freedom, so fraught with expectations of disaster. In the week that Gordon had been home, Dennis had criticized his every decision. His brother's confidence in him was strongest with visitors' Plexiglas between them.

"It's so damn dark back here." Dennis looked out the window into the leaf-tented patch of shade, the old tree's crown grown bigger than the yard. Now Gordon would hear how he should have gone to California: he'd have a fresh start there, complete anonymity.

"Damn!" he muttered, and Dennis started toward him just as the button went through.

"You're so nervous!" Dennis handed him the tie. "It's just an interview. What's there to be nervous about?"

Gordon turned his damp collar over the tie. The interview was too soon. He wasn't ready. Freedom was like this new suit Dennis had bought for him. It might look a perfect fit, but it felt as if it belonged to someone else. Gordon tried to knot the tie, then yanked it apart. "I never could do this!" He threw it down on the bureau.

"C'mon, big guy," Dennis coaxed, slipping it back around Gordon's neck. "Hey! After all you've been through, this'll be a piece of cake! You'll do fine!"

Gordon glared until Dennis stepped away. His hands trembled as he fastened the tie himself.

"Knot's too big," Dennis said, shaking his head.

Gordon pulled tighter, his face a mask again, eyes half-lidded to this speck in the mirror, not a man, but a point in time, that was all. No more than a moment. A moment. And then it would pass without pain, without anger or loss.

"Now what'd you do? You got the wrong end too long." Dennis chuckled. "Here, let me." He reached out.

Gordon stiffened. "There." He stuffed the longer narrow end into his shirtfront. "You can't even see it."

"No!" Dennis howled with dismayed laughter.

"That's the way I always did it," he said.

"Sure, when you were a kid. C'mere!" Dennis was undoing the tie. "We don't have much time left."

Gordon recoiled from the sour intimacy of his brother's breath. According to the corrections manual, each inmate had his own space, a circumference of twenty-four inviolable inches.

"That guy I told you about, Kinnon, my patient?" Dennis murmured with the last loop. "I called last night to double-check, and he said it was all set. He said he'd already laid the ground work. He'd already explained things."

"What things?"

"Things. You know what I mean, the details."

The knot dug into his gullet. Details. The scrapings of flesh—his—gleaned from under her fingernails. The cuts on his enormous arms measured, photographed: the quantifiable proof of her grasping, desperate struggle against the pillow. Details, twenty-five years deep, most like flotsam released in pieces, surfacing through dreams, or snatches from a song, certain smells: the damp sweetness of shampooed hair, or even abrupt silence into which would rise her muffled pleas, soft moans, the last earthly sounds of Janine Walters and male fetus. Kevin.

"He said he explained it all, you know, how young you were and everything," Dennis said as they got into the car.

Everything. Gordon stared out the window. As if it were one of those crazy things kids do? A prank? Just break into a house and kill a sleeping woman. His eyes closed. *"I hope you never forget! I hope every day of your miserable life is a living hell!"* her raw-eyed mother screamed with the verdict. She had wanted him dead.

"So now you just have to show them what a normal, regular guy you really are." Dennis grinned. "Plus, you've got all these letters." The folder between them was thick with testaments to his good behavior and trustworthiness from chaplains, wardens, guards. "The best one though's from Delores."

"What do you mean, from Delores?"

"Her letter. I told you I was going to ask her."

"No, you didn't!"

"Well, I thought I did. I meant to. I must've forgot, that's all. No big deal." Dennis backed into the street, then had to wait while a chunky young woman in a skimpy sundress carried an infant while maneuvering a sagging stroller across the street. Roped onto the stroller was a television set.

"And where the hell do you think she got that?" Dennis sighed and shook his head. "Don't forget: Keep everything locked. Mrs. Jukas said you even leave a window open and they're in like rats."

"You shouldn't have done that. I can't believe you asked Delores without asking me first."

"What? What're you talking about? It's just Delores! What's the big deal?" Dennis said. The minute the woman passed, he hit the gas and raced up the street.

"I don't want her to write a letter." He gripped the door handle. The contents of his stomach rose and fell with the blur of signs, sunstruck glass, cars passing, the honk of a horn. On the way home from Fortley, Dennis had to stop on the highway three times while Gordon dry-heaved alongside the car.

"What're you talking about?" Dennis shouted. "She already did! She wrote it! All it says is how she's known you all your life, and what a decent person you are. You know, things like that."

"No! Take it out!"

"But it's just a letter. She wanted to!" Dennis kept looking over, stunned. "It's not like I put pressure on her or anything. You know how she feels about you."

"No. I don't want it in there." Gordon reached for the file, but Dennis clamped his hand over it.

"Will you tell me why the hell not?"

"Because." He felt breathless, as if he were running up a steep hill. "Because she shouldn't have to have her name mixed up in this." Because he didn't want to owe her any more than he already did for all her letters and visits through the years. He had nothing to give. He had to be careful, careful of everything. More so now than ever before.

"Have her name mixed up in what? What do you mean? She's your friend, that's all."

Gordon groped for the handle to roll down the window, then remembered. It was a button now. "Can you slow down a little?"

"You want to be late?"

"My stomach, it feels funny."

"You're nervous, that's all."

"No, it's riding. The car, I'm still not used to it. It makes me feel sick." Eyes closed, he turned his face to the open window.

"Jesus Christ," Dennis muttered, slowing down. He said no more until they pulled into the Corcopax parking lot. "Oh, and one more thing. The only opening right now's in Human Resources."

"Human Resources? I thought you said laminating. They're not going to hire me for a job like that. Why didn't you tell me? I don't want to do this."

"Look, Gordon, let's get something straight here. I'm doing the best I can. I've got one hell of a busy life. I've got my practice, my family. I've got a million things I could be doing, but right now this is the most important thing. This! Being here! Helping my brother get off to a good start, that's all!"

"I'm sorry." He hung his head.

"You want me to butt out, you just say the word."

"No."

"Because I got so much shit going on right now, I can't begin to tell you," Dennis said with a disgusted sigh.

"I know. I'm sorry. I'm just nervous, that's all. It's just a lot all at once. I mean . . ." No company was going to hire him to work with people. Unable to say it, to give up even that much of himself, he rubbed his face with both hands. All he wanted was to be left alone. In Fortley he'd at least had that.

"Aw, c'mon, Gordo! You're going to do fine!" Dennis assured him as he got out of the car. He handed him the file. "I probably shouldn't get your hopes up, but I think this is a done deal. At least that's the way Kinnon made it sound." He waved, watching a moment, then pulled up alongside as Gordon trudged toward the gleaming glass-and-granite building. "Jesus! You've got to look more confident than that! C'mon, Gordo! Head up! Shoulders back! Go get 'em!"

In the lobby, Gordon slipped Delores's letter from the file into his pocket. All along the way, in the elevator to the third floor, then down the long bright corridor to the personnel office, he could feel people staring at him. Conscious of the sticky-sounding tread with every footstep, he walked quickly, met no one's gaze. He shouldn't have let himself be pushed into this. He wasn't ready. He woke up every morning disoriented to be home in his own room, as frightened as he was grateful to be free. He should have had Dennis come with him. Not into the interview, of course. Just to be close by. But, no. He couldn't always be a burden. As it was, Dennis had canceled three patients to bring him here. So far, every decision had been made for him: his new clothes, the house fixed up and ready, cupboards filled, even orange Popsicles in the freezer because Lisa, Dennis's wife, remembered his saying once how much he missed them. Personnel. His hand closed over the knob.

"Right in there." The receptionist's eyes swept over him. She pointed to the open door. "They're waiting," she said as he hesitated, caught between flight and paralysis. Her chair squeaked as she turned. Not every day she got to see a murderer.

"Mr. Loomis." A delicate woman in a hot-pink suit rose from her desk. After a lifetime of gray, colors came as a shock. As did beauty. Softness. His face reddened with the limp graze of her slender palm. He lowered his eyes to keep from staring at her face.

She said her name. Jamison. Then something about Brown. Who was Brown? He tried to follow her rushed explanation, then saw the bullnecked man in the corner. Mr. Brown would be just sitting in on the interview, a kind of monitoring process, that was all. She seemed extremely anxious that he understand this.

Gordon nodded. "I see. Yes, of course." He wondered how old she was. Or how young. He had no idea, no frame of reference for women. He tried to smile at Mr. Brown, whose emotionless stare never wavered.

"Let's see now." She opened a green folder, ran a glittering pink fingernail down the top sheet. "Your GED. A BS in business administration from Sussex State College." She glanced up. "Did you actually attend the classes?"

"Some."

"What did they do, bring you? I mean, you couldn't just leave the . . . the place, right?"

"The ones I went to, they had them right there. In the beginning. Those were the first classes. The first year. The courses, I mean. The ones everyone takes. Introductory, that is." His tongue swelled in his dry mouth. He kept swallowing. "Well, not everyone takes them. I mean, for the, you know, the ones that are . . ." He rolled his hand to churn up the phrase from the perfectly still, dead air. "Taking the courses."

She nodded, took up her pen.

He was making this easy for her. "Not just potentially dangerous, but inarticulate," she was probably writing.

"The rest were by mail."

"You've had some counseling experience, Mr. Loomis?"

"Counseling experience," he repeated to calm himself. His breathing was the only sound in the room.

"Did you work with any of the other . . ." She paused. "Men who were there with you?"

"No, ma'am. They had professionals for that kind of thing."

"What about peer-group activity? They must have had that kind of interaction. Most places . . . facilities like that do."

"They did. But I didn't. I didn't do that."

"Why not?"

"Because." He squirmed, wringing his hands. Because he hated talking about himself: the misery of it, the emptiness, the dead echo behind every word like footsteps through an endless tunnel. "Mostly I just kept a pretty low profile."

"For twenty-five years?"

"Yes, ma'am."

"But what did you *do*? I mean, how'd you keep busy? You must've done some kind of work." She closed the folder.

"Yes. Of course." He'd worked everywhere, in the library, laundry, kitchen, dining room, infirmary. But mostly in the sign shop. "I was a good worker. I always worked really hard. I like working. I always did."

"Hmm." She looked at her watch. "Well! I guess that about covers it. Unless there's something you'd like to add."

"Just these, I guess." He handed her the file. "They're letters. They're all from people I know. Well, people who know me. And who think I'm a good . . . worker." He'd almost said "person."

She thanked him, put the file into hers. "So what we'll do is go over everything and if something comes up, some position that's compatible with your particular experience, Mr. Loomis, then we'll certainly be in touch," she recited with a dismissive smile as she and Mr. Brown got up. Gordon rose in a panic. He couldn't very well go back to the car after such a short interview. The new suit. Dennis's canceled patients. "Excuse me! Could I just tell you about the sign shop?"

"The sign shop?" She glanced at Mr. Brown.

The prison shop made street signs for cities and towns all over the state. He had been in charge of the enameling process, getting the heat to the right temperature, then baking the signs. Well, in a manner of speaking, baking them, he added in a thin voice. "I did it for almost ten years."

"Really? Well, that's a long time." She was at the door again. "Well, in any event, Mr. Loomis, thank you. Thank you for coming."

"But I don't even want Human Resources!" he blurted before she could leave. "I'm much better with my hands. I mean, I'm quite conversant with the . . . the thing you make, the flashlight." He had taken it apart and then assembled it countless times last night. "In fact, I . . . I . . ." Breathless, he couldn't think. "I mean, actually making the flashlight, that's what I'd rather do. But of course I'll do a good job wherever I am. I just need a start. Someone to take a chance on me." He felt sick, weak for sounding so frantic. She stepped back, as if from cornered vermin. "I'm sorry!" he said quickly. "I'm nervous. I shouldn't be here. I'm not ready."

"You can always come back another time, Mr. Loomis."

"But that doesn't mean you'll hire me though, does it?" he asked quietly.

"I didn't say that!" Another step back.

"No, I know! What I meant was, it's my brother. He thinks this is all set, so if I say you said I could come back, then that's what he'll ask me. The same thing. But if I tell him, 'No, they don't want me'— that, he'll understand."

"It's not like this is anything personal, Loomis." And in Brown's growl Gordon felt the steel cold at his face, the warning in the guards' hard eyes.

"No," Miss Jamison added. "It's just a matter of no positions being available right now."

"Of course. Yes. I understand," Gordon said. He stepped into the hallway, then turned suddenly and stuck out his hand. She cringed, gasping. They regarded each other with mutual horror. "I was just going to say thank you. I forgot to say that." He felt like the same sideshow freak he'd been at the trial—the last time he'd had to convince someone he was a normal human being.

All the way back, Dennis tried to contain his anger. He reminded himself of what Lisa kept saying: that Gordon shouldn't be rushed; he would have to be coaxed from his numbness, eased into everyday life. But she hadn't known Gordon as a kid. He'd always been like this: thickly, maddeningly stubborn, to the point of oafishness, always being picked on, never fighting back or protesting, never telling anyone or even taking a different route to school to avoid their taunts, instead just plodding along as if it weren't really happening, as if he didn't care. But from the next room his younger brother would hear him cry out in the middle of the night, "Don't! Please don't! Please don't do that!" Don't just stand there with your head down, their mother had told them both. Act like a loser and that's how you'll be treated. Look people right in the eye and tell them exactly who you are! Who's that, Ma? Dennis would ask, not just to get her going, which it always did, but because it had really meant something. "The last name might be Loomis, but remember, up here you're Teresa Pratt's kid. And up here's what counts," she'd say, tapping her temple.

Of the two brothers, Gordon was most like his father, a shy, dull man, a cement worker for years until he injured his back pouring a foundation. When his father went on disability, Teresa's uncle, Jimmy Pratt, a records clerk at City Hall, spoke to his buddy the mayor. One phone call, and the next day perky Teresa was a secretary at the high school. She couldn't type, so they put her in charge of the copy machine, on which she printed out exams and study guides, reading them for typos and learning as much as she could about everything, preparing for the day opportunity knocked on her door. Education, she preached constantly—it was the surest road to success. But if their mother's determination had fueled one son, it had had little effect on Gordon, who was just as awkward around people as their father. Dennis still remembered the time his mother was too sick to attend his basketball banquet. Without her effervescent shield, his father and brother never once left their seats at the farthest table in the corner for fear someone might speak to them.

Dennis clicked on the door locks as he came off the highway. The minute he turned onto Nash Street, bleakness took hold, the gray net slipping over his eyes every time he came back. The neighborhood had never been much, but now it was a slum. Broken windows. Graffiti, the swaybacked, sinuous lettering, words that made no sense, it was everywhere. Here, the word *cargo* sprayed on the front door of the Langs' big old Victorian on the corner. Once the nicest house in the neighborhood, it had been chopped up into tiny apartments. Ten mailboxes flanked the door, their ragged strips of masking tape bearing the latest tenants' names. The house across from the Langs' had stood empty for years before it caught fire last winter. A homeless man had kept himself and his dog warm by burning papers and wood scraps in a bathtub. Plywood covered the windows, and with the slightest wind the blue tarpaulin on the roof puffed up and down over charred rafters. A man wearing a glittering gold necklace stood on the corner, lighting a cigarette for a skinny girl with pale, frizzy hair.

"Nice," Dennis said, watching. She was no more than thirteen or fourteen.

"Wait!" Gordon called, and Dennis hit the brake.

The man's hand slid to his pocket. He stared as the silver BMW slowed. "Go ahead, try it," Dennis muttered, staring back.

"What'd that sign say?" Gordon was trying to see out the rear window.

"What sign?"

"Back there. In the market."

"But you've got tons of food. For at least two weeks, anyway, Lisa said." He backed up, stopping in front of the Nash Street Market. Crooked, curling signs in the dingy windows advertised the week's specials. A square of red-lettered cardboard taped to the front door said HELP WANTED.

"Okay," Gordon said, turning back.

"No," Dennis groaned. "Don't even think of it. You don't want to do that. C'mon, Gordon. I mean, for chrissakes, it was just one interview. So maybe they did have security sitting in. I mean, what do they know about you? What does she know? You could be some screwball, some raving maniac, some kind of—"

"Killer." Gordon unknotted his tie.

"But she doesn't know what happened. The details. So naturally she's a little tense. But what're you going to do? You're never going to go on another interview? Instead, you're going to go what? Take up where you left off twenty-five years ago? Be a stock boy at the Nash Street again? What're you gonna do, wrap chickens? Juggle melons? Stack fucking tampon boxes?" he shouted, already knowing by the set of his brother's thick jaw that that was exactly what he wanted. Safety. A corner, a hole, some dark, out-of-the-way place to curl up in for the next twenty-five years. "Like Dad!" he exploded, then caught himself. "You know what I mean," he said more softly, then jabbed his brother's arm as they neared the little white house, their childhood home. Dennis's chest felt tight. Coming back here was a mistake, but Gordon had insisted. It was all he had, he said, the one thing he'd looked forward to all these years.

"C'mon, Gordon, just give it a chance, will you? I know people. Lisa's dad—I got all these contacts. I'm not going to let you down. You know I'm not!" He turned too fast into the narrow driveway, annoyed yet again with the hard bounce over the concrete berm, their father's barrier against rainwater surging in from the street, even though the driveway was pitched higher than the road: his life's energy squandered on petty projects, meaningless chores like his beloved rosebushes overrun now with weedy vines.

"I know," Gordon said before he got out.

A curtain moved in the window of the house next door. Gordon looked away quickly, but Dennis waved. "Always on duty, the old bitch," he said through a smile as Mrs. Jukas peered from the side of the curtain the way she used to when they were kids.

"She must be lonely without Mr. Jukas. He was a nice man," Gordon said.

"Yeah, nice man, always bird-dogging Mom." He didn't tell his brother, but after their mother died Mrs. Jukas had cornered him at the funeral home to say she hoped he wouldn't be selling the house to Puerto Ricans now the way everyone else had done. It wasn't his to sell, he'd said, enjoying the sour pucker of her mouth. His parents had left it to his brother.

Even freshly painted with new blinds and curtains, the wallpaper borders, and Lisa's delicate stenciling in the kitchen, it still looked the same. Tired, cramped, the kind of place you'd live in only because you had to. When Gordon had seen it last week, he had been amazed by the changes, the furniture, the big television on its laminate wooden stand, the cordless phone. Even the metal storm door, he had said, entering the kitchen, overwhelmed to think they'd bought all this for him to live here. Dennis had to explain that things seemed new only because he had never seen them before. Most of it had been bought by their parents after he went away. *Went away*, the euphemism, their code for imprisonment, for the wrenching turn their lives had taken. Gordon had gone away, taking along laughter and whatever good times there had been. Now they were gone and he was back.

Gordon's big feet thudded up the stairs. *He can't wait to get out of the suit and tie. What was that all about?* Dennis wondered. *Just a favor he had to do for me? Go through the motions, never being honest so people won't get mad at him? So they can't get too close?* Dennis called up to remind him that Lisa was expecting him for dinner Friday night. "She wants to know if you're bringing Delores," he added.

"It'll be just me."

"But you said you were going to ask her!" When Dennis had run into Delores the other day, he'd mentioned dinner, foolishly saying that Gordon would call her.

"I know, but I didn't."

"So call her now. She's dying to see you. She told me."

Looking down from the top step, Gordon shook his head. "I don't want to."

"Why not?"

"I don't know. I just don't feel like it."

"Jesus, she's your friend! I mean, she's been writing and going up there for how many years now?" Not much to look at, maybe, but she was exactly what his brother needed right now, a good woman and a good job. Gordon's impassive stare was maddening. *Goddamn sphinx, he should consider himself lucky Delores even cares. Lucky she's so desperate.* "You gotta call her, Gordon. It's the least you can do."

"What time should I come?"

"Anytime." Dennis grinned with the rare concession. "We'll probably eat at six-thirty or seven, but you know Lisa, the earlier the better!"

CHAPTER 2

As Gordon came down Nash Street, he wondered if the Dubbin family still owned the Market. He had been the same age as the Dubbin twins, Cynthia and Cornelius, though he'd hardly known them. They lived in Dearborn and seldom came into the store. He remembered their white-columned brick house from Sunday drives through Dearborn's tree-lined streets while his mother pointed out her favorite houses. First on the route belonged to the Dubbins, whom she felt she knew because her son worked for them. Next came her doctor's house, her principal's, Mrs. Jukas's sister-in-law's, and others she had never met but had read about in the paper.

Faded paint was peeling off the Nash Street Market sign. Warped green roof trim arched over the plate glass like an enormous eyebrow. A web of duct tape patched the shattered lower half of the exit door. Gordon pushed the door open, relieved it wasn't automatic. He always had the feeling he had to hurry through before they swung back and hit him.

The old smell of damp fruity dust seemed to grow right over him. He paused by the rusted office grate. One thing was different: the quiet, the strange emptiness for midmorning. No cashiers at the registers. Maybe it hadn't opened yet. He froze; only his eyes moved. What if something had just happened, and here he was, a week out of Fortley, first on the scene? Who would ever believe him? He started for the door when he saw a tall man with long curly hair stacking pasta boxes at the end of an aisle.

"Excuse me!" Gordon called with a weak wave. The man didn't

look up. Remembering Miss Jamison's startled reaction, Gordon jammed both hands into his pockets and cleared his throat. "Umm, I don't mean to bother you, but is the store closed?"

The man looked back and snorted. "Well, whaddaya think, you're in here, aren't ya?"

"Well, I know, but I didn't see anyone, so I thought maybe I was too early or something."

The man edged back with Gordon's approach.

"I mean, it just seems to be the two of us. And . . ." He took a deep breath. Sweat seeped into his eyes, making him blink.

"And what?" The man glanced past him.

"Well, I . . . could I . . . ," he stammered. "I . . . I need to . . . well, you see, I came in to . . . Are you the manager?"

"Christ! Another fucking holdup?" the man said, shaking his head. "Look, you don't need the manager. The safe's empty! They don't even bother anymore. They just put enough in the registers to get started." He pointed toward the office. "The register keys're—"

"No!" Gordon shouted. "This isn't a holdup! I'm not going to rob you! I just . . ." He started to take his hands out of his pockets, then stopped with the shock on the man's face. They'd been robbed before; the man might be armed. Gordon stared and kept talking. Knowing what to do in a precarious moment was second nature now. "I just want a job. I saw the sign. That's why I came in. That's why I'm here." He tried to smile. His eyes stung from the sweat.

"And that gun in there don't mean nothing, right?"

"No! No gun!" Gordon raised his arms. "See! Just hands, that's all."

Eddie Chapman explained that he was the owner's brother-in-law, as they walked to the rear of the store, past the meat counter into a sour-smelling storage area. One cashier was out sick, and the other was in the bathroom. He'd come in to help. "My wife's brother," he said with a rap on a black door. He shook his head, sighed, rapped again. "Neil! Hey, Neilie, you up?" he called, ear at the jamb. He lowered his voice. "His wife, she's giving him one more shot at it. A week, she said, and then that's it. Jesus Christ," he muttered, and hit the door harder. "Neilie!"

"What? What?" a thick voice growled.

Eddie opened the door an inch wide. "There's a guy here," he called in. "He wants the job."

"Later." A moan. "Yeah. Later."

"He's big, Neil. Really big."

"Oh, oh, oh," came a groan as the man on the narrow cot struggled to get up. "But no lights. Jesus Christ!" He shielded his eyes from the opening door. "What's his name?"

"What's your name?" Eddie asked, then repeated it back.

"Loomis," the man echoed from the murky darkness. "Loomis," he grunted, straining to raise himself up on one elbow. The only light came from the half-opened door. He held out his hand. "Jesus Christ, Eddie, I can't do this." He fumbled through blankets on the cot, then turned back, wearing sunglasses. "So, what? You want the job?" He belched. "You wanna be part of the Nash Street Market family? You wanna be on my team? Cuz if you do, I gotta warn you, I'm a son of a bitch to work for, right, Eddie?" Neil laughed, and so Eddie did. "I'm a real ball buster. Oh, yes, I am. Eddie'll tell you," he murmured, groping his way back down onto the cot. "You tell him, Eddie! You be sure and tell him now!" He turned toward the wall in a tight curl.

"So what should I do?" Eddie asked.

"Whatever the hell you want to do, Eddie," Neil Dubbin groaned.

The HELP WANTED sign stayed in the window even though his first day on the job had begun. There were two registers open. At the first was June, a tiny gray-haired woman with a hacking cough. She was the fastest cashier but couldn't bag groceries because of her emphysema. In the lulls between customers, she reached down and switched on her oxygen tank, then slipped the clear tubing over her head and adjusted the prongs in each nostril.

Serena was at the next register. She was a tall, coarse-skinned woman with large teeth and tendrils of ivy tattooed up each finger of her right hand. A small silver hoop pierced her left nostril. She and June seemed in a constant state of annoyance with customers. So far they'd had little to say to their huge, clumsy bag boy who kept filling the bags until they were too heavy. The bottom of the last customer's bag had ripped open, spilling cans all over the sidewalk out front.

"Hey, Gordon," Serena called as he double-bagged milk, juice, and cigarettes for a fat, bearded man in a dungaree jacket. "We're running low on plastic."

"Bags. Out back," June wheezed, then pushed a REGISTER CLOSED sign onto the belt.

Gordon hurried through the meat-cutting room.

"Whatever it is, tell 'em we're out," Leo, the butcher, called as he continued shrink-wrapping packages of ground beef.

Gordon stood in the middle of the poorly lit, chaotic storage area. He had already been back here on two previous futile missions for items customers couldn't find on the shelves. Stacks of torn, half-filled cartons were everywhere. Some had fallen, littering the floor with cans and boxes. There were no plastic bags. He was about to knock on Neil's door when he spotted them in a box by the walk-in cooler. He was filling a smaller box with bags when the wide double doors to the loading ramp swung open. Eddie Chapman pushed through a dolly piled with cases of milk.

"Just the man I need," Eddie said, and ordered Gordon to bring the cases up front and refill the dairy case. "There's six more cases on the ramp, but I gotta go see a guy, so if you could just put them in the walk-in, I'd really appreciate it." He zipped his jacket as he backed toward the door. "And for God's sake don't let anybody bother Neilie. He's gotta get through this. But mingya, I got a life to lead, too. I got my own thing. I can't keep doing this," he said through the closing door.

Gordon started to push the loaded dolly into the store, then realized he probably shouldn't leave six cases of milk out on the ramp to spoil or be stolen. He brought in the cases but couldn't see another dolly, so he carried them two at a time into the cooler. He was wheeling the dolly out to the dairy case when he remembered June and Serena. Hands flying, he got the milk onto the shelves in just a few minutes, then raced up front with the bags.

Five customers were lined up at Serena's register. June was gone.

"Is she all right?" he asked, and Serena rolled her eyes as she counted change back for a teenage girl with black lipstick and bright-red eye shadow. The girl pushed her cart through. In the baby carrier was a sleeping infant. Its tiny mouth opened and closed. He leaned closer. He'd only ever seen babies from a distance in the visiting room.

"Cute, huh?" Serena said.

"Like a little fish," he said, gazing down.

"And what the fuck's that supposed to mean?" the girl snapped.

His head shot up as she stormed by him. "I meant the mouth, the way it was opening and closing," he said quietly.

"Bitch!" Serena said, just loudly enough to be heard.

At the door, the girl turned, held up her middle finger. Serena burst out laughing. Gordon's face was red. He wasn't used to hearing women swear.

On the top step of the house across the street, the frizzy-haired girl was hitting a stringed ball with a wooden paddle. She had been out there doing the same thing late last night, until a woman called from a second-floor window and told her to go inside, it was way past her bedtime. The girl hollered something back. The woman leaned even farther out the window and threatened to call Social Services. With that, the girl ran onto the porch, then ducked down behind the railing. When Gordon went to bed, the girl was still crouched in the shadows, knees up, back against the wall.

His instinct was to keep his eyes down, but he forced a smile and mumbled a low hello. The girl stared out from cold, dull eyes until he looked away. The paddle continued its steady beat. He paused by the roses. His father's pampered shrubs had massed into a tangled hedge between his house and Mrs. Jukas's. The inch of new growth made it easier to tell which were dead branches. Trying to avoid the thorns, thick and curved like black talons, he reached in and broke off a long dead cane. He broke off another, then more, almost lulled by the steady *thwack thwack thwack* across the street. His hands and arms were getting scratched, so he looked in the garage for clippers. A lump rose in his throat at the sight of all the empty hooks and shelves that had once held his father's tools. The baby-food jars of nails and screws were gone, but their rusting caps were still nailed over the workbench. He went into the house and brought out scissors. Twenty minutes later, he had trimmed off enough to see which branch belonged to which bush.

The lowering sun was still warm on his back. A fat bee buzzed drowsily near his face. He had worked the last six hours a free man. He could do whatever he felt like, go wherever he wanted, could feel it pulse in his fingertips, the soles of his feet, electrifying, the shock of living, of just being here. The anxious chatter of squirrels rose to a high, quarrelsome pitch. In some nearby house, a baby wailed. A door squeaked open, then banged shut. Mrs. Jukas stood on her front porch, white-haired, dour as ever, tinier than he remembered, maybe not even five feet tall. Mr. Jukas had been a registry inspector. When Gordon failed the road test for his license, his mother called upon Mr. Jukas, who took him out every day, parallel-parking all over the city. By the end of the week, he could parallel-park better than he could drive. His second road test had been scheduled the day he was arrested. When the police pounded on the door early that morning, his mother first thought it was Mr. Jukas's idea of a joke, some kind of private road test he had arranged, until they shoved the warrant at her, decreeing not just entry, but their bounding surge up the stairs, five of them, guns drawn, shouting his name as they pushed open the bedroom door, then darted back, but needn't have because he was lying there waiting, still dressed in the clothes he'd worn the day before, eyes wide, waiting through the night, months, years to come, waiting for it to end, for it to finally be over. As they rushed him stumbling down the stairs, his mother's face had turned old, her hair wild from tearing at it as she screamed at them. *Leave him alone and get out! Get out! What are you, crazy? You're at the wrong house. You don't know what you're talking about. My son wouldn't lay a hand on anyone, much less murder someone. Not Gordon! No! No! No!*

"What do you think you're doing?" Mrs. Jukas's voice cut through the warm air. "You get out of here! If you don't get off my property right now, I'm calling the police!"

Gordon looked down at the base of the roses, wondering if the lot lines had changed.

"Just passing on through." It was the same young man with thick gold chains he had seen the other morning. He swaggered along the edge of her patchy lawn, grinning. Mrs. Jukas kept demanding that he hurry up. Gordon recognized the walk, the strut with its coiled, lethal bravado that could strike with pythonine force. The man crossed the street in slow, imperious fashion, looking neither right nor left, not even quickening his pace as cars bore down from both directions. He spoke to the girl who was sitting on the top step. The ball extended farther and thinner with each blunt *whack*. Suddenly he seized the ball, snapping it from its rubber tether. It rolled into the gutter. She shouted something. He grabbed her shirt and yanked her to her feet. She stumbled down a step, then caught herself on the railing.

He darted past her and rang one of the buzzers. The front door opened onto a scrawny young woman in skimpy shorts and a leather bomber jacket. She held her head at a dazed angle, squinting into the light. She gestured as if she didn't have whatever he wanted. She called to the girl. The girl answered back angrily. The man grabbed the girl then and forced her down the steps onto the sidewalk. Suddenly, as if from nowhere, a large purple SUV pulled up to the curb. The girl tried to get back up the stairs, but the woman shrieked at her to go. With that, the girl headed toward the SUV in her own version of the walk. She got in and it sped off. The man followed the woman into the house.

"Who is that? Who's down there?" Mrs. Jukas suddenly called. "I can see you. I see you down there hiding!"

"Mrs. Jukas." He stepped out from the bushes. "Gordon Loomis, Mrs. Jukas," he said quietly. He hadn't meant to startle her. Dennis had told him to go right over and say hello, and he should have, he said as he hurried up her steps. "But I didn't want to bother you." He'd been dreading this moment.

She hadn't moved. Her faded eyes darted between him and the relative safety of the street. One of her legs was bigger than the other, enormous in its casing of elastic bandaging. Instead of shoes she wore wide, soiled slippers.

"My mother used to tell me how after my dad's stroke Mr. Jukas would always come over and help her get him into bed at night," he said from the walk below.

"She was always asking for help," the old woman said.

"Well, it was nice of Mr. Jukas to do it."

"Your father had a hard life." She looked straight down at him. Thanks to you, she didn't have to add.

"I know. I know he did."

Her dark eyes went to his arms.

He nodded. "Well. I guess I better go. The thorns," he said, and tried to smile. "They certainly did a job on me. Next time I'll know enough to wear gloves. And long sleeves."

She didn't say anything. She didn't have to. She'd seen him last, being led, pushed from his house with bloody gashes down both arms. She watched him squeeze between the bushes into his own yard.

There had always been a constant glare in the cells from the corridor lights. He sat on the sofa, enjoying the darkness, though he still wasn't used to sleeping in it. Or in silence. In the beginning he'd had a succession of cellmates, most older than he was. He had managed to bunk alone these last few years by taking the smallest cell. His cot had been the length of the wall, with no room to stretch his feet over the end. For that modicum of privacy he had slept for years in a cramped coil.

A truck rumbled down the street, and he looked out the window. The sound of passing cars continued to be a strange sensation. Most of the tenement windows across the street were lit. Julia Kirbowitz had lived in the first-floor apartment. They used to walk to school together until sixth grade, when her family moved to a new house in Dearborn. The front door opened now, and a short, bearded man came onto the porch. He hurried down the steps and got into the old car parked below. As he drove off, someone rose up from the porch shadows. It was the same frizzy-haired girl. She ran to the window, looked inside, then ducked back. The door opened and another man emerged, then headed down the street, tugging his jeans over his hips as he went. The girl ran inside, wiggling as if she had to go to the bathroom. A light flashed on in the window, then quickly went off again.

A white car came down the street. It pulled up in front of Gordon's house. He watched from the side of the window as a stocky woman in a big purple shirt got out. Delores Dufault opened her back door and removed a large white basket. With the doorbell's sharp ring, his hair stood on end. *Go away. Please, just go away.* He didn't want her here. Didn't want to see her. Not yet. Not tonight. No. Not ever. This wild panic was completely illogical, yet so sharp in his chest that he could barely breathe. On visiting day he'd always come down to see her, even when he didn't want her there. But for this there were no rules, no assigned seats, no regulated time. He wasn't prepared. What would he say? Where would he sit? What would she expect? What did she want? After a few minutes, the treads creaked under her footsteps. Her car door closed. He sighed with relief as she drove away. He sat back down on the couch, then waited a long time before he opened the door. On the threshold was a large basket of cookies, brownies, and still-warm banana-nut bread. She had written a note on the back of a checking deposit slip:

"Welcome home, Gordon! Sorry I missed you. Call when you get a chance. Delores."

The telephone rang and he jumped. He groped along the coffee table for the portable phone, then pushed a button and said hello, baffled when the television came on and the phone kept ringing. He hurried into the kitchen.

"Hello?" he shouted into the wall phone. "Hello?"

"Gordon! You're home? Where were you?" It was Dennis.

"I couldn't find the phone!"

"Couldn't find it? What do you mean, you couldn't find it?"

"It's too dark. I couldn't find it at first!"

"Dark! Why's it dark?"

"The lights aren't on!"

"So turn them on, and why are you yelling like that?"

"I don't know," he answered sheepishly. At Fortley he'd had to shout into the phone to be heard over the din.

"Delores called. She said she was just there, but she didn't think you were home."

"I must have been sleeping."

"Yeah, that's what I told her." Dennis sounded skeptical. "She said she brought you some things. You better get them in before somebody takes them. They're out on the porch."

"Yes. Yes, I will."

"Oh, and Lisa says not to forget about Friday." Dennis paused. "So are you going to call Delores?"

"Well, not tonight."

"Look, just call her, will you? Thank her for coming over. Is that such a big deal?" Dennis sounded irritated.

Gordon said he would call, but not right now. He was too tired. He wanted to go to bed.

"So then they say, 'Fine, Doe. Put in the extra time if you want, but we're not. We've got lives to attend to.'"

With every chuckle her ruddy face glowed more. Delores Dufault was an incessant talker, yet after she left, Gordon could hardly remember anything she had said. Their visits always began the same way, with his squirming irritation as she told him how glad she was to see him again and how much his friendship meant. The garish colors and wild patterns she wore made him feel dizzy. Her shirt collar glittered with jet beads. Her long, squared fingernails were purple with yellow stripes painted through them. Everything glistened—her hair, face, teeth—but with a jangly sparkle that made her seem silly and oddly sad.

No sooner had he hung up the phone with Dennis than she was ringing the doorbell again. He was tiptoeing up the stairs when he thought of the long drive to Fortley. It was especially hard in winter along winding, mountain roads, as Dennis had told him often enough, though Delores had never complained. Once Dennis and Lisa had children, they couldn't come as often. Before Delores's first visit alone, he had written countless letters telling her not to come, that it was a difficult ride to an ugly, depressing place. Actually, he found any visits strained and unsettling. Small talk had never come easy, especially an hour of it with a woman he barely knew. Not wanting to hurt her feelings, he kept composing more letters, none of which he mailed. The few he ever did send were brief responses to questions asked in her letters. Silly rhetorical questions, like "What did you think of the bombing in Iraq last night?" As if his opinion mattered or made the slightest difference to anyone. And then one day, there she was in the visitors' room, in a ruffled powder-blue dress with a bright floral scarf on her broad shoulders. He asked if she'd come from church. Oh, no, she said in her effusive honesty that always made him cringe with embarrassment for both of them. People didn't get all dressed up for church anymore, she told him. It was a brand-new outfit she'd bought just for the visit. She'd wanted to look especially nice for him.

Not knowing how to respond, he had said nothing. Just as he was doing now in his living room, bright with every lamp on. These lapses were easy with Delores, who could leave no silence unfilled.

"So that way I figured I'd get the work done, then stop by here on my way home. I hope you don't mind, Gordon. I know you're trying to get reacclimated. Dennis said how he took you out to Corcopax. And like I told him—any time you need a ride there, or anywhere, for that matter, you should just call me. I'd love to bring you around and show you all the old places."

He looked away, embarrassed, as she readjusted her bra strap.

"Even though most of the changes are all for the worst. I think, anyway. Which reminds me—I ran into Susan Karp the other day. Remember her?"

He didn't.

"See!" Delores grinned, unpeeling a stick of gum. "Told you I'd quit." Her last letter had announced that once he got out she would not smoke another cigarette. He didn't say anything. She balled up the paper and put it on the coffee table. "Anyway, Susan and her sister were in our class. Annette, she started out a year ahead, but then she had some kind of, as they say, *trouble*"—she winked—"if you get my drift. Anyway, she stayed back. She was a really good basketball player."

"Oh." He had no idea who she meant. He put the wrapper into his pocket. At least her voice was pleasant, warm, with a kind of smile in it as if always on the verge of laughter.

"Well, anyway, Susan starts telling me about Annette's second husband, Eric. She said he works for some kind of food wholesaler. Cheeses, fancy jams, caviar, stuff like that. For, you know, delicatessens and all these trendy kinds of food shops that're all over the place now." She took another stick of gum from her purse. "And I'm thinking, Eric. Eric. I used to know an Eric. 'Eric Reese?' I said. 'Yah,' she said. And then we get talking about the past and everything, and she starts telling me how now that you're out of jail, the family's afraid you're going to try and contact them or something. So I said, 'Forget that! That's the last thing Gordon wants to do.' "

He had been staring at her. Eric Reese had been Jerry Cox's best friend, but there had been an argument. Jerry had stalked off, then run into Gordon on his way home from work that night, that horrible night when Jerry kept telling him not to let Janine Walters see him. Because Jerry Cox had been sixteen at the time, two years younger than Gordon, he had been tried as a juvenile. His sentence for the murder had been five years in juvenile detention. A few months after his release, he hiked into the snowy woods behind his family's house, put a gun in his mouth, and pulled the trigger. Someone told Gordon's father that Jerry had left a suicide note. Convinced the note would exonerate Gordon, he begged the family to let him see it. Alone at home all day, with little more to do than brood, the shy man became obsessed. He called them, wrote letters, even went to their house and begged Mrs. Cox to help him help his son. The Cox family took out a restraining order against Mr. Loomis. A reporter contacted them. Their long, front-page interview not only denied the existence of a suicide note, but reiterated Jerry's sworn testimony that the break-in had been Gordon Loomis's idea. Jerry had done everything humanly possible to stop him, they said, but had been powerless against gigantic Gordon's rage that night. They blamed their son's death on Gordon. They said poor Jerry never got over the shame and the guilt of being unable to help Mrs. Walters, who had always been so kind to him. To be again condemned and humiliated so publicly devastated Gordon's mother. She took a leave of absence from work and for six months seldom left the house. She stopped writing to Gordon and visited him only once. Soon after came his father's first stroke.

Gordon's hands locked on his knees. Everything in the little room seemed crooked and out of place. Delores's lavender pants were wrinkled. A long thread dangled from her shirt hem. She'd been like this as a girl, too, forever stumbling and ruining things, annoying classmates as well as teachers with constant talk and easy intimacies.

She winced. "Oh, no. You're upset with me, aren't you."

"I don't talk about that," he said stiffly. He wanted her to leave but couldn't say it.

Her fuchsia-coated lips trembled. "Oh! I'm sorry! I'm so sorry." She put her hand on his arm. "Actually, I thought it was funny. Well, not funny, but . . . but, well, weird that they'd think that. I thought you'd want to know. I thought . . . I mean, now that you're home . . . Oh, I don't know what I thought. I guess I wasn't think-ing, that's the problem. I'm sorry," she said, annoying him even more as she berated herself. "See? That's the thing, I talk too much. I just go on and on. That's how I work things out. I, like, talk them to death, and then nothing anyone says after that can bother me. But that's my way. And sometimes I forget other people aren't like that. My sisters, they're always telling me I don't have any respect for other people's boundaries. I'm sorry, Gordon. Really, I am. So let's be friends. Please? Let's just start over, okay? From this moment on it'll be like I never said it! There!" she declared, and slapped her thigh, the fleshy clap alarming him even more. "The most important thing is here and now, right?" She smiled and looked around. "So! Are you really going to stay here, I mean, live in the house?"

Well, she didn't blame him, she continued, not waiting for an an-swer. In fact, she'd still be in her old house, but after her mother died her sisters just about sold the place out from under her, they were so anxious to collect their share. "This lawyer I know says I should've billed the estate for all those years I took care of Ma, but what kind of person does that? I mean, she was my mother, and I was the only single one all those years, so naturally it was going to be me. But I never minded. I figure my time's coming, you know what I mean?"

He had been thinking of his own mother traveling all that way, weekly at first. Every visit had begun with her tight-lipped censure and ended in tears as each tried to tell the other how sorry they were for everything.

"Oh, Gordon." Delores shook her head and sighed. "I'm just boring the hell out of you, aren't I, with all my talk." Concern made her look even more unkempt.

"No," he said tentatively, as if it were a question. "I guess I'm just a little tired, that's all."

"Oh, poor Gordon!" She moved next to him and put her arm over his shoulder. "You do. You look so tired."

His thoughts roiled with the nudge of her breast against his arm. It was terrifying to be this inept, to not know what to say or do next. His face felt hot. She smelled like fruit, bruised and overripe.

"How about if I make some coffee? We can have dessert!" She started to get up. "Some nice, warm banana bread?"

"No, I don't want any," he answered too quickly.

She looked at him for a moment. "What'd you do today that made you so tired?"

"I don't know." He shrugged. If he mentioned the Market, she'd never leave.

She began to tell him about her boss's son, who had been terribly depressed since losing his job. "He never goes anywhere. He's always in the house. His mother wants him to see someone, but Albert says what he needs is a good kick in the behind, but it's like I keep telling him, everyone's got their own pace." She gave Gordon a quick look. "I've told you about Albert, right? He's a wonderful man, but he's had to make it the hard way, so he can come off seeming a little gruff sometimes."

Gordon felt he knew everything about Albert Smick. He used to think Delores had to be in love with the man, until he realized she was that effusive about everyone she liked.

After she left, he plumped the flattened sofa pillows. The wrinkled arm cover was on the floor. Leaving ripples in her wake, she disturbed things, left indentations in the rug, the door ajar, his heart beating uneasily. He never dared breathe too deeply when she was near. It wasn't her fault, he knew, but his. Her kindness always frightened him, and now he felt guilty. He hadn't even thanked her for all the pastry. He waited a few minutes, then called.

Breathless, she answered on the first ring. She said she had just gotten the key in the lock when she heard the phone. He hadn't finished thanking her before she was thanking him for being such a good friend all these years; he would never know how much his letters had meant. And as she was driving home just now, it had started to sink in that he was really here. He was home. Her best friend in the whole world was finally home! After an awkward silence, he said good-bye. Wait, she said before he could hang up. Would he like to come to dinner Friday night? She'd bought a prime rib, because she knew that was his favorite meal—he'd told her once, medium rare, right? With baked potatoes and green beans. He didn't remember ever telling her that, but it was true. He said he couldn't. He said he had to go to Dennis's that night.

"Oh!" There was a pause. "Well then, do you need a ride?"

"No. Thanks. I'm taking the bus."

"Don't do that. All those stops, it'll take forever. I can get you there in ten minutes."

"But I want to take the bus!" He paused to quell the panic in his voice. "I don't mind the stops. I was looking forward to it. I haven't been on a bus in such a long time."

"That's right. There must be so much you want to do now," she said slowly. "But if you need something, whatever it is, will you call me? Please?"

CHAPTER 3

I n those first days at the Market, the two women plied Gordon with questions. His reticence intrigued them, his shy discomfort eliciting not just their own secrets, but customers'. The lady over there in the miniskirt, Allie, nice legs, huh? Well, she was really a man. And Leo, the butcher, he had been depressed ever since his wife ran off with the eighteen-year-old girl who used to live downstairs. From Gordon's terse answers they learned that he had grown up in Collerton, then moved to the western part of the state. Hilldale, he said when they asked where.

"Hilldale! I never heard of that," Serena said.

"Yes, you have!" June turned quickly back to him. "The prison's there, right? Fortley. That's where the worst ones go."

The state prison, where everything was hard-core: the crime, the time, the men. He had few illusions. Exposure was inevitable, but for now he needed the anonymity of those blank spaces so that while pretending to be a normal man, he might learn how to be one. What he wanted most was to feel something. Anything but this deadness. For twenty-five years he had allowed himself only the present, this moment, this day. It was all he deserved or dared expect of time. He had not realized how strange freedom would be, how alien he would feel. They knew that he had worked in a library, a hospital, a laundry, a sign factory, that his parents were dead, that he lived alone, that he'd never been married. "No, never come close," he'd answered when Serena asked.

"Really?" June said with an eager smile. She wanted him to meet her sister, who was single—well, divorced. She had four kids, but none of them lived at home now. Yes, Serena confided later, because they were all wards of the state. Not the kind of person he would want to get involved with. Serena was one to talk, Leo said the minute she left. She and her husband smoked pot with their teenage sons and didn't see the least bit of harm in it.

On Friday, Neil Dubbin emerged from his fetid bunker. He spent an hour in the cluttered office, signing checks with a trembling hand between phone calls to his wife. She kept hanging up on him. When he started to cry, she listened long enough for him to apologize and beg her to let him come home again. Mary Dubbin must have said no, Serena reported back, because after Neil hung up he disappeared into his windowless room.

With the store empty, the women stood by the ladder while Gordon razored scraps of brittle tape off the front windows. June kept an eye out for Eddie Chapman, who'd been called back this morning to one of his construction sites.

"Eddie's an asshole, but he means well," Serena said.

The Dubbin family had been deeply disappointed in their daughter Cynthia's choice of a husband, but it was always Eddie in his steel-toed boots and with grimy fingernails who was sent in to hold the place together until Neil sobered up. June said the only reason the Market hadn't been sold long ago was that the family needed a place to stash Neil.

Gordon leaned toward the glass. The women's voices skirmished for his attention.

"She never comes in here," Serena said of Neil's wife.

"It's the city. She doesn't feel *safe* anymore," June said in a mocking tone.

"But the truth is, she just doesn't want to be around Neil."

"Drunk or sober."

"At least when he's drunk she's got some control."

"Yeah. See, the thing is, when he's sober, he can be such a bastard. Like mean. Like really, really mean."

"Yeah, you never know. You gotta be careful," Serena warned.

"But the thing is, poor Neil, it's like the meaner he gets, the worse he gets down on himself for it," June said.

"Yeah, he's like one of those people, the only time they're happy is when somebody else is miserable."

"So the thing is to just ignore him. That's what we do."

"Most of the time, anyway. Oh, shit," Serena groaned. "Hey, Eddie, you're back!"

"Where the hell is he?" Eddie stormed down the aisle.

"Up here," Gordon said. The ladder teetered as he hurried down. This was a project he had chosen for himself. "That old tape. I've been trying to get it off. I should've—"

"He said he was gonna work!" Eddie bellowed, looking around.

"He did." Serena explained how upset Neil had been after talking to his wife.

"He called her?" Eddie backhanded the new stack of *National Enquirers*, scattering them across the floor. Gordon began to pick them up. "I told him not to call her. Oh, Christ, I'm so sick of this. I don't know how much longer I can do this. I got a business to run. If he's boozing again, that's it!"

No, no. The women didn't think so. Neil hadn't left the store. Not once.

"Go look out back, then," Eddie ordered Gordon. "Tell him I'm here for one minute and I gotta see him."

Leo kept feeding chunks of beef into the grinder. He shook his head; he hadn't seen Neil. Next, Gordon asked the stock boy, Thurman, who was smoking a cigarette outside on the loading platform. "No. But I seen you last night," Thurman said, flicking the cigarette into the dirt. "You live near my aunt."

"I do?" Gordon said uneasily.

"Yeah," the boy said, rolling his dark eyes. Yesterday Eddie had cut the boy's hours in half. With so many holdups in the neighborhood, they needed someone big up front. So Thurman was hauling garbage and rounding up shopping carts, a humiliating demotion in a job he hated. As long as he stayed in school and kept his job at the Market, his grandmother would let him live with her.

Gordon made his careful way through the messy back rooms. This morning he had dislodged a stack of fruit crates, sending oranges and grapefruit rolling in every direction. It was a shame. Old Mr. Dubbin had been so organized, he used to know where every bit of stock was in the store. Neil's door was ajar. "Mr. Dubbin? Excuse me. Mr. Dubbin?" he called softly, then leaned into the dark, airless room. Water was running. He tapped on the bathroom door. Neil Dubbin emerged, patting his newly shaven face with a dingy towel. He nodded sheepishly as Gordon relayed Eddie Chapman's message. He said he'd be right out. He was almost ready.

"Wait," he called before Gordon could leave. "What's your name again? I forgot."

"Gordon."

"Gordon? Gordon what?"

"Loomis."

"Loomis?" The hand with the towel dropped to his side. "How long you been working?"

"Since eight."

"I mean, here. What day? When'd you start?"

"Monday. I came in the afternoon."

"Who hired you?" He leaned closer. "Wasn't me, was it?"

"Yes. Well, in a sense. But actually I guess it was Eddie. I mean Mr. Chapman."

"Mr. Chapman!" Neil laughed. "No. You were right the first time. You mean Eddie." He laughed again. "So how's Denny doing? I haven't seen him in a while."

"He's fine. He's doing well, thank you." Gordon kept trying to swallow.

"So, what happened? How'd you . . ." He twirled his hand. "You know, end up here?"

"The sign. It said, HELP WANTED."

"No, I mean, how'd you get out?" He laughed. "You didn't escape, did you?" Dubbin's gleeful wonder escalated. "I mean, you're not on the fucking lam or anything, are you?"

"I was paroled," he said, the word a stone's weight upon his tongue.

Delores Dufault checked her watch again. Almost six, and Albert still hadn't let her know about tonight. She had called him this morning at the Dearborn store, but he couldn't really talk. He'd have to get back to her on the details. All day long she had assumed that meant yes, that he was coming to dinner, but now she wasn't so sure. She was tempted to call again, but that would irritate him, so she'd been trying to keep busy until she heard from him. Their night together had always been Friday or Monday, depending on Albert's schedule. Holidays belonged to his family, of course. Lately, though, she'd hardly seen him at all. The new store was taking up all his time. It was already doing three times the business the old one was, he had said almost accusingly. But what did he expect with all their old customers going to the Dearborn store? Albert said people didn't want to drive into the poor, grim city of Collerton, which was precisely why he had opened the new store in Dearborn's affluent little downtown. Rents might be sky-high in Dearborn, but that's where the customers were.

Kiki said the handwriting was on the wall; it was only a matter of time before Smick Stationery closed, like so many other Collerton stores. Delores hadn't called her since. If she wanted to be put down, all she had to do was call one of her sisters. She didn't need it from her best friend.

When Delores finished refilling the greeting-card display rack, she noticed that the manila envelopes on the rounder were getting low. She looked out back but couldn't find any. As he had everything else, Albert must have taken them to the new store and forgotten to tell her so she could order more. He couldn't seem to keep things straight lately. Orders were always being messed up, and last month he'd sent three checks to the wrong suppliers. The problem was his family. They wouldn't be happy until they'd drained every bit of energy and happiness out of the poor man. All he got at home were complaints and coldness. It killed her to see that perky little wife of his in her sleek workout clothes breeze in here with her painted smile, calling everyone honey and sugar in her fiercely guarded southern drawl, when Delores knew what a calculating, self-centered woman she really was. His son was a leech, and his daughter was a spoiled brat whose prep-school tuition and brand-new sports car left her poor father too broke even to buy himself a decent pair of shoes. Two Christmases ago, Delores had bought him the expensive English cordovans he had worn every day since. It was depressing to see the heels all worn down, his wrinkled pants, and the frayed collars. Didn't his wife care? Or as usual, was Delores the only one who did? She slammed the storeroom door and stood by the front window, looking out at the street.

Here she was again, getting all worked up over a situation that had gone on for years. Maybe Kiki was right. If Albert was really that unhappy, why didn't he just up and leave? *But maybe that's it,* Kiki had said in that last phone call. *Maybe he just likes using you for his dumping ground, then when he's got it all out of his system he can just head back home and start over.*

Dumping ground. Is that all she was, a dumping ground? What a disgusting thing to say, but of course, Kiki didn't know the real story. No one did. Albert was just too decent and loyal to ever hurt his family. Every Sunday without fail, he spent an hour at the nursing home with his father, who didn't even recognize him anymore. Once when he bent down to kiss the top of his father's head, the old man slapped his face. Delores had never told Albert that last winter when he and his wife went to Aruba, she had brought flowers and home-made fudge to his father and watched the Mass on television with him. When it came time for her to go, the old man cried. He held on to her hand and wouldn't let her leave.

Two women had just come into the store. They brought a box of colored paper to the register. They said they were starting a cleaning service and needed paper for their first mailing. Only one spoke English. She said her sister and her sister's two grandchildren had just moved in with her. The sister's husband had died last month, and the grandchildren's mother and father were drug addicts. Delores asked the women if they wanted some names for their mailing list. They were all women who worked and could probably use help with the cleaning. Four of the names were her own sisters. Hearing this in translation, the badly bleached widow took Delores's hand and squeezed it, the fierce grip belying her tiny frame. Before they left, Delores had written twenty names and addresses on a piece of store stationery. *That's all it takes,* she thought, watching them go down the street, laughing, arm in arm. Now she felt good again. It never seemed to fail: whenever she got down in the dumps, along would come someone much worse off than she was.

She checked her watch: ten minutes to closing. Gordon was probably on his way to his brother's by now. She wished Dennis hadn't mentioned the cookout. Every time the phone had rung this past week, she had hoped it might be Gordon inviting her. God, he had looked so good the other night in regular clothes. But the minute she moved closer, she knew she'd made a terrible mistake. He had actually cringed as if away from some foul odor or contagion.

She picked up the phone. If he was gone, she'd leave a message. Saying what, though? She had to be careful. He was always so uptight around her. Dennis said he was like that with everyone, but the other night he'd looked almost panicky. The poor guy, he was obviously afraid to be alone with a woman. He probably thought one wrong move would scare her off. She'd just have to be patient. But persistent, she vowed on the first number. She'd say she was going to the mall tomorrow and would he please call her if he needed anything or felt like going. If he did answer, she'd offer him a ride. She could say she had to drop something off at Albert's house, which wasn't far from Dennis's.

"No!" She hung up the phone. She grabbed a rag and glass cleaner and scrubbed the front counter case. What Gordon Loomis needed most was a friend and not some lonely woman with too much time on her hands.

"Delores! Where's my jacket? Damn it! It's not here!" an irritated voice called.

"Oh, Albert!" She jumped up, smiling, then ran into the storeroom. "I didn't hear you come in. Oh, I'm so glad you're here. I've been waiting all day for you to call."

"I can't find my jacket." He was searching through the boxes in his office. "Where the hell is it?"

"I don't know. I haven't seen it. Here," she said as he scaled a notepad across the room. "Let me look. If it's here, I'll find it."

"Goddamn mess," he muttered as she went through the boxes.

"You just need to sort through it, that's all," she said, looking behind the desk.

"I don't have time!"

"Then I'll do it. I told you I would."

He stared at her, shaking his head incredulously. "Well, why haven't you, then?"

"Because you told me not to." She struggled to keep her voice steady. "That's all for the Dearborn store. You said you wanted to keep the two places separate."

"Well, you could organize it, couldn't you? At least do something. Put it all in one place, but don't let this happen!" He sounded so frantic that it was hard to be mad at him.

"Albert!" She touched his cheek, aroused as always by the late day stubble. For such a slight, fair-skinned man, he had a heavy beard. "What's wrong? Listen to you. You're a wreck."

He sighed and hung his head.

"Al! Honey, what is it? Come on, tell me." She put her arms around him, pleased when he didn't resist. "Come on, tell Doe-doe what's wrong. You're tired, aren't you. Well, you just follow me in your car and I'll have you fed and happy in no time," she whispered, kissing his ear and sighing when he shivered against her.

"I can't." He pulled away. "Cheryl's invited some people out to dinner." He hurried into the front of the store. He opened the copyroom door, still looking for the jacket.

"You're going out? Why didn't you tell me? You said you'd call. I haven't seen you in so long. I've just missed you so much."

"I'm sorry, Delores. It just feels like everything's coming down on me all at once, that's all. I mean, here it is my one night to relax, but what does Cheryl care? I mean, after all, who am I?"

"Oh, Al." She hugged him again.

He pulled away, almost pushing her back. "Not out here! What are you thinking? What if someone should come in?" He spoke out of the side of his mouth, his back rigid to the plate glass as if to a watching throng.

"It's after six. I'll lock the door."

"And then what?" he said with such indignant, widening eyes that she thought he was joking.

"Well, I don't know," she said, watching him. The first move had always been his to make. She had blundered horribly. "I . . . I just thought."

"You just thought what? That all of a sudden I'm going to throw propriety and good judgment right out the window? Right out there on the street for all the world to see?"

Humiliated by his disdain, she closed her eyes.

"Come on, Delores. Get a grip. Please! Will you, please?"

She shook her head, held up her hand. She was fine. It was all right. Really.

"Look," he said, hurrying to lock the door and turn out the lights. "It's like I just said. I can only do so much. You know what my parameters are." He went into his office, and she knew she had won. She followed quietly and unrolled the foam mat on the floor behind his desk, then took off her panty hose. He drew the bolt across the door and turned off the lights, talking while he undressed. "Instead of things getting easier, I have more pressure in my life right now than I've ever had. Ever! And I don't see any end in sight. Not with the way things are going now, anyway," he grunted as he lay down.

"I've missed you," she whispered, climbing onto him.

"I know you have." He sighed with an impatient squirm, his signal for her to begin.

"I just get so lonesome lately." She sat perfectly still.

"I know. I know you do. And I try. I do try. You know I do," he pleaded with an anxious groan. With its urgency came displacement, a strange distance, as if this ache had little to do with her head.

"We never spend any time together." The power was hers. She smiled through the darkness.

"But we are now . . . so let's not waste a minute of it," he gasped as she began.

"Talk to me, Albert. Please." She leaned forward.

"Don't, don't stop."

"Then talk to me. You know I like you to talk to me."

"Yes. Yes, I know. And that feels good," he whimpered, then moaned as she moved again. "That feels so good. You don't know how good it feels. Nobody makes me feel like this."

It was a technique from one of the manuals Albert had given her. She had a box full of them in a closet at home. She used to be proud of her ability to please him so completely, but lately her skills only left her feeling sad and empty. "Talk to me."

"Oh . . ."

"Talk to me. Talk to me, Albert."

"Yes. I will. I want to. I am. . . ."

"I said talk to me." Her eyes were wide open. His choked, guttural cries rose up from the dark. The words, and feel, and smell of him didn't matter. It was a voice she wanted, thick and deep with need, helpless with desire. *Gordon. Gordon. Gordon. Gordon,* beat the pulse in her brain.

CHAPTER 4

Gordon paused in his doorway before the ten-minute walk to the bus stop. He carried a small round watermelon in a plastic bag and a string-tied bakery box. What a luxury, what a privilege, to stand here staring through the thin glass of this door, his to open any time he wanted. The warmth of the late-afternoon sun made him smile as he watched a shabby old man hobble across the street. A small, matted dog limped after him.

The neighborhood was run-down, but its vitality was everywhere. Day or night there would be women on their front steps, children playing on the sidewalks, music blasting from idling cars driven by handsome young men who never seemed to leave them. Life might be a struggle here, but its energy charged the air, blind and unstoppable, as relentless a force as the thrust of new green shoots from the brittle rose canes; the clump of errant daffodils that had pushed up through the scrubby grass; the vines of bittersweet strangling Mrs. Jukas's shrubs. Even her gnarled, dying dogwood tree was half-alive with pink flowers on one side. He opened his door just as the old woman opened hers. Seeing him, she ducked back inside. She probably thought he was watching her house. It would give her little comfort to know this was the way prisoners awaited release from their cells for meals, work, visitors: they stood like this, staring, waiting.

As he came down the walk, a girl ran around the corner. It was the girl who lived across the street. She dove through Mrs. Jukas's bushes and disappeared behind her house. He hesitated, then just kept going. He knew the drill well. *Nothing to see, nothing to know,* old

Jackie McBride would whisper. *You don't want to be here forever, do you? You've still got a chance, a life out there.*

He started down the street for what would be his first trip of any distance alone into the world. Behind him, a car slowed and then drove alongside. He could only see the passenger, a young man with a curly black beard and small round sunglasses.

"Hey, buddy!" He stuck his head out the open window. Cupped in his palm was a badge. "A girl just run by here?"

"No, sir." The automatic response, respectful—and blind.

"What do you mean? She just came around the corner!" He lifted the sunglasses to squint up at Gordon.

"I don't know, sir. I just came out." His heart raced. Imagine! How many times had he heard of this? How many times? Guys like him doing it right, all by the book—only to be trapped in the wrong place at the wrong time.

"Out from where?"

"My house. That's where I live. Seventy-five Clover."

"Yeah, all right," the cop said, and the unmarked cruiser pulled into the street.

Gordon was the only passenger on the bus. His stomach felt a little queasy, so he got off at the first stop in Dearborn. He still had a mile-and-a-half walk to Dennis's. Apparently, not many people in Dearborn rode the bus. They all had cars, two or three or even four, he thought, counting the garage doors now on an enormous yellow house high on the knoll above the street.

He remembered that his brother's house was gray. He had wanted to go straight home that first day out of Fortley. Dennis had insisted they stop in Dearborn. He couldn't wait for Gordon to meet the children. And to see his spacious, sunny house. "Mom got such a kick out of this," Dennis had said with a click of the remote control that triggered a *whoosh* of flames through the birch logs in the fireplace. Gas, Dennis explained to his startled brother. "See this? She loved this." With the touch of another button, skylights slid open like enormous eyes onto the starry night. Dennis had been a wonderful son.

Gordon used to enjoy reading his mother's letters filled with the details of his brother's accomplishments and acquisitions. He couldn't bear to read the ones written when she was depressed and struggling to understand how such a horrible thing could have happened. What had she done wrong? she would ask. How had she failed him? What could she have done differently? She'd tried her best, loved her two boys, raised them both the same, hadn't he known that?

The watermelon bag thumped against his thigh. Just when he was sure he was lost, he came upon the black-and-gold DEARBORN COUNTRY CLUB sign and remembered that Dennis's house overlooked the sixteenth hole. Dearborn was cooler than Collerton, he noted, entering the deepening shade of linden and maple trees. He kept looking behind him. The stillness seemed unnatural. There weren't any sidewalks, but then there weren't any people or even cars going by.

He was halfway up Dennis's long front walk when the sprinkler system sputtered on, hissing out long watery arcs that swayed back and forth over him. He stepped back and waited for the spray to pass, then ran in a crouch, only to be drenched in the next wave. Head down, he clutched the cake box to his chest and darted off to one side to catch the lull. He started to run, then everything stopped with an eerie silence. The round black sprinkler heads retracted, disappearing like periscopes into the thick wet grass. Pollen-swirled water ran down the walk into the road.

"Gordon!" Lisa called from the French doors above. "Oh, you're all wet!" She was laughing. Water dripped down his face and arms. "I'm sorry. I'm so sorry. Come on," she coaxed, gesturing him closer. "It's all right. I turned it off." She started to laugh again, then apologized as she led him into the big square kitchen. "But you just looked so . . . so helpless out there. Oh, Gordon." She threw her arms around him. "I'm sorry. I'm just so happy and nervous, and I don't know what else, but it's just so wonderful to . . . to have you here!"

"It's wonderful to be here." He moved back stiffly.

She wanted him to change into something of Dennis's. He patted himself off with a dish towel and insisted he was fine. Dennis wasn't home yet, she said. Gordon felt panicky. He had never talked to her alone before. Pale ale, Harrington's newest, she said, taking a beer from the refrigerator. Her family owned the Harrington Brewery in Collerton. Before becoming Dennis's father-in-law, Mr. Harrington had been his patient, then his golf partner. The friendship had cooled, however, with Dennis's growing attention to Lisa, ten years younger and just out of college. Socializing with the brother of a notorious killer had been a bit of a hoot for the boozy, handsome Harringtons, but mixing bloodlines was the last thing they had ever imagined for their only child.

"How is it?" she asked with his first sip.

"Good," he lied.

"It's even lighter than the one last time," she said.

He sat on a stool at the long green-granite counter separating the kitchen from what Dennis had called the great room. At Fortley they called the day lounge the big room, though he had never known why, since it could hold only ten or fifteen men at a time. He had to be careful; the half bottle of beer he'd had his first night here had gone right to his head. He didn't even really like the taste. Lisa was making room in the refrigerator for the watermelon. He wished she'd open the cake box. He had remembered her saying once that chocolate cake with raspberry filling was her favorite dessert. Dennis found it strange that he could recall such random facts. It came from having so little contact with people, so naturally he would remember exactly who had said what to him.

Lisa sat next to him and guillotined the wire cutter down through the block of cheese on the marble tray. She was tall, olive-skinned, with thick chestnut hair that shone in the light. Her long legs looped around the stool. She was attractive in a rangy, boyish way, certainly not the prettiest of the girlfriends his brother had brought to Fortley. Gordon had hated those visits. Self-conscious with women, especially women he didn't even know, he could never think of anything to say. Not only did Dennis do most of the talking, but he would be so unusually loquacious, so focused on Gordon's reticence, that he found it necessary to explain in painful detail exactly what his brother was thinking, feeling, or trying so dismally to express. Lisa had been the only one to cut Dennis short. Leaning toward the small microphone in the glass, she had said in a robotic monotone, "Earth to Gordon. Earth to Gordon. Your brother thinks you've disappeared. Please inform him you are sitting right here in front of him."

As she passed him a slice of cheese, her hair fell across her face. He was glad she was growing it long again. Around her neck was a diamond-studded cross on a thin gold chain. Lisa taught a religious-education class one night a week and sang in St. Margaret's choir every Sunday. Gordon had felt guilty when Dennis said he'd never been to hear her sing.

Until his arrest, they had always gone to church as a family. When he first got to Fortley, the familiar ritual of Mass seemed his last link to a life he could no longer have. But it was also there in the blue block walls of the austere little chapel that his anguish and remorse were the worst. He would bury his face in his hands to muffle the sobs. Evil had invaded his aimless, blundering life, and he didn't know how he could live with the consequences of what he had done. He stopped going to church. Back home, so had his family.

"Is Delores coming?" Lisa asked. "Dennis said you were going to ask her."

"No. She's not. She's not coming."

"Oh no! Why?"

He felt guilty that he'd disappointed her. He'd been thinking only of himself.

"Does she have to work? Is that it?"

"I don't know. I didn't ask her," he added quickly.

"Well, that's probably it." She patted his wrist with consoling cheerfulness. "I'm sure that's the only reason. She probably thinks she'd be too late. Why don't you give her a call? Tell her to come when the store closes. Jimmy and Annie are still at swimming, and Lord knows when Dennis will get here."

"No. What I meant was I didn't ask her to come."

"Why?" She blinked and shook her head. "Why didn't you?"

"I don't know. I just didn't want to, I guess." He found it amazing how in their assumptions people tried to control others. Lisa and Dennis thought Delores would be good for him, so therefore it had to happen.

She looked at him a moment. "She's awfully nice."

"I know."

"She's so easy to talk to." She slid off the stool and threw the cheese wrapping into the trash. When she picked up the pastry box, he grinned. "And she really cares about you, Gordon. She really, really does." She put it into the refrigerator, and he was disappointed. He wanted her to know that he'd remembered. "Ooo!" She leaned over the counter. "I know that look. It's the old Loomis 'Get outta my face, lady.' Okay!" She waved her hand. "I said what I had to say, and now not another word about Delores Dufault."

"No! No." He had offended her. "It's okay. I don't mind talking about her. I guess I just don't have a lot to say about her, that's all. Or at least not now, anyway. I mean, I've just got so much else I'm trying to do right now."

"You sound like your brother," she said as she slid open the glass door. He followed her out onto the glistening white deck. She was telling him that Dennis's dream was to have his own medical complex. He seemed to spend every free moment looking at real estate parcels.

"That sounds interesting." Gordon eased carefully into a canvas chair that creaked and sagged under his weight. Afraid it might break, he was afraid to move.

"I think Dennis is tired of root canals and pulling wisdom teeth. What he really wants is to be some kind of mogul. Like that. That's what he wants." She pointed to the label on the beer bottle. "To have his name on something. Loomis." She scrolled her finger in the air. "The Loomis Dental-Surgical–Big Deal Medical Park."

Her laugh made him squirm. "It's beautiful out here," he said, looking toward the gently rolling green hills. Four golfers with pull carts moved through the rose-tinted twilight.

"Maybe you and Dennis can play this weekend."

"No, I don't think so. I mean, I don't know how. I never played before," he added, seeing her frown.

"Dennis'll teach you."

"No. It's too late. I'm too old."

"Not for golf!" she scoffed.

"But that's something you learn when you're young."

Dennis hadn't played golf as a kid, she said. But Dennis was a born athlete, he reminded her. Sports had always come naturally. "Like everything else. Dennis just had the touch. No matter what he did."

"That must've been a little hard to swallow, huh? I mean, you being the older brother."

"Actually, I was always very proud of Dennis. He was very, very gifted." He smiled. "And in a way, it diverted attention away from me. Which I wanted!" he added. "I was always so big. All I ever wanted was to fade into the background, and that's not easy when you're bigger than everyone else." He laughed.

"Oh! Poor Gordon." She patted his arm.

"I didn't mean it that way," he said stiffly. "I'm not feeling sorry for myself or making excuses. That's just the way it was. Actually, it wasn't until Fortley that I finally appreciated being so big."

"But . . ." She sighed. "But in a way that's part of it, when you think of it. I mean, being so big and always holding back. It all just seems so unfair. I mean, if you hadn't felt that way, you probably wouldn't have even gone with Jerry Cox that night, and none of this would have happened."

"But it did."

"But you didn't mean to . . ." She gestured for the unspeakable.

"No. I don't think that way. I can't," he said uneasily. If Dennis were here, he would have cut her off by now.

"You have to! You can't keep being so hard on yourself, Gordon."

At the trial his lawyer had portrayed him as a loner, a loser, a big, goofy kid so desperate for friendship that he had unquestioningly followed the sly, handsome, popular Jerry Cox into the house that night. *So what?* the prosecutor had roared during his closing argument. *So what if he was the most unhappy boy in Collerton? Or in the universe? What justification could that possibly be for taking the lives of two innocent people?*

"I have to be realistic, that's all. I did what I did. And nothing can change that. Nothing." If it were anyone else but Lisa, he would have gotten up and left.

"That's what you say, but that's not really what you mean, is it?"

"Yes. That's what I mean," he said coldly.

"I look at you and I see this . . . this tightness. Like a coil. Like it's all inside and you can't get rid of it."

That she might think him still capable of violence left him speechless for a moment. "It's hard. I—"

"Of course it's hard, because you're too hard on *yourself*, Gordon. God's forgiven you. I know He has. Now why can't you do the same?" She rubbed her arm, frowning. "You didn't mean to . . . It's · not like you wanted to . . . to do that. You were just a kid. You were scared."

What else was there to say? That Janine Walters had been so scared she wet the bed? That she wasn't supposed to have been there? Jerry Cox had said the house would be empty, that she and her husband were in New York for the weekend. But Jerry Cox had said a lot of things that night, that she was hot for him and always left the key in the garage for him to let himself in any time he wanted. He said the booze was in the back pantry, so the plan was to just help themselves and then be on their way. But then Jerry started opening drawers in the dark kitchen and feeling around inside cupboards for the money he said they owed him for yardwork. Probably upstairs, he said. She did that sometimes, left it in her underwear drawer for him, wrapped up in the silk panties she'd worn that day.

It had all been said, all written down somewhere, delivered in testimony no one believed. Why should they? And even if they did, which word, fact, or detail would change a thing? No matter what he knew and remembered, the truth was ultimately meaningless. Like her grave marker, there remained only this rock-solid, irrefutable pyramid of facts: Suffocated or strangled, Janine Walters had died and would always be dead, no matter how awkward, scared, misled, lonely, or gullible the boy Gordon Loomis had been. *It was murder!* the prosecutor had cried. *Murder! Nothing else.* It was what it was.

The front door flew open and the damp-haired children raced through the kitchen, calling for their mother. Gordon stood up as they burst onto the deck. "Come here, Jimmy, Annie," Lisa said, gathering them close as if suddenly for comfort.

With all three facing him, Gordon's self-consciousness boiled to a rising panic as Lisa told them how lucky they were to have their wonderful uncle Gordon back home again and with them forever and ever.

"Now you both go give him a great big hug and a kiss," she said, nudging them along. Jimmy forced a smile. His younger sister glanced back at her mother. "You'll have to bend down, Gordon," Lisa said. "Otherwise they can't reach you."

He bent forward, but sharing his discomfort, the children tilted their heads away from his clumsy embrace. He felt bad. He had positioned their pictures so that their beautiful faces were his first vision with the morning light into his cell and his last with sleep. Yet he was as much a stranger to them as they were to him.

"Now you go sit in the corner and tell Uncle Gordon all about yourselves," Lisa said on her way into the kitchen.

Gordon and the children had the same pleading expressions as they watched her go. Though he already knew the answers from Lisa's letters and visits, he asked Jimmy what grade he was in: Fourth. His teacher's name: Mr. Kelly. Did he like school? Well, sometimes.

"Sometimes he hates it," Annie confided, careful to look at her brother and not her uncle.

"No, I don't!" Jimmy fixed her in his indignant stare. "I never hate school. I just don't always like it the same, that's all."

"Yes, you did! You said you hated it, and Mommy got really mad because we're not supposed to say 'hate.' We're not supposed to hate anything."

"You're not?" Gordon said.

"No."

"Why not?"

"Because." The little girl wet her lips and brushed the long dark hair from her face, conviction growing as she explained that hating was ugly and if you hated something, then you'd be ugly, too, like a creature or some kind of monster everybody was afraid of.

Like your uncle, Gordon thought. His first night here, Dennis had leaped out of his chair when Jimmy pushed his sister out of his way.

"She's only six, that's why she still believes in monsters," Jimmy said, laughing.

"Mom!" Annie called, running inside, leaving Gordon alone with the boy. He couldn't think of a thing to say.

"What was the jail like?" Jimmy asked.

"Uh, big. It was big. There were a lot of . . . different parts to it."

"Did you ever try and break out? Like, saw through the bars or something?"

"No. No, I never did anything like that."

"How come? Didn't you want to get out?"

"Well, I knew I had to wait. Until it was time. Until—"

"I woulda climbed right over the wall, at night, with black stuff all over my face and these special things on my shoes, like suction cups that're so strong they—"

"Jimmy," Lisa said from the doorway. She sent him downstairs to apologize to his sister.

Gordon went inside and watched Lisa cover the zucchini and summer squash with foil wrap. "It's getting so late. Seven-twenty." She put the casserole back in the oven. "Maybe we should just start without him."

"I don't mind waiting," he said.

"I do. He's missed dinner just about every night this week."

Just then the floor vibrated as the garage door rumbled and then closed again. Dennis hurried into the kitchen, red-faced and breathless with apologies. He had taken a potential investor out to see one of the properties, but then the guy insisted on seeing the other one, which was clear across town, so the time just—

"The grill's already lit." Lisa handed him the platter of swordfish.

"I said I was sorry," Dennis said as she turned abruptly away. He looked at Gordon and rolled his eyes, then touched his shoulder. "Your shirt's wet. And so are your pants. What happened?"

"I got caught in the sprinkler."

"Well, go change. I've got things you can wear."

"He doesn't want to, Dennis. I already asked him," Lisa said. "Now will you go put the swordfish on? Please?"

Gordon followed him onto the deck. "What's that you're putting on?" he asked of the oily mixture Dennis was brushing onto the fish.

"I don't know, some kind of marinade." Dennis kept adjusting the flame.

"What does it do?"

"Keeps the fish wet. Moist. I don't know, something like that," he said with an irritable toss of his hand.

"If anyone asks me in the Market, now I'll know what it's for."

"Yeah." Dennis moved the swordfish to the back of the grill. He closed the hood, opening it again a few minutes later to turn the swordfish. He brushed more marinade onto the cooked side.

Gordon fidgeted in the silence. He regretted mentioning the Market. He bent over the railing and sniffed at the pink flowers in the window box.

"They don't smell. They're geraniums." Dennis sounded annoyed.

"Oh, that's right. Mom used to plant those. Red ones. By the front steps. Maybe I'll do that. I did some work on Dad's roses. Quite a bit, actually. Yeah, I got rid of a lot of the dead stuff. You should see all the new shoots."

"Oh, yeah?" Dennis glanced back as if to say something, then sighed and began moving the swordfish around on the grill again.

Gordon remembered these moods, even when Dennis had been little. Like black clouds obscuring the sun, they could pass as quickly as they came. But for as long as they lasted, everyone would feel not only their chill, but a kind of desolation. Gordon cleared his throat. "Boy, that's some grill. It's huge. It must be twice as big as the stove at home."

Dennis's head shot up. "It was the only one that would fit into that miserable little kitchen."

"No, no! I wasn't complaining. I just meant the grill, it's so big. I never saw one so—"

"You don't have to stay there." Dennis glanced toward the kitchen. "As a matter of fact, I was just talking to the Realtor. She said she'd be glad to get you an appraisal on the house."

"But I don't want to move. I—"

"Why? Give me one good reason you wouldn't rather be living in a brand-new condo with all the latest modern conveniences."

"I like it where I am. I know where everything is." He tried not to be rattled by his brother's smirk. They'd been all through this before. "It's comfortable, and I like puttering around. Plus I'm so close to work I don't have to—"

"So what was the degree for, then? All those courses? All the money, what the hell was that all about?"

"I said I'd pay you back. I always said that," he mumbled, feeling like a leech again.

"You know I don't give a damn about the money!" Dennis exploded, leaning close. A wind gust roiled through the trees. The swordfish sizzled, and the flames sputtered an orangy blue. "All I want is for you to have some kind of normal life, that's all I want. Jesus Christ! Is that so hard to understand?"

More than hard, it was almost unfathomable that Dennis could think normal life was possible. But then how could his brother understand his meager expectations when Dennis's had always been fueled by that relentless optimism and drive that delivered men like him to success? "I know," Gordon conceded rather than argue. "I guess I'm just trying to get a feel for things. I just need to take it slow at first."

"Fine! I can understand that. I just hate seeing you settle for less all the time, that's all." Dennis patted his shoulder. The light was back in his pale eyes. "So anyway, this gal I know, the Realtor I was talking about, she's going to call you. Her name's Jilly Cross. I asked her to show you some condos."

"Condos?" Lisa said, coming onto the deck with a large blue bowl of salad. "Don't tell me. Not condos again. Dennis should get his broker's license. Lately everyone he meets he's trying to sell condos to. Last week after church he's got Father Hensile by the arm, trying to talk him into one for his sick mother! Like all of a sudden condos are the answers to everyone's problems."

Dennis laughed, unfazed by the edge in her voice. "But it'd be perfect. Especially for someone in Gordon's situation."

"His situation?" Lisa turned back from the doorway.

"You know what I mean. He's stuck in a house that's depreciating faster and faster every day that goes by."

"But that's where he wants to live, Dennis, so isn't that the most important thing?"

"When you're living on Clover Street, the most important thing's not getting killed," Dennis called after her as she went inside to get the children. He turned off the grill and didn't say anything.

"We gather here together to thank you, Lord," Lisa said softly, bowing her head as they all joined hands around the table.

"For these thy gifts," Annie said.

"Which we are about to receive," Jimmy said.

"From thy bounty through Jesus Christ, our Lord," Dennis said with a sigh.

Lisa's eyes remained closed, but the children and Dennis looked at Gordon, waiting.

Annie squeezed his fingers. "It's your turn."

"Uh, thank you . . . thank you, Lord, for—"

"No!" Jimmy said.

"Just say 'Amen,' that's all," Dennis said.

"Oh. I'm sorry. I guess I forgot how it ends," Gordon told the children.

"Well, say it, then," Annie said, delighted that someone so big could mess up something so simple.

"Amen," he said softly. Mindful of the little grunts Dennis had criticized him for at lunch last week, Gordon tried to eat slowly. He was used to wolfing down his food. So accustomed was he to eating in a daze and not speaking to anyone that he wasn't sure where to look, at his plate or his dining companions. In an effort to do both, he kept dropping food onto the table, into his lap.

Jimmy was watching him. "Did anybody else ever try and break out of your jail?"

There was a *clink clink* as both parents put down their forks.

"No." Gordon shook his head. The children knew their uncle had gone to prison because someone had died. If they asked, he should just answer their question, Dennis had advised on the ride home. Tell them as much as they need to know. No details about the incident, of course. As if he ever would, Gordon had thought, amazed.

"You must've wanted to, though, huh?" Jimmy asked hopefully.

"Your uncle always did what he was supposed to do," Lisa said. "We may not always like our situation in life, but we do our best. Uncle Gordon was very brave."

The boy's eyes lit up. "How were you brave?"

Gordon had no idea. He hadn't been brave. He had only *been*. "I guess I just obeyed the rules, that's all. I did what I was told."

Dennis's hands were clenched. "So, Jimmy, tell us how swimming went today," he said, but the boy had already launched into his next question.

"Did any prisoners ever try and stab you or anything?"

"No." Gordon smiled as if that were a very far-fetched possibility. He caught himself. He had been about to say he had seen a few men stabbed and knew of many others who had been.

"My friend Jack said you killed a lady." Jimmy watched him closely.

Gordon nodded.

"That's enough now, Jimmy," Dennis said, and Lisa began to talk about Jimmy's swim meet next week. It was for the country club junior championship. Jimmy reminded her that she'd said he didn't have to be in it if he didn't want to. Lisa patted his hand and said they'd talk some more and then decide. Decide what? Dennis asked, staring at Lisa. Jimmy was on the team and he would be swimming in the meet, and it was as simple as that.

Gordon felt as if his mother had just spoken. He pushed vegetables onto his fork with his finger, then licked bits of squash from his thumb.

"Here." Dennis held out the basket of rolls.

"No, thank you," he said. He'd already had four, and there were only two left. He pushed more squash onto his fork and licked his finger.

"Please." Dennis set the basket in front of him. "Use a roll, will you?"

"I'm sorry," Gordon said.

"Dennis," Lisa chided in a low voice.

"Like this." Annie demonstrated, breaking a roll. "You just push it—"

"Thank you, Annie. I'm sure Uncle Gordon knows how to do it." Lisa looked at Dennis.

"So what happened to Delores?" Dennis asked. "You said you were going to bring her."

"No." Gordon wiped his mouth with the corner of his napkin. "I said I'd call her."

"And did you?"

"No, because she came over. She just came," he added, though his brother clearly didn't regard this as the intrusion it had been.

"Well, you dropped the ball, then, Gordon. I mean, after all she's done for you through the years. So now you're home and you don't even call her?"

"I . . ." He felt oddly winded. "I just didn't get to it." He took a deep breath. Then another.

"Dennis." Lisa sighed.

"She'd be someone to do things with, that's all! Get out of that depressing house and meet people!" Dennis said, not to Gordon but to Lisa, who glared at him.

"I get out. I meet people. Every day I meet interesting people."

"Where?" Dennis smirked. "At the Nash Street Market? Come on, will ya, Gordon! What kind of a life is that?"

"I—"

"I can't believe you're doing this!" Lisa's voice trembled with anger.

"Don't you see?" Dennis asked, looking at him now. "It's the same old thing, isn't it. Just like coming back here. Instead of taking a chance somewhere else, you'll just keep on settling for less, won't you?"

"No!" Gordon spoke quietly but firmly. "I'm just trying to ease into things, that's all. I don't want much. I don't need anything. I'm fine."

"But you've got to want things! You've got to be ambitious! Otherwise you might as well be back in there trying to hold up your pants with your elbows all the goddamn time!"

Lisa gripped the table edge with both hands. "How can you talk to your brother like that? Who do you think you are?"

Gordon was shocked. He had seen them bicker occasionally on their visits, but nothing like this. It pained him to be causing this deep anger between them, yet he understood. Dennis loved the idea, the concept, of having his brother back. It was the sweating, grunting, blundering reality of Gordon he couldn't tolerate. He stood up and said it was getting late; he probably should be going now.

"No. Please, don't," Lisa said.

Dennis apologized and asked him not to leave. Gordon continued to stand while on either side the children stared up in wide-eyed intrigue. Even for their sake he couldn't manage a smile. "Actually, I'm really tired. I think that little bit of beer did me in," he said, stooping to kiss the top of Lisa's head.

"I'm just trying to help, that's all," Dennis said, hand raised suppliantly.

"No, I know," he said as Lisa reached back for his arm. "I just hate causing you two any more trouble, that's all."

"Believe me, it's not you." Lisa squeezed his arm hard.

"She means me," Dennis said with a rueful smile, then told him again that he was sorry.

He let Dennis take him only as far as the bus stop. He found himself enjoying the rackety bus ride home. The driver, a woman with an orangy buzz cut, kept smiling at him through the mirror. A white-haired woman in soiled turquoise pants was the only other passenger. Clamped between her legs were three bulging shopping bags filled with smaller plastic bags. When he had gotten on the bus, she'd stared angrily out the window.

He knew how she felt. The hardest part of prison life had been not the lack of freedom, but being surrounded constantly by people. He'd always thought he would have been one of the few who could have endured solitary confinement without going off the deep end. But then of course he'd never done anything wrong or broken the rules. That was not to say he'd been a model prisoner. Not like Jackie

McBride, who worked at improving not only himself, but everyone around him. The old man thrived on the ruthless complexities of prison society. In another time and place, Jackie might have been an inspiring general or congressman instead of a steel-nerved Mob underling. It had taken Jackie a long time to break through Gordon's reserve. He had admired Gordon's pursuit of a college education. While other inmates openly derided Gordon as the "spook," Jackie considered his aloofness a sign of intellectual superiority. The old man had died two weeks before Gordon got out.

Prison life already seemed so distant that even when he tried to recall them, most details evaded him. The experience had often been so vile that little had seemed real or, in the end, just. What price had he paid? Two lives were lost, yet he still had his. The emptiness and the lost years could not have been the true punishment. Unless it was this constant dread like static in his soul. *No. There's more, more to come,* he thought as the bus rattled under the overpass into Collerton.

The pleated door closed quickly behind him. The tall arc lamps spilled a lavender glow over the dingy streets. Bradley Hill had once been one of the more desirable neighborhoods in the city. Now most of the large Victorian homes had been partitioned into apartments like this one on the corner, its massive oak doors flanked by rows of mailboxes and doorbells. Spray-painted on the porch wall was the word *Aurora.* Unmatched colored curtains hung in the windows, some too short, others knotted and wafting in and out over the sills. Leaving gaps like missing teeth, balusters had been wrenched or kicked out of the railing. Where the wide front lawn had once been green with tended grass and neat hedges, now six cars were parked on paving laid from the sidewalk right up to the granite foundation. The front door opened and a plump, bare-armed woman in baggy jeans came onto the front porch, carrying a bottle of beer by its neck. She sat on the top step and lit a cigarette. She stared down as he walked by. He remembered going to Joan Kruger's seventh-birthday party under the pear tree in the backyard there. Mrs. Kruger had silvery frosted hair, a fur coat, and a cleaning lady who came every week. A cleaning lady, and she didn't even have a job, which to his mother was the epitome of privileged indolence. In the front hall there had been an enormous mahogany hat tree, in its center an etched mirror surrounded by brass coat hooks, ivory hat holders, and a purple velvet bench flanked by two ornately carved receptacles, one for umbrellas and the other for walking sticks.

When he was curled up on his bunk with his back to the cell door, such recall of detail had been a vital nightly ritual. Under the constant glare, sleepless with the stink and groans and snoring around him, he would try to visualize each room he had ever been in, the furniture, where doors and windows had been, the color of walls and carpets. The one room he could never recall had been *that* room *that* night. It had been too dark, a hellish cave of lumpy shapes and shadows in the glowing red numbers on a clock radio by the bed: 9:16, that's what he remembered, that and her damp hair. The hiss of a startled cat. The rug sliding under his braced feet. The pillow feathers flattening until through them he could feel her jaw struggling against his palm. Her fingernails had been painted a bright red, but this he knew from the blown-up photos on the courtroom easel, showing two nails torn to the quick. *The heartbreaking proof of a young woman's desperate fight to live,* this delivered with the *snap, snap, snap* of the prosecutor's pointer on the glossy paper accentuating each word.

Gordon turned the corner and then stopped, toes curling in his shoes. The spinning blue light lit up the peaks and angles of the crowded rooftops. A cruiser was parked in front of Mrs. Jukas's house. The old woman's shrill voice cut through the night. "They were selling drugs. Right down there on the sidewalk. Right in front of my house. People kept pulling up and the girl, she'd go over to the cars and give them the drugs right there, bold as brass, then she'd come back and give the money to the one I told you about."

"Which one?" asked the bony-faced, older cop, his flat tone only fueling the old woman's agitation.

"I already told you! The one they call Feaster!"

Gordon had made it halfway up his walk when the cop called out, asking his name. Gordon, he answered. The cop asked if he knew Feaster.

"No, sir. Not—"

"Yes, you do! I saw you talking to him!" Mrs. Jukas shouted with an angry gesture over the railing. "Just last week! I saw you! With my own eyes I saw you!"

He wiped the sweat from his cheeks and explained that Feaster had spoken to him, that was all. He didn't know him.

"You new here?" the cop asked.

"I grew up here," Gordon said, eyes wide, waiting.

"You grew up here and you don't know Feaster?" the cop said.

"I just moved back. A couple weeks ago."

"Right when Feaster started coming around again!" Mrs. Jukas called out angrily. "The same time *he* came back." She pointed at Gordon.

Light flared behind her house. A second cop emerged from her backyard, crisscrossing his flashlight's grainy beacon from the foundation up to the roof. "There's no fire," he told the old woman. "Believe me, I checked everywhere."

"They were just trying to scare you, that's all," the older cop said. "That's what they do."

"Just trying to scare me!" Mrs. Jukas hit her breast. "He threatened me, that's what he did! And I want him arrested! You can arrest him for that! I know you can! Threatening a senior citizen's against the law, and I know that for a fact!" Chest heaving, she eased into her bent aluminum porch chair.

Both officers leaned close. Was she all right? Could she hear them? Was she having the chest pains again?

Gordon slipped onto his own narrow, little porch, his grip tight on the doorknob.

"Mr. Gordon!" the older cop called. "No need to call anyone! She says she's fine."

"Oh," Gordon said, turning.

"Can you come here a minute?" the older cop asked, gesturing.

"Yes, sir." Gordon hurried over. He stood in the shadows, shocked by the debris piled in the corners of her once-immaculate porch—leaves, papers, plastic cups, fast-food bags, empty cigarette packs.

The younger cop looked like an infantryman with his combat pants tucked into his boots. He shook his head in disgust as Mrs. Jukas described coming home last week from the doctor to find

Feaster stretched out on a lounge chair in her backyard. He had refused to leave.

"You should have called us."

"I did, but you never came!"

"We told her we'll keep going by all night," the older cop told Gordon in a low voice. "But I think she'll feel better if she knows you'll be keeping an eye on things, too."

Gordon doubted that, but he nodded, then asked what had happened.

Apparently Mrs. Jukas had told Feaster and his driver to stop having that girl sell drugs in front of her house. They said if she didn't shut up and go inside, they'd burn her house down. She told them she was going in all right, but to call the police! Which she did, but when they arrived, no one was here.

"Because it took you twenty-five minutes to get here!" the old woman shouted from her chair. "Twenty-five minutes! Next time I'm taking pictures. And I told them, too. That way I'll have proof!"

The older cop rolled his eyes at Gordon. The younger cop was trying to explain that for her own safety she shouldn't rile these people up. They could be very dangerous. Especially Ronnie Feaster, who lately thought he had free rein in this part of the city.

From now on, she should stay inside and just let the police handle it.

"Handle it! You call this handling it?" she said in a tremulous voice. With her arms crossed and hands clasping her shoulders, she looked frail and drained. "What good are you?" she asked wearily. "The minute you're gone they'll be back."

"Mrs. Jukas!" The older cop sounded almost irritated. "Your neighbor here says he'll keep an eye on things, so it's not like you're going to be alone or anything. Right, Mr. Gordon?"

"Yes, sir, that's right. I will. I'll keep an eye on things," he said.

"His name is Loomis." She stared at the cop.

"Sorry, thought you said Gordon," the cop said on his way down the steps.

"I did. Gordon's my first name."

As the cruiser pulled out, she looked up wanly at Gordon, the devil she'd been left with. She shrank deeper into her lopsided chair with its frayed and dangling nylon strips.

"Here." Gordon picked up a McDonald's bag and tore off a piece. He wrote down his telephone number. "You know, if you're afraid, or if you just hear something and you want me to take a look." He held out the paper. "Well, anyway." He laid it on the very end of her chair arm and took a step back. "It's good to have. Just in case."

Her stricken face belied the certainty that the very last thing on earth she'd do would be to call Gordon Loomis in the middle of the night to come murder her in her own bed.

It was the most vivid dream. He was in the Market, naked, stacking an applesauce display. Customers were pushing carts past him, up and down the aisles, but no one seemed to care. Suddenly, the entire pyramid began to shift. He threw out his arms to stop the rolling, tumbling jars, but they kept shattering all around him. He sat up, confused, then leaped out of bed with the alarm of breaking glass and a piercing wail. He opened the window and leaned over the sill.

"Help! Help me! Please help!" a woman pleaded through the leafy darkness.

He pulled on pants, then grabbed the Corcopax flashlight and ran outside. Mrs. Jukas clutched her porch railing. "They broke my window!" she cried as he ran up the steps. "I was sound asleep and then the window broke."

He said he'd look, but she wouldn't go inside with him. She stayed by the front door while he checked the three rooms downstairs. None of the windows were broken. Both kitchen doors were locked, the back door dead-bolted, the cellar door with a flimsy hook and eye. As he came through the dining room, she called in to ask about her Hummels. Were any broken? Were they still there?

"They look fine to me," he said, peering through the glass door of the floor-to-ceiling curio cabinet, every shelf crowded with the small ceramic figures of children with dogs, cats, umbrellas in the wind, buckets of flowers, musical instruments. For all his disciplined recall, he'd forgotten about her collection. These, his mother used to say, were the only children Mrs. Jukas could tolerate. He went back into the living room and asked if she'd called the police.

"Yes!" she answered immediately.

"I wonder what's taking so long."

"I'll call again," she said, hurrying into the kitchen.

She hadn't really called, he realized as he tiptoed up the stairs. She'd only said so to curb his homicidal impulses. The small front bedroom and bathroom were intact and empty. The next door creaked open into her bedroom. He flipped the wall switch and splinters of light glittered everywhere. On the floor beside the glass-sprayed bed was a brick. He peered from the shattered window into the new leaves of the old maple, so big now that it shaded both yards. Only a strong arm could have thrown the brick up into the branches and through the window. Another few inches and it would have landed on the bed, perhaps even on the old woman. Leaning closer, he saw a ladder propped against the house. His hand jerked back against the jagged glass edge with the sickening realization that someone had climbed up here and aimed the brick right at the sleeping old woman. He shone the flashlight on the ladder. LOOMIS, said the faded stenciling down the side. It was his father's old wooden extension ladder. His grip felt sticky on the flashlight; he'd cut his finger. He put his knuckle in his mouth and sucked on the cut. *His* ladder. *His* blood on the windowsill and floor. He tried to rub it away. Gordon Loomis, convicted killer, first on the scene and bleeding. A siren swelled in the distance, growing louder. Closer. *Is this the way it ends?* he wondered, looking wildly between the door and the window. *As stupidly as this?*

"The police're coming!" Mrs. Jukas called up, looking past him warily.

"There's nobody up here, but I just cut myself," he said, hurrying downstairs.

She turned on the water in the kitchen sink and told him to hold his hand under it. "It's not my fault. You should've been careful. I hope you don't need stitches," she fretted from behind.

"No, it's just a cut, that's all."

"Because I can't have any more claims on my homeowner's."

He shut off the water and told her about the brick, the explosion of glass, the ladder.

"Oh, my God!" Her mouth dropped open. "They were right out there, then, weren't they? Looking in! Watching me." Her eyes darted from window to door, ceiling to floor, as if they might still be watching. "They're here!" she cried.

The blaring siren filled the house. "It's my father's ladder," he shouted, licking his cut and following her onto the porch, repeating it until she turned. "But I don't know where they got it from. It wasn't where it used to be, in the garage."

"No, it's mine!" She said Dennis had given it to her a few years ago. She kept it out back in the bushes against the foundation.

Searching the yard, the police found only flattened grass directly below the broken window. These were different cops from the earlier pair. One was black and the other Hispanic. Sleepy-eyed neighbors watched from their porches and open windows. The few who came out onto the sidewalk were men.

"Just in case," Mrs. Jukas said as she put a nitroglycerin pill under her tongue. She'd had a heart attack last Christmas Day, she told Officer Pierce. He was black, a short, trim man whose erudite manner and hint of a British accent seemed to calm her. He suggested she spend the rest of the night with a friend or relative. "If I leave, they'll be in here like rats." She gestured down the street. "That's what happened on the corner." She told them how old Mr. Velez fell and broke his hip in the first snowstorm last winter. After a month in rehab he came home to find junkies cooking coke on his table, his kitchen ankle-deep in garbage.

"Yes, well, as they say, nature abhors a vacuum," Officer Pierce conceded wearily.

Mrs. Jukas's head snapped up. "That's not nature! They're worse than animals. They're dead inside. In here," she said, tapping her chest, "they're dead. My husband used to tell me what the war was like. And now I look around, the house on the corner, the two behind me. And now even my own bedroom, and it's just like he said, the fires and the glass breaking in the middle of the night. It is, it's like a war, and here I am in the middle of it. Never ever in a million years did I think I'd end up like this." A sob tore through her voice. "I'm afraid to leave my house, and I'm afraid to stay."

Officer Pierce put his hand on her shoulder. "Maybe if someone could stay with you, for the rest of the night, anyway." He raised his eyebrows at Gordon. "Maybe your neighbor here."

"No!" she cried. "Absolutely not!"

CHAPTER 5

A booming drum pulse heralded the purple Navigator's approaching splendor. The gilded hubcaps flashed in the damp morning light like spinning knives. The SUV stopped, and the sudden silence seemed amplified. Ronnie Feaster's driver climbed down from his high perch in black, unlaced sneakers. He was a huge young man with ribbons of fat curled round the back of his shaved head. Large gold hoops dangled from both ears. Feaster glanced up at Gordon, who had just stepped onto his porch, and gave a brief salute. The side door of the SUV opened on a woman who clung to the frame with both hands. She peered down at the road as if from a dizzying precipice. "Come on! Get out!" the driver demanded. He grabbed for her, but she kicked and pushed him away. Feaster's eyes held Gordon's over the long brown cigarette he was lighting.

"Leave me alone! Leave me the fuck alone!" the woman screamed through the early-morning quiet as the driver pulled her out.

In the tenement across the way, the front door opened. The frizzy-haired girl ran wobbling down the steps on thick platform shoes laced up her skinny ankles.

"Jada! Jada!" the woman bellowed.

"You leave my mother alone, Polie!" the girl shouted. Her fists pummeled his beefy back as he dragged her mother out onto the street. The girl reared back and kicked him in the knee. Howling, he gave the woman a shove that sent her staggering into a heap. The girl was trying to pull her mother to her feet when he limped up and hit the back of her head so hard that she collapsed across her mother's legs.

Feaster flicked his cigarette out the window. He smiled at Gordon. The driver reached into the van and pulled out a short, knobby club.

"Jada! Jada!" the woman wailed as he came closer. "Get up! Get off me!" she screamed. Raising herself, the girl swayed on her hands and knees. He lifted the club.

Oh, my God! No, don't! Don't do that! Gordon's mouth opened, but the words clotted in his throat. The driver jabbed the club into the girl's side, knocking her over. He said something, then climbed back behind the wheel. The monstrous pulse beat vibrated as they drove away. A thin trickle of smoke rose from the gutter where the cigarette still burned.

"Jada!" the woman pleaded as the girl hobbled up the walk and seized the railing. "You're mad at me, aren't you. I knew you'd be mad."

The girl dragged herself along the railing onto the porch.

"Jada! Jada! Jada!" the woman bawled at the closing door, then plodded up the stairs in the reluctant tread of the chronically misunderstood.

Gordon's chest felt bruised as he began to breathe again. Brutality had been as pervasive in his life as the low hum of Fortley's fluorescent glare, but what was this? What virulence had he just witnessed? And what mad absurdity had the other night been, terrorizing an old woman, sound asleep, in her own bed? . . . *I'm pregnant. Please, please, don't hurt me,* Janine Walters had gasped into the lowering pillow. He closed his eyes, overwhelmed again by the vastness of his own impotence. Who was he to be shocked or offended? What right did he have to judge the crime of another?

He started down the street, soon passing the same children he saw every day at this time. The oldest, Mike, dutifully gripped the hands of Jack and Tim, his younger brothers. Once around the corner, however, they began to wrestle, run, and tumble, grabbing one another's hats, jumping in puddles, tackling one another so that before they had even reached the crossing guard they were disheveled and wild with freedom. Gordon usually enjoyed watching them, but this morning their voices rang shrill and mirthless.

Thoughts of the girl filled him with the same degradation he'd felt when he first got to Fortley. Added to the weight of his own crime, everything there had come as a shock. It made him feel dirtier, more inhuman, unworthy of kindness, and utterly alone. Days could go by without a word from his lips. When he was forced to speak, his voice came as a whisper. Because he could not remove himself, the violence and torment had to be walled off from his consciousness. Night after night, men might scream or sob or even hurl their feces at passing guards. In that first year, a man was disemboweled in the shower, another set on fire while sedated in his infirmary bed, a boy, just a little older than Gordon, raped his first night there, but after a while the horror dulled. Menace droned on, but with the numbing monotony of distant battle or constant thunder. With his cell as sanctuary, it had little to do with him. Concentration and diligence became his barricades.

Dennis called at dinnertime. He was telling Gordon that Mrs. Jukas's call had come that morning in the middle of a difficult and excessively bloody extraction. It was an emergency, his receptionist had rushed in to tell him—something about an attack and his brother. The old woman told Dennis to come get his father's ladder or else she'd call the Salvation Army to take it away. She couldn't have it lying around out there anymore. Not after what had happened. Dennis had assured her he'd get the ladder out of there as soon as he possibly could.

"So could you please go get it?" Dennis asked.

"Now?" Gordon hungrily eyed the pork chops and spaghetti he had just put on the table.

"Would you just run over, please? I've been home a half hour and she's called me twice already," Dennis said.

He crimped tinfoil around the plate, then hurried next door and rang Mrs. Jukas's bell. He waited, rang it again. She wasn't coming and he was starving, so he went into her yard, where he found the ladder in a thicket of overgrown shrubs. He tried to pull it out, but it wouldn't budge. Sidestepping his way into the dense bushes, he saw that the ladder was tied to the dripping spigot in a rung-woven network of knots and loops. He tried but couldn't undo them, then remembered the box cutter in his back pocket. The blade sliced easily through the brittle rope.

Above him, the back door creaked open. "I've been watching you. I know you're down there, Gordon Loomis. Don't think I don't."

Shielding his face from the battering branches, he worked his way out and explained what he was doing. "But I had to cut some of the rope." He reached in and slid the ladder free.

"You cut it?"

"With my cutter." He held it up and she cringed from the screen. "I hope you don't mind. I was just trying to get it out. I'm sorry. I guess I should've asked first," he said as she continued to stare down at him. He gestured up at the plywood nailed to the window. "If you want, I could go up and measure for the glass. Might as well, now that the ladder's out."

"No, thank you." She shut the door.

He lifted the heavy wooden ladder onto his shoulder and carried it into his garage. It gave him great pleasure to slide it over the rafters where his father had stored it.

He had just sat down to eat when the phone rang. Dennis said Mrs. Jukas was very upset. She thought Dennis would be taking the ladder. She didn't know it was just going to go into the garage right next door where anyone could still go get it to break into her house.

"I locked the garage," Gordon said.

"That's what I told her, but she says she's calling the Salvation Army to come for it."

"No! That's Dad's ladder. You tell her I want it, I'm keeping it." In the silence his voice faltered. "It was Dad's."

"Jesus Christ, don't you get it?"

"Yes. I know. She's scared."

"She's scared all right. She's scared of you."

Delores Dufault called the Dearborn store and left a message for Albert that she had to close early today because of a dentist's appointment. She outlined her eyes in dusky blue, put on fresh lipstick and generous spritzes of Sweet Freesia, the cologne she'd always worn to Fortley. At four-fifteen she was steering a grocery cart through the Nash Street Market. She pushed it all the way back to the meat counter, moving slowly as she looked down each aisle. Gordon was in the farthest corner, arranging mounds of green and red grapes in the slanted case. Every time he reached forward, his shirt hiked up his bare back. His red apron ties dangled at his sides.

In a smaller person, shyness often bestows obscurity, an easy invisibility. But with Gordon's size it seemed to convey a brooding force, as contradictory as it was intimidating. In school she had understood his ducked head and averted eyes when he entered the classroom, then his quick cringing slide into the seat. Always big herself, she knew the misery, after some blunder, gaffe, wrong answer, or startling barrage of allergic sneezes, of wanting to disappear, to just shrivel up and die.

Delores had managed to keep her Fortley visits a secret from her family until one day last year when Lisa Loomis had rushed Jimmy into the clinic with a bad reaction to a bee sting.

"Loomis . . . Loomis . . . My sister Delores knew a Loomis once." Her sister Karen, the triage nurse, had pretended to struggle for the connection, when everyone of a certain age knew exactly who the Loomises were. There had been only one Loomis family in town, and the trial had been covered by all the Boston papers. Jerry Cox's father had been an all-American football player, and until that unthinkable night, Jerry had been on a similar track. The papers had even printed variations of Gordon's hated nickname: Gloomis. The Gloom. Gloomer. Loomer. The stories had depicted a dramatic contrast between Gloomis and the handsome, sandy-haired Jerry Cox, who had made the mistake of trying to be kind to the class creep.

"Oh! So you must be Delores Dufault's sister," Lisa had said in her easy way. "Delores is great. She always manages to make our trips to Fortley seem like fun."

With that revelation, the four Dufault sisters had descended upon Delores the very next morning. What was wrong with her? My God, hadn't she read enough Dear Abby letters to know what happened to women who got mixed up with prisoners? Was she that lonely? If she had that much time on her hands, then why not spend some of it with her nieces and nephews instead of trying to impress Lisa Harrington with what a good sport she was?

"I hope you're not going to be seeing him now that he's home," Karen had said just the other day when she called. She'd heard that Gordon Loomis was back living in the old house on Clover Street and working at the Nash Street Market.

"Maybe. I don't know," Delores had answered, hurt that she had to find out from her sister where he worked. She neglected to say she had already seen him, not to allay her sister's fears, but because of her own regret at dropping in on him like that. And now, wasn't this the very same thing? My God, what was she turning into, a stalker? She didn't even have food in the cart. He would know she was here to see him. That stricken look would darken his eyes, and once again she would feel so desperate and pitiful.

"You looking for a special cut, miss?" A droopy-eyed man leaned out from the meat-cutting room, his apron stiff with blood.

"No. No, thank you." She hurried back the way she'd come.

"Delores!" a voice called when she was almost at the front door. Gordon. She turned, grinning, only to see Neil Dubbin atop a ladder, removing stained tiles from the ceiling. "Hey, how've you been?" he asked, climbing down quickly.

They knew each other from the Chamber of Commerce. At the last meeting he'd sidled up, whispering how they'd better stick together. There weren't many of them left in Collerton. Many what? White faces, he'd said.

He was telling her how the roof leak kept triggering the alarms. "One of these times the cops just aren't gonna come." His brown-spotted hands trembled, and his hair was a lank, yellowish gray. They were all aging, but his seemed like decay. "And then what happens?" He sighed. "I mean with all the crap that goes on around here. I used

to park my car out back, you know, leave the prime spots for customers," he said, pointing to the narrow front lot. "But no sir, not
anymore. Now I'm right out there. Right by the door."

"Well, that's good."

"Yeah, well, my customers don't have cars anyway." He laughed.
"If they did, they'd go shop someplace cheaper. Same as your place,
right? It's like this captive clientele we got." He leaned closer. "They
don't get no choice cuz they got no choice." He laughed.

"Well, anyway," she said as she moved toward the door. She
thought she'd seen Gordon's approaching reflection in the plate glass.

"Last month I had two break-ins and one holdup, this stupid
junkie shaking so much he dropped his food stamp ID card trying to
shove the bills into his pocket."

"Oh, that's right." She took another step. "I read about that."

"But not anymore. Cuz now I got the best security of all." He
held his hand to his mouth. "You remember Gloomis, don't you?"

It *was* Delores Dufault. Gordon froze halfway down the coffee and
baking aisle. She was talking to Neil. He turned, then hurried into
the back room, where he busied himself moving pallets so he could
mop the floor.

"This one's out on Lowell Road." Jilly Cross handed him the listing
sheet. Gordon had agreed to look at the condos only to pacify Dennis. The ladder incident had escalated. Mrs. Jukas had called Dennis
three times, demanding it be removed from Gordon's garage. Dennis
kept assuring her he had spoken to his brother and it would be taken
care of. This morning an Attorney Martin had called Dennis at his
office to say that his client, Mrs. Elsbeth Jukas, wanted her ladder
back. She claimed the ladder had left her property under false pre-
tenses, that Dennis had led her to believe it would be going to his
house, not next door into the hands of a convicted murderer. Dennis
canceled his last two appointments and drove over to Gordon's and

pleaded with him to let the Salvation Army take it away, but he refused. Their father's ladder was not going to end up with strangers.

"Because it's such a fucking precious heirloom, right?" Dennis
shouted, and Gordon went silent. Dennis apologized. All right, then,
he conceded. He'd keep the ladder at his house and drive it over to
Collerton whenever Gordon needed it. "For the sake of peace, all
right?" Dennis said.

"But that's ridiculous," Gordon said. "I mean, why should we
both be inconvenienced? Especially you."

"Jesus Christ! You want her calling the parole office, is that what
you want?"

What Gordon didn't want was Dennis mad at him, so the ladder
would go to Dennis's and now a Realtor was showing him a condo-
minium he had no intention of buying.

"It's expensive," Gordon told her. Too expensive to even hold the
listing sheet. It kept sliding off the dashboard. He held it down with
one finger as they rode along.

"Not really." She turned onto a road lined with identical brick
buildings with small wrought-iron balconies. "Not when you consider today's market."

Today's market. Gordon glanced at his watch. He hadn't eaten yet.
He wasn't used to being hungry. He couldn't seem to follow what
she was saying. Every day for twenty-five years he had eaten at the
exact same times. His stomach was growling. He pressed his knees
together, clearing his throat and coughing to cover the gassy rumbling. Dennis had said not to be nervous, that she was very nice, and
she was—easy to talk to, no pressure. Just sit back and let her do her
thing, Dennis had said. That's all he wanted, he'd said, just to have
Gordon see what was out there. He kept glancing at her. She was
beautiful, long blond wavy hair. Everything about her was delicate:
her turned-up nose, her perfect white teeth, her slender fingers on
the wheel, her pink nails glistening in the light. She stopped the car,
and he realized he hadn't felt carsick once.

"Here we are. Building sixteen. Dennis said to show you everything. Both ends of the spectrum," she said on their way inside.

"Which is how I do it anyway. At this point in the process you're being educated." In the closeness of the elevator, she smelled of flowers. Tiny white flowers. Her head didn't reach his shoulder.

She unlocked the door. Her voice echoing through the empty unit made her seem smaller. The kitchen was not only big enough for a table, she was saying, it even had room in the corner for a good-size wine rack. Or an office niche.

He wasn't sure what that meant.

"Do you have a computer?" she asked.

"No. No, I don't. But I learned. They had classes. I mean, I know how to use one," he added, relieved when she didn't ask where. She didn't seem the least bit nervous. If she did know who he was, it didn't seem to bother her.

The long living room was as big as the entire first floor in his house. He kept wanting to tell her that so she'd laugh, but he hated to interrupt. Her voice was so soft, he had to bend and tilt his head to hear her. She had a wonderful laugh, surprisingly strong and rich for such a small woman. He had made her laugh before, trying to fit into her little sports car. To demonstrate the spaciousness of the walk-in closet, she extended both arms and turned without touching the metal-gridded shelving. "Almost big enough to sleep in. Well, maybe for some people. Not for you," she added, laughing.

Actually it was, he realized. His cell had been about that size.

On the way back, she told him about an even nicer complex she would show him next time. It had a clubhouse with an Olympic-size pool he'd love.

"I don't swim!" He laughed and wasn't sure why, other than this lightness he was feeling.

"You don't know how?" She pulled in front of his house.

"No, I know how! I just . . . never do it much."

The purple Navigator cruised down the street with its brilliant hubcaps and booming bass. It stopped in the middle of the road. Gordon said good-bye and quickly got out of the car. He didn't want her to see anything as ugly as the incident last week. Feaster got out and lowered his sunglasses with a sly smile as she drove by. "Hey, big man, that's nice. That is really nice," Feaster called as he swaggered over. "Hey, I just found out. You used to be from around here. But a long time ago, right?"

Gordon nodded.

Feaster lowered his glasses again. "You know Jacinto? JumJum, he's at the Fort."

"No."

"Yeah, well, JumJum and me, we were close. Like that." Feaster clasped his hands together. "Till he screwed up, and now it's just me." He smiled. "You need anything, big man, you let me know. I'm always around." Just then a car screeched around the corner, music blaring and honking its horn. Feaster waved for them to slow down. "Busy place, huh? But cool. Everything's cool. I make sure of that."

"My side's tight." Dennis tossed the rope over the roof of his Land Rover. Gordon slipped the end around his side of the ladder, then knotted it quickly. Mrs. Jukas watched from her window. "Happy, you old bitch?" Dennis said through a smile, and waved. When they were done, Gordon offered his brother a beer. He'd bought a six-pack of Harrington's for him. Dennis came in for a minute but said to save the beer for another time. He had to get home. Father Hensile was going to be there. It was Lisa's night to host PreCana class, and it wouldn't do to have hubby dragging in late and half-crocked.

"Hey, the place looks good." Dennis sat on the couch. He clasped his hands behind his head and stretched out his legs. He asked about the condo. It was very nice, Gordon said.

"Well, that's good." Dennis grinned. "So you're interested."

"No."

"Jilly said you liked it, but you thought it was too expensive. Like I told her, I'm willing to help. You know that, right?"

"No."

"Well, I am."

"No, I mean that's not the point. This is fine. I'm fine here."

Dennis looked at him. "All right. I'm not supposed to say anything yet, but Lisa's going to talk to her father about a job for you at the brewery. You'd make three, no, four times what you're making at the Market."

"No!" Gordon said as the phone began to ring.

"That's probably Jilly," Dennis said, getting up. "I told her I was stopping here."

Gordon listened as Dennis answered the phone. He didn't want to look at any more condos, but he did want to see Jilly Cross again.

"No! You're not interrupting anything," Dennis assured her. "Oh, that's great. I bet he'd like that. Here, you ask him. He's right here." He handed Gordon the phone.

"Hello?" Gordon's smile faded. It wasn't Jilly, it was Delores apologizing; she didn't want to bother him with Dennis there. She sounded nervous. If he wanted, he could call her back after his brother left. No, that's all right, he said, not wanting the burden of owing her a call. It somehow seemed safer talking to her with Dennis here. His brother looked on, smiling as Delores invited him to dinner Friday night.

"Oh. Well. I don't know. I don't know if I can." Sweat beaded his furrowed brow.

Dennis shook his head in disbelief. If the problem was work, Delores was saying, he could come after. Later would be better for her anyway. She was doing inventory at the store. Mr. Smick wanted everything counted right down to the last paper clip. Her voice trembled. So later would be good.

"Well, I'm not sure." He turned, shading his eyes from Dennis's frantic gestures.

"What're you doing?" Dennis paced around him and whispered. "Just say yes. Go! You want to be stuck here all the time?"

"All right," he said, wincing with her whoop of delight. That was great. Wonderful! That was just so wonderful, she was still saying when he hung up.

"Yeah! Way to go, Gordo!" Dennis let loose a flurry of jabs at his arm the way he used to. "You gotta loosen up! You gotta get out there! You gotta let life happen, my man!"

Astonished, he looked at his brother. The last thing on earth he'd ever do would be to let life happen.

"And the same when Jilly calls." Dennis shadowboxed around him, feinting jabs at his face, which he disliked as much now as when they were kids. "Trust her. She's a great gal. And she likes you, so let her show you what's out there in the world. What you been missing all this time."

CHAPTER 6

After a long night's shivering refusal to turn on the furnace, Gordon hurried to work through the early-morning chill. With his first bills had come the shock of how expensive everything was. As he scuffed through the litter of faded scratch tickets in front of the drugstore, he considered buying one, but five dollars was too much to spend for a few seconds of hope. He had asked for more hours, but Neil had said he couldn't afford it.

Ahead at the corner, his young neighbor Jada waited to cross. Remembering the incident in front of her house last week and not wanting to embarrass her, he pretended not to recognize her.

"Assholes! You're supposed to stop," she muttered as cars whizzed by. "That's it, I'm going." She stepped off the curb.

"Look out!" he said. "They're still coming."

"What're you, some kind of crossing guard?" she said over her shoulder.

"There's too many cars. It's not safe yet." Traffic still unnerved him.

"Yeah, right." She was trembling. An empty bookbag hung from her bony shoulder. She wasn't wearing a sweater or jacket, just a thin T-shirt. Goose bumps covered her arms. "So can I go now?" she asked with the last car.

He looked both ways. "Seems pretty clear now."

They crossed and she walked fast to keep pace. He glanced over, then looked again, startled by the incongruity, the strangeness, the hybrid confusion that was her exotic freckled face. Her tight curly hair was a pale rust color. Her green tilted eyes seemed almost lidless. She had a fine, hooked nose above a mouth so wide and full that it seemed to take up the lower half of her small face. Her skin was of indiscernible color, not white, brown, or yellow. Even her boyish, lanky stride seemed contradictory, wrong on so female a body, tall and skinny as it was.

"What do you want?"

"Nothing." He slowed down, wanting her to get ahead.

"How come you keep looking at me, then?"

"I was just wondering if you were on your way to school," he said quickly, uneasily.

"Well, yeah!" As proof she lifted the bookbag.

"Which one do you go to?" He slowed even more, and so did she.

"The Craig."

"Oh. Craig Junior High. I went there." And hated it, he remembered.

"It's middle school."

"What's the difference?"

"Don't know." She shuddered in the sudden biting wind.

"What grade're you in?"

"Sixth. Same as last year."

"How old are you?"

"Thirteen."

There were boys walking behind them. He had run out of questions. The Market was still two blocks away, with the Craig a block on farther. When they came to the Shoe Fix Shop, a small white dog darted out from the alley and ran snapping at their heels.

"You fucking mange! Get the fuck outta here!" The girl's kick sent the dog yelping into the street.

"Hey, what'd you do that for?" called one of the boys. They all wore jackets or sweatshirts under their sagging backpacks. "Yeah, Jada, you freak, what're you doin' kicking a little dog!" another yelled.

Without a word or break in gait, she hoisted her middle finger up over her head and kept walking.

"Freak! You freak!" they all jeered. "You crazy, fucking freak!"

Her eyes narrowed and her mouth curled in a snarl, yet she seemed amused by their taunts, if not proud, as they ran by screaming.

"Was that their dog?" Gordon asked.

"No!" she sneered. "It's Cootie's. Plus, he's not even a real dog."

"Looked real to me."

"Yeah, well, he lives in a box, all winter, him and Cootie—like, under the bridge! They even eat the same food."

"That's not the dog's fault, though, is it?"

She shrugged. "Maybe. Maybe Cootie'd have a whole better life if he wasn't stuck with such a friggin' loser dog."

Her logic made him laugh. "He could always give him away."

"Or kill him," she added.

He didn't know what to say.

"But the thing is, he can't. They're, like, stuck together. Like, like they got no choice, you know?" she said as they kept walking. "Fucking pathetic, huh?"

"Who's Cootie?"

"The crazy one. He's always smoking. He wears this, like, ski-hat thing. Even in the summer he does. And he stinks."

"Oh, I've seen him around." Gordon stopped when they came to the Market. Cootie had been in the store the other day, trying to buy cigarettes with food stamps, but June made him leave. When he returned later with a bag of empty cans and bottles, she would redeem only a few, saying the rest were brands they didn't carry. While she sorted through the bag, Cootie slipped four packs of Camels into his pocket. June called the police, who told the old man to stay out of the Market. If he didn't, they would arrest him. Later that day someone dropped part of a cinder block from the loading dock onto the roof of June's old car. She called the police again. They said they couldn't do anything unless she could prove Cootie had done it.

"Well, anyway." Gordon stood by the door. "I've got to go work now."

"My friend works here. Thurman Dominguez. He hates it, but his grandmother, she said if he quits, that's it, he's out. And nobody else wants him."

"That's too bad. He's so young." Gordon wasn't surprised. The boy smoldered with anger.

"Not that young. Sixteen, I think. 'Least that's what he says. His mother moved to New York just to get away from him. Nice mother, huh?"

"I better go in." He started to open the door.

"That old bitch still work here?"

"Which one?"

"The one with the things." She poked two fingers into her nostrils. "The tubes."

"Yes, June. She's still here."

"Fucking bitch. She, like, kicked me out for life." Jada shaded her eyes to peer through the glass. "I don't see her."

"She's probably out back. Well, I better get inside and get started."

"Hey!" she called before he could leave. "Do me a favor, will ya?"

"What?"

"Will you let me know when the bitch dies? Because of her I gotta go all the way down the Shop and Save every time I need friggin' milk or something."

"Well, just tell me, then. I can get it for you. I live right across the street."

"Yeah, I know." Her ropy mouth quivered with a faint smile. "You know JumJum?"

"No. I don't."

"He's there, too." She grinned. "At the Fort. You probably heard of him, though, huh?"

"Yes, I did hear that name," he said stiffly. "Just the other day, as a matter of fact." He looked at his watch. "You better get going or you're going to be late."

"What'd you hear about him?" She watched him closely.

"Well, what you just said. That he was there."

"He offed somebody, too." She looked around and leaned closer. "He blew this guy's brains out all over his girlfriend's brand-new Celica. But that's not why. He's there for something else. Dealing, but that's not the real reason."

"I better go."

"Yeah, well, see ya." She held out her hand and shook his, her grip hard as a man's.

"You better check your pockets, see what's missing," Serena called when he came inside.

"What do you mean?"

"You know who she is, don't you?"

"She's my neighbor. She lives across the street."

"The Fossums aren't neighbors!" Serena scoffed. "They don't move in or anything. They, like, infest the place and then you can't get rid of 'em."

Gordon had never worked so hard as in these last few days. According to the women, each new bout of sobriety forced Neil Dubbin to even higher, steeper peaks of ambition, so vast was his trail of broken promises. His pledge to turn the Market into a first-rate business had few believers in his family, but at least his creditors were extending him three more months of their patience. To Gordon had fallen the verminous task of tearing out the rotting cabinets to make way for new storage. Neil tried to help in between the violent headaches that drove him, nauseated and squinting, to his sour room, where darkness was his only antidote, other than alcohol. He had just reemerged and now sat on an overturned crate, shoulders hunched, wincing with every hammer strike. Again, Gordon offered to stop.

"No, keep going. Please. I need you to do this. It's too important," he insisted. Neil's surest skill was entrusting others with his well-being. He needed not just their help, but their loyalty and affection in a way that validated their self-importance. And maybe he genuinely did; Gordon couldn't be sure, not when his own natural distrust of people blotted out such nuances. He had known other men like Neil, irresistibly bitter men whose sins seem more affliction than failings. Even Neil's eager fascination with other people's pain made them think he truly cared about their troubles.

"You're pretty good at this," Neil said. "Is this the kind of thing they teach you there?"

"I used to help my father a lot," Gordon said quietly.

"Just the opposite of me and my dad. They never wanted me wasting my time around here. I think I was supposed to be a big-time accountant or lawyer or something, I forget. But thank God they never sold the farm!" he declared with a bitter sweep of his arm. "Where the *hell* would I be without it?"

Gordon kept tapping the crowbar, to drive it deeper behind the cabinet frame.

"Just so you'll know," Neil continued. "I haven't said anything. I mean, about you, back then. I haven't told anyone."

Shoulder braced to the wall, Gordon wrenched the heavy bar back and forth. A persuader, his father used to call it. A persuader. They didn't know. Not yet. In a way it would be a relief to get it over with.

"I mean, what's the point? You know what I mean, they'll just get all worked up. The girls, I mean. They'll start thinking weird things, you know, like . . . like . . . maybe they can't be alone back here with you or something. But then how long can you keep a secret like that? It must've been hell, huh, just a kid and being locked up all that time? I never could've done it. I would've checked out my first night there—broken glass, sheets, something. You ever try anything like that?"

The crowbar fell to the floor. Grunting, Gordon pulled as hard as he could.

"You must've thought of it, though, huh? You must've." Neil's harsh breathing scratched at the silence. "Hey, I saw you get picked up the other day. Pretty lady. You must be making up for a lot of lost time, huh? I mean, twenty-five years! Jesus Christ, what does a big, healthy guy like you do? You gotta have something more than a warm hand, right?"

The rank dust of food-fouled wood exploded into the air as the cabinet gave way.

"You probably did what you had to do, right? Well, anyway, I haven't said anything to anybody." Neil sighed. "I just wanted you to know that."

It was Friday, and Gordon was on his way home from work, still hoping Jilly Cross might call. In his bag there was an angel food cake, a pint of strawberries, and a can of real whipped cream for dessert tonight. He was surprised to be looking forward to dinner at Delores's. He was tired of his own pathetic attempts at cooking. Nothing ever came out right. Last night's steak had been so dry and tough, he'd had to cut it into slivers to chew it.

The phone was ringing as he unlocked the door. "Hello! Hello!" he shouted into the dial tone. Reading from Jilly's business card, he dialed the first three numbers, then hung up. It didn't seem right, asking to see condos he would never buy. But if she called him— well, that was different.

He waited by the phone a moment more in case it rang again. When it didn't he went down the narrow wooden stairs into the cellar. He stripped off his soiled, sweaty clothes and put them into the washing machine so they'd be clean for tomorrow. It hadn't occurred to him he needed more clothes until June asked the other day if that blue sweatshirt and pants were all he had.

He was lathering his arms in the shower now and trying to remember the last time he had actually bought clothes in a store. Vague images rose through the steam: his elbows banging into tiny dressing-room walls as he hurried to undress before the curtain parted, then crouching from the gash of light as his mother handed in a shirt with sleeves inches short of his wrists and pants with cuffs she would tear out and then hem in her long, clumsy stitches. The first woman in her family not to do piecework in the mills, she had been proud of her ineptitude with needle and thread.

He put on the chinos and yellow shirt Dennis had gotten for him to wear home from Fortley. As he sat on the edge of the bed, tying his shoes, he could see down into Mrs. Jukas's backyard. In the full swell of late-afternoon sun, the trees seemed even thicker with leaves than this morning and the grass darker in the deepening shadows. The only trees through Fortley's windows had all been distant, the land cut close, allowing no shrub or stump of growth for a man's concealment.

Neil Dubbin had asked, but the truth was Gordon had never considered suicide as a way out. The most vital elements had died inside, died before he got there. After a while he stopped noticing the horizon's lethal scroll of razor wire. The letters and visits he initially yearned for soon became cruel reminders of a lost world. His father's trembling head and stroke-frozen face seemed only further proof of his crime. In a way, he had been glad when his father finally died, glad for his father, relieved for himself and his mother, who seemed happier, less burdened. From then on, her letters brightened with details of Dennis's busy life or her trips with friends, and then her pride in Lisa, who was exactly the kind of girl a mother would want for her only son, one letter so guilelessly confided. But he knew what she meant. He understood. It was all part of the price.

The phone rang and he grabbed it on the first ring. A breeze lifted the curtain as the room filled with Jilly Cross's voice. She apologized for not calling sooner. The condo had gone under agreement, but another had come on the market this afternoon. It was perfect, just the right size, still in Collerton, which she knew he preferred, but in a much better neighborhood—and, she added, still in his price range. "I thought of you immediately!" she said, and he grinned. "Can you see it tonight? I've got to make a few more calls and then I could pick you up."

"Yes, of course." He had to check on something first and then he'd call her right back to tell her when.

He dialed Delores's number, then hung up quickly, confused when he got the recording. He was supposed to be there in twenty-five minutes, so why hadn't she answered? Maybe she was busy cooking. He called again, listened to the tape. "Hello, Delores?" he said in a rush at the beep. "Delores, this is Gordon. Gordon Loomis. I can't . . . The thing is, I have to . . . that is, you see . . . well, let's see now, what should I do? Maybe you're at the store. Maybe you're not home yet. I'm going to call you there. That's what I'll do. I'm going to call you at the store."

Listening, Delores froze, hand inches over the phone. She'd heard that tension in so many men's voices. If she answered, he'd say he couldn't come. But at least he wasn't leaving the message on her machine the way others had done. The phone rang again. He sounded frantic. "Hello, Delores? Delores, this is Gordon Loomis calling you back. I mean, I called before and you weren't there, so now I'm calling back. I just called the store, but you're not there. And now you're not home, either, so I don't know. I'm not sure, maybe I've got the wrong night. I thought you said this Friday. But maybe you meant—"

"Gordon!" she cried, as if in a breathless run for the phone. "I couldn't really hear who it was. I was busy cooking and then I realized it was you, and yes, you're right. I did say Friday. Tonight. In fact, everything's just about ready. . . ." The countertops were cluttered with cucumber peels, onion skins, and discarded lettuce leaves, bottles of spices and oils, the sink filled with bowls and pans. Her shoulder crimped to the phone, she turned on the hot water and began to scrub the encrusted fry pan.

He couldn't come. There was an appointment, a very important appointment he had forgotten until just a few minutes ago. "I'm sorry—"

"No!" she cried. It was all the unanswered letters, the long, hopeful drives to Fortley, her prideless efforts to keep the conversation going, telling him things he so obviously had little interest in, her sisters, nieces, nephews, neighbors, the store, her boss, and the illicit sensation of speaking Albert's name to another man, this man she had grown to care deeply about. But then, as with Albert, the secret had taken on its own life, its significance swelling with an imagined complicity that required no acknowledgment on his part. It suddenly seemed so twisted. Yes, it was. It was. She knew it was, but she could not, would not, continue to be unloved, and so his cold disinterest and her desire had to exist on parallel tracks, unexamined. And now with their collision she wasn't sure who she was berating, the fantasy lover or the socially blunted ex-convict. "You can't just be calling me up twenty minutes before you're supposed to be here! I've been expecting you! I've got everything cooked." Her voice faltered as she looked around. "I mean, what am I supposed to do with all this—"

"I'm sorry. I should have thought. I'll be right there. I'll still be on time. I just have to make a phone call and then I'll leave . . . I'll be right there!"

Bag clutched to his side, Gordon hurried down his front walk.

"Hey, how's it going?" Jada's mother, Marvella, called in a lazy voice from her top step as he crossed the street. She waved.

"Hello." He gave a stiff nod and walked quickly by. Serena knew Marvella's brother, Bob, the only near-normal one in the family— well, the only one that worked, she'd said. He had his own business— his own truck, anyway—cleaning out septic tanks.

"Come on over sometime. Sixty-four Clover, come over, come over, first floor, door on the right, where there's always a party going on, going on, going on, always a party . . ."

Her bawdy voice pursued him to the corner.

He had to hurry. He wasn't enjoying this walk at all. His feet hurt. Winded, he took the steps two at a time to Delores's second-floor apartment.

"I'm sorry . . . I'm sorry," they both said with the opening door.

"I shouldn't have spoken to you like that," she said.

"I shouldn't have called at the last minute like that." He was trying to catch his breath.

Their uneasiness continued through the brief cocktail time. She had a mug chilling in the refrigerator, but all he wanted was a Coke. The can was fine, he said before she could pour it into the frosted mug. "No sense dirtying a glass."

"That's no problem," she said, pouring it anyway. She spilled her Manhattan onto the sofa, then drank the next one much too quickly. They sat at the round table dragged in earlier from the kitchen. She had covered it with an embroidered linen tablecloth and positioned it in front of the living-room window. She struck a match, and her hand trembled as she lit the tall green candles. The two salad plates were the only ones left of her mother's pattern, Desert Rose. Some-day she would complete the set, she was telling him, but he looked at her blankly. Yes, she thought, when she did her registry. She poured them both Cabernet, Albert's favorite with any kind of roasted meat. She felt better now. He looked at his watch again. *Such a big man, he must be hungry.* The ruby liquid glistened through the facets as she raised her glass in a well-practiced toast. "To your return home, Gordon." She paused, but he didn't take up his glass. "May your days be filled with good food, good times, and good friends. And may your heart know only love." He began to eat, so she made a little swoop of the glass and then took a sip.

"Thank you. Thank you very much." He was halfway through his salad. "That was delicious," he said when he was done. He glanced around the table. She thought he was embarrassed to have finished so quickly while she was still eating. She offered him more; there was a whole other bowl in the refrigerator. "Oh, no. No, thank you." He told her how Fortley's salads had been a slimy mush of limp lettuce and crushed tomato chunks. "What's that cheese called?" He pointed to her fork.

"Goat cheese," she said, keenly aware that his lips parted as she raised the fork to her mouth. She took his plate into the kitchen. When she returned, he grinned to see the cheese-covered salad she placed in front of him.

Everything was delicious. It was, he said again as he ate the last baked potato. It was the best meal he'd ever had. "Leave room for dessert," she warned. She hadn't even mentioned her chocolate cake, so touched was she by his thoughtfulness in bringing dessert.

"I hope you like strawberries," he said with such hopeful concern that a trickle of warmth seeped from her chest up into her cheeks.

"I do."

"They're right in season now."

"Yes, this is the best time."

"I can't wait to try them." He glanced at his watch again.

She thought he was concerned about walking home in the dark. She had already said she'd give him a ride.

"That was something I really missed," he was saying. "Fresh strawberries. So many other things I forgot about . . . well, not really forgot. Just never gave much thought to. It all just kind of faded. The possibility—I guess that's what I mean." He shrugged uneasily.

It was the most he'd ever shared of his feelings. Tensed on the edge of her chair, she stared at his face, the strong chin, the smooth cheeks and wide brow, boyish in spite of all he'd been through: depravities she could only imagine, loneliness more terrifying to her than death. *Twenty-five years,* she thought, heavy eyed with this blinding ache in her belly, *twenty-five years and he's never been held or touched by a woman.* There was an odd agelessness about him. He was both young and old, but with no experience, no connection in between. Her head trembled with the struggle to keep her fists clenched on the table. *Let me help, let me touch you and hold you, give me your pain and I will show you how good life can be, how beautiful.* There wasn't a morning she didn't wake up knowing that this was the day she had been waiting for. Love, with its mysteries and excesses, children, food, laughter, it was all such a wonder. Even grief had its own allure. At wakes and funerals she could give the best and most of herself, consoling, weeping, embracing even mere acquaintances in their time of need. She had never been afraid to feel any of it. Being unable to love, that would be the worst torment of all.

"Some things never go away, do they?" She wasn't sure what she meant. She had to be careful. She had drunk almost the entire bottle of wine herself. This time she had vowed there wouldn't be even the suggestion of intimacy, no touching or sitting too close. First there had to be an emotional connection. "It must have been so hard. I mean, I can't imagine it, being so young and then suddenly it's all gone, everything you've ever known or wanted. Your future, I mean, what does that do to a kid?" His implacable stare seemed too high a wall to surmount. She waved her hand weakly. "How do you live without . . ." What was the word he'd used? "Without possibility? How do you do that?" she asked, voice and heart quavering with the message in his cold, unblinking eyes that she had gone too far again, not with the bulk of her flesh this time, but with her own pain—when it was his pain she was feeling, his wounds she would help heal.

"That's just the way it was, that's all." He looked at his watch.

"But you had to be so strong. I mean, when you knew—"

"I had to be realistic."

"But Jerry Cox lied. You know he did. He went back there after. He went back by himself." She felt herself stumbling toward him now but couldn't stop because she had read all his testimony on microfiche and needed to help, needed him to know that if no one else on the face of the earth believed him, she did. He may have left the woman unconscious under the pillow, but he had left her alive, not strangled to death the way they said.

"I'm not going to talk about that." His face blurred over the long blue flame. "If you don't mind," he added quietly.

"I'm sorry." She stood up. "I'll get your dessert. It'll only take a minute." She patted his shoulder and he looked at her with an expression of such anguish, such loss, that from now on, whatever this poor man wanted, she would do it. Anything. Anything at all, her eyes told him.

"I have to leave in a half hour. I'm being picked up."

"What do you mean?" She turned dizzily. "Who? Who's picking you up?"

"A real estate agent. Jilly Cross. That was the appointment. Remember? When I called—so I changed it. I changed the time." Clearly nervous, he checked his watch again. "You don't have to slice them, you know. I mean, they're just as good whole." He swallowed hard. "And maybe even better that way."

"You have an appointment with a real estate agent?" He hadn't said date, but then, under the circumstances, would he?

"To see some condos. She had new ones she wants to show me."

"Condos? You're going to sell the house?"

"No! No, I like it there. It's Dennis. It's like a favor for him. I mean, he wants me to move, but I'm not. The favor, I guess, is to give Jilly Cross some business." He smiled.

"Well, if you're not going to buy anything, it sounds more to me like you're just, you know, wasting her time. Stringing her along." *Wasting his own time,* she thought, irritated by Dennis's influence. He hadn't even wanted his brother back here.

"I know, but I told her." Gordon followed her into the kitchen with his soiled plate. He dropped his knife and fork into the sink with an unnerving clatter. "She knows I don't want to move." He put a strawberry into his mouth. "I don't know, maybe she thinks she's going to change my mind or something." He grinned and a thin red trickle ran down his chin. He wiped it away with his cuff.

In her rush she cut herself, so now she was trying to slice the strawberries with a paper napkin wrapped around her thumb. Bits of tissue kept sticking to the fruit. She tore it off, only vaguely concerned that her blood might be mixing with these raggedly sliced berries. She carried his bowl to the table. A dull ache had started at the base of her skull. Her period. What a waste that was. *The monthly reminder of emptiness. The soon-to-be-ebbing tide of . . . of possibility,* she thought, standing over him now with the chilled can, shaking and shaking and shaking it, then giving a long, vicious spurt of curled cream onto the strawberries *he shouldn't have brought here without asking,* she thought as flecks of cream sputtered onto the tablecloth, angering her even more. *Now, everything is ruined, and he doesn't even know.*

"Thank you," he said, chewing. "Oh, this is so good."

Suddenly, she was glad he was leaving. She would have the rest of the night to herself, to do whatever she wanted. She wasn't a young woman anymore. This constant solicitude was draining, bewildering to never have it returned. She sat down, but he didn't look up. She sucked at the tip of her finger and watched him tilt the bowl for the last spoonful of juice. *It's more than reserve. Or caution, even. No. He's missing something. Something inside. Or maybe it's me. Maybe there's nothing in me for a man to love or hold on to.*

"As it turned out, there's only one we can see," Jilly Cross said stiffly as they drove down the street. Her voice sounded different tonight, strained.

He was afraid he was annoying her with his struggle to get his seat belt buckled. Eight o'clock was too late for the people on State Line Road, which left only the Meadowville condo, she said, but that was vacant, so it would be better to go when he could see it by daylight.

"That's all right. I can see it tonight," he said quickly. He didn't want to be taken home. He pressed the seat belt against his hip so it looked buckled. It was these small ineptitudes that made him feel most out of step with everyone else.

"There's another one that just came in, but the woman has cats so she has to be there when it's shown. Or something like that, I don't know." She seemed distracted.

"Why, do they bite or something?"

"No, they're house cats. She's afraid someone'll leave a door open and they'll get out."

"How can they be house cats if they live in a condo? They must be condo cats," he said with a broad grin. He wanted to make her laugh. He almost felt giddy as they drove toward the fast-rising moon, tangerine in the blue-black sky. The evening air was sweet.

"That's right." Her nose and cheeks were red, as if she'd gotten sunburned. Her lips were a soft coral, the same shade of the scarf knotted around her neck.

"I like cats," he said. "We never had our own pet cat, but they were always around. My mother was always feeding stray ones. My father didn't like them too much. He said all the milk bowls and cat food on the back steps used to attract every kind of animal for miles around. Stray dogs and raccoons and skunks. And the squirrels! Oh, my Lord, he hated squirrels most of all. Rats with bushy tails, he used to call them. I forgot about that." He sighed and shook his head. "It's funny the things you forget."

They were coming off the highway now. It felt good just to be able to talk. About nothing, really, and yet something wonderful was happening. He felt so much looser and more open. He could be himself. He didn't have to watch every word the way he did with most people, especially back there with Delores. He kept trying to think of something clever to say. Jilly drove slower, maybe, like him, wanting the trip to last.

At the security gate she showed her Realtor's pass. Meadowville was an enormous complex with at least ten five-story buildings. She parked in the visitors' lot and left the motor running. The headlights shone onto a rock garden of white flowers. In the center a fountain dribbled water from a sculpted fish's gaping mouth.

"Gordon . . . Oh, I don't know what to say. You see, I didn't realize . . . I mean . . . well, I knew you'd been away for a long time, but
Dennis never said why."

"Oh." He turned, forgetting to hold on to the seat belt. She gave a
start as it snapped back. "I'm sorry. I thought you knew." He shifted
his feet. His knees jammed into the dashboard.

"No, he just told me. Right before I picked you up, as a matter of
fact." She touched her flushed cheek, then her throat.

"Well, I'm sorry." He took a deep breath. "I don't know what to
say." Ahead, the wet stony gills seemed to pulsate in and out.

"I was telling him we could only see one, the empty one, because
of how late it was, and I said how that's something I never do unless
I really know the client, but of course with you being his brother and
everything." She sighed.

"We don't have to go in. I understand."

Her mouth kept opening and closing, then she blurted, "He said it
was a murder. A woman, the same age as me."

He nodded.

"He said it was an accident. That you were trying to keep her
from seeing you, but the pillow smothered her."

He rubbed his eyes.

"I mean, how can that be an accident?" She shivered and folded
her arms.

"I know," he said dully. The air had turned heavy, the moon paler.

"An accident's something you don't mean to do. But you broke
into her house, right?"

"We didn't think anyone was home." It hurt to speak.

"And that's when she woke up?"

He nodded.

"Why didn't you run?"

He glanced at her beautiful face, then had to look away from such
innocence. How many times had he asked himself that very question?

"Why didn't you just leave?"

He shook his head and had to close his eyes. Even with Jerry
screaming at him to cover her face he had wanted to run, knew he
should, could have still run and saved his life and hers, instead of

grabbing the pillow next to hers, the one on which her husband's head would have, should have been but for her swollen ankle sprained earlier in the day so that she could not travel with him, so that when the intoxicated, giddy intruders blundered into her bedroom, she was lying there alone. *Fresh for the kill,* the prosecutor had whispered to the jury. *Unable to move, Janine Walters and her unborn son lying there, waiting with only minutes left to live.*

"It must be so awful to think someone's . . . I mean, it's like . . . like there you were and there she was . . . I don't know." She shivered again. "Dennis said it was the worst thing that ever happened to him. The whole family. He said after that everything changed."

Gordon's stomach rumbled with the ferment of cream and strawberries rising sourly into his throat. Dennis was right, he never should have come back. People did not know how to deal with such a thing. And why should they be expected to? It was an aberration so beyond the boundaries of normal life that at first even he had not been able to comprehend its enormity and impact. Though his own tearful confession had been derided, when he did run from her bedroom, crashing into tables, lamps, the telephone, and then stumbled down the dark stairs out into the soft night rain, he had known she was still alive. *All he could do was sob as they ran through alleys and backyards while Jerry kept asking if she'd seen him. Was he sure she hadn't? What was it she kept saying? "Please don't," was all he'd heard. And then just grunting sounds.*

"Is she dead? You think she's dead?" Jerry demanded, grabbing the back of his shirt to make him stop running.

"No!" he insisted. Of course not.

"But she wasn't moving. She was so still."

"Yes. But she was making sounds."

"What kind of sounds?"

"Moaning. Like soft moaning."

"Jesus Christ, then we gotta go back!"

"No!"

"We have to, you fat, stupid fuck!"

"No, I can't! I can't!" he kept panting as he ran, arriving home in time for the popcorn his mother had just made and insisted he share with them,

huddled in the dark little living room, staring at the television, while his mother, father, and Dennis watched the Red Sox, hating himself, sickened by his cowardice for hurting the poor woman and then for not going back with Jerry to help her. Please be all right. Please, please, please be alive, he was still imploring batters, pitchers, umpires, and screaming fans, who all seemed to be leering at him, when the phone rang in the kitchen. It was for him, his mother said.

"She's dead," Jerry whispered.

"No!" he said so loudly that they all looked up at him.

"Shut up! Nobody's gonna know we were even there—so shut up! Just shut the fuck up! About everything—you hear what I'm saying?"

Then his mother was next to him, demanding to know who that was, then, with a gasp, held up his hands to look at the gouges down both arms. It was the bushes, he said. The rosebushes had scratched him when he came through the side yard. She called in his father, who said his rosebushes could not have made cuts as deep as those, enunciating each word as if he knew there was evil among them and would not have his roses in any way tainted by it. Then he said it was a fight. He'd been in a fight. With who? A girl? Dennis jeered.

"And look!" his mother said. "You lost your ring, didn't you? His brand-new class ring," she told his father, who had defied her by allowing Gordon to order the most expensive one.

"He'll get it back," his father said. "His name's inside. I told him to have it engraved and that way he'd always get it back."

The next morning a policeman was banging on the front door. Holding up a clear plastic bag, the officer asked if that was her son's ring.

"You found it! Thank you. Thank you so much," his mother said, joining the disembodied chorus, their voices chanting the warrant's directive of names, dates, places, his right as to what to say or not to say, to speak, to be represented by counsel of his choice, and if not, the court would provide one.

Jilly drove him home. They would see the condo another day in better light. That was fine. He didn't care about condos. All he cared about was not frightening her. She parked in front of his house. Across the street, two younger boys watched Jada Fossum reel out a yoyo then snap it back until it wobbled crazily on the taut string. Two dark figures stood in the porch shadows above her. A phone rang and one of the men paced back and forth as he talked on his cell phone.

"Gordon, wait," Jilly said as he started to open the door. "I'm sorry. I mean . . . I'm sorry."

"No, don't you be sorry."

"It was just such a shock. I mean, it was all so . . . like, new and fresh in my head, I didn't have time to get it all straight."

"No, I know." He tried to smile.

The purple Navigator was parked down the street. The two hooded men came down the porch steps. Polie said something to the boys and they ran away. Feaster put his arm around Jada's shoulder and whispered in her ear. She walked between the men to the SUV.

"Do you think it was, like, fate or something? I mean, what happened. The murder," she said, watching him.

"What do you mean?" he asked with a faint note of amazement. Fortley had been filled with fatalism's disciples, hapless victims of their victims.

"Well, like, there you were and there she was, and then all of a sudden everything just kind of came together. In such a horrible way. I believe in that," she added.

"What? That things aren't our fault?" he asked quietly. Suddenly she seemed so young.

"Well, yes. In a way. And now science is actually proving it. I mean, in a way it's all decided ahead of time, when you think of it. Who we are, what we become—it's all in the genes."

Stars, he had expected her to say, which meant we were no more than inconsequential fleas jumping through our preordained hoops in a meaningless cosmos. Hopeless, helpless, blameless.

"So in the end, there's only so much a person can do with whatever they've been given. And of course, that's really the thing, isn't it? I mean, doing your best, no matter what. No matter what happens or doesn't happen, or whatever you have or you don't have." She sighed. "I'm not putting this very well, but do you know what I mean?"

Her equation made him a born killer, genetically programmed and predisposed to murder, helplessly adrift in the tide of natural homicidal urges that could be incited by any random, intersecting force. If he knew nothing else, he knew that wasn't true.

"I'm not sure, but maybe. I think so," he answered slowly. She didn't realize the scope of what she'd said, but he was touched by her need to exonerate him.

As she drove off, the Navigator came down the street. In the backseat Jada rolled down the window. She smiled, waving wildly at Gordon.

CHAPTER 7

Jada crouched by the toilet, squinting at the outlet. She finally unscrewed the wall plate with the steak knife. Mouse turd and plaster grit spilled out with the crimped bills she pulled from the outlet box. Eighteen dollars, it was all she'd been able to find in her mother's jeans when she came back from Lowell or wherever the hell her mother had ended up this time. Jada hated leaving her alone for too long, but there wasn't any food in the house.

The phone rang. She ran to get it before her mother woke up. Probably the guidance counselor again. Or Ronnie Feaster. Either way was trouble. She hadn't been to school all week. Her mother had had another fight with Ronnie. She owed him too much money as it was, so from now on she paid cash like everybody else, but she was too sick to hustle. She woke Jada up in the middle of the night, crying and saying she had to go someplace but she'd be right back. Three days later, she dragged home with black eyes and cuts all over her face. At first she hardly moved in the bed. Jada kept checking to see if she was still breathing. Today, though, her mother was waking up more. She kept telling Jada to call Ronnie. Jada lied and said she'd already left at least twenty messages for him.

Her mother groaned as Jada snatched the ringing phone from the bed. She ran into the bathroom. If it was him, she'd say her mother still wasn't back. In a couple more days the worst would be over. She'd be clean again.

"Hello," she answered in a low voice, hand cupped at the mouthpiece. "Yes, this is Marvella Fossum," she told the attendance secretary, who then asked why Jada was still absent. "It's the flu. She can't eat or get out of bed even, she's so weak." It was almost the truth. All she'd eaten today were pretzels and such lousy-tasting milk she'd had to hold her breath to drink it.

"That's a long time to be so sick," the attendance secretary said. "Has she seen a doctor?"

"Oh, yes, twice I brung her, as a matter of fact, and both times they said the same thing: a lotta liquid drinks and that she should sleep. A lotta sleep. Get it all outta her system," she added, on a roll now. She should be an actress, JumJum said once, and Marvella said, Yeah, but in what kind of movies with a mutt face like hers?

"Who's Jada's doctor? What's his name?"

She couldn't remember. She needed a name. "Gordon," she said, looking out the window. "Doctor Gordon."

Pages were turning. "Gordon . . . do you know his first name?"

"He just said Doctor."

"Well, where's his office, then?"

"Uh—maybe at the emergency room. That's where we went, her fever was so high."

There was a pause. "Jada! I know this is you."

"No, I told you, this is Jada's mom, Marvella," she said indignantly.

"Well, I guess I have no choice, then, but to send the attendance officer out."

"Fine," Jada said huffily, panicking the minute she hung up. She would tell him how her mother had the flu and was too sick to talk to anyone. Jada put on pajamas and spent the rest of the day waiting in front of the TV, but no one ever came. At three-thirty the moaning started up again. Jada went in and sat on the edge of the bed. Shivering, her mother lay curled in a tight ball. Had Ronnie called? She needed to get high. She'd die if she went much longer, she groaned. Her teeth were chattering. She smelled of sweat and stale urine.

"It'll be all right," Jada said softly. "Pretty soon it'll be over and you'll feel so good. Just like before, I know you will."

"Fuck off. Just fuck off, will you?" She raised her head, then withered with the effort. "Get Ronnie. You gotta get him!" she begged.

"Okay, Ma, I know, I know. Just lay back and you'll feel better. I'm taking good care of you, Ma. I won't let anything happen to you."

Her mother sobbed, and she started to touch her arm, then drew back. Sometimes she'd be so flipped out, she'd think Jada was trying to hurt her. "It's okay," she whispered. "It's okay, Ma. Don't cry." She went into the bathroom and wet the end of a towel. "Here, Ma." She barely touched it to her mother's hand. "Maybe this'll make you feel better."

"Give me the phone," her mother cried, flinging away the towel. "I said give me the phone."

"Just try, Ma. One more day, that's all. You can do it. I know you can. Please! Will you just try?"

"Give me the goddamn phone! Give it to me, you ugly little bitch, you, or I'll leave! Is that what you want? You want me to leave? Cuz this time I'm not coming back. You hear me? You hear me?" she was still screaming when Jada ran in with the phone.

Hunched on one elbow, she tried to sit up. Her shaking hands kept hitting the wrong numbers. She gave Jada the phone and told her to do it. Her mother left a teary message, telling Ronnie how sorry she was and how she was so sick, she was afraid she was dying. "Please," she begged. "Please bring me something. A five-dollar rock. Pieces. Anything. Please, I'll do anything, I promise. Please, please, please."

Jada ran down the hill through the cold drizzle, hating everyone in every house and store she passed for having a better life than hers, hating her mother, hating Ronnie, but most of all hating herself for doing this, for trying to find him when this was all his fault. After the last rehab, her mother had stayed clean almost four months, her longest yet. She had a job with a big cleaning service, and she started going out with JumJum again, which really got to Ronnie. Nobody dared say it to his face now, but everyone thought Ronnie had set JumJum up just to get Marvella back. Not that Ronnie was the least bit nice to her once JumJum went away. That's the way Ronnie was. He had to be in charge, had to be the boss all the time of everyone.

Jada figured JumJum was probably her father. At least he was the most likely one. Her mother had been with him off and on since dropping out of high school her freshman year. Sometimes when Ronnie wasn't being such a vicious, mean asshole, she imagined how it might be him. According to her mother, it could have been any one of four different guys. Or maybe it *was* all four, she'd laugh, teasing Jada about her strange mix of features.

The thin rain pressed her close by the storefronts. Her pace quickened when she saw two guys smoking outside the pool hall. One was that fat creep Polie Valens. He was Ronnie's cousin from the Bronx, so that made him the man. He said he didn't know where Ronnie was, but then nobody ever knew where anyone was. Especially Ronnie Feaster. Polie gestured, and the other guy went inside.

"Whachoo want him for?" Polie asked.

"Nothing. I just gotta give him something."

"Give itta me, then," he said, bringing his wide face closer to hers. "I'll make sure he gets it." He yanked her inside the doorway.

"I can't." She tried to pull back, but he held on to her arm.

"C'mere, kitty-kitty-kitty," he said through pursed lips. "That's whachoo remind me of." His huge body engulfed hers, pressing her against the plate glass. He smelled of butts and beer and musky cologne. The whites of his eyes were glazed and yellow, his nose and chin raw with zits.

"Don't! Don't! Don't do that." She whipped her head from side to side.

"Come on, come on, come on, just one time, one little kiss and that'll be it, I promise."

"No! Leave me alone!" She butted her head into his shoulder.

He laughed. "I got what she needs. That's why she keeps calling, right?"

"She didn't call you."

"Same thing. I get the messages. Ronnie, he had to go someplace." He squeezed her chin in the cup of his warm, puffy hand.

"So when's he coming back?" She pushed his hand away.

He smiled. "Too late for Marvella. By then she'll be long gone. But here, feel." He guided her hand down his leg. "Right here in my pocket."

"How much? I only got a few bucks."

"One nice kiss and it's free, that's all."

"I got ten bucks." The other eight she needed for food.

"That ain't enough."

"Yes, it is! Ten—I got enough for a rock."

"Not anymore. Price's gone up, but not much. Just a kiss, that's all. Wait much longer, and you know where she'll be."

Toilet plunger, she thought, shuddering as his full wet lips clamped over hers. His fat tongue swelled inside her mouth, and now he was sliding both hands inside her pants. She couldn't talk or push him away. *Please,* her eyes implored the dull, low clouds, the wet, empty street. *Please make him stop. Somebody please stop this pig,* this disgusting, sweating pig that was grunting in her mouth. She choked and began to gag. He drew back quickly. A car slowed close to the curb, then cruised by, a customer in orbit.

"Here." He pressed the crack into her hand, then hurried into the pool hall. She looked down at the tiny white rock wrapped in clear plastic. It was too small to be a ten-dollar. He'd ripped her off, but she wasn't about to chase him into the pool hall. Besides, her mother would be too strung out to care as long as she got something.

All the way down Nash Street, she kept spitting onto the sidewalk, trying to get rid of the pig taste. Her whole mouth was sore. It tasted the way Uncle Bob's truck smelled after a pump-out. She stopped in front of the Nash Street Market and spat again. Gum would take it away. Her stomach rumbled with hunger. She couldn't see Thurman. The only cashier was some lady, not that bitch with the tubes. She moved closer to the window. That guy Gordon was at the end of the aisle. If she got food here, she wouldn't have to go all the way downtown to the Shop and Save. She went inside and grabbed a quart of milk, a box of Cap'n Crunch, Coke, Mountain Dew for her mother (the bottle, so when it was empty she could use it to smoke), two Hostess cupcakes, Reese's peanut butter cups, Tostitos chips, hot salsa, and two frozen pizzas for supper. She was starving. "Hey!" she called.

Gordon turned from the meat case he'd been scrubbing and said hello. Water dripped from his rag.

"You got any of them green apples? I can't think what they're called." She didn't even like apples, but every now and again she'd make herself eat one for the vitamins. Her gums were always bleeding, and her two back teeth were so sore and rotted that in her dreams every time she opened her mouth teeth drifted out. She didn't want to end up looking like the loser Burdle sisters down the street, not even twenty yet and no front teeth. Drugs instead of food, that's what happens, she'd warned her mother. She should have been the mother and Marvella the daughter. There was so much stuff her mother didn't know.

"Granny apples." Gordon pointed, but she couldn't see where. "Over there, next to the oranges."

She shifted her armload of groceries and hurried off. Her mother was probably climbing the walls by now. Ninety-nine cents a pound. How the hell much did an apple weigh? She tried to find the smallest two without dislodging the display. An apple avalanche, that's all she needed.

"What're you doing in here?" a shrill voice demanded.

"Shopping." Jada clutched an apple as the bitch bore down, dragging her wheeled tank.

"You get out. You get outta here right now!" June grabbed the apple and now was trying to get the milk.

"No! I got money! This is mine! I'm buying it!" Jada yelled, pulling back.

"Then I'm calling the cops, is that what you want? Cuz if you don't, you better put that stuff down and get the hell outta here."

"What's wrong?" Gordon asked, wiping his hands on his apron. Both spoke at once, June saying the girl was a thief while Jada insisted she had money. "So you're paying for that stuff?" he asked uneasily.

"Well, yeah!" Jada said, rolling her eyes. "I got the money right here in my pocket."

"And what else've you got in there, you little thief?" June reached toward Jada's pocket.

"Don't you touch me, bitch!" she warned. The crack was in the same pocket as the money. She'd forgotten to put it down the front of her pants.

"See!" June crowed to Gordon. "What'd I tell you?"

Leaning, Jada released her armload of groceries onto the lemons. "Here!" She took out the bills and waved them in the bitch's pinched gray face. "Eighteen bucks!"

Gordon assured June he'd bring Jada through the checkout himself. He carried the groceries up front, then bagged everything as Serena rang it through. Jada tossed a pack of bubble gum onto the mat.

"Twenty forty-nine," Serena said.

"Oh." Stunned, Jada checked one of the pizza boxes. Two forty-nine. "Take this off, then. I only got eighteen." She'd have cereal, and her mother could have the other pizza.

"Oh yeah, like she wasn't going to steal anything," June crowed from the next register.

"Bitch!" Jada shot back.

"Here. Here, it's okay. Take this." Gordon was trying to put money into Jada's hand.

"Count your fingers, make sure they're all there now," June cackled. "Fossums'll steal anything."

"Go fuck yourself!" Jada cried, shoving past his outstretched arm. Coins fell and rolled across the floor.

"I don't need shit. I don't need anybody's shit," she panted as she ran home through pelting rain. The front door was wide open. The television was on and all the lights, dresser drawers dumped out onto the bed, the corners of the kitchen linoleum torn back, the dented trash can tipped, its stinking contents spilling onto the floor, while from behind the couch a voice in perfect diction repeated, "Please hang up and try your call again. If you need assistance, dial your operator. Please hang up now. This is a recording." She reached down and fished up the phone. It was cracked. Directly above was a hole in the wall. She threw herself onto the couch. She was eating soggy pretzels and watching cartoons when the doorbell rang.

"Here." The big guy, Gordon, held out two bags of groceries.

"Yeah? What do you want?"

"Well, here. They're yours."

"How much do I owe you? I forget," she said, hoping he'd say it was all right, she didn't have to pay.

"Eighteen's fine."

"Yeah, but now I only got five left." She slipped one bill from the rest. "I had to get some stuff, some medicine for my mother."

"Oh," he said with a look of consternation as he took the five.

"But I'll pay you back."

"Oh. Okay. All right, then." He nodded as if to convince himself.

The minute he left she tried to light the oven. It wouldn't go on. The gas must have been shut off. "Goddamn her," she muttered, emptying the frozen pizza onto the counter. She'd have to eat it raw. Or maybe that guy Gordon would let her use his stove. She could see him out in the rain, picking dead branches off his bushes. She ran to the front door, then closed it quickly when the Navigator pulled up. Polie was driving. Ronnie Feaster ran up the steps. He rang the bell, then banged on the door.

"Give her this, then," he said when she told him her mother wasn't home. He handed her a piece of folded paper. His new pager number. He was always getting new ones—just to be safe. When she started to close the door, he blocked it with his foot. He needed a favor. Twenty bucks he'd pay her, and all she had to do was wait by the swings on the South Common for a guy and a girl in a black Jeep Wrangler. Same deal as last time: they'd pay and she'd pass the stuff. She said she couldn't.

"Me and Polie'll be in the bar. It's right across the street. The Tower. We'll be there. We'll be watching."

"Yeah, like a cop's not gonna know, right, me standing out in the rain."

"Say you're waiting for a ride, for your mother to pick you up."

"Yeah, right."

"C'mon. I told you before, you're like my star. The cops, they don't stop girls. They don't want to be checking your underpants and have you start yelling rape or something. C'mon, piece of cake." He held out his hand.

She thought of Polie and shivered. "No, I can't. Plus, I got a ton of homework. I got all these tests tomorrow."

"Tomorrow's Saturday." He grinned.

"They're special tests. I been sick."

"Come on! All right, how much you want? Twenty-five?"

"Yeah, like I ever see it."

"That's Marvella's fault. So this time we don't tell her. C'mon!"

"I can't. I'm hungry. I was just gonna eat."

"C'mon. Twenty minutes this'll take, and after, you can have whatever you want to eat. Anything!"

"Burger King?" Without a car, she never got to go there.

"Sure! Whatever!" He mussed her hair, and she grinned.

She sat in the backseat, trying to avoid Polie's eyes in the mirror. Disgusting creep, he wouldn't dare put a move on her now. She studied the shiny black hair curling over Ronnie's collar. She wouldn't mind him being her father. A mean son of a bitch, but at least he cared what happened to her. She hated running drugs, but her mother usually made her go, and besides, she liked being needed, liked being able to help him out in a bind. If she got caught, she wouldn't face nearly the time an adult would, but they'd definitely take her away from her mother, and if they didn't send her to juvie, they'd put her in foster care again. And that scared her more than anything else.

Gordon came outside the minute Jilly Cross pulled up. She had called a while ago to say she'd be right over if he still wanted to see those condos. She looked tired. Her eyes were puffy, and her hair was twisted into a tight bun at the nape of her neck. "I'm sorry about last week," she said as they turned the corner.

"That's okay."

They drove for a while. Finally, he asked where the condo was. Collerton, she said, but so close to the line that part of their service road was in Dearborn. Her voice trailed off. He tried to think of something to say, something to tell her. Anything to get her attention.

"Look! See? See that? That used to be the hot dog plant." He pointed to the dreary clump of cement-block buildings they were passing. "Every month we'd go there and buy hot dogs. My dad and me. A five-pound box. Half skinless and half natural casings." He

smiled, recalling how his father hated to pay full price for anything.
New shoes came from the factory store that sold seconds and over-
stocks. "It was great! The whole city was like that, so many interesting places to go and things to do." There had even been an
underwear factory in the city then and one that made jackets and
coats. For half price they could buy juice by the case from Whip-
ple's, the fruit-juice company. "If you want, I can show you sometime where they all are," he said as she turned down the road to the
condo complex. "Where they were, anyway," he added as she parked
the car.

"So, what's your sister-in-law like?" she asked, throwing him off
base a minute.

"Very nice. She's a very nice person." He looked out at what appeared to be clusters of attached English Tudor cottages. "I don't
know, it looks pretty expensive here."

"Kind of, but Dennis said your sister-in-law's getting you a job at
Harrington's. You'd make a lot more there."

"Oh, no. No, I'm fine where I am. I like it there. I don't want to
work at the brewery."

"That's not what your sister-in-law wants."

"I haven't discussed it with her. Maybe she thinks I do, I don't
know."

"What is she, some kind of control freak?"

"Lisa? No, she's wonderful. She's a wonderful woman."

She opened the door and got out. They went quickly through the
model condo, then Jilly drove to the next one, which was smaller and
cheaper. Except for a few questions about Dennis, she had little to say
on the way back. He felt deflated when she turned onto Clover
Street.

"The house looks like it's in good condition." She peered over
the wheel. "A lot better than any of the others here."

"It is! Dennis took really good care of it." He smiled out at the
neat little house. "Even the roses are doing good now. See all the
buds?"

"He's a good brother, huh?"

"Yes. Very good." He looked at her. "Would you like to come in?" he asked, then froze.

"I can't," she said too quickly. "But thank you."

"I mean the house, to see what condition it's in."

"Oh, you mean an appraisal."

He nodded. A second chance, that's all he wanted.

"But first, you were telling me about your sister-in-law. What's she like?"

He'd already told her. "She's very kind and patient, and she's got a really good sense of humor. She always made me feel . . . well, comfortable—I guess that's the word."

"She's really religious, huh? Like really into the church."

That was an odd thing to say. He wasn't sure how to respond. But maybe this was how men and women got to know one another, after a certain amount of awkward probing. He'd have to think of a question about her family. "I don't know much about that part of her life, but one thing's always impressed me about Lisa. She's one of those people who know what you're trying to say before you can even get it out." He saw her fidget with the key chain. Afraid she would turn the ignition, he amazed himself and continued talking. He was telling her how of all the women Dennis had brought on visits, Lisa had been the most natural. He said he still didn't know if Dennis wanted his approval of the women or theirs of him.

"Probably both," she said, smiling.

"Yes, but when I heard her last name, Harrington, I was really nervous. I kept thinking, Here's this pretty young woman from one of the richest families around, and to hear her laughing and talking in the visitors' room you'd've thought she was in my living room or something."

"Sounds like someone's got a real thing for their sister-in-law," she said with raised eyebrows. "Well, anyway." She reached into the console for a card. "Here. Hillman Appraisal. That's who I use most of the time. Ask for Randy. He's the owner."

He kept looking at the card.

"Is that okay?" She started the car.

"Yes. Yes, Randy—I'll remember that." So maybe that's all this was, a business relationship. A favor for Dennis, compelling her to go through the motions with his loser brother. But no, there was something more here. Her interest in him went deeper than that. He could feel it. He could see it in her uneasy eyes.

CHAPTER 8

Neil Dubbin had hired one of his brother-in-law's carpenters to install the new vinyl shelving and display racks. After three outrageous painting estimates, he had assigned the job to Gordon. The work had gone slowly at first, with Gordon not only performing his routine store duties, but trying, when he found time to paint, to make each brush stroke perfect. Now that his pace was faster, most of the storage areas were finished.

He was back on the ladder, touching up some ceiling molding, when Leo said he was needed up front. He had been called down twice in the last half hour, to help unload truck deliveries, now this time to fix June's register tape. Every few days the tape would snarl, jamming the register and locking the cash drawer shut. Neil was trying to remove the rolls from the cartridge, but he was so nervous that his hand shook. Gordon took his place and peered into the frozen cartridge, while behind him Neil launched into another litany of failure. He was still using thirty-year-old manual registers when every place else had been computerized. "I must be nuts. I've wasted how many years in this dump, and Jesus Christ, here I am, still trying to make a go of it. What I should do is just walk out that goddamn door and let my sister and her idiot husband run things if they want to keep this dump going so bad."

"Almost got it," Gordon grunted, wedging the tip of the slender screwdriver down alongside the tape spool. "Same thing," he muttered. "That one little wheel's slipped."

June sat on a crate, sipping blue Gatorade. She'd just had a weak spell. Six customers waited in line at the next register. Serena was ringing up orders and doing her own bagging.

"This is ridiculous!" said a disheveled woman in a stained white uniform. Her two small children wailed because she'd just smacked their hands for taking gum after she'd said no.

"Can't somebody do that register?" another woman asked, pointing.

"Where's the kid? Why isn't he bagging?" Neil asked, looking around for Thurman.

"He went out to round up carts," June said, wheezing, and smirked at him. "Ten minutes ago." He had gone out for a cigarette.

"Oh, Jesus." Neil started for the door. Out on the street, a slight, thin-haired man in a gray suit was shouting at Thurman, who was a head taller than he was. Just yesterday the boy had blown up at Leo and stormed out. When his grandmother got home from work, she'd marched him into the store and made him apologize to Leo and Neil.

"Fuck you!" Thurman's voice exploded through the opening door. With Neil's arrival, the man gestured angrily at Thurman, who stood in the hot sun, glaring in his long-sleeved white shirt and baggy prison pants. Neil patted the man's shoulder and tried to bring him inside, but the man looked back and said something. The boy lunged and the man shoved him away, but the boy came at him again. Neil pushed between them. The man's round, fair face blotched with rage as he strained against Neil to get at Thurman.

"Gordon!" June implored, pulling her tank to the door, but he was numb, frozen.

"Oh, my God!" a woman in line cried out, saying she knew the boy's grandmother.

"He pushed them right into me," the man panted as he came through the door.

"They're hard to stop sometimes," Neil said, then, seeing the boy on his heels, ordered him to go home and cool off. With that, Thurman charged inside, shouting that the asshole had driven into the carts on purpose, that's how his car got scratched.

"He wouldn't wait!" Thurman insisted.

"Yeah, right," the man said, straightening his tie. He stared at Gordon.

"Ask him what he called me!" Thurman said to Neil. "Go ahead, ask him!"

"Get the hell outta here! I'm not going to say it again. You go home and cool off. Now!" Neil ordered.

"No!" Thurman bellowed. "I'm not leaving! I didn't do anything! He's the one, not me! Ask him what he said! Go ahead!"

"Look, that's it! I've had enough of your mouth, you hear me? What do you want? You want me to fire you? I don't think so. I don't think that's what you want." Neil had gotten Thurman to the door.

"You're Loomis, right?" The man's eyes raged with turbulence. His head trembled.

Gordon nodded.

"I want you to ask him! Go ahead! Ask him what he called me!" the boy demanded as the man advanced on Gordon.

"Here, look! Look at this." The man held out his open wallet with shaking hands. "See! See that beautiful face? That's all that's left because of you! A picture," he said, his low, anguished voice running into Neil's and Thurman's.

Gordon's head jerked away from her joyful smile. Twenty-five years ago, her pictures had made her seem so much older than he had been then. Now he realized how young she had been, how pretty.

"Fucking spick, that's what he said! That's what he called me," Thurman said through the closing door.

"You son of a bitch," the man spat. "You don't even care, do you. At least Cox had the decency to blow his fucking brains out as soon as *he* got out."

Gordon stared down at his huge, sweaty feet in these absurd blue-and-white sneakers. At least in a cell the bars had been visible.

"But it's over for you, right? You did your time. You just come back, start over, what the hell do you care! She wasn't anything to you, right?" He paused, mouth quivering. "But she was my sister. Janine! Oh God," he moaned, and covered his face, still holding the wallet. Business cards and photographs slid to the floor.

Neil picked them up. "Tom," he said, holding them out.

"My sister's gone," the man sobbed in his struggle with the inexplicable, this monstrous and simple fact. "And my parents, they died of broken hearts. But you, you're still here. Why? How *can* you be? What kind of person are you? Look at you! You can't even look me in the eye, can you?"

Gordon shook his head. No.

"Do something!" the man screamed, slapping the wallet at Gordon's chest in a frenzy of rage and impotence. "Say something! Don't just stand there, you fucking coward, you no-good bastard, you stupid son of a bitch!" He hit him in the neck, and Serena screamed.

Gordon stood there. He could not express it, could not say that the very fact of his emptiness meant something, that never for a moment had he denied or relinquished guilt, and so in that ineffable way did mourn and suffer her loss. Even his torturous memories were meaningless, as futile as this brother's outburst. What possible atonement was there for taking her life? What reparation might balance the loss? None, of course. Not even execution or suicide could plug the hole he had made in the universe. And in his own soul. "I'm sorry," he whispered. "I'm so very sorry."

"Sorry! Sorry! What's sorry? What's that? That's nothing! That's a word! A fucking, useless, empty word, that's all the fuck that is!" The man's voice broke with a rubbly gasp, the unseen wreckage of a cave collapsing in on itself.

The door above him opened. "Gordon? Gordon, are you down there? . . . Gordon?" Neil paused halfway down the creaking cellar steps. "What're you doing?"

"Looking for a ladder."

"It's already up here. You were on it."

"I thought there was another one. A higher one."

Neil almost seemed to be grinning. "No, you're hiding down here, that's what you're doing."

He felt sick to his stomach, so drained that his bones ached.

"I didn't know who he was at first," Neil said. "Even when he said the name, Tom Ferguson. I didn't make the connection. He said he just found out you were working here and something snapped inside. He was on his way to work and he just kept driving. From New Jersey. Six hours—he never stopped. All he knew was he had to see you. He said it all blew up, all those feelings, things he hadn't thought of in years."

Gordon remembered him sitting between his bewildered-looking father and devastated mother, the younger brother who often wept during the trial. He used to wonder why they subjected him to that, why he wasn't in school. Now he knew. So that he wouldn't forget. So that when they were gone, some part of them would still speak her name.

"I told him you're a good guy, and that's all I know."

Gordon nodded.

"What else could I say? You never talk about anything."

Gordon shrugged.

"You keep it all in, huh? Not like that Dominguez, always mouthing off at somebody. If it wasn't for his grandmother, I'd fire the sour little bastard." Neil picked up a sooty coal bucket by the handle and swung it back and forth. "You know, this may come as a surprise, but I envy you. No commitments, no anchors, nothing to hold you back like this shithole here." He laughed, his gleaming eyes skittering over the dusty crates, teetering stacks of pallets, and cobwebbed signs and warped shelving. Propped against the wall was the original marquee. NASH STREET MARKET, proclaimed the red glass script, dull with grime and dead fuses. "Feels like a tomb down here, doesn't it? A fucking grave!" He let go of the bucket and dropkicked it into the marquee.

Gordon jumped with the explosion of neon tubes.

"I should have sold it when I had the chance. But all I could think was, Yeah, and then what the hell do I do? I figured it was too late to start over. I mean, I had a family to support. What was I gonna do, go sell cars someplace? It was like being frozen, like I was encased in this block of fucking ice I'm always trying to see out of, and then one day there you are, and it hits me. I don't have to do this anymore. I served my time. I can be free, too. Do you know what I mean?"

"I don't know. I'm not sure."

"But the thing is, it's gotta at least look like it's worth something if I'm ever gonna sell it."

"You're going to sell the Market?" A lump rose into Gordon's throat.

"Sure. If I can find someone stupid enough to buy it."

Lisa called a few days later. Jimmy's eleventh-birthday party was going to be two weeks from Sunday. Dennis could pick him up, or he could take the bus if he'd rather. "And if there's anyone you'd like to bring, Gordon, feel free. We'll probably be outside, so the more the merrier!"

"Oh, okay," he said, trying to hide his dread.

"Oh, and another thing, Gordon. I meant to call the other day and tell you, but guess who I ran into at the mall? Delores Dufault! It was just a quick visit, but I enjoyed seeing her so much. She's so nice!"

"Yes. Yes, she is."

"And I told her how much I miss her. I used to love our rides up to see you, she'd be so funny. Well, anyway, she said you'd been to her house for dinner a couple weeks ago."

"Yes. That's right. I did."

"Was it good? I'll bet she's a great cook."

"Yes, she is. It was good. It was very good." What he remembered was the sweetness of the strawberries and his excitement at the prospect of being with Jilly, who he thought about all the time, last night even dreamed about.

"So you had a good time?"

"Yes, very nice." He smiled, thinking of the dream. Jilly and his mother were playing cards on the deck of a dry-docked boat over-looking the ocean, where the waves had been too loud for him to hear their conversation.

"But you haven't called her or anything since then, right?"

"Well, I've been busy. I . . ."

"I know, that's what I told her. I said how busy you've been and how maybe she should just give you a ring. But then I felt bad. She said she'd stopped calling because she didn't want to bother you anymore."

"Oh. Well, I don't know. I have been putting in a lot of time at the Market."

"Why don't you give her a call? Just say how busy you've been. Ask her what's going on, and . . . well, you'll know what to say." She paused. "You shouldn't be alone so much, Gordon. You need someone to share things with."

It was early morning. The cloudless sky was a brilliant blue, and the sun already felt hot. Gordon knelt in the damp grass, measuring out a quarter cup of fertilizer from the hardware store. The label said to pour it in a circle around the base of each bush. That done, he tilted the old watering can and thoroughly soaked the harsh-smelling granules into the humusy black soil. Every day the bushes were greener and fuller. He could almost feel their gratitude after so many years of neglect. Sometimes when he was done he would glance back, half expecting an anxious voice begging him to stay. He gathered up his tools and started toward the house.

"Hey! What're you doing?" Jada Fossum called from across the street.

"Good morning," he answered, then continued inside as if he couldn't hear her still calling to him. Last week, she had asked him to bring her home some milk, bread, and peanut butter. He had almost said no because she had never paid him for the other groceries. But he did, and then when he brought them to her, she said she'd have to pay him later, her mother wasn't there and she didn't have any money. Two days later she came into the store and bought ten dollars' worth of food, for which she had only three dollars and fifty cents. The rest must have fallen out of her pocket, she said. Serena asked her which things she wanted to put back. Gordon kept sweeping. He didn't know what to say when she tapped him on the shoulder and asked to borrow the six fifty difference. She'd pay him back that night, swear to God.

"No, you can't do that!" Serena told her. "You can't come in here and be hitting people up for money!"

"I'm not hitting people up!" Jada spat back. "I know him. He's my friend. He can help me if he wants." Edging closer, she peered up at him. "I really need this stuff. I'll pay you back, I swear," she said in a low, hungry voice. "Thank you! Thank you so much!" she squealed when he gave the money to Serena.

He gazed out the window as he washed his hands in the kitchen sink. Bright yellow dandelions covered Mrs. Jukas's yard. Yesterday she had been out in her bathrobe, stuffing blown papers and twigs into a trash bag. When he'd gotten home from work last night, a woman in a pink uniform and dreadlocks had been shaking rag rugs over the back railing. Mistaking her for a nurse, he had asked if Mrs. Jukas was sick.

"If she is, she didn't tell me," the woman said, then told him she was the cleaning lady. She came once a month.

He sprayed glass cleaner into the sink, then dried it with a square of paper toweling he kept there for just that purpose. Every week he'd start a new square. Thriftiness gave him some small sense of control in his life. The hardest part of freedom was his accessibility. Like Tom Ferguson and Jada Fossum and Delores, anyone could get to him at any time. Instead of being pleased, he was irritated by invitations. He didn't want to go to Jimmy's birthday party. He dreaded meeting Lisa's parents and seeing the horror in their eyes. At least Jilly Cross had been honest about her reaction. So far no one at work had said anything, but he could feel them watching him. Serena and June had become nervously solicitous, as if they needed to stay in his good graces now more than ever. Neil hadn't said another word about the incident with Ferguson. He had given Gordon two hundred and fifty dollars yesterday to thank him for all his hard work and for never saying no to him. Not once, no matter what he ever asked him to do, he had said.

Gordon made up his mind. As soon as he finished breakfast, he would call Jilly. His toast had just popped up when the doorbell rang.

"Hey!" Jada grinned up at him through the screen. "I was calling you. Didn't you hear me?"

"What is it?" he said, unable to hide his irritation.

"Here!" She held up a fistful of bills with a furtive glance back at her house.

He opened the door and took the money. She dropped a handful of change onto the bills. "I was in kind of a hurry, so if it's not right, let me know and I'll bring over the rest."

"Thank you," he said after a quick count. Eighty-nine cents short, but he'd let it go.

"You didn't think I was going to pay you back, huh."

"Well, yes. Of course I did."

"Good, cuz I'm very honest, you know."

"Yes, well, anyway, thank you for bringing this over." He started to close the door.

"Umm, that smells good." She sniffed against the screen. "What kind of coffee's that?"

"Just regular, that's all."

"High test, that's what I drink. That decaf stuff, it's like, ugh. I mean, why bother?"

"Well, anyway—"

"Could I have a cup? We don't have any. We ran out."

Saying he'd be right back, he went inside and quickly poured her a cup. He glanced at the clock. Jilly would be leaving for work soon. When he came back with the coffee, Jada was in the living room. She asked if he had any milk. She could drink it black, but if he had milk, she'd like it a lot more, she said, following him into the kitchen. He had a really nice house, she said, looking around.

This was a mistake. She was taking over, but he couldn't very well ask her to leave. He handed her the milk carton.

"Thanks!" She pulled out a chair and sat at the table. She poured milk into her cup, then took a long, slurpy sip. "Hey! Don't forget your toast." She pointed to the toaster. After each sip she added more milk. "What do you put, butter on your toast? Or jelly?" Sip. "I like both." Sip. "Actually, I like everything." Sip. "I don't care, I'll, like, try anything." Sip. "I'm, like, always hungry." Sip. "Sometimes my mother says, 'I think you got worms, you must—nobody can eat that much food and be so skinny.' " Sip. The cup was filled with milk. "You gonna eat that toast?"

"In a minute." Determined to outwait her, he wet the sponge and wiped off the countertop.

"If you don't want it, I'll eat it." Her eyes fixed on his with a hard swallow. "But can you pop it down for a minute?" she asked as he started to take it out. "That way the butter'll melt. I love this house, it's so nice. Where I live it's just like nobody gives a shit, oops, sorry, but you know what I mean? The landlord, all he cares about is his rent." Her voice grated like the scrape of the butter knife on the dry toast. "We're gonna move. I'm not sure when. But pretty soon. We were gonna move in with JumJum, but then that turned to shit, I mean, like, well, you know what I mean. Thanks!" She snatched a slice before the plate was even on the table. "The problem is, we only got one bedroom. I hate that. My mother's like this wicked loud snorer. Could I have another piece?" she asked, licking her fingertips and leaning close to the dish as she pressed them into the crumbs. "I'm not getting on your nerves, am I?" she said as he gave her the second slice. "My mother says I'm a pain in the ass I talk so much, but I can't help it. I don't like quiet all the time. I mean, it's like there's nothing there, you know what I mean?"

"Actually, I like things to be quiet," he said as deliberately as he could.

"Whoa! Well, I guess I better go, then." She stuffed the rest of the toast into her mouth and headed for the door.

He'd played this out in his head a thousand times, and now he was finally dialing the number. He winced with each ring. He had everything planned. Dinner at the Yellow Brick Inn, which he'd overheard June say was the best restaurant around. When Jilly picked him up, he'd show her the roses. He'd break one off and give it to her. Or maybe he'd have a bouquet already cut and waiting. But they'd probably wilt in the car. So maybe the restaurant could put them in a glass of water for her. And there they'd be all through dinner, those red petals, velvety soft like her cheeks.

"Hello?" she answered breathlessly.

"Hi." The restaurant, roses, her sweet voice, it all ran together in his head. He didn't know what to say next. "This is Gordon. Gordon Loomis."

"Oh, sure—Gordon! How've you been? I've been meaning to call you. I was wondering what you thought of the condos I showed you."

"I liked them. They were very nice. And I really appreciated seeing them. I mean, I appreciated your time . . . the time it took to show them to me."

"Well, I'm glad to do it. Did you get your appraisal yet?"

"No. That's not why I'm calling. I wanted to know if you could go to a restaurant. That's what I wanted to ask you."

"A restaurant?" She sounded confused.

"Yes, to eat dinner. That's what I meant. And any time's fine. Any night, whenever you want. I mean, I know you have appointments and things sometimes at night."

"Oh, I'm sorry, Gordon, but I can't."

"Oh. Well. Well, that's okay, then. I . . . I don't mean to bother you."

"You're not bothering me! No, it's not that at all. It's just that I'm—I'm seeing someone right now. I'm sorry. I'm so sorry, Gordon."

"No, don't be sorry. I mean, you don't have anything to be sorry for."

CHAPTER 9

He had been a fool to think that such a beautiful young woman would ever be attracted to him. He had to remember not to expect too much. Reentering the world didn't make a man free. It was enough just to be here, on his way home from work in the warm afternoon sunshine. As he turned into the front walk, Jada Fossum ran across the street carrying a puppy.

"Isn't he so sweet? Oh, I love you so much, you sweet little beebee!" she squealed, nuzzling the folds of its plump brown neck.

"He's a nice little dog." He thought of her kicking the old man's ratty little dog.

"Pet him. Go ahead!" She grabbed his hand and placed it on the dog's warm head. "See! He likes you!"

The dog yipped and wiggled toward him. "He's friendly."

"Yeah, these druggers, they were gonna take him to the pound, but my mother said, 'No, you can't do that.' She can't stand seeing animals be hurt. She said, 'They'll just put him to sleep, and the poor little beebee's never even been outside or anything.' They kept him in a cage all the time, the zombies. They did, didn't they?" she murmured in his floppy ear. "Poor little thing, he keeps pooping all over the house. I'm trying to train him, but every time I put him down he takes off. Hey, you don't have an old leash or anything, do you?"

"No," he said. Then, seeing her disappointment, he remembered the old pieces of clothesline in the garage. She tied the shortest length to the collar. The collar seemed loose, but he knew better than to get too involved. The minute she put the puppy down, he squirmed out of the collar and tore through the bushes, onto Mrs. Jukas's front porch. Yelling, Jada chased after him. The door opened as the girl dove onto the yipping dog, trying to snare him with the collar.

"What do you think you're doing?" Mrs. Jukas demanded through the screen.

"I'm just trying to get my dog, that's all!"

"Get out of here!"

"I am. I'm just tryna get the thing on him, that's all!"

"No! Get out of here! You get off my porch right now!"

"I am! I am! I just have to do this!" Jada said as the collar slipped off the dog's head again.

The commotion had summoned Marvella Fossum to her front door. She seemed confused at first, then hurried down the steps and across the street onto Mrs. Jukas's narrow porch. "What the hell're you doing?" she screamed. "If you can't take care of him, then you're not gonna keep him. Didn't I tell you that? Didn't I? Well, didn't I?" Jada picked up the dog and was trying to untangle the rope from the leg of the aluminum chair the dog had pulled over. "Answer me! I said answer me!" Marvella cried in the frantic tone of baseless authority.

"Get out of here! Both of you! You get off my porch right now!" Mrs. Jukas said.

"Fuck you!" Marvella kicked the door panel.

The old woman's head recoiled. "That's it! I'm calling the police. I don't have to put up with a tramp like you coming onto my property!"

"Ma!" Jada pleaded as Marvella charged the door again.

In the driveway, Gordon raised his hand.

"Stop it, Ma! Stop it!" Jada cried, and grabbed her mother's arm.

"So she can call me any name she wants?" Marvella screamed. "Like I'm nothing? Like I'm just some piece of garbage?" she bawled as Jada managed to get her off the porch with the joyful dog straining at the lead.

Delores couldn't believe her ears. Not a word from Albert in days and suddenly here he was with his mousy little Dearborn clerk, Katie, in her denim jumper, saying he was closing the Collerton store in a few weeks.

"It seems like short notice, I know," he said.

"Short notice!"

Katie was tallying the merchandise count in a steno notebook, but Delores knew she had been brought as Albert's shield.

"It was one of those what I call lightbulb decisions," Albert intoned in that chest-deep voice he used when he wanted to impress someone. "All of a sudden you go, What are we doing, why do we keep carrying this deficit from month to month? . . ."

Katie looked up and nodded.

We? Who's we? He and Katie? How can he do this? How can he be so insensitive?

"And then it hits me! Why not just end it now?" he said.

"What do you mean?" Her voice quavered. She stared into his eyes, as if they were the only two there.

"Close it. Clear everything out, just lock the door," he declared.

"And that's it?"

"Well, what would be the point really of a going-out-of-business sale? I mean, when we can just take it all over to the new store," Katie called from behind the glass case where she knelt, counting Post-it pads.

"We can probably get it all out in a day," Albert agreed.

"If that!" Katie scoffed.

"What about me?" she asked him.

"We're still working out the details." He opened the storeroom door. "Hey! Where'd the old copier go?"

"That's the last thing we need, Albert Smick, another copier!" Katie laughed and jumped up. "He can't throw anything out," she told Delores. "You never know when you're going to need it, right, Albert?"

That night Delores called her youngest sister. Babbie was the one she called when she needed to sound off but didn't want a lecture. Of the five Dufault girls, Babbie was considered the featherbrain in the family, even though she was the only one who'd gone to college. Babbie said she should be grateful the store was closing. She'd never understood why Delores had stayed there all this time.

"All right! All right, I'm coming!" Babbie called away from the phone. She had to go. Dwayne was waiting. It was their line-dancing night at the Elks.

Maureen wasn't home, and Linda had her daughter-in-law on the other line and would call her right back. Delores was on the phone with her oldest sister, Karen, now, chewing her inner cheek to shreds while she tried not to cry. "You had to know this was going to happen. There's no loyalty with a boss like Smick. He's a creep! He's always been a creep."

"No, he's not. He's a good man. And a good friend. A very good friend," she added.

"So is your very good friend going to make you manager of the new store, then?"

"I would imagine."

"Well, is he or isn't he?"

"Yes. Of course. I'm sure he is. He's just been so busy, he—"

"Delores! Don't you get it? This is it! In a couple of weeks you're out of a job!"

"No, I'm not!"

"You could make so much money somewhere else. I never understood why you stayed there. How many times did I tell you about openings at the post office? You would've been a supervisor by now. You would've had security plus a pension. You're so smart: I don't get it, Delores. What were you thinking all those years? That somehow there was going to be some future there? I mean, even Mom saw this coming. She'd say, 'What's she doing still living at home? Why isn't she out on her own like the rest of you?'"

"I took care of Mom! She wanted me there. She needed me. Who else was going to do it?" Delores cried, though she was sure Karen was once again putting words into their dead mother's mouth.

"What she wanted, Doe, was for you to have your own life like the rest of us."

"I do. I have my own life. I always have. It may not meet your standards, but I'm very happy the way I am." She felt better for saying that. She took a deep breath. "And if you can't accept me for who I am, then that's your problem."

There was a pause. "Oh, my God."

"What do you mean, 'Oh, my God'?"

"You're gay, aren't you. You're a lesbian, that's it, that's what you're trying to tell me. I feel so stupid! I mean, here I am, a nurse, and it went right by me. All these years, my own sister, and I never even put it together. Of course! It was like you always wanted to tell me something: I always had that feeling. Now it all makes such sense."

"It does?"

"You always had so many girlfriends! You never went out with guys."

"Yes, I did."

"Yeah, but they were always more like buddy things."

"Buddy things?"

"You know, either they were seeing someone else or, God, probably even gay themselves, now that I think of it. Or like Gordon Loomis, right? Jail, now isn't that the ultimate cover? But listen, Doe, it doesn't matter. Really. You're my sister and I love you just the way you are! No matter what you are!" Karen declared with the fervor of liberation, sisterhood, relief—something.

"I'm not gay, Karen."

"It's all right. I can handle it."

"But I'm not!"

At nine the next morning, Delores sat in her idling car in the narrow lot behind Smick's in Dearborn. She noted the brand-new wheeled trash receptacles. All the Collerton store had were old galvanized barrels she could barely drag when full. There were even two lawn chairs and a small plastic table for employees to use on warm days. Albert pulled into the space beside her.

"What are you doing here?" His shiny pate pinkened with her approach.

"I have to talk to you."

"All right. Yes. Of course. We do, but does it have to be right now?" He glanced at his watch. "Shouldn't you be opening now?"

She shrugged. "Why? What does it matter?" Her heavily made-up eyes burned in the morning light. She hadn't slept all night but had taken pains to look her best, wearing a bright fuchsia pantsuit and parrot-green scarf.

"It's not as if this comes as any big surprise, right?" he said in a low voice.

"Why did you have to bring someone with you? Do you know how I felt? We've always been able to talk. My God, how many years have we . . . known each other?" she added quickly when his eyes widened.

"I'm sorry."

"You hurt me terribly, Albert. I've always been so loyal. You know I have. And I've tried to be understanding. No matter what was going on, I always tried to see your side of it. So how could you do that to me?"

"I'm sorry."

The emotional restraint she had found so sexy was breaking her heart. "I feel so empty," she whispered, unable to stop the dreaded tears. "I don't know what to do."

"We can't very well discuss it here. Not when you're like this! I'm sorry!" He spoke through a ventriloquist's frozen smile. "This is our big personalized-stationery sale. There's a calligrapher in there right now. He's waiting for me!" The grin widened. "You couldn't have picked a worse day for this!"

"I'm sorry." She turned away.

The back door opened. "Oh! Albert! There you are!" Katie said.

"So I'll come by and we'll get it all figured out," he called, his tinny jollity a blade up her spine as she walked to her car.

She was surprised to find her sister waiting for her at the store. Karen had just gotten off her shift and couldn't wait to tell Delores who had come into the emergency room last night. "So here it is three in the morning when this cab pulls up and this huge guy runs in—I mean, he was enormous—and he's all worked up because there's a woman with him—a woman out in the cab and she's having a heart attack and he's afraid she's going to die. 'She's in real bad shape,' he says, 'so can somebody please get out there with a stretcher and bring her inside?' And I'm sitting there with my jaw hanging open, looking up at him, and all I'm thinking is, Oh, my God. I don't believe it. It's Gordon Loomis—wait until I tell Delores."

"Who was the woman?"

"I wrote it down." She unfolded the paper. "Jukas. Elsbeth Jukas."

Delores tried to hide her relief. "Why didn't they come in an ambulance?"

"He couldn't get her to. He said she wanted him to drive her car, but he doesn't have a license. Naturally! I mean, I didn't even think of it until he said that, but he probably doesn't even know how to drive, right?"

"Probably not."

"Twenty-five years. God! I mean, think of all the things you've done in the last twenty-five years. Can you imagine?"

For eleven years there had been her job in the bank and shy Robert Cleary, five years younger and a high school English teacher. He told her through the teller window one fine June morning that he had accepted a job in Japan and would be leaving immediately. She wrote, but he never did. After Robert, there had been other men she met in clubs, on singles cruises, men she worked with, bowled and played softball with, single and married, blind dates, personal ads, it hadn't mattered until she found herself spread-kneed on a paper-lined gurney with her feet in stirrups, hands muffling her ears against the ravenous sound of the suctioning. She was still bleeding and hating herself the day Albert Smick shuffled up to her window with his store's deposits and a weary sigh. His salesgirl had quit just when he was finally able to take his wife and children to Disney World. He couldn't afford to close down the business, so he was on his way home to tell them they'd have to go without him. Go, she said; she'd run the store for him. She had tons of vacation time, and if ever she needed a change in her life, it was then.

"It's weird," Karen was saying. "He's older, of course, but he stills looks the same. It's like nothing's changed. Like not having his license, like nothing's happened, nothing's left its mark on him. It's like he's not really real, you know what I mean?"

"Did he know who you were? Did you say you were my sister?"

"I did, but he was, like, out of it. He just sat in a corner, staring down at the floor while they worked on her."

"Is she all right? She didn't die, did she?" *Poor Gordon, having to go through that alone.*

"No. They took her up to Cardiac Care, but the whole time he's like, wringing his hands together, and all I can think is, Oh, my God, they're so huge, that poor Janine Walters, she never had a chance." Karen leaned over the counter. "When you went up there on those visits, did he ever do anything, you know, to make you nervous?"

"No."

"He just seems so . . . so, like, coiled."

"He's just quiet, that's all. He's shy, reserved."

"Did he ever say anything about the murder?" Karen's eyes gleamed. "He did, didn't he? Come on, Delores. You can tell me."

"No. But I wouldn't say anything even if he did."

"Oh, come on, you know you would. You've never been able to keep a secret, Delores, and you know it."

Mrs. Jukas was still in the hospital. "She's a tough old bird," the nurse had told Dennis when he called. Gordon felt almost as useless as the night Mrs. Jukas called, gasping that she was having a heart attack. There was little she'd let him do, other than wait on the porch for the cab, then help her into it. The only thing she'd said before they wheeled her away was, "Keep them away from my house." Her grass needed mowing, but he wouldn't dare cut it without her permission.

Sticking out from her door was a white card that hadn't been there yesterday. He hurried onto her porch. It was from the gas company, a postcard for reading the meter. He slipped it through the brass mail slot in her door, so no one would know she wasn't home. A brief but violent windstorm had littered both yards with broken branches. He bundled them all and left them on the curb in front of her house for pickup along with one of his own trash bags for additional signs of life.

Across the way, Jada's puppy was caught in a frenzy of barking at the end of his tangled rope. Tied to the railing, he had only a few inches of slack left after all his jumping and running in circles. Gordon felt bad for the frantic creature but continued on his way to work. The kinder he was, the more the girl wanted from him.

That night he had just finished dinner when Jada showed up with the puppy in her arms. He spoke to her through the locked screen door. She asked if he had any leftovers. She had run out of dog food.

"What about your mother? Can't she get some?" He had seen Marvella Fossum leaving the house only moments before with Ronnie Feaster.

"She's asleep," the girl said, lowering her voice as if not to disturb her. "And Leonardo's hungry. My poor little baby's starving, aren't you?" She kissed the puppy.

"That's what you named him? Leonardo?"

"Yeah! Cool, huh? That's who he reminds me of."

"The painter? Leonardo da Vinci?"

"No!" she hooted. "Leonardo DiCaprio! The guy on the *Titanic*," she added, seeing his blank expression.

"Just let him have the meat. He might choke on the bone," he said when he came back. He passed the foil-wrapped packet through the door, then locked it.

"Smells good." She and the puppy sniffed at the packet. "What is it?"

"Chicken."

"Oh! KFC? I love their new barbecue kind. But this isn't, though. I can tell by the smell."

"It's baked. I made it."

"Oh!" She parted the foil. "Well, I gotta see how good a cook you are, then, right?" With the dog straining to get at it, she bit into the drumstick. "Delicious," she said, then took two more bites. "You're a really good cook!"

He smiled. "Maybe I should get you another piece, huh? I think you're as hungry as he is."

"Well, I am, a little. We were gonna have takeout, but then my mother had to . . . go and fall asleep."

As he ripped off a larger sheet of foil, he heard the door handle jiggle against the lock. He wrapped up another drumstick, a cold baked potato, and some green beans. She thanked him, then glanced across the street. "I'm not supposed to be over here. My mother, she thinks every guy I talk to's tryna come on to me."

Two nights later she returned with the puppy. Her mother had bought dog food, but Leonardo hated it, and her mother said, well, too bad then—it could just sit there on the floor and rot until he got hungry enough to eat it. "She said she doesn't need two fussy eaters in the house!" Jada called after him as he headed into the kitchen.

She was halfway across the street with her packet of steak and macaroni and cheese when Ronnie Feaster's SUV pulled up. Her mother got out and started yelling at her. Gordon closed the door. A few minutes later, Ronnie Feaster knocked on his door. His smile was like the flick of something sharp in the night.

"What do you want?"

"No, it's not me, man. It's Marvella. She's like flipped out over there. She's knocking the kid around, she's gonna call the cops, she doesn't know what the hell she's doing, so that's why." Each phrase was punctuated by his open hand across his chest. "I'm just the messenger, that's all. She's a weird kid, you know, like way too . . . well, you know what I mean, so just don't be . . . don't be thinking, you know, cuzza Marvella, it's okay or anything." His cold eyes fixed on Gordon's. "Cuz it's not. It's really, really not."

"What do you mean?" he asked, horrified.

"Like I said, I'm just the messenger."

"I gave her food for the dog."

"That's what she said, but that Jada, she's got more stories. Like, she says you're always tryna give her things." Feaster's eyes narrowed. "Just don't try giving her *that* thing. Okay?"

"Hey, wait up!" Jada called the next morning. He walked faster. He didn't want Marvella Fossum to come screaming out her front door. "Wait! I gotta tell you something!" The girl ran after him. "Guess what today is," she said, catching up. Her quick smile had a glare to it. Like light in a dingy room, it made her young face seem haggard and gray.

"I don't know," he said, relieved to be turning the corner. "What day is it?"

"My birthday!" That's why she was going to school early. To tell all her friends, she said in that glass-bright, too easily shattered voice that was held together by lies and hope. He thought of Rodney Swift, whose high-pitched, breathless tales of wealth, fame, and thousands of sex partners ringing through the night only brought him threats and kidney punches the next day. No matter how they bruised and bloodied him, nothing could ever make Rodney sad. His irrational joy only seemed to thrive on the abuse.

"Happy birthday. How old are you?"

"Thirteen."

"Well, that's a good age, thirteen." He didn't remind her that she'd told him a few weeks ago she was thirteen.

"How come?"

He tried to think why. "Well, now you're a teenager. That's a big step."

"Yeah, but I still can't do anything."

"What do you want to do?"

When they got to the drugstore, she scurried around grabbing handfuls of scratch tickets from the sidewalk. She peered closely at each one, discarding them as she talked. "Like go in there and buy my own cigarettes. Jeez, one more spade and I'd have a free one," she said with the next toss.

"You smoke?"

"Yeah, sometimes. But now I gotta buy them from Thurm."

"Thurman? He sells cigarettes?"

"Yeah, in the parking lot, but not whole packs. Just like fifty cents a butt. I used to sneak them off my mother, but I can't now. She keeps them on her all the time. Bummer!" She threw the last card into the gutter. "There was this guy once, he won a million bucks off a card he found. He just picked it up and next thing you know he's got like a chauffeur and a butler and this big mansion with a heated pool."

"Really?" He wondered if Thurman was stealing the cigarettes from the Market.

"Yeah. And a stretch limo and his own jet."

"He certainly was lucky."

"Yeah, like me. I'm lucky. I'm wicked lucky."

"You win things?"

"Yeah! I win stuff all the time. Like Leonardo. I won him."

"Where? Where'd you win him?"

"From a pet shop! Where the hell do you think?" She laughed. "They had this humongous jar in the window. It had like all these . . . these dog-bone biscuit things in it and the person that guessed how many won. Every day I went by that window and I couldn't figure it out, and then one day I'm walking by, and all of a sudden my brain goes—9,834 dog bones. And guess what? That was it! The exact right number. I couldn't believe it!"

"Good-bye now," he said when they came to the Market. The new line was being delivered today. PREMIUM GOURMET COMESTIBLES, read the gilt-edged black lettering on the door of a small red van in front.

"Hey, that steak, that was good. That was so good," Jada called after him.

Neil was already slicing open the boxes. The Premium salesman squatted next to him, filling the lower shelves.

"Hey, Gordon! C'mere and see," Neil called, gesturing. "This is it. The icing on the cake." He held up a jar of capers. "So what do you think? Is this a first-class operation or what?"

The salesman looked up and started to smile.

Gordon hurried past them into the storage room.

"What was that all about?" Neil asked, coming in a moment later. "I ask you a question and you just walk away?"

"I had to do something."

A smile quivered at Neil's mouth. "You know who that was?"

Gordon nodded. Eric Reese, Jerry Cox's best friend. At the trial, Reese had testified that he and Cox had skipped school. They spent most of the afternoon drinking at Reese's house, which was across the street from the Walterses'. Cox told Reese that Mrs. Walters was always trying to come on to him. Whenever he did yardwork, she walked around inside half-dressed. Wishful thinking, said Reese. Cox then made similar remarks about Reese's girlfriend. They argued, and Reese told him to leave. A little while later Gordon turned a corner and ran into Cox, who was angry and drunk. Gordon was pleased Cox knew his name and flattered by his confidences as they hung out in the park. He didn't know who the horny Mrs. Walters was, so Cox said he'd show him where she lived.

"He's as surprised as you are." Neil stepped closer. "He didn't know you were out. Nice guy, you ought to go say hi to him."

"I don't think so."

"He said he always felt bad for you. He said right after Jerry got out they went drinking, and Jerry starts crying and telling Reese the thing he felt worst about, worse even than the girl's dying, was you. He said you got screwed. The next day he blows his brains out. Reese said after that he always wondered. He just asked me, he said, 'What's he say about it?'"

"I'm not going to talk about this."

"Well, I've got a right to know. I mean, I've got obligations to those people out there." He pointed to the door. "They don't know what to think. All they know is what they heard. The girls, they won't ask you, but ever since that thing with Ferguson, they're scared."

"Well, if they are, I'm sorry. There's nothing I can do about it."

"Yes, there is. They want to know, they keep asking me, what's the story. What am I supposed to tell them?"

"Whatever you want, Neil. It's up to you."

CHAPTER 10

Gordon was getting ready for his appointment with his parole officer. Their first meeting had been little more than a bureaucratic checklist, restating the terms of parole along with names of various social service agencies and temporary shelters if he needed them. He showered, shaved again, shined his shoes: nothing left to chance. Mazzorio would have no doubts about his suitability as a free man. He was struggling with his tie knot when the phone rang.

It was Delores. Her sister Karen had told her about Mrs. Jukas coming into the emergency room, and she just wondered how she was doing. All right, he told her. As it turned out, she hadn't had a heart attack. She was supposed to come home in a few days.

"What about you? How are you doing?"

"I'm fine. I'm okay. Busy, I've been really busy." *That's really why she called,* he thought. Surely her sister knew more about Mrs. Jukas's condition than he did.

"Karen said you were so nice to the poor old woman."

"She was having a lot of pain. I think she was scared more than anything."

"That must be so awful, getting a call like that in the middle of the night."

"She was pretty upset."

"Poor thing. Especially being all alone like that. My neighbor upstairs, she's eighty-six. Sometimes I'll think, Oh jeez, now when was the last time I saw Edna, and then I'll go running up. And usually she's in—"

"Um, excuse me. I'm sorry, Delores, but I can't talk. I have to go. I have to do something."

She apologized. She hadn't meant to bother him, she said, but if he ever felt like going somewhere, or if he needed a ride, anything, he should feel free to call her. Anytime. Oh, and that was the other reason she'd called, to tell him her boss was closing down the Collerton store, which meant she'd be in the Dearborn store soon, so she'd give him that number in case he—

"Delores! I'm sorry. I can't talk anymore. I'm really in a rush here."

He arrived at the district courthouse fifteen minutes early. His trial had been held around the corner in superior court. But they looked the same, smelled of the same old wood and papery dust. He felt big again, bigger than anyone else, as he came down the corridor. He started into the crowded elevator, then changed his mind with all the irritated faces staring back. He hurried up the stairs to the parole office on the second floor, where eleven men sat in the waiting room. He settled into a corner seat. The men were all younger. He was the only one wearing a suit and tie. An hour later, Mr. Mazzorio called him into the office.

"So, how're things going?" Mazzorio wore a red golf shirt. He was fumbling through stacks of files on the floor by his desk.

"Very well, thank you." Gordon folded his arms. Afraid that might seem threatening or arrogant, he clasped his hands in his lap.

"Any problems?" Mazzorio's voice rose from the far side of the desk.

"No. None that I can think of." Other than Neil, but if he said his boss was acting strange, Mazzorio might think he had done something to cause it. Which maybe he had. He was beginning to wonder.

"Jesus Christ," Mazzorio muttered. "I can't find anything in this mess. Here we go!" He popped up with a file. "Okay," he murmured, flipping pages. "Okay. Okay. Let's see now." He ran his finger down one page, continued on the next. "Okay. All right, so we got no sex crimes, no rape, molestation, nothing with kids, right? Just the one homicide, which was, what—here we go—twenty-five years ago, so you don't have to register as an SO."

"No." An SO was a sex offender. They'd covered all this in the first visit.

He looked at Gordon. "So you know the drill, then? All you gotta do is keep it clean, live straight, show up here on time, and you're home free." He scribbled on a smudged form, then pushed it across the desk. Gordon signed, handed it back. Mazzorio said he would be notified by mail when his next appointment would be.

"So will that be it?"

"Far as I'm concerned. Unless you got a problem." Mazzorio peered over his glasses, looking at him for the first time.

"No, no problem. I just wanted to make sure, that's all." A missed appointment, an unreturned document, an anonymous complaint, the merest hint of suspicion, anything might send him back.

As he came up Essex Street, a gust blew from a narrow alley, and his stomach turned with the stone-deep stench of urine and the memories it brought back of Fortley. He hurried on ahead, past a pizza shop that had once been Coco's Photography Studio. He'd had his senior yearbook picture taken there. His mother hated the picture. She insisted he have it retaken. By the time she got done convincing him how thick-faced the picture made him look, how dull-eyed and lethargic, he wasn't about to let a camera betray him again. Rather than argue, he said he would, but never did. It became the wire services' official schoolboy-killer shot.

"Oh no!" his mother had cried, showing him the paper the first time it was used. "It makes you look so cold and mean. Like you actually could have done it."

"Well, I did," he said, and she slapped him, then burst into tears.

"What're you trying to do, destroy me? Is that what you're trying to do?" she sobbed.

Farther up the hill, St. Theresa's white steeple pierced the treetops. His family had attended Mass there in the small wooden church. Next door was the parish grammar school, a one-story building of brick and glass blocks that with its gated school yard had been his first prison. The buzz of an electric bell cut through the stillness, and there he was again, stepping into formation, shuffling from the safety of his cell into clamor and constant watchfulness. Lines of children streamed through the opening doors into the playground. Some things were still the same, the girls' plaid uniforms and white blouses, the boys' dark pants, white shirts, and plaid clip-on ties. Teachers led the march to the chain-link gate. It would be opened by the student of the week. She was a tall, skinny girl with red hair down to her waist. There seemed to be only one nun. Instead of a bulky habit she wore a blouse, skirt, and short pale-blue veil. At her nod the gate was unlatched and the children surged onto the sidewalk. Cars stopped as a stout woman in black pants stood in the road with her arms out against the traffic while the children crossed. He smiled as they ran past.

"Excuse me, sir," the woman said when the last child was on the sidewalk. "Can I help you?"

"No. No, I'm just watching the children, that's all." He smiled at her.

"Why? Are you waiting for someone?" She came toward him.

"No, I was just going by. It brought back memories, that's all, seeing all the children." He could see it in her probing eyes. Something was wrong here. She could tell. There was something odd about him. Too nervous. Too furtive. The twitchy smile. His flat voice. "Well, anyway. I guess I better get going."

"Do you live around here?"

"A few blocks away. Not too far."

"Do I know you? You look awfully familiar."

"I work at the Market. The Nash Street Market? Maybe that's it."

"No, you look like someone I used to know. A long time ago. When I was a kid. I'm Cecilia Reardon."

"I'm Gordon . . . Loomis."

"Oh. Yes," she said quietly. "I was a little girl. You were a couple years older than I was." She could control her voice, but not the mind-racing shock on her face. The little girl's bogeyman had come home.

"Yes, well, it's been very nice meeting you." He nodded, then hurried down the street, wanting to run, hide, disappear. Anything was better than being out here alone. Had she run into the school yard to tell all the teachers? Or was she on the phone calling the police: *Guess who I just stopped, standing there, staring at innocent children?* This must have been his family's humiliation all those years. Running into neighbors, old friends, strangers who knew everything there was to know about them. The shame, the terrible shame he had brought upon them. Turning the corner, he realized Delores's store was somewhere near here.

The pitcher of iced tea and Albert's favorite butterscotch squares sat on his desk as he delivered his dismal accounting of the Collerton store's sales in the last six months. His eyes were rimmed red, as if he'd been up all night. Everything she wanted to say dissolved when she saw his agitation and fatigue. She couldn't bear to be angry with him. None of her calls had been returned other than a terse notice of this meeting, and that had been left on her answering machine at home when he knew she'd be here. There was an edge to his voice, as if it were somehow all her fault: the neighborhood's steady decline, his old customers' reluctance to come here, their preference for the safer, tree-lined streets of bucolic downtown Dearborn. "This is so hard." He sighed. "I've been dreading this moment."

"I know. All right, so the store's closing, Albert. You don't have to keep telling me why. I know why! So let's just get on with it. I can handle it. What do you think, this place is my whole life? That I can't function anywhere else? You think I can't handle working in the Dearborn store? For God's sake, Albert, you know me better than that. God, I'm probably the most flexible person you know." She sat down so that he could be the taller one. She was trying to make this as easy for him as possible, but he wouldn't even look at her. He was always too hard on himself.

"I don't think you understand. I mean, I know what you've done here, how hard you've worked, and not just that, but your loyalty to me. I mean, all that we've . . . the thing is, I don't need you in the Dearborn store. Katie's the manager there."

"That's okay!" Her voice trembled, but she forced a smile. "I'd just as soon be a salesgirl anyway. Do me good, just to show up every day and not have to worry about inventory and—"

"No, Delores. That won't work! And besides, there aren't any openings. There's no place for you. Everything's taken."

She couldn't speak. She was as shocked by his indifference as by her own blindness. Beads of sweat frosted the pitcher. This was the second batch of squares. She'd thrown out the first; the bottoms had baked too dark. She picked one up.

He paced back and forth. He'd be glad to write reference letters, however many she'd need. With the economy so good right now, there were an awful lot of jobs out there. In the meantime she should apply for unemployment compensation. Stretch it out as long as she could. Enjoy the summer. All he wanted was for her to be all right.

Her thumb flattened the doughy mass. *The baby would have been a teenager now. Thank God it had been spared such a pathetic mother.* She couldn't even get mad. Here it was, that same emptiness again and again, the same weak smile with his hand on her shoulder, assuring her that all things work out for the best in the end, "down the road when we look back," he was saying, when she should be doing something, anything rather than suffocating in his slimy sympathy. If she had a gun right now or a knife . . . *that pitcher, just pick it up and throw it.* At least she'd be doing something, instead of sitting here with her thighs stuck together, just taking it and taking it, once again letting all the life and love be sucked right out of her. Papers rustled. He was reading order forms. *Problem solved. It was over, gone, but what was it? No one knew. Or if they did, they never said.* And she would not ask. How could she? The secret would be her only possession of it. She did not deserve such knowledge when she had no regard for its existence. How could she have done that? And now this? To be so empty again. At least pain kept her among the living. But this was unbearable. This was worse than death.

"Hello? Delores?" a man called from out in the store.

Albert's head shot up. "Shh. Someone's out front," he whispered, horrified to see her crying.

"I don't care," she sobbed. "I don't care who's out there. I don't care about anything anymore."

"Stop it, Delores! There's someone out there. A customer!"

"Good! Well, they'll just have to help themselves, then, because I can't. Take what you need!" she called between teary gasps. "Whatever you want! Take it all, I don't care! Because Albert Smick is a liar! He doesn't care who he hurts."

"My God, Delores, what if——"

"And now he's got little Katie in her crunchy-granola jumper, so he doesn't need me anymore! Oh, God," she bawled.

Albert Smick could stand no more. He fled from the back room, through the store, and out to his car.

"Delores?" Gordon Loomis peeked through the doorway. "Are you all right?"

She closed her eyes and shook her head.

"I just stopped in. I was so abrupt on the phone. I'm sorry. I was going to leave, but then I was afraid maybe something was wrong."

"That was Albert. My boss."

"Oh."

"He just fired me."

"Well, I don't blame you for being upset, then," he said so somberly that she almost laughed.

"People always say that, don't they? As if you shouldn't be upset unless you have a really good reason," she said with a sob. "Well, you want to know something? I never do. I never get mad at anyone. Even when I should. I don't, and that's my whole trouble. I always try and figure out why people do things. Why they're so mean or thoughtless or selfish. So I can understand. So I can try and help them and forgive them. Oh, I'm sorry, Gordon, I'm so sorry," she wept, feeling even worse to see him look so troubled. "You've just caught me at a bad time. Oh, God, listen to me—a bad time. A terrible time, that's what this is. A horrible time."

"Should I leave? Would that be better?"

She nodded.

"All right. I will, then," he said, backing away. "And if there's anything I can do, just . . . please, let me know."

"I'm sorry. I'm so sorry," she said as the door closed. She covered her face with her hands. Now she'd done it. In one fell swoop she'd driven both men from her life.

"Yo!" Ronnie Feaster called from Mrs. Jukas's porch. He sat tilted back in the aluminum chair along with Polie and Thurman, who wore a tank top. A tattooed snake curled up the boy's forearm. His wary grin faded with Gordon's approach.

"You shouldn't be up there. That's Mrs. Jukas's property," Gordon said from her walk.

"I know that," Feaster said. "That's why I'm here. I'm taking care of it for the old lady."

"She doesn't want you up there. You know she doesn't."

"We're not doing anything. We're just here," Feaster explained, glancing at the beeper on his belt. "We're establishing a presence. You know, like cops do. A little time here, a little time there, and that way everything's cool, people know."

"Look, would you just get off her porch? All right? That's all I'm asking."

"You know how many cops've been by since we got here? How many, Polie?" Feaster asked.

Polie's thick index finger met his thumb in a zero.

"I mean, somebody's gotta do it," Feaster said.

"You don't want me to come up there, so why don't you just get down?" Gordon's throat was so dry, it hurt.

Feaster sighed and shook his head. "What? You're gonna do something stupid, the cops're gonna come, and all they're gonna say is, 'Loomis, what the fuck're you doing with known felons?' And what can I say? You think they're gonna listen to me? No, you just go in your nice little house over there and everything'll be cool, I promise. Really. Ask anybody, they'll tell you. That's what I do, right, Polie? Right, Thurm?"

"Yeah."

"That's right."

It was a long walk to his door. He looked out from time to time.

The boy squatted on the porch floor, smoking a joint. Feaster seemed to be dozing in the chair. Sometimes his cell phone would ring and Thurman would go running down the street. A while later Jada came out of her house, carrying the puppy. She set him down on the strip of yellow grass. Bending, she held on to the collar while the dog urinated. Polie got up and started across the street. She grabbed the dog and hurried back inside.

On Saturday morning Dennis stopped in with Lisa and the children. They brought him a quart of strawberries they'd just picked at a farm in Boxford. Dennis was leaving that night for a three-day dental conference in Hartford, so he and Lisa were spending the day doing whatever Jimmy and Annie wanted. The children asked if they could go outside and climb up the old maple tree. Dennis and Gordon both said no, but Lisa said they could as long as they didn't leave the yard. Gordon kept getting up and going to the back door to check on them. Feaster and his pack weren't out there. It usually wasn't until late afternoon that they dragged onto Mrs. Jukas's porch.

Lisa and Dennis invited Gordon into Boston with the four of them. They were going to the aquarium. While he made coffee he explained why he couldn't go. Thurman had been let go yesterday after an argument with Neil. His grandmother had come into the store last night and begged Neil to take him back. He had already been expelled, and she was afraid with so much time on his hands he was going to get into some really big trouble. "So Neil finally said he would, but she wasn't to tell him yet. He wants the boy to spend the weekend stewing. But the thing is, it's only a matter of time before he ends up in detention or worse," Gordon was telling them as he set their coffee cups on the table. Nervous when they first came, he was enjoying their company now. "The grandmother, she used to work for Neil, but in any event, I have to cover for him today."

"So some kids flips out and you're the only who can do his job?" Dennis asked.

"Well, no, I—"

"So come with us, then!" Dennis said.

"I already told Neil I'd do it."

"So? Now you've got something else to do! Like the rest of the world! Just call and tell him you're busy. No big deal."

"I can't. I'd like to, Dennis, but he's counting on me."

"That's all right," Lisa said uneasily, looking at Dennis.

"You don't go anywhere. You don't do anything. What kind of a life is that? Come on, we're your family. Spend some time with us," Dennis said.

"Well, maybe next week."

"You know who you're reminding me of, don't you?" Dennis said over his raised cup.

Sighing, Lisa stared at her husband. Gordon returned the milk to the refrigerator, then looked out the back door. The children were hanging from the lowest branch.

"Dad never went anywhere. God, I used to hate coming here, see him sitting there in front of the television with the blinds closed."

"Dennis!" Lisa pleaded.

"You've got to grow, you've got to do things, Gord. You can't just *be* here."

"I'm not."

"*Yes, you are!* Tell me one thing you've done since you've been home, one place you've gone."

The condos with Jilly Cross, though he knew better than to say it. He stared into his coffee. Dennis had no idea. The simplest things seemed so difficult, like picking up the phone to call Delores and ask how she was doing. He wanted to, knew he should, but by the time he had considered every possible scenario—whether she might be busy or embarrassed or think he was interfering—all his resolve would be gone.

"Dennis just wants you to be happy. We both do." Lisa patted his hand.

"I want you to have a life, Gordo. That's all," Dennis said with a jab at his forearm.

After they left he went outside and picked up twigs the children had broken from the tree. Their footprints were deep in the newly seeded patch of lawn by the fence. The watering can had been knocked over, and the garage door was open. He closed it but couldn't find the key. They weren't very well behaved children. Dennis was too quick-tempered, and Lisa was too easy on them.

He was getting ready for work when the phone rang. It was Delores, inviting him out to dinner tonight.

"It's last minute and I know you're probably busy, but I figured I might as well try," she said.

"Oh. Well, I have to work. In fact, I'm getting ready now, but I—"

"That's all right," she said quickly. "I should've called earlier. I'll let you go, then."

He paused, his entire body tensing with the effort to force out the words. "Well, I was just going to say I get off at seven. Is that too late?"

"No! Not at all! Seven's perfect. That's a good time. A really good time. Where do you want to go?"

"Well, I'm not sure." He couldn't remember. That place Jilly had mentioned. "I can't think. It's something about bricks. Yellow bricks." He'd show Dennis that his life was more than the Nash Street Market.

Poor Gordon, Delores kept thinking through dinner. It was all new. Everything. He had been so self-conscious and stiff giving his order that the waitress began talking to him as if he were retarded. Watching him replace his water goblet at the point of his knife, Delores wondered if he thought it had to be exactly where the busboy had placed it. He kept glancing around as if to make sure everything he did was in accordance with other diners. She should have suggested something less formal. He had been quite talkative during the fifty-five-minute drive here, but as soon as he stepped into the candlelit foyer he fell silent. His conversation since then came in hushed tones of wonder.

"That was the most interesting salad I ever ate," he whispered as the waitress took their plates away. He glanced around. "What were those little black beads?"

"Caviar."

He smiled. "Really? Huh. Imagine that! I just ate caviar," he said so softly she had to lean forward to hear him.

"I thought you saw it on the menu."

"It was making me too nervous. I didn't really read it. That's why I ordered the same as you."

"Don't be nervous. Most of these people are probably here for the first time."

He looked around more slowly now, moving only his eyes. "How do you know?"

"It's not the kind of place you come to every week."

"It's not?"

"No, it's more of a special occasion kind of place."

"Oh." Looking vaguely troubled, he nodded.

She began to tell him about Cheryl Smick's surprise party here for her fiftieth birthday. Delores had planned everything, the jazz band, party hats in lavender, Cheryl's favorite color, and the favors, gold and silver heart-shaped frames containing Cheryl's picture.

"I thought you said you'd never been here before," he whispered.

"I didn't go to the party. I just helped Albert, that's all. There were so many things to do. Like the guest list, the invitations. And the menu. Albert's no good with details. It was a surprise, so all the RSVPs had to come into the store, of course. It was almost like planning a wedding, which I also did, by the way, for my baby sister, Babbie. You probably don't remember Babbie, though, do you?" The wine was light on her tongue. Her cheeks felt flushed. "She would have been just a little kid then when we knew each other."

"No, I don't remember her."

"Babbie lives in Dearborn. She has two girls. They're so adorable. Her husband's in software. Dwayne, he makes all kinds of money. And I love him, but he is the cheapest man I have ever met. Whenever my sister buys clothes she has to lie and say they're from me." Delores could feel herself talking with the same reckless extravagance as Babbie's shopping, the dizzying spree of confidences spent with full knowledge of the inevitable regret. Disloyalty was the greatest sin, yet intimacy continually demanded it of her. He asked about the sisters he remembered, Karen and Linda. They were finishing their racks of lamb when she realized she was still answering him. Stopping abruptly, she apologized. Here she was going on and on about herself while he just sat there being so polite.

"No, I'm really interested. There's so much catching up to do. Everything's so changed." The neighborhood, for example; Ronnie Feaster and his crew hanging out every day now on Mrs. Jukas's porch.

"Ronnie Feaster!" she said. "He's horrible. Absolutely despicable. Albert caught him selling drugs once in the alley behind the store. He told him to leave or else he was calling the police, and that very night someone broke into the store and trashed the place. But worst of all, you know what they left on Albert's desk?" She leaned forward. "A pile of—oh, I shouldn't say it while we're eating, but you know what I mean. It had to be the worst thing anyone ever did to Albert. He's very finicky. Poor man, he can't even stand the sound of someone blowing their nose. Turns his stomach. Some people are just so sensitive. It's the same thing with being hot or cold. Or pain. It's got to be something in the nerve endings. He just feels things so much more intensely than the average person."

"Then how could he just fire you like that if he's so sensitive?" Gordon asked.

"Because," she began, relieved now as the busboy arrived to clear their plates. Because she had been too strong a force buffeting his delicate nature. Because her every offering had to be momentous, the biggest and best. Because her generosity frightened people, made them wonder what she wanted in return. "Because he had no other choice," she explained after the busboy left.

"But he's the boss. He should be able to find a place for you."

"Well, I guess he couldn't," she said, teary-eyed.

"I'm sorry. I didn't mean to make you feel bad."

Touched by his concern, she nodded. The blurred dining room with its flickering candles and myriad conversations seemed to flow into a low, dark thrum. She loved eating out. It was such a sensual atmosphere, feeding off everyone else's hunger until her belly ached with it. *When was the last time he'd had a woman? If ever. My God, what would his first time be like? Stop it,* she thought, even now hearing her mother tell some aunt, neighbor, total stranger, *I've never seen such an appetite. She's the only one of all the girls.*

Before Delores could stop her, the waitress had handed the bill to Gordon, his brow knit, lips moving, as he stared at it. She asked him for it. After all, she was the one who had asked him out.

"I'll pay for it." He took a deep breath, then began counting out twenty-dollar bills onto the pewter bill tray. She removed his money and replaced it with her credit card. He tried to argue, but she absolutely insisted. Next time would be his treat, she allowed with breezy confidence as he followed her into the lobby, where a few couples sat on plump, tapestry-covered sofas, drinking brandy from cut-glass snifters. She waited by the door while Gordon went into the men's room. She was reading a framed poem on the wall, "Ode to a Demanding Diner." In the glass reflection she noticed a handsome couple coming down the stairs. They paused on the landing, laughing and leaning into each other. The young woman was a tiny blonde in a short red silk dress. The tanned man in the canary yellow blazer was Dennis Loomis. He and the woman waited arm in arm by the lectern for the maître d' to lead them into the dining room. The men's room door opened, and Gordon was walking toward them. They spoke at once, the woman joining in as if she knew Gordon. The maître d' appeared, and Dennis gestured irritably for the woman to go on ahead into the dining room. He and Gordon stepped aside in the shadowed hallway. Dennis did all the talking.

For once she kept quiet. Gordon stared out the window as she drove.

"I can't believe he'd do that to Lisa," he finally said.

"Maybe it's not even what you think it is."

"He was mad. Mad that I caught them together. It was so obvious."

"But you don't know for sure. Maybe she's just an old friend or something."

"She's twenty-five years old."

"He told you that?"

"No. I know her. She's a real estate agent. Jilly Cross. The one who showed me the condos. I can't believe it," he said again.

She drove slowly into Collerton. Seeing sexy Dennis and his

clingy little girlfriend, along with the wine and the nearness of Gordon in the dark, rolling car, made her ache. She wanted to reach over and touch him. She pulled up in front of his house, trying to think of a way to invite herself inside.

"Well, thank you. And I'm sorry it had to end this way," he said.

"What way?" she asked, alarmed.

"Well, seeing Dennis like that. I mean, it's so disappointing. I never expected anything like that. Never in a million years." He looked sick.

"Sometimes things like that happen. They just happen whether people want them to or not."

"Lisa's such a good person. She's his wife. The mother of his children. I thought they loved each other." He sounded so sad.

"I'm sure they do."

"How can he if he's doing that? Because then everything's a lie. Everything!"

"But he's still your brother, right? No matter what he does, no matter what happens, right?" She touched his arm, leaving her hand there. "Right?" she whispered, turning in the seat. His hair was starting to recede. He had the softest blue eyes, especially now with so much hurt in them.

He nodded. "I just can't believe he'd do something like that."

"Don't worry." She squeezed his arm. "She's just some dippy little thing. He's not going to leave his family for someone like that. Dennis is like you. He's got character, he wants stability in his life. Everything's going to be fine."

"I don't know, maybe it can't be."

"Oh, Gordon. Don't say that. You're going to have a wonderful life. Everything's just so new right now, that's all."

Across the way, a girl bounded down the tenement steps. She ran in front of the car and leaned down at Gordon's window. "Guess what happened," she said breathlessly. "Some guy tried to break into your house, but Thurman told Feaster, and him and Polie pulled him off your back porch. Polie beat the shit out of him." Her eyes glowed with excitement as Gordon scrambled from the car toward his house. Delores and the girl followed him inside. "I seen you here before," the girl said to her as Gordon turned on the lights. All the windows and doors were locked. "Yeah, right after he moved in," the girl continued as Gordon returned to the living room. Everything seemed to be in order, but he had to check upstairs to be sure. Delores introduced herself as an old friend of Gordon's. "That's cool," the girl said. "He's a really nice guy. But not too many people come here. I can see right out my window there. That's where I live. Right there." She lifted the blinds and pointed.

"What's your name?" Delores asked, fascinated and repelled by the rawness her full wet mouth seemed to convey.

"Jada Fossum, nice to meet you," she said with a sure, hard grip. "Hey, Gordon," she called as he came downstairs. "Next time you go out I'll bring Leonardo over. He can guard the house for you." She flopped onto the couch. "He's a wicked good watchdog."

"He is?" Delores said, and like Gordon remained standing, looking down at the sprawled girl.

"Christ, all he does is bark." She laughed. When neither one replied, she sat forward. "Oh, you're probably on a date, right?" She gave a lewd, crooked grin. "And you're waiting for me to go, right?" She jumped up.

"Thank you, Jada. And thank you, too, Delores. It was good getting out," he said, leading them to the door.

Delores found herself on the sidewalk with Jada Fossum while room by room the lights went out inside Gordon's little house. A dog was barking from somewhere across the street.

"I like him. He's so nice," Jada said, batting mosquitoes away from her fuzzy curls that shone under the streetlight.

"Yes, he is, isn't he."

"Everybody's scared of him, but I'm not."

"Why are they scared?"

"He killed somebody once. A girl and a baby. You didn't know that?"

"I guess I just forget sometimes."

"Jesus, how can you forget that? My mother's wicked scared of him. I'm not even supposed to be over here."

"Gordon would never hurt you." She opened her car door. "But you better get home. You don't want to get in trouble with your mother."

"I'm always in trouble with her!" the girl said, laughing. As she crossed the street, the barking grew frantic.

CHAPTER 11

June had already told Thurman that the aisles didn't need sweeping, but he ignored her. Headphones on, he swept his indolent way through the store. His grandmother might have made him come back to work, but she couldn't make him like it. When Gordon thanked him for preventing a break-in Saturday night, his sour shrug made clear that he hadn't done it to help Gordon. He had yet to do one thing June or Serena had asked. Gordon tried to avoid him as best he could. The boy was a powder keg, aching to be set off.

The store was empty. It had been raining since early morning, and only a few desperate customers had braved the downpour. He didn't like days like this—too slow, too much time to think. The plate glass rattled with the sudden boom of thunder. He pressed in another floor tile. Seeing Dennis with Jilly the other night had thrown everything off-kilter. It was vital that the few people in his life stay the same, to be who he needed them to be. He felt betrayed. And foolish. He thought he had been moving ahead but now saw how stuck he was. He wouldn't even answer the phone anymore. If it was Dennis, he didn't know what to say, and if it was Delores, she would want to talk about it and he couldn't.

He had replaced almost all of the cracked tiles by the front doors. Working had always been the best therapy. He sat back on his heels. A few more to go. Little by little, one step at a time, that's all it took to make things look better. These black and gray tiles matched the rest of the floor. Last week, he had found them down in the cellar in a soot-covered box. When he showed Neil, he was told not to bother, the new owner would probably gut the place and start over. But then after Neil's letdown this morning, Gordon had taken to his knees, scraping and gluing. Maybe the next potential buyer wouldn't be so quick to write the place off. His lower back ached, and the cuts in his hands stung from the acrid glue. He felt a little light-headed, and his stomach was growling. He hadn't even stopped for lunch. His enthusiasm for these projects seemed to irritate Neil. It was the same reaction Dennis had whenever Gordon mentioned repairs around the house, the brass hooks he had screwed over the sink for dish towels instead of hanging them on the oven door the way his mother used to, the stops he had glued in their old maple bureau to make the drawers line up evenly, the shims he had painstakingly shaved from the handle of an old paint stirrer and then wedged under the hinges so that the coat-closet door would finally latch shut. Dennis had given him that same look in the lobby the other night, as if he still didn't get it, did he. *Get what, though? That nothing was worth anything anymore? Not even people?*

June and Serena were concerned about Neil. After two days of almost giddy happiness, he was curled up on his cot now in a migrainous fog, clutching a bottle of Fiorinal. The Realtor's very first client had wanted to buy the Market. He was an intense young black man in a pale-blue suit that glowed under the fluorescent lights. He drove a silver Mercedes and owned two other grocery stores, in Haverhill and Lowell. His goal was a chain of stores catering to the ethnic makeup of their particular locales. He had returned last night with his accountant to look at the books. This morning the Realtor called to say the accountant had declared the books rigged and the store a financial sinkhole. The only way to make a go of the business would be to double its size, and no bank was going to make that kind of investment in this part of the city.

"That guy, the accountant, he's from Dearborn. I mean, what the hell does he know about a place like this?" Serena said.

"All he needs to know." June sighed as she popped open a Diet Coke. "Where the hell's Thurman? Three times now I told him to bring the carts in."

"Yeah, there's only one left."

"I'll go get them," Gordon called as he brushed glue on the back of the last tile. "I'm almost done."

"No. You've got enough to do," Serena said.

"Yeah, that's Thurman's job," June said.

"I know, but I feel a little funny," he said as he stood up. He needed some fresh air.

"Then go home! To get some rest, I mean," June added uneasily.

"I know. I can barely keep my eyes open." Serena yawned.

"It's the rain," June said.

It was the glue, but he was afraid to persist for fear they would think he was in some fume-crazed, murderous state.

"It's like night out there, it's so dark," Serena said.

Suddenly, an ungodly wail filled the store. "What is that?" Gordon yelled, lurching toward the women. They shrank back, white-faced and gasping, while Thurman continued to push his broom toward them, singing to music only he could hear. Hand at her chest, June took off down the aisle. With a frantic tap on the boy's shoulder, she ordered him outside to bring in the shopping carts.

"There's nobody here," he protested, lifting an earpiece.

"But there will be," she said.

"So then I'll get 'em."

"No, now!"

"It's, like, pouring out there!"

"Go get the goddamn carts or I get Neil, whichever," she wheezed.

"Yeah, right." Thurman laughed, then replaced his earpiece and headed back up the aisle, singing in a high-pitched, scratchy voice.

"I'll go. I don't mind. I like the rain," Gordon said, fumbling the torn store poncho over his head. The women's eyes met: *He likes the rain—of course, deviant that he is.*

Hurrying into the downpour, he was immediately calmed by the steady rain-beat on the visor. He took long, deep breaths, trying to clear his head and lungs as he struggled to push the carts through the rutted lot. He lined them up outside the front door, then headed down the street looking for more, sloshing through puddles. The few cars that drove by had their lights on. Their wheels sprayed up waves of water, drenching him. He took his time coming back with the rest of the carts. He was so wet now that it didn't matter. He held his head back and let the rain sting his face. He pushed these carts into the others, then reached for the door. He froze. The eerie tableau through the blurred glass couldn't be real. The rain streaming down the cloudy panes gave the fluorescent lights inside a pulsating, garish yellow glow. The man in the black ski mask and hooded sweatshirt pointed a gun at Serena as she hurried out of the office with two cash boxes in her arms. Huddled by her register, June held her tubes to her nose and stared out at Gordon. Thurman's head bobbed along the back aisle in rhythmic oblivion. It was after three, so Leo had already gone home. With empty storefronts on either side as well as across the street, the nearest phone would be in the liquor store around the corner. By then it would be too late. He could run around back onto the loading dock to use the meat-room phone, then he remembered that door was always locked. Two more aisles to go and Thurman would be in sight of the gunman. Serena set the cash boxes on the counter. She started to back away, but the gunman spun around, screaming and gesturing with the gun. With each demand he sprang forward on one foot, then lurched back again to scream at June. Terrified, Serena seized a handful of plastic bags, most drifting to her feet as she tried to get one inside the other. She dumped the money from the drawers into the bag. June began to cry. A car was coming down the street. Gordon ran toward it waving his arms, but the horrified woman at the wheel veered into the oncoming lane, then sped away. The Market door flew open and the man ran outside. Gordon watched from the road with dirty water gushing past his feet.

"He's got a gun! He just held us up!" Serena screamed from the doorway as the man sprinted down Nash Street, hugging the bag to his chest.

Gordon's heavy, sodden sneakers splashed down the street, but once around the corner, the thief disappeared into the foggy rain. When he got back, three cruisers were in front of the Market, parked at the chaotic angles in which they'd arrived. Questioning Thurman was futile, though both women agreed that his sudden caterwaul of song had triggered the thief's flight. Serena couldn't stop shaking.

June was hyperventilating. Her son was on his way to bring her home. This was the first holdup in which they'd actually seen a gun. Befuddled by pain and medication, Neil hunched in the front window, wearing a Red Sox cap and sunglasses over his light-sensitive eyes. "I was asleep," he told silver-haired Detective Warren, who with his forearm kept shifting his belly into place. He asked the women to describe the thief's voice. Shaky, they agreed. No accent. Not deep or high or soft.

"Scared," Serena said, hugging herself. "Like if we didn't do what he said, he'd just shoot. Like he couldn't even help it."

"So where were you again?" Detective Warren hefted his girth toward Gordon.

"Out there. Getting the carts."

"For how long?"

"Five minutes. I'm not sure."

"Five minutes. That's a long time to be out in that."

"Just about all the carts were out there. Some were even down the street."

"So when you finally got them all collected, you were right there by the window."

"Yes," he said, the details already blurring through the curtain of jailhouse blindness.

"So you must've seen something. You were standing right by the window there."

"I wasn't really looking. I was trying to get the carts lined up." June stared at him.

"So you didn't see anything until when?"

"He ran out the door and Serena yelled. That's when I started chasing him."

Warren's eyes were cold on his. The detective wet his thumb and flipped a page in his blue spiral pad. "According to Serena Rimsky, you were standing in the middle of the road waving your arms when she yelled at you."

"Maybe. I might have been. I don't know. I'm not sure." *Admit it,* he thought as the detective stared at him. *Tell him the truth, that you*

*weren't thinking straight. That once again at the crucial moment you pan-
icked.*

*You don't know anything, kid, remember that. You were there, that's all—
you were just there:* Jackie McBride's first rule for survival.

"How long you been out?" the detective asked in a low voice.

"Since May first."

"You don't remember me, do you."

"I don't know, sir. I'm not sure."

"It was twenty-six years ago. I remember, my wife was pregnant.
My daughter, that's how old she is." His thin wet smile said all the
rest, though the steady overhead hum of the fluorescent tubes was the
only sound anywhere.

There was a short article in the paper the next day reporting a
holdup at the Nash Street Market, owned by Neil Dubbin. Gordon
was relieved his name hadn't been printed. That night Dennis called.
"Lisa just showed me the paper. That's why I'm calling. About the
holdup. We wanted to make sure you're all right," he was saying into
the answering machine. Hearing Lisa in the background, Gordon felt
safe picking up the phone. He said he was fine, then explained how
he'd been outside while it was taking place. Well, that's good. That's
good, Dennis kept saying, then handed the phone to Lisa, who
wanted to talk to him.

"Gordon, it's not safe. You can't keep working there. That's it. I'm
going to call my father and—"

"No, Lisa. I'm fine, really. I don't want you to do that."

At work he would look up to find the women staring. With his
approach they would look the other way, pretending to be busy. Leo
had stopped talking to him altogether. Now when his teenage
daughters came into the store, Leo hustled them into the back room
away from Gordon.

Neil was disgusted. "What do you think you're here for? Cuz
you're a good bagger? Cuz I want the fucking floor there fixed? No!"

For one reason and one reason only—to prevent exactly what had just happened. But where the hell had he been at the moment of crisis, of conjunction, when once again the planets lined up in the inexorable constellation of bad breaks and failure under which Neil was doomed to live out his life? What the hell had he been doing rounding up carts when that was Thurman's job?

"I'm sorry."

"Sorry's not gonna cut it. Not when I'm out three thousand dollars."

Three hundred, Gordon knew but didn't say anything. The police weren't around the corner before Neil was running new tapes through the registers for his insurance company.

"Tell me something," Neil said, following him out to the loading dock the next day. He was unshaven and his clothes were wrinkled. "You must have connections, right? I mean, you know, people that know people, well . . ." He lowered his voice. "Like for instance, people that are good with . . . fires."

"No, I don't." He just stood there, holding on to the empty crates.

A look of disgust came over Neil's face. "I don't get it. You're supposed to be inside, but no matter what June says you gotta get outside. You have to, you want to because you love the fucking pouring rain so much. Then what do you do, you take off, you go for a walk. But meanwhile there's a fucking holdup going on. You come back, but what, just a little too early, though, right, so you take off again. And now I'm supposed to go, 'Oh, what a fucking coincidence'?"

"It was. But if you want to fire me, that's all right, I understand."

"Get outta my fucking way!" Neil gave him a shove and pushed past him, then paused as if to accommodate the expected or desired attack.

The next morning Neil was about an hour late opening the store. His hands shook and everything had to be repeated before he seemed to understand. Later that afternoon there was a commotion by the register. Serena shouted for help.

Thurman had Cootie pinned up against the wall.

"Those're mine! I swear to God, those're mine!" the old man insisted as Thurman fished packs of cigarettes out of his pockets. He pulled three more packs from the lining of the ragged jacket. Eleven in all.

"That's it." June picked up the phone.

"No! No, please don't! Don't let her. Please, Neil! Please!" Cootie begged. "I'll work, I'll pick up all the papers out there. And the cans, they'll all be yours. You let me before, Neil. And I did a good job. You know I did," the old man bawled. "Please, Neil, please!"

"Why? Why the hell should I?" Neil sounded as desperate as the old man.

"My dog. My poor little dog." Cootie pointed to the animal tied to the parking meter. Briars studded his matted fur. "They'll put him to sleep. They told me last time, they said they would. Please, Neil, please. I'll do anything."

Neil took him outside, then stood close by, talking, while Cootie untied the dog. The bedraggled creature rose on his shaky legs, then limped down the street next to his master, who hunched forward, trying to light a cigarette against the wind.

The next day Gordon went into the storeroom, surprising Thurman as the boy was stuffing two cartons of Newports into his backpack. Gordon asked if he'd paid for them. What the hell business was it of his? Thurman sneered, zipping up the backpack.

"It's Neil's business," he said quietly.

"Oh, fuck, yeah, right." Thurman laughed.

"Just put them back, and that'll be the end of it," he said.

Thurman was already heading out through the store.

Neil had enough trouble, he didn't need this, Gordon thought as he followed the boy onto the street. "What're you, in some big rush to get in a cell? Because that's what's going to happen. You know that, don't you?"

"Fuck off!" Thurman kept saying, trying to get away, until Gordon finally yanked the backpack from his shoulder. He took out the cigarette cartons and brought them inside. The women had been watching from the window. Without a word Gordon put the cartons back on the shelf. That night Neil called Thurman's grandmother and fired him.

Delores was ringing his doorbell. He came quickly onto the porch so he wouldn't have to invite her in.

She had just made oatmeal cookies. "Here, have one while they're still warm." She started to open the tin, but he said he wasn't hungry right now. "I'm not disturbing you, am I?" she asked.

He said it had been a long day. Across the street two men were trying to light the grill they had just carried onto the strip of grass in front of their house. The door above them kept opening and banging shut as women carried platters and bowls of food onto the porch.

"I read about the holdup. And I kept calling to see if you were all right, but you didn't answer, so then I started worrying," Delores said.

"I'm fine."

"That's good. So, what have you been up to? What have you been doing?"

"Nothing much. I don't know." He knew by her hungry smile that she wanted to talk about the other night.

"The paper said the guy had a gun." She paused. "Have they caught him yet?"

"No. Not that I know of, anyway."

"Did you see what he looked like?"

"No, he had a mask. Plus I was outside."

She asked if he thought there was any connection to the attempted break-in at his house the other night. He assured her there wasn't. She asked if that girl Jada had come around again since that night. That night. So that was how she would get to talking about Dennis cheating on his wife.

"She did, the other day with her dog. But I was eating, so I didn't go to the door. She always seems to come at dinnertime."

"She thinks you're lonely. Aside from me, she said she's your only company."

"I don't like her thinking she can just run over here anytime she wants," he said slowly, as pointedly as he could without coming right out with it. "I feel like telling her it's not very polite."

Delores laughed. "You can try, but I don't think polite's in that girl's dictionary."

"I know, but it's annoying. I mean, I have things to do. And you know how it is, after being around people all day, you just want to be quiet when you get home. And alone."

"Alone? Around here?" Delores said as a flurry of children sped by on bikes.

If I could go inside, I would be, he thought. Across the street, family members continued to stream from the house onto the porch steps. Below them a young man in baggy army pants was grilling sausages and hamburgers. The old woman, Inez, sat on the top step. She kept reaching back to serve everyone from the salad bowls and platters arrayed behind her on the porch floor. Salsa music blared from a second-floor window. A dog was barking. A woman with long black hair backed out the front door now with drink coolers and a stack of paper cups under her chin. A thick cloud of greasy smoke hung over the sizzling grill.

"Smells good," Delores said.

A passing car blew its horn, and the young man waved his spatula overhead.

"Yo!" Delores laughed when he did it again as another horn blared in greeting. "It's so muggy tonight." She blew the hair off her forehead. "Do you mind if I sit down?" She was dragging a white plastic chair closer to the railing.

"It's dirty," he said, but she had already plunked herself down.

He continued to stand, holding out the cookie tin like a priest's paten. The tapered cuffs of her yellow pants were tight on her legs. A gnarl of purple veins bulged out from one ankle. Something about her battered feet saddened him, the slender white sandal straps that cut into her callused toes, her constant search for what would never be possible. "Could I get you something?" he asked. "A cold drink?" His dirty dishes were still in the sink. His coffee was probably cold now. Irritated, he tried to remind himself how much he had enjoyed her company at dinner the other night. Until they had run into Dennis and Jilly.

"No, thanks. I'll be leaving soon," she said, flipping back her hair. The inappropriate long black curls gave her a look of awkward desperation, made her seem older, bigger than she was. "It's just that I wanted to ask you something," she said with a hopeful smile. "Did you tell Lisa to call me?"

"No," he said uneasily.

"That's what I thought. She invited me to Jimmy's birthday party, and I just don't want you to feel—well . . ." She threw up her hand as if he'd know the rest. "I mean, I know how that goes. My sisters did it to me for years. I'd show up, and guess who else'd be there? Some bozo, the brother-in-law's divorced cousin they just knew would be perfect for me. I don't know, maybe they ran out of bozos or maybe they finally just got tired of it, but now Auntie Doe can just go stag if she wants." She laughed. "I'll tell her no."

He realized she'd meant that as a question. "No. Go. I mean, if you want."

"Would you mind?"

"No." What else could he say? he thought, irritated all over again.

After she left he sat in his darkened living room, drinking luke-warm coffee while across the street the party had swelled to twice as many people. A radio up in the window filled the night with rap music. On the sidewalk some of the younger boys were entertaining everyone with their dancing, most of which seemed to Gordon spas-tically gymnastic. An older man did the cooking now. Ronnie Feaster's SUV had just parked in front of Mrs. Jukas's house. The man at the grill paused as Feaster and Polie walked toward him. See-ing them, a pretty young woman in a red halter top ran to the porch railing and waved, but the man at the grill barked at her in Spanish and she sat down. Two younger girls covered their faces and giggled. The red flare of the cigarette jerked up and down in the man's mouth as he spoke to Feaster. The man didn't want him there. Inez stood up, arms folded, glowering down at them. The man gestured angrily with the spatula, and Feaster and Polie crossed the street. They took up positions on Mrs. Jukas's porch, slouched and laughing as if their banishment were of little consequence.

A dog was barking. Gordon's head snapped up, eyes opening wide. He wasn't sure how long he'd been asleep in his chair, but there were even more people across the way. In the distance a skinny girl in black pants hurried down the street. It was Jada. As she came closer, the barking intensified. Gordon checked his watch. Ten P.M. She ran into the house, then came right back out carrying her dog.

The minute she set him down, he ran onto the grass and lifted his leg against the now unmanned grill. Jada grabbed a hot dog, then devoured it in the hunched pose Gordon had noticed before. The dog ran back and forth between people's legs. A few kicked him away. A boy tossed a roll over the railing and the dog sank down, hind legs sprawled as he ate it. Inez called to Jada, and she climbed past the scowling women on the steps and filled a floppy paper plate from the various bowls. No one said anything. Even the children kept their distance as she sat on the steps, scooping food into her mouth with two fingers. When she was done she filled another plate and carried it down to her dog.

The women shook their heads. One called out angrily, but Inez said something and the woman went inside. Jada shrugged and kept eating.

Gordon wondered where her mother was. Jada had come into the Market looking for him the day after the holdup, but he had been unloading a truck. Leo told him later that June had thrown the girl out. Late last night Polie had come to Jada's door with a paper bag that seemed heavy the way he passed it to her with two hands. She took it and closed the door quickly, but Polie didn't leave. He rapped on the door until she finally opened it, peering at him over the lock chain. He was still talking when she closed the door again. He left. Halfway down the steps he turned and ran back up. He banged on the door, then kicked it. He went to the window and rapped on the glass, then took something from his back pocket and tried to pop out the storm window. A car pulled up in front of the house then, and Polie hurried down the steps and up the street.

The business Ronnie Feaster ran from Mrs. Jukas's porch was swelling in volume. Cars parked down the street, while up on the porch Feaster's cell phone rang with each arrival. After a brief conversation, which would be relayed to Polie, one or another of the boys, some looking as young as nine or ten, would appear from nowhere. After a word from Polie they would swagger along the sidewalk, then pause at the parked car's window. Each transaction took less than three minutes. The boys would trot past Mrs. Jukas's porch, then slip into her backyard. So far Gordon had seen no drugs

or money pass between the boys and the men on the porch. At Fortley there had been a loose tile in a shower room and behind it a lid-
ded soap dish to contain whatever currency was expected.

Mrs. Jukas had been home for a week. She arrived in a taxi and
walked into the house unaided, but for a cane. A visiting nurse
stopped by the first few days, but Gordon hadn't seen her there since
Tuesday. He kept wondering if he should go over and see how the
old woman was doing, but he didn't want to upset her. An older
woman had brought her a fruit basket yesterday. A little while later
the senior center van tried to deliver a hot meal, but Mrs. Jukas
wouldn't take it.

Each day he pinched off more diseased leaves. The first sign of
blight had been small black spots on some of the leaves. Every morning before work he sprayed the bushes with baking soda, water, and
dishwashing detergent, a concoction recommended in a *Better Homes
and Gardens* magazine he'd been reading free at work, a few pages a
day. The soapy froth dripped down the spray bottle onto his sneakers.
The roses were drenched, the leaves glistening a brilliant green as his
last few sprays sent a stream of bubbles into the air.

"Hey, look!" a boy called, wiping his mouth as the bubbles
floated by.

"Yo! Whatcha doin', mister?" another hollered as four boys strut-
ted around the side of Mrs. Jukas's house. Feaster and his runners
hadn't been around since the old woman had come home. The last
boy out of her yard sported a thick gold chain around his neck and
diamond studs piercing both ears. Like those of the other boys, the
front of his shirt was wet.

"You shouldn't be over there," Gordon said in a low voice. "She's
an old woman and she's very sick."

"We're not doin' anything," the biggest boy scoffed. He looked
like a young Buddha with his round thick head and small dark eyes.
Rolls of fat tubed his midsection.

"That doesn't matter. You're not supposed to be there."

"Feaster said for us to wait here," the boy said.

Gordon stepped through the bushes. "No. You wait out there. On the sidewalk. Now."

Their eyes held his. They left the yard, glancing back until they turned the corner.

A few minutes later he thought he heard water running. He followed the sound to the back of Mrs. Jukas's house, where the outside faucet had been turned on. He turned it off as tightly as he could, but it continued to leak. He mounded some nearby rocks under the drip. A window rattled open. Mrs. Jukas called down to ask what he was doing. He explained about the faucet, then asked if she was feeling better. No, she said. As a matter of fact, she felt terrible, worse than she ever had. But that's the way it was, and there wasn't anything anyone could do about it. Before she could shut the window, he asked if she needed anything from the Market. He could bring it by on his way home from work. "No, thank you," she said, closing the window.

He went into his house and washed his hands. As he came down the walk, Mrs. Jukas shuffled onto her porch and called to him. She had lost a lot of weight. Her head trembled, and as she leaned on her cane with both hands, the front of her housecoat parted, revealing her sagging underpants. She needed coffee and orange juice, whatever brand was cheapest. She'd pay him now or later, whatever he wanted, it didn't matter. Later was fine, he said, pleased that she wanted his help. Have a good day, he said, but she was already on her way back inside.

After work he rang her doorbell. Waiting, he was shocked by the mess on her porch. Cigarette butts, Styrofoam cups, empty cans, crumpled fast-food bags. He was kicking some of it into a pile when the door opened.

"How much?" she asked, taking a coin purse from the pocket of the same housecoat she had been wearing that morning. She paid him, and before she could close the door he asked for a bag to put this mess in.

"Don't bother," she said.

"It's no bother. It'll take me a second, that's all," he said, pushing another pile together.

"I don't even care. Do what you want. I'm too tired," she muttered, closing the door.

He went home, then came right back with a broom and a trash bag. He had just finished sweeping when Feaster's SUV pulled up. Polie ran across the street and banged on Jada's door. Inside, Jada's dog was barking. When no one came, he peered in her window, knocked a few times, then returned to the SUV. Feaster got out then and came up Mrs. Jukas's walk as Gordon came down the steps with the broom and bag. He asked Gordon if he'd seen Jada or her mother around. He hadn't. Not for a couple of days, anyway.

"Look, do me a favor, will you?" Feaster said, scribbling on a piece of paper. "Give her this. Her mother. Tell her it's the new number."

"No."

"No? What do you mean, no? It's a fucking cell phone number, that's all. Here."

Gordon walked past him.

"You can't do me a favor, is that what you're saying?" Feaster fumed as he followed him onto the porch. "Is that what you're saying? You can't do this one fucking simple little thing, is that what you're saying?"

Gordon tried to open his door, but Feaster stepped in front of it. Polie lumbered up the walk in his huge flapping sneakers.

"Is that it? Is that what you're saying?" Feaster demanded.

"I didn't say anything," Gordon said, head lowered, staring.

"You don't get it. See, I'm, like, tryna help her, that's all. When she gets this strung out she doesn't care. She's crazy. She'd slit your throat for a nickel and not even know you. Just give her this." Eyes gleaming, he offered the paper again.

"No."

"Take the fucking paper," Polie growled, the club by his leg.

"I got a better idea," Feaster said. "How's this? You don't wanna give her the number, so we'll just sit here and wait till she comes home."

Feaster pulled two chairs close to the railing and sat down, hands behind his head, his feet up on the railing. Polie sat next to him and did the same.

Inside, Gordon sat on the couch with the bag of trash in his lap. He felt sick to his stomach. He could handle Thurman, but these two were liable to pull a knife or gun on him. He could hear them laughing and calling out to people. A cruiser hadn't been by in days, and now two were racing around the corner, sirenless but with lights spinning. They turned at the corner and were gone.

A few minutes later a car pulled into the driveway. Dennis was halfway across the lawn when he stopped.

"Nice car," Feaster said to him as Gordon came to the door.

"Who're you?" Dennis asked, chin out.

"I got a better question. Who're you?" Feaster said, and Polie giggled.

Gordon held the door open.

"What's going on?" Dennis asked him.

"They're waiting. The woman across the street, they're waiting for her," Gordon said with an awkward gesture. He hoped Marvella didn't show up now with Dennis here. "Are you going to come in?" He opened the door wider.

Dennis came inside, then stood by the window. "What am I missing?" he asked, looking out. "Would you mind telling me what's going on? What do they want? What're they doing out there?"

"They'll be leaving soon. The woman, she'll—"

"They're punks. You want them out there, right? On your front porch? With their feet up on the railing like it's theirs? What're you thinking? You can't let punks like that just do what they want. Next thing you know they'll be coming in the house anytime they want."

"They'll leave soon. I just don't want any trouble, that's all."

"You don't want any trouble!" Dennis shook his head with a derisive hoot. "Jesus! That's good, that's really good. You don't want any trouble! You don't want any trouble."

"I don't."

"Then go tell them to get the hell outta here."

He glanced at Dennis. It wasn't disgust or pity that finally made him look away, but the venom in Dennis's eyes. And Gordon knew why. Because of what Gordon had seen and knew. Because of Dennis's own weakness.

"Then I will." Dennis stormed outside and ordered Feaster off the porch. His brother didn't want them there. Polie stood up, a head taller than Dennis.

"Fuck off," Feaster said without even looking back.

Dennis leaned over and knocked Feaster's feet off the railing, almost tipping him out of the chair. Polie's lunge sent Dennis stumbling across the porch. He caught himself on the post, and Gordon rushed outside. There was a dull black gun in Polie's hand.

"Jesus Christ!" Dennis gasped. "What're you doing? What the—"

"Don't move, asshole," Polie growled as Feaster came toward Dennis.

"That's my brother," Gordon said in a low voice.

"I don't care who the fuck he is," Feaster hissed, face twisted, his eyes never leaving Dennis. "He keeps his fucking hands off me or else he's fucking nobody's fucking brother. Now go in the house. Go in the fucking house!"

Dennis followed Gordon inside. The minute the door closed, Dennis picked up the phone.

"Don't!" Gordon said.

"Don't? He's got a gun out there!"

"No! They're leaving. See?" Gordon pointed. They were. Feaster and Polie were getting into the SUV. "They're gone," he reported as they drove away. "It's all right." He held out his hand for the phone.

"All right?" Dennis shook his head, and now Gordon saw how hard his brother was breathing. His face was gray. "You think this is all right? Then Jesus Christ, you're even more pathetic than I thought."

"You don't understand."

"I don't *understand!* Jesus Christ! How can you say that?"

"Because you don't. You don't understand how careful I have to be. All the time, every minute, every day. I have to stay away from trouble. I've been doing it so long now it's like second nature. I keep my head down. I look the other way. I don't hear, I don't see, and I don't ask questions. Somebody bumps into me, I apologize to them. And you're right, it is pathetic, but that's the way it is. That's the way it has to be for me."

"I'm sorry." Dennis rubbed his forehead in a dismal gesture of shame and resignation. "Look, I just want things to be all right for you, that's all. I don't mean to be dumping on you like this. Things are just so screwed up right now." He sighed and turned to look out the window again. "The reason I came is . . . well, it's about that night. I mean, there's certain things you don't understand. I mean, how can you? You're not married, you don't know how these things work. Oh, Christ! What I'm trying to say here is, what you saw, it's not what you think. It's just this . . . this thing that happens sometimes and who the hell knows why!"

"You don't have to tell me this."

"Of course I do. It's important. I want you to know. Jilly's a sweet, sincere girl. She cried all that night. She's still upset. She thinks she's done some terrible thing."

"Well, she has, hasn't she?" Gordon blurted.

"Well, no," Dennis said slowly. "That's what I mean—she hasn't—not in the big scheme of things, that is. But what she's really upset about is you."

"Me? Why?" He almost smiled.

"That's why I came over. She's afraid. She said she tried to be nice and show you places like I asked her to, but you took it the wrong way. You tried to come on to her."

"I asked her out to dinner, that's all I did."

"Well, the whole thing's got her really freaked out now. You, me, her!"

Gordon's face burned in a turmoil of shame and anger. "What about Lisa?" he asked.

"What do you mean?"

"Are you two breaking up?" The words sickened him.

"No! Jesus Christ, is that what you're thinking?" Dennis looked incredulous. "No! I'd never do that. Never! My family, I mean, that's my whole life!"

CHAPTER 12

Gordon ran up the cellar stairs. Someone was ringing the bell and banging on the door. Jada. She looked terrible: acne on her forehead and nose, cold sores on her mouth, red, teary eyes. Leonardo had worms. Her little dog was dying, and she didn't know what to do. He'd been on the bed whimpering all morning. He wouldn't eat or drink anything. Gordon said he probably needed to see a vet. He might as well have told her the dog needed to go to Tibet. A vet? Where? How?

"Find one in the phone book." His guide to life, everything he needed to know, was in there. "Veterinarians," he said, thumbing through the pages. "Here they are. A whole page of them."

She held the book close, then drew back her head. "They're all someplace else. There aren't any here." She handed it back.

Dearborn, Hilliard, Plainfield: all in the suburbs. She was right. There weren't any in the city.

"Maybe you can get a ride from somebody," he said.

"I can't."

"What about your mother?"

"She doesn't have a car, and besides, she's not home."

"When she comes back, then."

"Can I have a piece?" She gestured to the loaf of bread on the counter.

He handed her a slice. "She might know someone to call."

"Polie," she said, chewing. "But I'm not going anywhere with him. That asshole."

He offered her another slice. When he saw her devour that one, he asked if she'd like a ham sandwich. She grinned, watching closely as he made it. Did she want mustard? Yeah! A lot or a little? A lot, she said. Especially when she ate mustard sandwiches.

"I never heard of a mustard sandwich."

"Well, yeah, if there's nothing else to put in."

He added another slice of ham. "Here. Sit down." He started to put it on the table.

"That's okay." She ate standing by the counter. "What's that?" She nodded at Delores's tin.

"Nothing." He was saving the last few cookies for dessert tonight.

When he turned to give her a glass of milk, the sandwich was gone. She guzzled down half the milk, then asked for a paper cup. A little milk might make Leonardo feel better. He didn't have any paper cups. She could take it over in the glass if she brought it back. "Are you out of milk?" he asked.

"Yeah, but there's still some Coke left," she called back.

After she left he felt guilty. He should have given her the cookies, he thought as he cleared the table and counter. He hadn't seen Marvella Fossum for a while. Maybe she was sick. No, because Jada said she wasn't home. He remembered Jada's ravenous consumption at the cookout that night. Like a stray no one dared confront. Her dog probably wasn't even sick. She'd just needed an excuse to come begging. He stared out the window. Was it possible? Was there a hungry child over there? He couldn't recall such a thing ever happening when he'd been a boy. Not here, not on Clover Street. There'd been an old man over on Liberty Street, once, who fell down his cellar stairs and broke his hip. Days later the mailman found him incoherent from hunger and dehydration. Twenty-five years, and everything was different now. Children screamed at their mothers every day in the Market. Holdups were so commonplace, Neil had gone through three in four months. Last week a gang of girls had beaten up Serena's teenage niece in the school library for e-mailing one of their boyfriends. Expecting order and sanity, he had found a world gone awry, the planet tipped. Instead of meteors, airplane bolts and metal chunks fell from the sky. Untended babies plunged through open windows. But who was he, what right did he have to expectation, disappointment, indignation, of all people, him, Gordon Loomis, *so insignificant, so lost in his own life, that he had surely been on his way long, long before the night she dead-bolts her door, hobbles on one crutch from the shower into bed, where the last book she reads is* The Healthy Woman's Guide to Happy Pregnancy, *never suspecting that in minutes it will be over. Everything, past and to come. Ended. He would be twenty-five years old. Almost twenty-six.*

Kevin, the father testifies, and Gordon's lawyer jumps up in protest, not wanting it allowed humanness or gender. What does its name have to do with the facts of that night? "Everything!" the father bellows back. Gordon burrows deeper into the stony silence of shame one newspaper describes as "an unflinching disregard for the victims. During testimony, the young man stares into the distance, making eye contact with no one, not even his own family." But in the years since, he has found solace knowing the fetus was allowed that—at least a name in his father's mind, if not a memory, a name on some brittle page of court transcript, a name never entered on a birth certificate, but perhaps carved into granite, a name to mark his existence. Kevin Walters, a fact in the eyes of the defense, not a being.

It was four o'clock and they still weren't back. One more favor he'd owe Delores now. He wished he hadn't called her, but when Jada returned later in the morning, the dull-eyed puppy panting and limp in her arms, Gordon panicked.

"He's dying. Look at him, he's gonna die, I know he is. His heart's hardly even beating," the girl wailed. "My poor sweet baby's gonna die."

He tried to explain over Jada's sobs, tried to apologize for calling Smick's, but there was an emergency. That's all Delores had to hear. She didn't even hesitate. Help was needed, so she closed the store and got there in less than ten minutes. Dr. Loop in Hilliard, that's where she used to bring her mother's cats, she called back as Jada's long skinny legs folded into the front seat with the dog wheezing at her chest. "He's really good!" Delores called before she drove off, leaving

Gordon confused but strangely energized, as if there were a thousand things he might do, if only he knew what they were.

When they finally returned, Jada had four different kinds of medicine for the slightly livelier dog that was sniffing the leg on the coffee table. Delores told Jada he had to go to the bathroom.

"Here." Jada grabbed a section of the newspaper and tossed it. Leonardo squatted, spraying the paper. The long yellow stream dribbled over onto the floor.

"Jada!" Delores said.

"What?" Jada said.

"You can't let him do that in somebody's house!"

"But he's paper-trained," Jada said as Gordon hurried out of the kitchen with paper towels and Pine-Sol.

"Here . . ." Delores took the roll from him and handed it to the girl. "Clean it up and then bring him home. Poor thing's had enough excitement for one day."

After a quick wipe of the floor, Jada gathered up Leonardo and his medications. She had already thanked Delores and said good-bye, but she lingered in the doorway. She asked Delores how long her nails had to grow before they could be manicured.

"I already told you—you gotta have some white showing. At least to the tips of your fingers," Delores said.

Jada frowned over the dog's head at her chewed nails. "How long's that take?"

"Not long. You'll be surprised," Delores said.

"What if they don't grow?"

"They will. And if you'd wash your hands once in a while, they'd grow even faster."

"What if they all grow, then one breaks?"

"Then we'll go anyway!" Delores laughed. "Now will you please leave now so that poor thing can get some rest?"

"Oh, yeah, you sweet little baby," Jada murmured, nuzzling his ear as she left.

"Wow! Is she a piece of work or what?" Delores sighed, watching through the window.

"I'm sorry, I shouldn't have bothered you. I just didn't know what to do," Gordon said. He felt foolish for having dragged her into this.

"No!" She was glad he had called her. What she meant was that she'd never met anyone quite like Jada Fossum. Amazing—in spite of the neglect, there was still a sweet girl under all that craziness. "Do you know how long she's been alone over there?"

He didn't know she'd been alone.

"A week, anyway. Her mother's in rehab somewhere, she said, but she doesn't want anyone to know. She's afraid of being put back in foster care, so she gets up every morning and goes to school, then comes home right after. Funny, huh, kid like that trying to do all the right things because her mother's not around. The one she's most afraid of finding out, though, is Ronnie Feaster. Every day he comes by looking for her mother."

"He even asked me if I'd seen her."

"Yeah, she owes him money, so now he wants Jada to work for him and pay it back."

"That no-good bastard," he muttered, then was embarrassed that he'd sworn, but she didn't seem to mind.

"I know. I told her she shouldn't be living alone like this, but she said her uncle comes by almost every day to see how she's doing. She said he doesn't like her living in this neighborhood, but she told him how there's a real nice family across the street that's always helping her out."

"Really? What family's that?"

"You."

In constant motion, each child had the presence of three or four, halfway up a tree one moment, then crawling out from under the deck the next, now trying to throw tennis balls over the roof. Gordon didn't want to be here. He had expected a children's party, but most of the guests were friends and neighbors of Lisa and Dennis. The only one he knew was Delores, and she was busy helping Lisa. He headed toward the deck when he saw Delores come outside with a tray of toothpick-studded fruit wedges.

A tall, barefoot woman in a long gauzy dress was suddenly walking beside him. "We haven't met yet. I'm Gretta Deacon."

"Hello."

"I live in the green house. We just moved in a few weeks ago. I'm still working, so I haven't met too many neighbors yet. I'm not due till October, so I suppose I will then. I'm not going right back to work. Not until the baby's a year old, anyway. At least! And then who knows, maybe I'll—"

"Excuse me." He turned, slipping into the cool shadows alongside the house. Snatches of conversation floated by.

"You try losing ten pounds in . . ."

"Lee and Kendra's littlest boy . . ."

". . . how they lost the entire front to grubs when . . ."

"And who's got that kind of . . ."

"Hey! Hey, mister! Are you Jimmy's uncle?"

Gordon nodded. The boy bit his lip, then glanced back at Jimmy and two boys watching from the hammock.

"Are you really?"

"Yes."

The boy raced back to the hammock.

While everyone around him laughed, Dennis knelt at a croquet wicket, measuring his last shot with the mallet shaft. He and Lisa were playing with a couple whose names Gordon forgot the moment the woman said she'd been wanting to meet him for a long time. Why? What did she mean by that? What did she want? Relieved they hadn't seen him, he came around the front of the house. The street was lined with parked cars. If he kept walking, he could be at the bus stop in twenty minutes, home in another twenty.

"Gordon!" Lisa hurried down the sloping lawn, followed by a chubby man in rumpled black pants and a short-sleeved shirt. "I've been dying for you two to meet," she said, and introduced him to Father Henry Hensile.

"Hank," the priest said.

"Nice to meet you." Gordon shook his soft, moist hand.

"Father Hank used to be at St. Theresa's in Collerton," Lisa said, adding that he had been in Dearborn for the last five years.

"Oh. That's good," Gordon said.

"St. Theresa's was Dennis and Gordon's parish growing up," she told the priest.

"It's a great parish. Probably different, though, than the way you remember it," the priest said.

"Yes," Gordon said uneasily.

"Gordon works at the Nash Street Market. The Dubbin family owns it. You know Cindy, Father," she said.

"Oh, sure! Yes. Of course. Without Cindy there'd be no Las Vegas Night," the priest said.

"Las Vegas Night's a fund-raiser," Lisa explained to Gordon. "Actually, I think it's the biggest one of the year, isn't it, Father Hank? Maybe in the whole diocese."

"Shh," the priest said, looking around. "I don't know how proud we should be of that."

Lisa turned as a sleek black car came down the street. "My mom and dad are here!" she cried, then ran to the driveway. Mr. Harrington hugged her while Mrs. Harrington removed two elaborately wrapped gifts from the backseat. Lisa's father was a portly, balding man, shorter than his slender wife and daughter. Lisa's mother was dressed in white—shoes, pants, and sweater—with her silvery blond hair pulled back from her tanned face in a small, smooth ponytail.

"I wonder how their trip went," the priest said, watching the reunion.

"I don't know. I've never met them," Gordon said.

"Oh, you'll like them. They're very nice. You'll like them a lot."

Lisa hurried her parents over. "Mother, this—"

"Father Hank!" Mrs. Harrington said, pursing her lips in concern. "How's your mother? Poor thing, how's she doing?"

"Holding her own," the priest said.

"We lit a candle for her in Balaton, didn't we, Tom? It was the most darling little stone chapel, stained glass—"

"Mom! Wait! You haven't met Gordon yet. Gordon, this is my mom, Mitzi, and my dad, Tom."

Mr. Harrington's florid, freckled face was belied by steady, deep-watching eyes.

"Nice meeting you." Gordon shook their hands.

"Yes, and it's nice meeting you," Mrs. Harrington said through a forced smile, her pretty face frozen with discomfort.

"You any kind of a golfer like your brother?" Mr. Harrington asked.

"No, sir, I'm not."

"Smart man! But I'm sure Dennis'll take care of that in no time," Mr. Harrington said. "Speaking of whom, where is my favorite son-in-law?" he asked, then headed off with his wife in a bluster of eagerness to tell Dennis all about their trip.

"Don't feel bad. They were just nervous about meeting you," Lisa said.

"I understand," Gordon said before she left to catch up with them.

"I suppose that's happened a few times," the priest said as both men started to walk. "People don't quite know what to say, do they?"

"No, I guess not. But that's all right," he said, looking past the priest for his own escape.

"Well, I give you a lot of credit for coming back. It couldn't have been easy. Most people in your situation wouldn't have."

"I don't know." He paused by the front steps. "If you'll excuse me, Father, I have to go inside for a minute."

"Oh, sure, go right ahead, Gordon. But can I just tell you something first? Lisa's told me a lot about you these last few years. She's very fond of you. And . . . well, there's no point beating around the bush here, Gordon—she asked if I'd make a special effort to get to know you. And I'd like to do that, but I also don't want to force myself on you. So I thought maybe we could go out for a cup of coffee—or something. That is, if you'd like sometime."

"Well, I don't know. Maybe." Sometime. In the far, far distant future.

"How about Monday? Nine-thirty? Ten?"

"I work in the morning," Gordon said, relieved.

"When you get off work, then."

"I don't know my hours yet."

"It doesn't have to be coffee. How about a beer some night?"

"I don't drink."

The priest paused in that unspoken assessment Gordon was getting used to. "Okay. All right, then. Here." He slipped a card from his worn, flattened wallet. "Here's my number. Just give me a call when you know your hours. Or anytime, for that matter. I'd really enjoy talking to you."

No one was in the house. Gordon wandered through the dining room and living room. He had to be careful. He didn't want to break anything. He had never seen so many pretty ornaments, ceramic dishes, Oriental vases, statues, gleaming lacquered boxes, leather-bound books, carved birds so perfectly painted that from a distance they looked real. In the cabinet under the window, Dennis's collection of antique glass paperweights dazzled in the sunlight. On the piano was a framed wedding picture of Dennis and Lisa with both sets of parents. He leaned close. Obscured by shadows, his father's face was bleak with illness, his eyes faint in their hollows. Gordon smiled at the image of his mother's feisty happiness—Teresa Pratt, head high, chin out, glowing with pride. He started into the great room, then stopped, alarmed to see his brother at the other end of the kitchen.

"Come on in," Dennis called before he could get away. He was filling a bowl with ice from the refrigerator-door dispenser. "Sure beats those old metal trays, remember?" Dennis said over the racket of cubes clunking into the bowl.

They both looked up with the gritty slide of the opening deck door. A perspiring, buxom woman leaned in to say Lisa needed the ice. "Not as much as you," Dennis said, handing her the bowl.

"And Lisa says to take the cake out of the fridge," she called as she left.

"Hey, will you look at this," Dennis said, sliding out a cake decorated in the shape of a soccer field with goal nets, scoreboard, and miniature players kicking a ball. "Here, count the candles, just to be sure." He held out the cake.

"Twelve? I thought he was eleven." The card he'd bought said "For an Eleven-Year-Old."

"He is, but one's for good luck, right?"

"Oh, that's right. Good luck. I forgot."

"Hey, will you relax? Look at you, sweat pouring down your face, you're a wreck. Those punk bastards, they're not hassling you again, are they?"

"No. No, they haven't been back." He tensed, expecting more talk about that night, about Jilly.

"Good. You can't ever show blood, Gordo. The least little thing and they'll be on you like vultures. Remember that now."

Gordon nodded, amazed. How did his brother think he had survived the vultures in prison? Was Dennis so blind about some things, or was it just a way of compartmentalizing his life? And wasn't it the same for him, who wandered among these perfectly normal people as if he were every bit as decent as they were, as if no one knew who he really was?

"Hey!" Dennis called as he carried the cake onto the deck. "In my next life I want to come back as one of Lisa Harrington's kids."

"You already *are* one of her kids!" a woman shouted back, and no one laughed harder than Dennis.

Delores dragged a lawn chair close to Gordon's under the sweet flowering linden tree. With the cake served and presents opened, the children were absolved of any responsibility to behave like guests. They ran between the yard next door and this one in fitful bursts of Frisbee and kickball and now for the most part were just running and shrieking. The adult voices and laughter came faster and louder. The almost frantic clamor reminded him of the prisoners in the last moments of rec time. He was tired. Just being here had been a strain. With rain threatening, the sky sagged low overhead.

"What a nice party this has been." Delores sighed, settling into the chair. "See those two women over there? The one in the long blue skirt? She's Albert's sister-in-law's cousin, Mary Bianci. She was two years ahead of us in high school. Apparently things haven't been going too well this week for poor Albert. Mary said his daughter totaled her very expensive sports car, and then the next day his big beautiful house in Dearborn was broken into." She shook her head. "So much for the safety of suburbia. You can say what you want about Collerton, but I've never been broken into, never once!"

"You live on the second floor, though."

"So? I have a fire escape. They could get in that way. If they wanted to. Sometimes I even leave that window open on hot nights."

"You shouldn't do that," he said, thinking of Mrs. Jukas.

"Why?"

He squirmed under her scrutiny. She probably thought his warning harkened back to his own crime. "It's not safe, that's all." He broke off a blade of grass and wrapped it around his finger.

"There's no such thing as safe." She was looking at him.

"Uncle Gordon!" Annie cried, running up from behind. She leaned over the back of his chair. "Mommy said to ask you if you're having a good time."

"Yes, I am. A very good time. Thank you, Annie."

She swung around the chair arm so that her pert, sweaty face was at his. "I'm supposed to find out if you want anything. Some more cake? Ice cream? Punch?"

"Punch would be nice."

"Okay! Here you go!" She laughed and drove her fist into his shoulder. "Have some punch!"

"Oh," he said after a moment. "Some punch. I get it." He tried to smile.

"I think you hurt him! Poor Uncle Gordon," Delores called as Annie ran off, giggling. "She's beautiful, isn't she? She looks so much like her mother. And Jimmy, God, he reminds me so much of Dennis." She sighed. "It's amazing when you think of it. I mean, having a child that's so much like you and yet they're their own person. My sister Babbie said with her first baby it was all like such a miracle. But then when the second one came along it hit her, that these were really real people and not just babies she was bringing into this really real world." '

In the corner of the yard, an intense badminton volley continued over a drooping net. Dennis watched with his arm around Lisa, talking to Father Hensile and a man he'd met earlier, an older man leaning on hand braces.

"That's Ernie," Delores said. "He owns a company that makes umbrellas. They're famous for their golf umbrellas."

Umbrellas, he thought with a pang. *The poor guy can't even hold an umbrella.*

"They look so happy," Delores said after a moment.

"Do you think she knows?" Gordon said. There was a rasp of leaves in the quick wind.

"You mean about that night?" She leaned toward him, continuing in the same informative tone. "Probably not that. But she knows Dennis, so she knows. How could she not? He's always been a ladies' man."

He stared at them, his family, his stability and mooring point. Without them he had nothing. No one. Dennis's hand dangled over Lisa's shoulder. Her arm was tight around his waist. If Delores was right, he didn't know which was more upsetting, their easy pretense or the false intimacy. *It changes everything. Cheapens it.* His brother had everything but wanted more. Didn't he know what could happen? Didn't he care? One wrong move, a misstep, that's all. He gripped the chair arms, but he wanted to leave.

"Gordon?" Delores touched his wrist. "What is it?"

"Nothing."

"You look so . . . so sad. Do you feel all right?"

Dennis and Lisa walked hand in hand toward Lisa's parents. Annie was sprawled in her grandfather's lap, head back on his shoulder. Mrs. Harrington gestured, and Dennis leaned close. Whatever she whispered made him suddenly seize Annie as if to run off with her. With all the adults laughing, Annie struggled free and leaped back into her grandfather's outstretched arms.

"How could he do that? What's wrong with him?" Gordon said.

"Nothing. Nothing's wrong with him." Her hand pressed on his arm. "Some men just . . . well, they need more than others, that's all."

"Need more what?"

"They need the respectability and the security that comes with being married, but they have other needs, too. They need someone who understands them, who knows what . . . what those needs are. Someone who . . . someone who doesn't expect much back." Her voice faltered. "He'd never leave Lisa, though, if that's what you're thinking."

He watched her try to scrape a ketchup stain from her pant leg with a fingernail thick with fuchsia polish. *She has no good sense, no judgment,* he thought. Her kindness to Jada Fossum now seemed only careless and indiscriminate, an act of giving, meritless because of its easy availability, because she couldn't say no. Her charity was earthy and promiscuous. She had done it not for the girl's sake or his, but for her own. In helping others, she was pleasuring herself. It was a way of insinuating herself into people's lives, feeding off their needs and their loneliness.

Delores drove slowly. She lingered at stop signs, waiting so long after lights turned green that cars had to sound their horns before she moved on.

"Well, thank you," he said, opening his door when she finally pulled up in front of his house.

"I wonder how the puppy's doing. I hope Jada's still giving him the medicine. Dr. Loop said she should use it all up."

"Well, thanks again." He managed to get one foot out onto the street.

"Do you know she can barely read?"

"Really? She seems smart enough."

"I don't think it's that. I saw her trying to read the directions on the medicine box. First she held it this close. . . ." She held her palm to her face. "Then out like this. I think the poor thing needs glasses."

"Maybe she does. Well, anyway—"

"You'd think her mother would do something. I mean, doesn't she care? There's something about Jada—she's got this spark inside, you know, like a fire nobody's going to put out no matter what happens to her." Delores almost sounded angry.

"I don't know," he said, looking back now. "I've seen a lot of fires go out." Billy Leeman had gotten his head bashed in for nothing more than refusing to talk to his psychotic cellmate. All he had wanted was to be left alone so he could read race-car magazines and write letters to his wife.

"But yours never did, did it?"

"I never had one."

"Of course you did. You do. It's how you've gotten through everything."

"No. It wasn't that way with me. All I did was wait. That's all."

She laid her hand over his, and he froze. "You're a good man, Gordon. A really good man. I hope you know that. You need to know that."

Jada's legs ached. She had walked from one end of the city to the other. It was all uphill now, and she was carrying Leonardo. He kept sitting down and she would have to drag him along on the rope to get him going again. This last time he began to howl, so she had to pick him up. She looked at every house, trying to find her uncle's. She hadn't been there in a couple of years, not since his adopted baby's christening party. Bitchy Aunt Sue had accused her of stealing her fourteen-carat-gold kisses-and-hugs chain. Marvella had taken it, and what could Jada do but keep insisting it wasn't her? So then Aunt Sue pulled her out onto the porch, her beery, garlic voice hissing how they'd wasted a lot of time and money, a whole year of their lives, taking care of her when the state took her away from her mother, and how Uncle Bob was always telling her that underneath it all Jada was a nice kid, but this just proved she was like all the rest of the Fossums, trash from start to finish. Uncle Bob quit on her after that, which hurt, because he was the only relative who'd ever cared what happened to her.

"There it is!" she told Leonardo. The truck in the driveway said BOB'S SEPTIC SERVICE in gold letters on the green tank. The house was a duplex her uncle had converted into a three-family. An ankle-high white wire fence bordered the narrow strip of lawn. Lining both sides of the short front walk were small American flags her mother said he was always taking from people's graves. She put Leonardo down, then wet her fingers and tried to brush the dog hairs off her black T-shirt before she rang the bell.

Jada had lived with them for a year the first time Social Services took her away. Her mother said she'd never let them have her again because she'd come back "spoiled rotten," crying if her pants were wet or every time she was told no. It always pleased her to hear that. Not just because it meant her mother cared what happened to her, but because it seemed proof of some value, some genuine worth, about herself. When she was seven, the state took her again, but she had to go to a foster home because her aunt and uncle refused. They said it was too painful to have her sent back to her mother, who just undid all their good work.

"Hi, Uncle Bob!" She grinned as he opened the door. His hair was the same gingery color as hers. Anglo straight, though, not kinky like hers.

"Jada," he said in a flat voice.

Leonardo barked. Her uncle stepped outside and closed the door. "What's that?" He pointed down at the dog jumping on his legs.

"My dog. Leonardo. He really likes you!"

"You shouldn't have brought him here. Tiffany's allergic to animal dander. Deathly allergic," he said with a look of horror.

"Oh! I didn't know that. Who's Tiffany?"

"My daughter."

"Oh yeah, that's right. I forgot." The fat drooling baby that wasn't even theirs. "She's like, what, six or seven now?" It seemed that long since she'd been here.

"Tiffany's just turned four. Last month, as a matter of fact," he said with the twinge of a smile.

"I'll bet she's really cute, huh?"

"She is. She is, she's really cute."

"Hey, you ever need a baby-sitter, I got lots of experience," she said, grinning.

"How'd you get here?" He looked toward the street.

"I walked. Me and Leonardo. Well, *I* walked. But not him, the spoiled-rotten little thing, he got carried most of the way."

"You walked? Why? What's wrong? You're not in some kind of trouble, are you?"

"No! I'm not in any trouble." She laughed. "I just need to borrow some money, that's all, and I was hoping maybe—"

"Why? What's going on with your mother?"

"Nothing. She's got some kind of flu thing or something. One of those viruses, I guess you call it, and she's been—"

"She sent you here to ask me for money?"

"No! No, she doesn't even know I'm here. I just figured you could help me out. I got this, like, field trip, this thing I gotta go on, and I'm supposed to bring the money in tomorrow. For the tickets. For the bus. The bus tickets." She swallowed. "It's gonna cost like . . . fifty dollars," she said, plunging full-speed ahead. Might as well go for it, because from the look on his face she probably wasn't going to get anything anyway, so what the hell.

"Where's the field trip to?"

"The aquarium." The first place that came to mind. She had missed out on a lot of field trips there over the years.

"Fifty dollars to go a few miles into Boston?"

"No, not that aquarium. The one in New York. New York City." Jesus Christ, she didn't even know if there was one there. Probably not, from the red-faced way he was staring down at her now, like something inside getting ready to explode.

"All right, look, Jada. I'm gonna help you, but just this one time. But first you gotta tell me the truth. Who's the money for, you or your mother?"

"Me! I swear!"

"Because if it's for her, all you're doing is helping her kill herself. You know that, right?"

Even her nod felt like betrayal.

"You know how many times your mother's screwed me? How many times she's lied and cheated and even stole things from me? Last summer we went to the beach for the weekend. One lousy weekend, and my house gets broken into. And all Sue's jewelry gone and her little TV in the kitchen. Right away I knew it was her." He folded his arms. "So tell me, tell me the truth, what do you really need money for?"

"The field trip." If she said food, he'd know she was alone and he'd call Social Services again.

"You sure?"

"Yeah! I'm sure! I got a book all about it. I'm gonna read it to-night. All about whales, sharks, swordfish, codfish—" She stopped just short of saying *cakes*. "Catfish."

"Who's your teacher?"

"Mr. Ansaldo." She watched his hand slip into his pocket.

"Sam Ansaldo? He's a client. I just pumped him out last fall. What time's school start?"

"Seven forty-five."

"Okay. At seven-thirty I'll be right there and that way the mon-ey'll be safe. I won't have to worry about Marvella ending up with it. I'll pay your teacher myself." He started to open the door. "See you in the morning!"

"Uncle Bob! It's not for a field trip."

"So you lied to me."

"No! I do need the money. But not for a field trip. That part's not true." Her mind raced with reasons. She could say for clothes or shoes, but he might offer to buy them for her. "It's for medicine."

"Medicine? You got Medicaid, right?"

She had no idea. "For him, for Leonardo," she said, pointing. The dog lay curled, asleep at her feet. "He was, like, really sick, and this wicked nice lady, she drove us to Dearborn to this vet and we got all this medicine, and she paid for it, but now I gotta pay her back, so I—"

"Jada! You sound just like her now. Like all the rest of them with their lying and cheating. I'm gonna tell you something. I wasn't much older than you when I just took off on my own, and if you're smart, that's what the hell you'll do, too! Find some good people and stick with them."

"But it's true. I'm not lying. Her name's Delores. She's this big lady, and I owe her money. I do! I swear!"

Behind him the curtain parted and a fist rapped on the window-pane.

"My supper. Your aunt Sue, she wants me to come in. Here." He held out his hand as if to shake hers. She felt cash pass into her palm. "You be good now. And no more lies."

As the door opened and closed behind him, the spicy smell of spaghetti sauce made her ache inside. As she bent down, lights pinwheeled behind her eyes with this brilliant image of pansies and daisies and roses bubbling in a thick red sauce. She picked up Leonardo so they wouldn't have the satisfaction of seeing him refuse to walk with her. "Cheap bastard," she muttered. Two lousy dollars. A landlord with his own business, clients even, and that's all he'd given her. It wasn't fair. Well, he could just go fuck himself for all she cared. They all could. Every goddamn one of them. The whole fucking goddamn world. Who the hell was he telling her not to lie, when that's all they did, all the time, him and his bitch wife, everyone, every motherfucking fucker she'd ever known? "I'm so hungry," she whispered at Leonardo's ear. "So fucking hungry, I could cry." And then she did. Tears ran down her cheeks, and she laughed out loud. A little old woman walked toward her, pulling a wire cart filled with bags. A brown cloth pocketbook dangled from the crook of her arm. What could be easier? Just grab it and run like hell. Even with Leonardo she'd be long gone before the old lady knew what hit her. Closer. Closer now. Alarmed by her fierce grip, he began to bark. "Don't, don't," she hissed, squeezing him. "Shut up! Will you shut up!" The barking intensified.

The old lady smiled. "What a cute puppy. What's his name?"

"Leonardo." Damn, she shouldn't have said his real name.

"Leonardo, hello, Leonardo," the old lady crooned, and tickled his straining neck. "Can I give him a doggie treat? I just got some. I keep them for when my son's dogs come over. They're these little black poodles. They're in here somewhere." She set her purse on the ground and began digging through the bags. Jada stepped closer. Her foot was touching the pocketbook. "Here!" The old lady ripped open a box and held out a small dog biscuit, which Leonardo lapped from her hand. She gave him another one, then glanced up at Jada with a fading smile. "What's the matter? Why're you looking at me like that? What's wrong?" She picked up her pocketbook and brushed it off.

"Nothing. I'm just hungry, that's all."

"Oh, I'm sorry. I shouldn't have held you up like this. Well anyway . . ." She put the box back into the bag. "I'll let you go, and it was very nice meeting you. You, too, Leonardo," she called, pulling her cart to the curb. She paused, looking both ways before she crossed the street.

CHAPTER 13

"Good morning," Gordon said over the pallet of cereal boxes he was wheeling down the aisle.

"Good morning," Serena and June answered in dull unison, heads lifting like startled birds at his approach.

He asked where Neil was. He hadn't written an egg order, so the Hensmen driver said he'd stop by again at the end of his route.

"He's out back, slicing boxes," Serena said.

"He is?" He stepped around the pallet. "Why's he doing that? I always get them done in time." After the holdup, a fire lieutenant had come into the Market to tell Neil not to store boxes at the front of the store anymore. A violation, they were a fire and safety hazard. "This whole city's a fire and safety hazard," Neil had said, laughing bitterly.

The women continued to look at him with wide-eyed, blank expressions, as if holding their breath against fouled air. He could feel their eyes on him all the way to the back of the store. Neil was outside, stacking the flattened boxes by the loading dock. "You don't have to do that, Neil. I'll take care of it." He hurried down the rickety steps. Since the holdup, Neil had been barely speaking to him. He couldn't seem to please him no matter how hard he worked.

Neil grunted and cut another box.

"Go inside. I'll finish the rest."

"I'm almost done," Neil said, slicing all four sides.

"I'll put them in the Dumpster, then," Gordon said. He began dragging cut boxes toward the back of the lot.

"No! Leave them there!" Neil barked.

"But they won't pick them up over here," Gordon reminded him. The drivers took only what was in the Dumpster.

"I want to see about recycling them. Get a few bucks, maybe."

"That's a good idea," Gordon said.

"Yeah." Neil stood up, smiling. "It is, isn't it."

"You know, something else you might want to do is give the outdated bakery stuff to the homeless shelter. I go by there. I could drop it off." He had seen Lida's Bakery truck delivering day-old bread there the other night.

Neil drew in his chin. "Now why would I want to do that?"

"Charity?" Gordon said with a shrug.

"Charity my ass! Let them fucking work like the rest of us! Like you and me! The lazy fucking maggots, why the hell should I bust my hump just to keep them alive another day. Huh?" He continued to shout in Gordon's face. "Nobody ever fucking helps me! Nobody gives a fuck if I live or die!" He caught himself and smiled that thin wet smile again. "But so the fuck what, right, Gloomis?"

Every muscle tightened. His eyes flinched from Neil's. All these years, and it still stung.

"I'll tell you what," Neil said, taking a matchbook from his pocket. "Here. Next time you go by just give it a toss and do them all a favor."

For the rest of the day he managed to avoid Neil, whose angry voice carried through the store now. He was berating Leo for ordering sides of beef without asking him first.

"That's how much we always get!" Leo looked at him as if he were crazy.

"From now on you ask. You check with me, goddamn it!" Neil roared.

At three o'clock the store began to get busy. Gordon was bagging at Serena's register for a woman with silver rings on all her fingers. When Serena rang up the total, the woman removed a white envelope from her purse and counted out the food stamps.

"Naturally," Serena said under her breath.

The woman looked up, but Serena was smiling at her. Gordon was relieved when she left.

"But don't sell the jewelry," June said from the next register.

"God forbid," Serena said with a sigh.

Leo stood at June's elbow while she rang up an order. He was complaining about Neil again. His face was white, his dark eyes bulging from their sockets. "I'm telling you, he's a psycho. He's a friggin' psycho. And something's gonna happen, something bad," he said in a low voice as June's fingers flew over the keys.

"Come on, Leo, Neil's just . . . just being Neil," Serena said as she started ringing up the next order.

"Well, I'm sick of taking his psycho crap. I been ordering without his okay so long I can't remember. Now all of a sudden he's pissed? I'm telling you, something's very wrong with this picture. The man's headed right off the screen, and you mark my words when it happens, cuz it is. It's gonna happen."

A little while later, when the rush was over, June went into the office to rest. Gordon told Serena he was going to stock the dairy case. He'd be right back if she needed him.

"Hey," she said before he could leave. "There's something I been wanting to say. I mean, when you first started I kept thinking, I know this guy. And like the name, Loomis—I kept thinking, Damn it, I know that name, but from where?" She leaned closer. "It must've been tough, being so young and having something like that happen."

He nodded. She had turned twenty-two a few days before she died.

"I mean, you probably thought your life was over, right? That when you got out you'd be an old man or something."

He realized she was talking about him.

"And look, you're what, in your forties? You got your whole life ahead of you. So really, all you did was miss out on the rat race." Her husky laugh dragged through him, and he tried to smile.

———

After work the next night, he called Dennis. No matter what was going on in his brother's life, they had to stay close. Dennis had never given up on him, and he owed him at least that now.

He wasn't home yet. "He should be there pretty soon," Lisa said. Dennis had called from the office to say he had to run some errands and then he was going to stop by Gordon's and help him with the pipe in the cellar. *Pipe?* he wondered as Lisa continued.

"I don't know about you two." She laughed. "I mean, at this point, why not just call a plumber? Or is this some macho trip you're both on? Some kind of plumbing bonding thing?"

He forced a weak laugh.

"I mean, after all—three nights in a row! Is somebody not getting the message here?"

Yes, you, he thought sadly.

"I'm only kidding, Gordon. Actually, I'm glad you're spending time together. Dennis just seems so much happier lately." She told him how glad she was he'd come to Jimmy's party and how great it was seeing Delores again. "She's such a wonderful woman. Oh, and I almost forgot. Father Hensile—he enjoyed meeting you, and he'd really like to get together with you sometime. He's a very nice person," she continued when he didn't say anything.

"He seemed to be."

"I think you'd enjoy his company."

"I'm just a little busy right now."

"What about this weekend? Saturday? We could—"

"No. I can't. I'll be doing yardwork. The roses—the leaves, they've got black spots on them."

It was Sunday. Gordon looked out the window again: raining and still no sign of clearing. Dennis would be here soon. Gordon had called him at home this morning and said he needed to talk to him. Lisa had called last night looking for Dennis. He had told her he'd be with Gordon most of the day. When it was almost dinnertime and she hadn't heard from Dennis, she'd called Gordon to say she and the kids were going to pick up pizzas at Lida's and they'd be right over with them. She'd asked Gordon what he liked—sausage, pepperoni, anchovies?

"Dennis isn't here," he told her.

"Oh, darn! It would have been fun. I wish I'd thought of it earlier. What time did he leave?"

"I'm not sure."

"I'm going to hang up. Maybe I can catch him on the car phone." She called back minutes later. "That's funny—he's not answering. But I'll keep trying, and if I do get him, I'll call you right back."

Her next call came two hours later. It was seven-thirty. She hadn't heard from Dennis and she was worried. She wanted to know exactly when he'd left there. Gordon said he didn't know. Wasn't sure. Couldn't remember. There was a pause. "You're lying to me," she said. "He hasn't been there at all today, has he?"

"I—"

"Tell me. Tell me the truth, Gordon. Has Dennis been there today? Has he?"

"I don't know what to say."

"Lie to me. Tell me he's been with you all day. Since early this morning. Tell me he's there right now and he's in the middle of something and he just can't come to the phone right now. That's all you have to tell me. That's all I need to hear."

He couldn't tell if she was laughing or crying.

"That's how ridiculous this is. How pathetic I am."

"Don't cry. Please don't cry, Lisa. He'll be home soon. Something probably happened, that's all," he said, though he doubted she could hear him, she was crying so hard.

Even with the wipers on high, rain blurred the windshield. Dennis floored the accelerator. He drove at the same furious speed of his thoughts. Lisa didn't believe that he had run into an old classmate yesterday and they'd gone into Boston for a few drinks and ended up meeting Charlie's cousin in some bar, where they watched the Sox-Yankees game on television. *Charlie who?*

Ross.

From where? she had demanded.

Dental school, he had said, annoyed to be caught, annoyed to be doubted when it had always been his right to be believed, annoyed that she not only insisted he give her details, but annoyed that she would write them down, as what? Proof, evidence, of what? That he didn't love his family, that he wasn't doing the best he possibly could under the circumstances, and now Jilly said he had to choose, her or them, which of course was no choice at all, even though he didn't want to lose Jilly, couldn't bear the thought of her leaving him, but his family was the most important part of his life, as well as the most complicating. There wasn't anything on earth he wouldn't do for them. It was the pressure he couldn't take, the constant pressure of always having to be more for everyone. Nothing was ever good enough. Lisa had known what he was all about when she married him. He'd never made any bones about who he was. She was the one who'd changed. What did she expect, with all her sweet piety and constant optimism? It was like living with a goddamn nun on Prozac. He was sick of always being told to look on the bright side and love his fellow man. He was sick of trying to understand people's fears and forgive them their shortcomings. How could she call him selfish when he'd spent his whole life doing for others, making up for his family's shame, his brother's misery? And here he was, still at it, still being sucked into the miasma of weakness and ineptitude that was Gordon's life. That's the part she didn't get. And never had.

Brakes squealing, he pulled up in front of the house. He hit the front door with his wet fist, banging, banging, banging harder, harder. "Open the door! Open the door! Open the goddamn door, you—"

"You're all wet," Gordon said in all his volitionless inertia, not letting him in, continuing to hold the door ajar, standing there in his tight gray pajamas, the sleeves skimpy, the cloth dull as his eyes.

He pushed his way inside, wanting to tell his brother how he'd gone through this once and he wasn't going to go through it again, having his life turned upside down and everything he cared about threatened and compromised. He had known this wouldn't work. What had he been thinking? He should have just sold this place a long time ago and forced his brother to go his own way, instead of always thinking he had to be the one to pick up all the pieces and put everything back together, because that's the way it had always been, because that's all he knew how to do, it seemed, anymore.

"What is it? What's wrong?" Gordon asked.

He sank onto the couch, for a moment bewildered that he had not said it and could not, because the wound that was his heart continued pumping its spasm of bloodred heat in his chest while his eyes tried to adjust to the dimness of this shabby room.

"Can I get you something to drink? A glass of water? A beer? I have one. I keep it there." He pointed toward the kitchen. "For you. It's cold. It's in the refrigerator. I can go get it."

Dennis laughed. He couldn't help it. "What do you do here? What do you do when you come home?"

"I read. I watch television. Sometimes. If there's something good on."

"Tell me something. Am I the only one who ever comes here?"

"No," Gordon said, blinking.

"Is that where you sit?" He pointed to the chair in the corner. "It is, isn't it. That way you can see the street and the TV all at the same time." He chuckled. "Gordon's window on the world, huh?"

"Don't be mad at me, Dennis. I didn't do anything."

"But I did, right?"

"I didn't say that."

"You know all those letters you got? All the family news, the stupid jokes, the newspaper clippings? Well, did you ever wonder what was really going on here? Or did you think it was all the same?"

"I knew it was hard. How hurt you all were." Gordon stared down at the floor, head bobbing faintly up and down in that maddeningly goofy way that made him look so stupid and inept. "I know what it did to everyone."

"I don't mean that! You're still so caught up in self-pity you think everything's about you, don't you? Poor Gordon, nothing ever goes right for him, does it? Well, guess what, poor Gordon, while you were licking your wounds, *I* was the one alone here. Because of you *I* didn't have a father or mother anymore. From that point on it was all up to me. Me! They expected *me* to make everything right."

"I'm sorry, Dennis."

"You're sorry? Well, what the hell good is that?" he exploded, fists so tightly clenched that the nails gouged his palms.

"What do you want? What do you want me to say?" came the slow, dead voice.

"Nothing." Dennis had forgotten just how obtusely cold his brother could be.

"The truth is, I didn't really think of what it did to you so much as what it did to Mom and Dad. You always seemed so lucky, I guess, so on top of everything all the time."

A chill passed through Dennis and with it deflation, a sense of his own diminishment. He looked away. He didn't want to hear this. He didn't want to be having this conversation. What did he want, then? He didn't know, didn't even know why he'd come. Gordon droned on. Hearing Lisa's name, Dennis looked up.

"She sounded so sad. I didn't know what to say."

"What the fuck're you talking about?"

Gordon's face flushed. His chin quivered miserably. "You shouldn't . . . you shouldn't do that to her."

"You don't know what the hell you're talking about." He stood up to leave and, seeing the two hideously wide white sneakers side by side at the bottom of the stairs, facing the door, waiting, wondered why, for what? For the same thing he had been waiting these twenty-five years? For nothing, he realized, for absolutely nothing, if it meant eating and sleeping, then waking again to discontent, this sense of il-limitable loss. His brother was here, so what was this yearning for? It was supposed to be over now.

"You're married, Dennis. You should be faithful to your wife."

Dennis spun around. "Look, there's only one way this is going to work. You want to come back here and live like this, fine. But *my* family is *my* business, not yours. You got that, Gordo?"

They stared at each other until Gordon looked away. Dennis started to open the door.

"They're my family, too," Gordon said under his breath.

It usually took only a few swings to get the right momentum, but some of the trash bags felt like dead weight. Two crates of rotting cantaloupes had come in, and the supplier said to throw them out. Another shipment was on its way. Gordon grabbed the bag with both hands, ready to heave it, when he heard a loud clang inside the swill-streaked Dumpster. He froze, listening. Too loud to be a squirrel or a rat. Something heavier, big, like a raccoon, maybe. Or a skunk. He stepped back.

"Fuck!" came a thin voice from inside.

He put down the bag and peered in, unable to see much over the piled trash. He jumped back as a crushed box of doughnuts flew past his head. He walked to the end of the Dumpster where a loaf of flattened bread and a deeply dented can of pineapple chunks lay on the ground among glinting splinters and rusted shards, the man-made till from years of trash haulings.

"Fuck!" There was a painful groan.

"Who's that? Who's in there?" For a moment there wasn't another sound other than flies buzzing and, from the lone spindly tree beyond, the high-pitched, scolding chatter of a squirrel whose larder was being pilfered.

"I said, who's in there?"

Still no reply. Up on the loading dock, the metal door creaked open, then banged shut. Neil was dragging out another stack of cartons to flatten and pile against the building. Seeing Gordon's guarded stance, he hurried over. Gordon gestured to indicate someone was in there. Neil nodded, then disappeared for a moment under the loading dock. He returned dragging a long, rusted section of drainpipe. He began to pummel the trash in the Dumpster with it, all the while cackling, "Come on out, you beggar! You fucking beggar, you!"

A head popped up on the opposite end of the Dumpster, then came arms and a torso in a roll over the side, with Neil sprinting close behind. "Mother o' God, look at this," he said, pulling the girl from the straggle of paper-blown bushes. "Look what was in there, the very bottom of the food chain."

The long cut on her left arm was bleeding down her fingers onto her pants.

"Jada!" Gordon said. Her wild hair was snagged with bits of trash and what at first appeared to be torn flesh, until, seeing seeds, he realized it was the slimy skin of a rotten tomato.

"Tell him to let go-a me!" she snarled through clenched teeth.

"Tell her to shut up!" Breathless as a cat with prey, Neil grinned, eyes gleaming with the pure, high-octane thrill of her pain. "Nice, huh?" He pointed at her. "Nice country we live in."

Every time she tried to pull away, he yanked her back, laughing.

"What hole did you crawl out of?" he said.

"Fuck you!" she shot back.

"Or maybe you live in there with the rest of the maggots."

"She's my neighbor. I know her. She lives across the street from me," Gordon said.

"I wouldn't admit that to too many people if I was you, Gloom."

"Tell the asshole to let me go!" Jada shouted.

"I don't think she was doing anything wrong, Neil. See." He showed him the box of broken doughnuts. "She was probably just looking for food."

"Food? Jesus Christ, what planet are you from? She was out here trashing cars, and then she needed a place to hide."

"But there aren't any cars out here now," Gordon said.

"Yeah, because she trashes them all!" Neil cried. "Come on!" He jerked her arm, pulling her up the steps onto the loading dock. "I'm calling the cops. We'll let them figure out what to do with trash like this." He opened the door.

"Okay! Okay, you do that and I'll tell them you were tryna get me to do something on you and that's how I got cut—tryna get away from you, you creep, you pervert, you fucking molester, you. Help! Help!" she screamed. "A man's tryna molest me! Help! Somebody help me, please!"

Leo charged through the doorway, bloodied cleaver in hand.

Neil released her arm, and all at once in a long, feral streak, the girl sprang from the platform, disappearing into the verge of weedy trees behind the Dumpster. Leo stared in horror at Neil.

Jada had been avoiding Gordon. That same night he'd come to her door, rung the bell, knocked hesitantly, then hurried away. She hadn't seen him since. It was midafternoon, and she was hungry again as she walked home from school. Her stomach ached all the time now. Even when she'd be eating, it would feel empty because she'd start wondering where or when she'd eat again. She wasn't sure what day today was. Not Friday, she hoped, because the weekend meant no hot lunch, the one thing she looked forward to, her main reason for going to school. Today she had slipped an extra slice of pizza onto her tray to take home to Leonardo, but the bitchy aide made her put it back.

As she came by the drugstore, she looked to see who was working. *Please, not the Indian guy with the turban and eyes like periscopes.* He could see around corners. He had almost caught her with her hand in the box the other day.

"Yes!" The girl in the cape was behind the register, the one who told everyone she was a witch. She bent over the counter, too busy polishing long black fingernails to even notice the tiny Cambodian woman's struggle to push her baby stroller in through the theft detectors. Jada held the door for the woman, then hurried to the back aisle where the few food shelves were. She reached behind the cookie display for the box she had opened last time. She stuffed a handful of Oreos into her pocket, then meandered over to the magazine display. She flipped through *Cosmopolitan* while the woman came down the aisle, balancing a jumbo package of diapers on top of the stroller. When the woman got to the register, Jada went back, filled her other pocket with the rest of the cookies, then shoved the empty box behind the others. "That's a very pretty baby you got there," she said on her way outside.

"Sank you!" the woman called after her.

"No, sank *you*," Jada said, laughing to herself.

She ate half the cookies before she got home. She wet her fingers, stuck them in her pocket, then licked off the crumbs. The other half were for Leonardo. Last night, Inez had made her a peanut-butter-and-jelly sandwich, which she'd tried to eat in the bathroom until

Leonardo's whimpering snuffles along the door bottom had made her feel so guilty that she'd given him the crusts. She had told Inez that her mother was going to be late, so could she have something to eat just to tide her over. Jada could tell Inez didn't believe her, but the lie was easier between them.

Jada wasn't sure anymore how long her mother had been gone. She had come home in the middle of the night with a scrawny guy with long hair called Tron. When Jada came out with her pillow and blanket so they could have the bed, her mother said no, to stay there, she and Tron were on their way somewhere, but they needed to get high first. His nose was running, and he reeked of cigarettes and sweat. "Hey, little pooch," he said, and Leonardo jumped into his lap and licked his neck as he cut a hole in the empty Mountain Dew bottle. He stuck a straw in so they could smoke. Her mother went first.

Jada had drifted in and out of sleep to their crack-agitated voices from the other room. It was almost funny, the way they could talk to each other at the same time. Tron said he had been on the detox waiting list in Lowell for a long time. A hell of a long time. He should let her know when he got the call, Marvella said. She'd been through it, so she'd help him. She knew the drill. She'd been there, so let her know and she'd go with him. Moral support, that was the most important part. Yeah, moral support. Because, see, like that's what she never got. Moral support. Yeah, that's all anyone needs. So as much as Jada hated being alone, it would all be worth it if her mother was in some detox center right now with Tron.

The minute she got home she jumped onto the couch and fed Leonardo the Oreos, one at a time. When they were gone he burrowed his snout into her pocket, looking for more. She closed her eyes, laughing as his scratchy tongue licked her face. "I love you. I love you so much," she said, holding him still so she could kiss her favorite place, the warm, musky underside of his silky ear. Everything would be different this time when her mother came home. Jada vowed to treat her better. She wouldn't bitch so much about everything, and she'd keep the apartment so clean her mother wouldn't want to ever leave it, and she'd study hard and get really good grades, so then her mother would probably start going to all those parents' nights things they were always having and she would come back and tell Jada how proud she was to have her for a daughter, and all the mean things she'd ever said, like calling her "the abortion that lived" all the time, how it hadn't been her talking but the drugs, because her Jada was the most beautiful girl in the whole world.

A loud banging made her sit up with a start. It was after five and she had fallen asleep watching television. Afraid Ronnie Feaster was back, pounding on the door again, she crept to the window and peered over the sill. Inez's son's old car idled at the curb, music booming from the speakers. In the distance came Gordon Loomis lumbering down the street with two full grocery bags. She didn't dare go out. Ronnie Feaster and Polie had come by twice in the last hour. The last time, he said he was sick of waiting for the money Marvella owed him. Jada hollered out that her mother wasn't there, but he didn't believe her. He said to open the door before he kicked it in. Inez leaned out her window then and yelled at him to go away or else she'd call the cops. After he left, Inez came downstairs and asked where her mother was. "Asleep," Jada lied, adding that she'd been sick for a few days. The whole thing was tricky: Jada had to be careful. She was pretty sure it was Inez who'd called Social Services the last time.

When he got to his porch steps she opened the door and ran across the street. "Gordon! You mad at me?" she asked with a big grin. She could tell he was.

"No." Even though his eyes held steady, his face, as usual, revealed nothing.

"I'm sorry for all that, but that guy, your boss, he, like, went psycho on me, and what was I gonna do, just, like, 'Oh, okay, here I am—have me arrested for looking through your friggin' garbage'? That's all I was doing. You saw me, right? What was I doing? Was I doing something wrong?"

"The Dumpster's private property. You shouldn't have been in it. Plus it's filthy. What if there was a rat in there or something?"

"What do you think, I'm scared of rats?"

"You should be, climbing into a Dumpster. They could bite you."

She laughed. "I was looking for a bone, that's all. A friggin' bone for Leonardo."

"How's the cut? I hope you put something on it. Ointment or something."

"Oh yeah, that." She lifted her sleeve and licked the scab. "See? That's all you have to do. It's like some kind of natural, antigerm juice in your mouth. Hey, you got anything good in there?" Something smelled good. She sniffed at the bags. Apples. Or maybe bananas. Her stomach was getting that weak, wavy feeling again. And the worst of it was, once she ate anything it would only feel even emptier right after, but she couldn't help herself. He held his bags close, as if he were sure she was going to grab something. Spooky guy, all he wanted was to do his own thing, same as her. She wasn't afraid of him like most people were. When he was out in his yard, Inez wouldn't leave her apartment, and the old lady, Mrs. Jukas, would move from window to window the way she was now, peeking out at him. Last week, when Polie tried to pull her inside the SUV, she told him Gordon was watching out his window. Then, to make it even better, she said Gordon told her to let him know if anyone tried to mess with her. Polie made some dirty remark about her and Gordon, but he'd let her go real fast.

"Here." He handed her a peach. "They're small, but they're really ripe. They're sweet."

She ate it so fast, it had no taste. She moved the pit around in her mouth, sucking on it as if it were hard candy.

"You're hungry, aren't you."

"Well, yeah! I mean, it's suppertime, right?" She took out the pit and nibbled off the stringy bits caught in the grooves, then stopped when she saw how he was looking at her. As if she were disgusting him. She put the pit into her pocket.

"How's school?"

"It's school." She shrugged.

"Do you get good grades?"

She just laughed.

"School's important, you know that, right?"

"Did you like school?"

"I tried to." He seemed to be struggling with a thought.

"But there were too many assholes around, right?"

He laughed. "I guess so. Something like that. But I did like it when I was older. I got a lot more out of it then."

"I had this one teacher, Mr. Cesster, once he gave me all these books to read. And I'd try, but it was like, *Little House on the Prairie*! Give me a break, will ya? I mean, stuff like that—I can't get worked up because little Laura forgot to lock the gate and the friggin' goat gets out. I'm like, yeah? There's a lot worse things that can happen. How come nobody writes about those?"

"Well, maybe you should. Why don't you?"

"Yeah, right. Hey, can I have another one?" She tried to eat more slowly. This peach was so delicious it made her ache inside. "Hey, how's that friend of yours? That lady, the one that helped me with Leonardo." She wished she hadn't said anything about her mother being gone, but Delores had been cool about it.

"Delores?"

"Yeah, how's she doing?" She chewed each little piece.

"Good. She's doing good."

"I like her. She's a nice lady. And she really loves dogs, but where she lives she can't have one," she said between tiny bites. "She used to have a dog. When she was the same age as me, but then it bit one of her sisters, so she had to get rid of it. She said her father took it someplace and she cried for two whole weeks, and everyone kept getting mad at her and saying she felt badder about the stupid dog than she did her own sister. Which wasn't true because she loved her sister. What she really felt bad about was that it wasn't the dog's fault in a way." She held out her hands. "Because he was a dog! You know what I mean?"

"I remember that dog! Everyone was afraid of him." He smiled yet looked troubled.

"So what's the story? Are you and her going out?"

"We're just friends."

She didn't believe him. Not with the way Delores looked whenever she said his name. "Next time she comes over, will you let me know? I like talking to her." She dropped the second pit into her pocket.

Behind her a car door slammed. Gordon's eyes sank low again. Feaster was getting out of the SUV. Polie was at the wheel. Feaster called for her to come down off the porch. Just for a minute. He had to talk to her. No, she called back, enjoying his anger. She could hear him just fine from up here, she said.

"It's about your mother!" he shouted.

Thinking he'd seen her mother, she hurried down.

"Look," he growled, his unshaven face at hers. "You better tell me where she is."

"She went out. I don't know where."

"Don't tell me that. I don't wanna hear it."

"You just did." She shrugged, then started off in the cockiest strut her shaky legs could manage.

"Little bitch." He spun her around. "You think it's funny?" His fingers were almost cracking her arm in two, but she wouldn't cry. "Here!" he snarled, squeezing harder. "Here! Go ahead, laugh some more."

She did. She threw back her head and laughed. As loud as she could, even though he was just about breaking her arm, the bastard.

"Let go of her," Gordon said, and Feaster tightened his grip. "I said, let go of her."

"Fuck off! You just fuck off!" Feaster warned Gordon, who was on the top step, still clutching his bags. "This has nothing to do with you! This is business! This is *my* fucking *business*, you hear me?" He hissed in her face now. "You hear what I'm saying? You better tell me where she went or I'll cut her name all over that monkey face of yours."

She sucked in deep, then spat right into his face. The back of his hand hit her with such board-blunt force that her teeth clamped onto her tongue and her eyes rolled to the back of her head, the men only purplish shapes in the yellow glare, their dark voices too low to grasp as she staggered into the thorns. Blood trickled down her chin.

You hit her!

Get the fuck out of my way!

She's a kid!

Move, I said . . .

She's just a little kid!

Hasn't stopped you, though, has it?

It was the middle of the night. She got up again to see what the noise was. This time she curled up on the couch and stared at the window. Someone was out there. She heard footsteps, then a scraping like something being dragged across the sidewalk. She crawled to the window, nose against the sill. No one was out there. The few parked cars were empty. Maybe it was an animal, a raccoon or skunk dragging garbage around. Yeah, that must be it. But then why wasn't Leonardo barking instead of sound asleep still on the bed? A truck was coming down the street. The Navigator. Polie was in it alone. He parked near the corner, then got out and came quickly along the sidewalk, carrying something by his side. She ran into the bedroom, opened the window, then grabbed Leonardo and slid down the pitched shed roof. Holding his snout so he wouldn't bark, she edged along the side of the house. Above her on the porch, Polie grunted as he tried to pry open the door with a crowbar. She sprang across the street, down Gordon's driveway, and onto his back porch. There wasn't any bell. She tried to turn the knob, but the door was locked. The second-floor window was open. She picked up a small rock and tossed it at the screen, but it hit the side of the house. "Gordon! Hey, Gordon!" she whispered, and threw another one.

"What're you doing down there?" He peered from the dark window.

"Shh," she whispered, struggling to keep Leonardo quiet.

"What do you want?"

"Polie's tryna break in my house."

He opened the back door. She followed him into the dark living room, where they watched Polie through the window. Now he was trying to pry open the window. Gordon asked if her mother was in there. She said no.

"Do you want to call the police?" he asked.

"Jesus, no! Then he'd really kill me."

"What do you want to do, then?"

"Stay here. Just till morning," she added quickly. "Then me and Leonardo, we'll go home."

"No! You can't stay here!"

"Please, please," she begged.

"Why? What does he want? Why's he doing this?"

"It's Feaster. He says my mother owes him money and he wants it back."

"Look," Gordon said.

The front door opened and Inez's husband came out with his son, Carlos, the burly truck driver. The two men shouted at Polie. He yelled back, then hurried toward the Navigator. Lights had come on in the adjacent houses. The men watched until he drove off.

"This was my brother's bedroom." Gordon turned on the light. It was a small, perfect room with a bed, bureau, desk, and chair. The walls were the same beige as the curtains and bedspread. As he closed the door, she thanked him again, then curled up in the clean sheets and pulled Leonardo close.

She lay awake for a long time until she heard snoring; then, taking Leonardo with her, she tiptoed down the stairs to the kitchen. She opened the refrigerator. She had never seen so much food, most of it leftovers, a few string beans, half a chicken wing, a scoop of mashed potatoes. She stood in the glare of the open door and ate from the bowls, a little bit of everything. She tried to reseal all the plastic wrap. She was thirsty, but if she used a glass, then he'd know she'd been down here snooping around, so she drank the milk right out of the bottle. She crept back upstairs, into bed. Leonardo lay with his back to her, sound asleep. She struggled to stay awake. If she fell asleep, then it would be morning and she would have to leave this clean, quiet place. She didn't know how much longer she could last on her own. A few more days, maybe. The last time she'd been in foster care, her mother's rehab had taken five months. Pretty soon she'd have to be running crack full-time for Feaster. And one of these times Polie was going to get the thing he really wanted. Maybe she should just close her eyes, hold her breath, and let him, pig that he was. "Do you love me?" she whispered, and Leonardo squealed a little in his sleep. The wind stirred the leaves at the window. Hearing a creak, she sat up and listened. Was it a door? No, probably a branch in that old tree. No matter what was out there, she was safe in here.

If only Gordon would let her stay. She wouldn't be any trouble. She'd clean the house, and every night when he came home from work she'd have his supper ready. On weekends they'd cook out on the grill, then maybe go to a movie after, and people would say, Well, will you look at that Jada Fossum—she's certainly taking good care of that poor Gordon guy. . . .

All she could see from the doorway was a mountainous white sheet. She tiptoed to the side of the bed. He slept with the pillow over his head like she did. She lifted the sheet and slipped in, inching closer until the heat of his body met hers. He groaned, then muttered something and turned. His ragged breath blew on her neck. She curled into the hollow of his long torso. He muttered again and she froze, then smiled when he sighed against the back of her head. She lay perfectly still while he huddled closer, pulling his legs up under hers. "What do they want?" he groaned softly. She felt him stiffen against her thighs. She reached back to touch him, and his hand clamped over her belly. He moved, then sat up so suddenly that he almost knocked her off the narrow bed.

"What? What're you doing? What're you doing in here?"

"I got scared."

"Get out! Get out of here!" he shouted.

"I heard a noise and I got scared."

"Get out of here! You get out of here right now! Just leave! Leave! Will you please leave!"

"I'm sorry. Don't be mad. Please don't," she begged, but he continued to demand that she leave as he stood in the corner, clutching the sheet around him. Leonardo charged in, barking at him. "I'll go downstairs," she said, picking up the dog. "I'll wait there. On the couch. Just till morning. Please?"

Thick, milky clouds massed in the dawn sky. There was a damp, stony chill in the room. Maybe it had been a dream, but he knew it hadn't been. He sat on the edge of the bed, afraid to go downstairs and find her here. He stared down at his hands. A girl, a child. He felt empty inside and numb.

CHAPTER 14

T he priest was still talking about his family. He had been the youngest of six brothers. Before her marriage his mother had been a Broadway dancer. A real hoofer, he said, and laughed, recalling her annual performance in the parish musical. "The sweetest little lady, but the minute the spotlight came on—oh boy, talk about Ethel Merman."

"Really?" Gordon murmured again. *What's the point? Why is he here?* Now Father Hensile was telling him his own vocational call had come as a seventeen-year-old lifeguard at Salisbury Beach when he had rescued a woman from a riptide. It was in that ferocious struggle to get her back to shore that he realized how much help we all need just to survive.

Of course: saving and taking a woman's life. I shouldn't have answered the door. Such terrible aimlessness, the priest was saying. *Need, such great need.* The need for youth activities. The parish was renting a gym for basketball and volleyball games. With enough donations they hoped to buy weights and a Nautilus machine. *So it's money he's after.* The smell of unwashed supper dishes hung in the air. All he wanted was to clean up the kitchen and watch television. And to be alone. He glanced toward the window and saw Jada Fossum crossing the street. His face flushed with shame. He had made her leave as soon as the sun came up this morning. *No, don't come here. Not now.*

Father Hensile checked his watch. "I should be going. I don't want to be taking up your whole night here," he was saying when the bell rang.

"Can I come in? Just for a minute?" she asked through the half-open door.

"No. Someone's here. I've got company," he said in a low voice.

"I just want to explain, that's all."

"No, that's all right. You don't have to." He stepped outside and closed the door.

"But I want to. I was scared, that's all. I thought I heard a—"

"No! Go away! Just leave, will you?"

"But that's why. You're mad at me. . . ."

"No, I'm not mad."

"Then what are you? You sure look mad."

"I'm not mad. I'm not anything, but I have to go back inside. So will you leave? Please?"

Her eyes moved in shrewd assessment between him and the closed door. "You got a couple bucks I can borrow?"

He only had six dollars, a five and a one.

"Five's okay. I'll pay you back. I promise." She ran off down the street.

"That was my neighbor," he explained, coming back in. "She lives across the street. She's only thirteen."

"Actually, that's why I'm here," the priest said.

"What do you mean?" His voice trembled.

"The new youth center. I was hoping you could maybe give us a hand now and then. No set schedule or anything, I don't mean that. That's the beauty of this, it's all kind of free-form. Random. Just come by when you feel like it."

"No, I don't think so. I wouldn't be very good at it," he added because the priest continued to look at him.

"But there's nothing to be good at. All you'd have to do is be there."

"No. No, I can't."

"I could really use your help. I'm afraid I've gotten myself in pretty deep," the priest said with a wan smile.

"I'm sorry, but I can't."

"Can I ask why?" The hounding eyes held his.

"I'm sorry, Father. I don't mean to be rude, but I can't. I have a lot to do here. I'm very busy. I don't have a whole lot of free time. I'm usually pretty tired after work. And I . . . To tell you the truth, I prefer being alone. I need that now."

"Forgive me, then. I've overstayed my welcome." The priest started to get up.

"No. I meant generally. In everyday life. I mean, after . . . after all that time."

"Yes, of course." The priest hunched closer. "And you were so young. All those years, what a terrible price to pay for an accident."

"It wasn't an accident."

"It wasn't?" The priest didn't move. "But you didn't mean for it to happen."

"It doesn't really matter, does it?"

"A terrible price all the same," the priest said with all the dismissal of absolution.

He was stunned. *The only terrible price is that I'm here and she's not.*

"Well, after all this time I hope you've come to some sense of acceptance, Gordon," the priest said, obviously reading his shock. "I mean, how else do you live with something like that?"

You don't, he thought, looking straight into his eyes.

"It all has to be put into perspective. You have to understand that some things happen for which there is no earthly explanation. And that what you did or didn't do in a particular moment doesn't condemn you—forever," he added uneasily. "Not in the eyes of God, anyway."

Gordon sighed and looked away. This was the mission, to rescue the sinner from his sin. He could feel himself clinging to a crumbling window ledge while this priest tried to coax him back inside.

"Don't you think God has forgiven you?"

"To tell you the truth, Father, I don't think about it."

"Why not?"

"Because . . . because it's so irrelevant!" he said in exasperation, shocked by his disrespectful tone yet empowered by it.

"Why? Because you can't forgive yourself?"

"Because no matter what I think or say or do, she's gone, she and her baby," he blurted, as close to anger as he would allow himself.

Like so many others, it was the priest who needed to forgive him, the priest who needed to make sense of what he had done. "Because it's an emptiness that can never be filled. And it would be wrong for me to even try."

The priest had been shaking his head. "Do you think God wants you to suffer forever, to keep on punishing yourself like this?"

"He doesn't want anything from me." He would not speak the name.

"Of course He does!" The eager benevolence spread like warm honey. "You're here for a reason, Gordon. We all are."

"So in other words, everything's all really out of our control."

"No! No, not at all. What I'm saying is that we're born, we're human, we're here, and so it's up to us to find out why."

Now more than ever Gordon wanted this intrusive little man to leave. He disliked him intensely. Any further pretense seemed unnecessary. He stood up. "I'm very tired now. I need to wash the dishes."

It was long past midnight when the dog jumped off the bed, barking. Jada stumbled after him to the front door, then, still benumbed by sleep, stood staring at the turning knob.

"Ma!"

Her mother rushed past her into the bathroom. "Don't turn on the light," she said from the toilet.

"Where've you been, Ma? I've been here all alone."

"You should've called Uncle Bob. I told you to."

"No, you didn't. You said you'd be right back. That's all you said."

"Well, I don't have to tell you everything, do I? I mean, you should've known. You should've called him."

"The phone's shut off."

"You should've gone up and used Inez's."

"I didn't want her to know you were gone."

The toilet flushed, and Jada turned on the light. "Oh!" she gasped as her mother cringed from the glare. She was deeply tanned, but so skinny that her arms and legs were like sticks. Her hair was lighter and had been braided in cornrows. "You look so nice, Ma. Your hair, I like it like that. Who did it?" she said, following her into the bedroom. She sat cross-legged on the bed, holding Leonardo while her mother undressed in the dark.

"Some guy. I don't know, it's like this thing they do. They just come along the beach and they do it. Here, feel." Her mother held out a braid, but Jada didn't move. "They even put these little bead things in."

"You were at a beach?" She was wide awake but deeply tired. Her mother hadn't been in detox. She wasn't clean at all, just high on the curve between hits. Leonardo wiggled, straining toward her mother, but Jada wouldn't let go.

"There was so many different ones I don't even know where I was half the time. There's so many boats parked, you can't even see the water, they're all crowded in so close. And to get on the dock you just walk on the boats, one to the other." She lay down. "That's all you have to do." She yawned.

"You were on a boat?"

"Yacht's more like it. You should've seen it, baby, you wouldn'ta believed it," she said as she petted Leonardo, who'd burst from Jada's resentful grip. He sprawled on her mother's chest, squealing and trying to lick her face. Her mother clamped her hand around his snout. "They even have, like, their own private chef."

The window rattled and Jada sat up. "What's that?"

"Chef. It's a French word. It means a cook that cooks fancy food."

"Ma, Feaster wants his money. He said you did this big buy and then you took off."

"Why do you have to ruin everything all the time?" her mother groaned. "I should've just stayed there, that's what the hell I should've done. The only reason I came back is because of you, and now you won't even listen."

"I am, I'm listening, but—"

"You know what I ate every single night?"

"No, but Feaster's mad, Ma. I been really scared. Him and Polie both, they made me—"

"I said I don't want to talk about them. All right?" She paused, then shook Jada's arm, her voice girlish and cozy again. "Guess what I ate every single night?"

"I don't know." *There's this and then there's that, there's here and there, but never any connections. Except me,* Jada thought.

"Here's a clue—it's one of the most favorite things you like."

Jada shivered. Without Leonardo's warmth, she felt raw, as if a layer of skin had been stripped off.

"Come on, Jada! Every night I told everyone, I said the same thing, 'This is my kid's most favorite food in the whole world.' Oh, all right. Shrimp cocktail!"

"So what about Tron? Was he there, too?"

"Tron?" There was a pause. "Oh, no, he wasn't there."

"How come? Did he go in detox?"

"Huh?"

"He was gonna go in detox and you said you were, too."

"Tron's an asshole."

"He seemed nice to me."

"He's a crackhead, that's all he is, baby. . . ." Her mother's voice trailed off. "That's all he'll ever be." She was already snoring.

Jada reached for the dog, but he growled through the darkness. "Leonardo," she whispered, hurt.

"Jesus Christ," her mother whined, then snored again.

Jada covered her face with her hands, refusing to cry. She slipped out of bed and groped along the floor for her mother's purse. She opened it in the bathroom. Two twenties and a lot of ones. Three cellophane-wrapped rocks lay at the bottom of the purse among grains of sand, matches, hair clips, casino tokens, crimped roaches, and loose cigarettes. She held one rock over the toilet, smiling as she let it go. The minute it splashed she panicked. She scooped it out and wiped it on her shirt, then put it back.

She crept back into bed and drifted into fitful sleep, curled as close to Leonardo as she could get without waking her mother.

The next morning Jada sat on a stool in the Donut Shop, eating breakfast. She finished the onion bagel with cream cheese, then ordered a chocolate-covered jelly doughnut and another coffee. Reflected in the mirror behind the coffee urns were three boys coming down the street, Thurman and two buddies, Colt and Ray. She ran to the door. "Hey, Thurman! You guys want a doughnut or something? I'm paying," she yelled, waving the twenty. They scrambled in and sat at the counter, careful to leave an empty stool between themselves and her. They each ordered two doughnuts, which they wolfed down in silence. When they were done they jumped up and hurried outside.

"Wait!" she called, running to catch up. They ran even faster. "Wait up! You want a smoke? Hey! I got some Camels here."

The wind kept blowing out the match, so they went into the alley next to the drugstore and huddled over the flame. Thurman lit up first. Lighting hers last, she took a deep drag. As they continued walking, Thurman had them staggering with laughter. He was telling them about his crazy sister. She was always messing up her paper route, but nobody ever said much because she was the only one the newspaper could get to deliver, the neighborhood was so bad. If Thurman needed a few bucks, he'd go collect from some of her customers. Then when the time came she'd try to collect. Her customers would say they'd already paid, and she'd just get confused and think she'd forgotten to write it down.

"Who you talking about? Peggy Triker? She's your sister?" Jada said, walking faster to keep pace. Peggy weighed at least three hundred pounds and delivered the papers on a gigantic tricycle. "She's, like, grown-up. I mean, how can she be your sister, she's too—" Old, she was about to say as Thurman shoved her against a parked car.

"Careful, freak-face, or else I'll knock those crooked teeth right down your throat."

"Go ahead, try it," she grunted, laughing but mad as hell as she tried to knee him. His face was at hers. He butted his pelvis into hers. The two boys watched with ruttish glee.

"Hey! What're you doing? Leave her alone!" a man called.

Heedless, Thurman was just about breaking her wrists.

"Thurman! I said, leave her alone. Get off her!" Gordon's shadow fell over them. Eyes glazed, Thurman stepped back with a nervous giggle. Gordon glanced at her, then continued walking down the street.

"Wait! Wait a minute." She ran after him, but he only walked faster. "Don't be mad," she pleaded, running to catch up, then hurried alongside.

Gordon looked around in embarrassment.

"Please, please don't be mad . . . I told you . . . I told you what happened . . . I was scared. . . ." She grabbed his arm. "That's all. I wasn't tryna come on to you or anything."

Mouth agape, he stood there.

"I wasn't!"

"I have to go to work."

"Fuck you," she whispered as he rushed off. He'd had that same look as Uncle Bob, as if she hadn't fooled him at all and he knew what a hopeless piece of shit she was.

Ray waited, with his shirt wrapped around his hand. Thurman sliced the back-door screen with his knife. He unlocked the storm, then tapped the glass with the knife butt just enough to crack it. Ray punched in the glass the rest of the way, then reached inside and turned the latch. "When's he get home?" Ray asked as they ran into the kitchen and began looking for money, drugs, or booze. Thurman wasn't sure. He hadn't worked at the Market since the asshole got him fired.

Jada hadn't even tried to stop them. She was too high. Plus, it was Gordon's fault. The least he could have done was listen to her. She liked walking around up here like the lady of the house. Everything was so neat, his closets and drawers, the rows of stacked change on his dresser. She studied the picture on the nightstand, instantly disliking the two kids with their fake smiles and stupid pose, the girl sitting close in front of the boy.

Downstairs, cupboards and doors opened and then banged shut. The television came on. Colt and Ray kept calling out to Thurman. The sweet smell of weed drifted up the stairs. Thurman had bought some on the way here with the rest of her money. She sat on the bed and opened the nightstand drawer. Not much in here. A real estate–agency business card with a woman's picture: Jilly Cross, it said. A Bible. A Holy Roller, maybe that's why he was so spooked about the other night. It didn't look like it had ever been read, though. A couple of paperback books that also seemed new. A list of telephone numbers. In the back of the drawer were two folded magazine pages. She opened them and giggled. They were pictures of naked women, the creases worn in places to little holes. She felt a pang of jealousy. They were both blondes. At least Miss July had thick lips and long skinny legs like she did. Forget Miss May, though, with those supersize white boobs that weren't even all hers—she could tell. She stood sideways in front of the mirror with her hand on her butt like Miss May. She pulled her shirt tight behind her back. It was never going to happen. Not unless she got some of that silicone stuff someday. From downstairs came a crash, quickly followed by another. Then another. She dropped the pictures and ran down to the kitchen. Ray and Colt were emptying cupboards onto the floor.

"Stop it! Stop it!" she screamed from the doorway. "What're you doing?"

Ray paused to chug down the rest of the beer he'd found, then opened the narrow closet by the open cellar door and threw out mops, brooms, ironing board, more cans and boxes. Colt walked around the countertop to get to his beer. He finished it with a loud, convulsive belch then smashed the bottle in the sink. Thurman came up the cellar stairs. "Jesus Christ . . ." He laughed as he kicked his way through the shattered and tumbled debris.

"Make them stop!" she screamed, but Thurman brushed past her into the living room.

"That's all the fuck there is?" He pointed to the VCR on the floor by the front door. "How 'bout up here?" he said, taking the stairs two at a time.

Ray and Colt charged out of the kitchen after him.

Footsteps overhead. Swearing. Something fell with a heavy thud. They howled with laughter. She felt sick to her stomach.

"Look at her fuckin' tits," Ray shrieked.

"Cops! Cops!" She ran up the stairs. "They're coming!" she yelled from the doorway. "I just saw them."

The mattress was halfway off the bed. Thurman rolled over it and landed in the hallway. Colt and Ray stumbled down the stairs, out the back door.

She stood the chairs back up and righted the table, but the rest was hopeless. The floor was slick with jelly- and syrup-covered broken glass and oily salad dressing. All this wasted food. She rinsed her hands in the sink. Every nail had been bitten to the quick except for her pinkie finger. At least she had one. It was a start, anyway. From now on things would be different, she vowed as she ran out the back door. She made her way through a warren of little backyards until she came out on Green Street. She took her time walking home.

Her mother's head lifted slightly from the pillow as she crept into bed next to Leonardo.

"Where you been?"

"School."

"I need my pocketbook. Go get it."

"Why don't you wait, Ma? See how long you can go."

"Why?"

"Don't you even want to try? For me, Ma."

"Yeah, okay, I will, I'll try."

Jada buried her smile in Leonardo's warm neck.

Her mother sat up in a burst of dismal laughter. "There! Okay, I did it, I tried. Now go get the fucking pocketbook. Now!"

Delores had called asking if he could help her move some things on his way home from work. The stationery store would be closing for good this weekend. Gordon was on his way there now, but first he had to buy stamps.

Many of the signs downtown were in Spanish. The buildings he remembered most clearly were the huge granite banks. Mostly vacant now, they seemed smaller. The post office had been built when he was in high school, but the ensuing years had dulled it with the same grime and fatigue as all the other buildings. He hurried inside to the end of a long line. A few minutes later he realized these people were all waiting outside the door to the passport office. He went around the corner and bought eight stamps for his bills.

He was leaving the post office when a woman in a yellow suit and red sunglasses stepped in front of him.

"Oh! Gordon! I'm in such a rush I didn't realize it was you," Jilly Cross said with a quivering smile.

"I just bought some stamps." He watched his reflection in her sunglasses foolishly hold up the strip.

"I've got to get my passport renewed," she said, pulling her shoulder bag close.

"It's a long line. I was just in it. Well, by mistake, that is."

"I know. I should've come earlier. I've just been so busy lately. Running around like crazy." She glanced ahead to the door. "Trying to get ready for a trip. To Bermuda."

"You better go in, then. It's pretty long." His face felt hot. Hadn't he just told her that? Tiny beads of moisture dotted her cheeks. Could she tell how fast his heart was beating? He was short of breath.

"Yes, I better, but . . . well, how've you been?"

"Fine, thank you." He paused and then, when she didn't say anything, felt he had to keep talking. "I've been really enjoying this nice weather." Looking troubled, she stared up at him as if there were something she needed him to say. "After all this rain we've had. I mean, it's nice to get out, out in the sun. The roses are so . . . so beautiful."

She smiled and seemed relieved. "I know you're probably not interested, but the other day I got this great new listing and I thought of you immediately." She removed the sunglasses. "It's on the first floor with its own little . . . well, courtyard, I call it, but you could have plants out there. And just be able to sit outside when you want. Dennis is right, you know. Staying in Collerton just doesn't make any sense. There's so much crime and . . . he worries about you, Gordon."

He felt it building—this anger, this indignation, the need. She was so pretty, so sweet, and what she was doing was so wrong.

"It really bothers him. He's always—"

"You shouldn't be going out with my brother," he heard himself saying. "It's not right. He's got a wife, a very nice wife. And his children . . . I mean, he's a happily married man. A father. Doesn't that matter? Don't you care? Don't you think that's important?"

"Well, I . . . I . . ." She turned and then hurried, almost running, back toward the parking lot.

The front door was locked. Delores had already left. She must not have needed him. She had already left. He felt agitated, yet strangely, euphorically, relieved. He had finally done something, the words having come so swiftly and from so deep within that only energy surged through him, a sense of expansiveness, as if there were nothing he could not do right now. He knocked again, then through the door glass saw Delores hurry from the back room.

"I didn't think you were coming!" she said, letting him in. She wore black pants and a black sweatshirt. Her hair was pulled back from her face. Without makeup she looked younger, the way he remembered her in high school, freshly pleasant. "I was just starting to bring some things out to the car. The rest Albert can deal with." She gestured at the stacked boxes. "Most of it's all packed and marked." She sighed. "I don't know what else to do. I'm not calling him anymore, I know that. I keep leaving messages, but I guess this is the way he wants it." Covering her mouth, she seemed to take a deep breath. "Eleven years. It's hard to believe. Excuse me, Gordon, I'll be right back." She hurried into the office.

He waited a minute, then stepped into the storeroom. The bathroom door was closed. Water was running. She came out carrying a small round mirror framed in seashells. Her red eyes glistened. "I made this." She tried to smile.

"You did?"

She nodded. "I found all these shells. Me and my sister and her husband, we used to rent this cottage two weeks in July, and every morning early I'd go for these long walks with my nieces and we'd pick up shells, then on rainy days we'd make things."

"It's very nice."

"Here, then. You take it." She held it out.

"Oh no, I—"

"Please. Just take it. Please?" She looked ready to burst into tears if he didn't. He thanked her.

After they had put her possessions into the car, a rug and a small table and a few boxes, she locked the store, then jumped behind the wheel and backed quickly down the alley. "Boy, it's a good thing you're here," she said at the red light. "Because if you weren't, I'd pull right in there"—she pointed to the drugstore—"and buy a pack of cigarettes. That's what always happens, every time I quit the sky starts to fall, and next thing I know I'm lighting up."

"It's better than having to drink, though, right?"

She looked over and laughed. "I don't know. One kinda goes with the other when you're feeling like that."

He was surprised when she turned onto Clover Street. "Don't you want me to help you carry all this up to your apartment?"

She shook her head. "That's okay."

"I don't mind. In fact, that's what I thought we were going to do." He patted the musty rolled rug jutting out over the seat between them. "I mean, you can't carry this up all by yourself."

"I don't even want it. I don't want any of it. I just don't want to give *him* the satisfaction of throwing it all out." She pulled up in front of his house. "I'm sorry. I guess I'm not my usual sparkling self tonight." Her forced smile dissolved in weariness.

"That's okay. I understand. When you feel like this you just want to be alone, that's all."

"No. I hate being alone. I hate that more than anything. Sometimes I get scared and I think, What if I fall down and break my leg or pass out or something? No one would know. Or care, probably. Except the paperboy or the mailman." She tried to laugh, then quickly covered her face, struggling not to cry.

He didn't know where to look or what to say. Once again it was the wantonness of her emotions that most frightened him, her easy

intimacy a contagion requiring constant vigilance. His mind raced to
change the subject. Anything. "Oh. Yes, the mailman. That reminds
me," he said stiffly as she wheezed and snuffled into her hands. "I was
coming out of the post office and I saw that woman, the one with
Dennis. It was awkward. I mean, it was the first time since that night
at the Inn. And all of a sudden it just kind of came out of me. I certainly didn't plan to say what I did. And she was, well, dumbstruck, I
guess." The oddest thing happened as he spoke. He didn't want to be
telling her any of this, knew he shouldn't, yet he was relishing every
word, savoring the moment relived, in a way that made it all seem not
only quite right, but even better than he had realized.

"What do you mean?" She wiped her eyes. "Gordon." She
touched his arm. "You actually said that? You told her to stop seeing
your brother?"

"I had to. Dennis and Lisa, they're my family. I can't just stand by
and do nothing. It's not right. I mean, you'd do the same. You know
you would."

"No. No, I wouldn't do *that*."

"Yes, you would. You care for people. I've seen you. You speak
up. Like that time with Jada. You dropped everything. You came
right over."

"Because you sounded so nervous."

"Because you care for people," he said, straining toward her, wanting to help, to convince her of her own worth.

"Because I care for you."

He had an image of himself as a child walking out too far into the
pond and then suddenly having to tread water. And in his panic realizing that if he stopped for even a moment, it would be over. "And I
care very much about my brother. And his family. Lisa and Jimmy
and Annie."

Reaching over, she patted his hand. "Of course you do, Gordon.
And even if he does get mad, at least you know you did the right
thing. And that's really all that matters, isn't it?"

He nodded.

"And who knows, maybe it'll work. Maybe now she'll break it
off, that . . . that what's-her-name."

"Jilly," he said, sinking into the warmth that came from speaking her name.

Delores touched his arm, stroking it with her fingertips. "Yes, and then everything will be the way it should be." She brushed her lips against his cheek. For a moment his eyes felt much too heavy to open.

She followed him up the walk. She said she had to go to the bathroom. He didn't believe her, and the odd thing was he didn't really mind. For the first time in a long time, he didn't want to be alone.

The minute the door opened, the sharp smell of mustard stung his nostrils. Then vinegar. He kicked something. The VCR. Why was it on the floor? He turned on the light.

"My God." He looked toward the trashed kitchen, unable to comprehend what he was seeing.

"Those bastards," Delores muttered, stepping closer.

He looked at her. "Who?" She seemed to know what had happened here. He watched her pick up an unbroken saucer from the shards.

"Was there any money hidden in here?"

"No."

"That's why, then. They probably got mad."

"Who?"

"Kids, probably." She picked up an intact plate. Then a bowl. Another saucer. "Hopefully your insurance will cover it. You better call the police."

"No."

"But if you don't report it, then—"

"No. I don't want to."

"Well, you better look around, then. Check the other rooms."

He didn't move, though. He stood there surveying the incomprehensible.

"We should start cleaning this up." She stepped carefully through the mess. She righted the trash basket and began dropping large pieces of glass into it. It filled up quickly, and she removed the sagging bag, tied it, and set it out on the back landing. She shook out a new bag, which she began to fill. "Damn!" She sucked her thumb where glass had nicked it. She asked for a bandage. This snapped him from his paralysis. He hurried upstairs to get a bandage from the medicine cabinet. The phone was ringing. He hurried back down, but Delores had answered it. He was shocked to hear her glib invasion of his privacy. Had he come upon this alone, he would have told no one. No one at all. She had no idea how horrified he felt.

"It's absolutely unbelievable. . . . Yes, the whole kitchen. Everything. Even the fridge," she said, opening the door. The empty shelves were oddly dark. She peered in. "They even smashed the bulb. . . . No! I don't know, but I'm assuming it was more than one person. . . ." Listening now, she looked at Gordon. Her mouth dropped open. "Are you sure? Well, tell Gordon, then. He's right here. It's your neighbor, Mrs. Jukas." She handed him the phone.

The old woman's voice cackled in his ear. "I knew something was wrong. I could tell just by the way she was running. Like a bat out of hell, right down your back steps over into McGinty's. I should've called the police, but she's been over there before. You've even let her in your house! So I didn't know, I thought, What's he doing, just turning the place over to her any time she wants."

She was still talking as he handed the phone to Delores. He found the broom and began pushing glass-splintered pickles and glittering chunks of meat loaf into the dustpan.

Delores was telling the old woman she was sure it hadn't been Jada; her running through the yard was probably just a coincidence. He knew it wasn't. Of course it had been Jada. She was paying him back for the other night.

Chocolate syrup and tomato juice sloshed underfoot. Delores had cleared enough of a space to open the back door. The soft chirp of crickets through the twilight was obliterated with each glass–rattling sweep of the broom.

"We're getting there," she said.

He looked at her.

"Gordon. It wasn't Jada. She adores you. In a million years she wouldn't do something like this," she said, shoveling two hundred paper napkins into a sodden mound. "If she wanted something, she'd ask you." She leaned the broom against the table. "Oh, Gordon!" She threw her arms around him. "I feel so bad for you. Here you are just getting started, then something like this has to happen."

CHAPTER 15

Mosquitoes kept buzzing at her ears. If there were any crickets, the other night sounds drowned them out—a far-off burglar alarm, sonic bursts of music from car radios, the intermittent cries of a woman for "Melio! Melio!"—all to the beat of a dribbled basketball, the gritty scrape of running sneakers, then with every *clung* of the rim a scuffle of male voices. "Get that shit outta my house!" one laughed now.

"Yeah. Get that shit outta my house," Jada whispered in echo, the dull incantation steadying her in the darkness of the bandstand steps. Her uneasy eyes scanned the street. The Navigator was parked by the Liberty Rooming House. It looked empty, but Polie said he'd be watching. The bites on the back of her neck stung as she scratched them with the rough edge of the beeper. Knees to her chin, she tugged her shirt over her knees and ankles to keep the bugs away. She hadn't been to school in a couple weeks. Not since her mother had been back. Vacation must have started, though. They'd probably keep her back again. If they did, she'd just quit and get a job. She'd be fourteen pretty soon. July 24, which shouldn't be too far off from whatever the hell day or month this was. Like her mother would even remember. Like anyone would. "So fuck it," she said aloud, then laughed, said it again.

She'd seen Gordon from a distance, going back and forth to work, or mowing his grass, or bringing groceries to Mrs. Jukas. Last night Delores's car had been out there until midnight and Jada felt really jealous, then confused because she didn't know who she hated more, Delores for being with Gordon, or Gordon for being with Delores, or both of them for not being with her. She gnawed the side of her thumbnail until she tasted blood. She sat on her hands and waited.

A low red car slowed down. She stood up. She couldn't see if it was the Toyota Spider or not. No beep from Polie. The car passed, so she sat down. Her hand closed over the bulge on her belly, the bag of rocks in her shorts. This deal was huge. She was supposed to count it first, twenty hundreds, before she passed the bag. Beep, Polie had said, then head straight back. Any trouble, just keep on going right by the Navigator. Stuff the money down her underpants and run like hell.

Polie and Feaster had bought her a Big Mac and a large Chicken McNuggets on the way here, but her stomach was rumbling again. She was hungry all the time now. Eating only made it worse. Maybe Polie would get her a Coke or something. Water, even. She jogged along the path up the rise to the SUV.

"Jesus Christ! That's them!" Polie shouted as a red sports car stopped on the far side of the park. She ran back and sat on the bottom step.

Their headlights went off. She slapped her leg, and the mosquito flattened in a sticky mess. "C'mon! C'mon!" She ground her knuckles against the concrete step. Maybe they couldn't see her. She stood up with her hands on her hips to make as big a target of herself as possible. One of these times something bad was going to happen. She was getting in too deep, but her mother owed Feaster all that money from before plus for the crack she needed now, and that wasn't even counting anything for food or rent. Yesterday the electricity got turned off, but her mother called from a pay phone, crying and saying she had a new baby in the house. It came back on this morning. The sheriff had come by twice already with eviction notices, but they wouldn't let him in.

Both car doors opened. A runty guy in a shiny black shirt started down the path. Arms folded, the other guy leaned against the car, watching. Halfway along, the runty guy called out and asked if she had something for him. She said she did.

"Bring it here, then."

"First you gotta give me something." She came off the path a few feet, then stopped.

"C'mere, then." He gestured her closer. "Here. You gonna take it?" He held out a brown paper bag.

She grabbed the bag. It wasn't supposed to be taped up. "Stupid ass," she muttered, ripping it open. She counted quickly: twenty hundreds. Well, twenty bills; it was hard to tell what they were. She tried to see.

"C'mon! Hurry up!" He kept looking around. "C'mon!"

She pulled the bag from her shorts. The white guy hurried down the path. The Navigator was gone. Polie had taken off. Something was wrong.

"C'mon, give it over! I ain't got all day!" The runty guy stepped closer. The other guy had a beard and his hair was longer. Fuck! It was the cop who'd chased her and Thurman on their last deal together. His arm went out. Thinking he had a gun, she threw the bag and the beeper in his face and ran toward the Liberty. They were close on her heels now. Cars came at her from both directions as she ran into the street. Men yelling.

"Stop, you little asshole! Stop! Police! Stop! Police! Police!"

Holy shit! She had their money. Horns blared. A car braked onto the sidewalk. She opened her fist and flung the money up into the air before darting down the alley behind the Liberty. She ran and she ran, all the way to Gordon's garage. Hours later, when no one had come, she ran home and fell onto the couch, exhausted and still shaking.

CHAPTER 16

The still morning air was soft with the fragrance of roses. Gordon was spraying the bushes with his baking soda elixir when he saw a long broken cane on Mrs. Jukas's side. It had been split at the base. Last night Delores had brought a slice of cherry pie over to Mrs. Jukas. Instead of using the walk, Delores must have blundered her way between the bushes. *Typical,* he thought as he pruned off the perfectly healthy cane. In her slavish need to please, she did more harm than good, he thought, then immediately flushed with guilt and desire for her.

Delores was the first woman he had ever slept with. The experience continued to be both profound and disconcerting. Though he wasn't naive enough to think he was her first partner, he was sure there hadn't been many others. She just didn't seem the type. The sexual aspect of their relationship was far more exhilarating than anything he had ever imagined. He had never felt so much a part of another human being, so vulnerable and yet so strong. But the moment it ended he would be overcome with desolation. She would curve her body to his, wanting to be held, wanting to talk, when all he wanted was for her to leave so he could be alone. As soon as she got home she would call, and he would force himself to answer the phone. She deserved the same unfailing kindness and tenderness she gave, but it just wasn't in him. Maybe it never had been. Maybe he had achieved nothing and this was all a charade, everything, everything about him. Maybe he would always be a shadow trailing truer, more substantial lives than his. Emotional intimacy came easier for women, Delores had said last night in another attempt to get inside his head. He couldn't tell her how that kind of talk frightened him, left him feeling shallow and inadequate, wondering which realization was worse: that he had nothing to give or that there was nothing he wanted or needed from her. Or from anyone else, for that matter.

When he stirred now in the depths of night, it was Jilly Cross's sweet face he saw in his dreams, and this was deeply disturbing. He would wake up feeling like a hypocrite, unprincipled, corrupt. In his prison fantasies he had struggled to be faithful to the same centerfold women. When he did have to replace one, it was always with guilt and self-loathing. Paper-worn but ageless, his women never parted their legs for the camera's ugly eye or touched themselves or stared out with brazen seduction. Instead they gazed off shyly, bodies turned ever so slightly as if they had been just about to cover themselves when the shutter clicked.

He was finishing his cereal when the doorbell rang. He rinsed the bowl quickly and was on his way into the other room when the frantic banging started. Ever more cautious since Jada's night here, he checked the window. His brother's car was in the driveway.

"Dennis!" he said, opening the door.

Dennis rushed inside. "What the hell's wrong with you? Don't you ever think anything through?"

"What do you—"

"She's scared out of her mind! What're you doing, following her now? Stalking her?"

"I wasn't—"

"She just told me! She comes out of the post office and there you are? Warning her? Telling her to stay away from me?"

"I just told her . . . I said you were married, that's—"

"Like she didn't know that, right? Look," Dennis said, shaking his head in wordless fury. "I don't know how else to say this to you. But you can't be doing this. You can't keep fucking up my life! I can't handle it anymore. I mean, all these years I've been trying to put it all back together. You . . . you can't do this! If you want this to work, if you want us to have any kind of relationship, you've gotta stay way,

way out of my way, Gordon! Do you hear me? Do you know what I'm saying?" He threw up his hands. "Jesus Christ, are you even listening to me?"

"I just don't want anything to happen to you and Lisa. And the kids. You're my family."

"Nothing's going to happen. There's just some things you don't understand. Just because you want things a certain way . . . I mean, life's not like that—*I'm* not like that."

"What are you like, then?" Gordon asked, then coughed to clear his wheezy throat.

"I'm like you," Dennis said with a forced smile. "I make mistakes, but fundamentally, deep down, in here"—he pointed to his heart—"I'm a good, decent guy."

"Not if you can't be faithful to your wife, you're not."

The smile curdled. "You know, I could always see right through you. Same thing with Dad. He could never say what he really meant. He was always avoiding people, slinking around corners, trying to change one thing into something else. Like after you went away, no matter what I did, it was never enough. Nothing was going to make him happy. Nothing! No matter how hard I tried," Dennis spat. "He never said it—how could he?—but deep down he resented every lousy little bit of happiness Mom and I tried so hard to have. Somehow we became the bad ones—like we were the murderers!"

Gordon struggled not to flinch or blink. "I'm sorry."

"No! Just be honest—with yourself, at least. You're trying to scare Jilly away because *you* want her." Dennis glanced at his watch, then opened the door. "But that's not the way it works, big brother." He patted Gordon's arm and smiled. "Uh-uh, no sir, no way."

Dennis's words kept coming back. It had been years since Gordon had felt this angry with him. He'd always considered his brother not just his best friend, but his only friend. And all this time Dennis had resented him, his visits to Fortley made out of the same sense of duty that kept him married to Lisa.

The store stayed busy through the day. Neil's sour mood worsened when June called in sick. Gordon was relieved when Neil left at noon to play golf with his accountant. Serena always seemed to have at least three people lined up at her register. He tried to stay up front to help bag or run price checks, but a few times he had to hurry out back to receive a delivery. A brief lull came at five-thirty. Without June there, Serena had been surprisingly friendly all day. She was complaining about Neil again.

"Does he play golf much?" Gordon asked as he rolled up his sleeves. When the late-afternoon sun poured through the plate glass, the balky air-conditioning had little effect.

"He's not playing golf," Serena scoffed, putting on her red sunglasses. "He's in a bar somewhere. I can tell. I can always tell. Like his voice, the way it was so shaky, and when I said how he should just hire a new kid for the summer he couldn't even look me in the eye, he was so out of it."

"I think he's under a lot of pressure right now," Gordon said. Yesterday the produce wholesaler had called to say there would be no more deliveries until the bill was paid.

"Oh yeah? Well, welcome to the club, then, but you don't see me taking off at noon. Like tonight—when I get home I got eight people waiting for me. Eight mouths I gotta feed and clean up after."

"I'll help close. That way you can leave sooner."

"Oh, Jesus, not again!" Serena groaned as Cootie limped through the door carrying his rheumy-eyed dog.

"Neil here?" The old man winced with every step of his right foot. "He back yet?"

"No! I already told you, he's gone for the day. He's not coming back," Serena said, fanning herself against the stench.

"But he said to come, that he'd be here. This bum foot, it's hard, I can't keep coming back like this."

Gordon tried to hold his breath, but the smell was overpowering. The old man must have soiled himself days ago. There was no way Neil wanted him here.

"He'll be here in the morning," Gordon said.

"No! No, he told me, he gave me the time. I wrote it down. Here," he said, spilling the dog onto the counter so he could look in his pockets. The dog licked Gordon's wrist, then wiggled toward Serena, wagging a dry clump of feces with its tail.

"Pick him up! Get him offa there!" she cried. "He's filthy!"

"It's in here somewhere." Cootie was emptying his pockets onto the counter. "Neil wrote it down so I wouldn't forget." He opened various wads of paper, unable to find the right one. "He said two-thirty. Yeah, I know he did. One thing I never forget is time, tell me a time and I never forget. Okay, okay, here, here we go, I got it." He shook out the scrap, reading at arm's length. "Two-thirty! I told you!" He showed Gordon. "See?"

"Yes, but right now it's five forty-five," Gordon told him. "This says two-thirty A.M."

"It does? Well, what day is it, then?" Cootie asked.

"Thursday," Gordon said.

The old man looked about to cry. "Where'd Wednesday go? What the hell happened? Are you sure?"

"Yes, positive."

"I fucked up," the old man cried. "I missed it!"

"That's it," Serena declared. She locked her register and hurried toward the office. "You won't leave, so I'm calling the cops."

"No, no, no, no—we're going, we're going. See, here we go, c'mon now, little doggie, c'mon, we gotta figure out what we're gonna do," he muttered, scooping up the dog and limping toward the door.

After he was gone, Gordon picked up the paper the old man had dropped. "Halefield Dairy" was printed at the top. There was a Halefield Dairy pad in Neil's office, but why would he want the old man here at that time?

At six, it got busy again, with the steady run of suppertime shoppers lasting until seven. "God, my feet are killing me." Serena sat on a milk crate, wincing as she rubbed one instep, then the other.

"Go home," he said. "Go ahead, I can finish."

"You sure?" She got up quickly and put on her shoes. "Thanks again," she said as he unlocked the front door for her. "I really appreciate this. And don't forget, we're three carts short," she called on her way out.

He watched until she turned the corner, then continued wet-mopping the front of the store. Pieces of the old rubber tiles kept breaking off in the mop strands. He had gone from that first unaccustomed anger with his brother to feeling hurt. He dumped the black mop water down the double sink in the storeroom and felt the anger churning again. He hadn't done anything wrong. But somehow Dennis had made it seem that way. He'd only wanted to help, but Dennis made it all sound so desperate and perverted. Was his brother that cruel and self-centered? Or like their mother when feeling cornered, quick to turn their strong bright lights on everyone else's flaws, missteps, and ineptitudes? He hated the way he felt right now. For all these years he had managed to control his feelings, to rise above cruelty and perversion. But how could he now? He couldn't just look away, isolate himself. This was his brother. His insides felt as if something had broken loose and was clanking around between his head and gut. The best remedy was work. He had to keep busy. If Dennis was willing to risk everything for some woman, then that was his problem and there wasn't a thing he could do about it. He had to stay focused. In control. No one could harm him unless he let them. Like the girl Jada. He had let her get too close. He had gotten careless, had followed his feelings instead of his head.

After one last check, he locked up for good. Halfway down the street, he remembered the missing carts. They were probably in the strip of woods behind the store. Last week there had been a brush fire in there. Right before the fire trucks arrived, a pack of boys had darted out of the smoky scrub, each in a different direction. He'd look first thing tomorrow. A night in the woods wasn't going to do any more damage to those rusting old carts.

He wasn't too far from the Market when he spotted a cart in an alley so narrow, it ran like a crease between two tenements. He had to lean in sideways to pull it out.

"Hey, mister!" A round little woman with green-streaked hair chased after him. "What're you doing? That's mine! You got my cart! You can't just take my cart!"

"It belongs to the Market. The Nash Street Market." He gestured ahead.

"Like hell it does! I got that cart. It's mine," she said, pulling on it.

"I'm sorry, but it's not."

"Yes, it is, because I got that cart. It's from Shop and Save. See!" She pointed.

"Where? Where does it say that?" The plastic store strip had broken off the handle. It belonged to the Market, he repeated as he pushed it away.

"Please, mister!" she implored, hurrying alongside. "Okay! You're right, it is your cart, but the thing is I need it. I got nine-month-old babies, two twins, and last week they stole my stroller right outta my hallway, and the babies, they're too big, I can't carry them both at the same time plus go get food and formula all the time, not to mention Pampers. I go through these, like, humongous packages, and I just want to use it, that's all. Just borrow it. A week. Just a couple days." Breathless, she tried to keep pace. "My girlfriend Wanda, she works in the Goodwill. She's tryna find me one. Please!"

"I'm sorry." The cart's rattle over the cracked pavement vibrated up his arms. He felt terrible, thick and obdurate. But how could he give what didn't belong to him? And if he did, what if she was accused of stealing it? Then, of course, she would say he had given it to her, and that might be it, the stupid mistake, the one moment of weakness that would bring everything to a wrenching stop.

"Please, mister! A few days, that's all, and then I'll bring it back. I swear. Please! I need it! Please!" she shouted after him. "You no good son of a . . ."

The minute he turned the corner he saw a funnel of black smoke rising behind the store. Papery cinders drifted past like black snowflakes. He left the cart by the doors and ran out back. Flames licked up to the roof. The mountain of boxes Neil had piled against the building was ablaze. Fragments of fiery cardboard floated up through the smoke.

He ran around the loading dock and uncoiled the hose from its hanger. As he reached under the stairs to turn on the faucet, he heard a *whoosh* and then flames erupted in a pile of boxes that hadn't been under there this morning. He aimed the high-powered nozzle directly into the smaller fire, dousing it immediately. He struggled to pull the taut hose around the dock. It wasn't long enough, so he had to duck down to bring it under the smoky platform. As he crawled out the other side, he saw the old man disappear into the woods, his dog skittering after him. His heart sank as the first blast of water only seemed to feed the fire. Burning strips of siding curled away from the building. Moving closer, he aimed the water into the core of the blaze until there was only thick black smoke. Coughing, he sprayed the fiery siding, waving the hose back and forth between the loading dock and the building. Streams of black muck puddled around his feet. The blast of water was all he could hear. Someone jostled his arm. Startled, he jumped. He kept trying to hand the shouting fireman the hose until he realized they had their own. They wanted him out of their way.

The police had located Neil at the Dearborn Country Club. The cleats of his white golf shoes clicked on the asphalt as he ran to the back of the Market.

"It looks a lot worse than it is," the fire lieutenant said. He continued writing his report as he talked to Neil. "You're lucky your man here came back when he did."

Gordon shrugged and tried to smile. Poor Neil, he could use some breaks.

"He called you?" Neil asked.

"He put it out," the lieutenant said. "With the hose there. It must've just started."

"How'd it start?" Neil asked.

"Probably set. All that cardboard there," the lieutenant said, snapping shut the thin metal cover of his report. The fire marshal's office would be investigating, he added, then told Neil they had to check inside now.

Why? What were they looking for? Neil wanted to know. Did they think someone might be in there?

No, they had to make sure the wiring was all right.

While Neil went through the building with the lieutenant and two other firemen, the rest of the crew waited by their trucks, drinking bottled water and arguing about some new player the Red Sox had just traded for. Gordon lingered by the Dumpster. He folded his arms, unfolded them, paced back and forth, then decided to look in the woods for the missing carts. The first one lay on its side in the dry streambed. Nearby was the second one, jammed into a snarl of brush. It was filled with empties and covered with a tattered brown blanket. Cootie's stash, he realized, dragging them from the woods. With the ruckus of cans and bottles clinking in the rattling carts, the firemen stopped talking. They knew who he was. He took a deep breath. What if they thought he had set the fire?

Satisfied there had been no electrical or structural damage, the lieutenant was leaving.

"It's those goddamn kids. I don't know what more I can do," Neil called through the closing door. He locked it. Gordon had been filling a trash bag with the cans and bottles. He and Neil watched the smaller truck pull into the street, where it held back traffic so the hook and ladder could turn out of the lot.

"Neil, it was the old man. Cootie, he's the one who set the fire. I saw him."

"You saw him? You saw him set it?"

"Well, no, not setting it. But he was right there. I was trying to get the hose around and I saw him. He was running into the woods."

"Did you tell them that?"

"No. I thought I should tell you first."

"Well, that's good. That's really fucking good," Neil said with a deep sigh.

"It's a mess out there, huh? But it shouldn't take too long to clean up. I can get started first thing in the morning."

Neil looked out at the street.

"At least you don't have to shut down, that's one good thing," Gordon continued.

Neil turned, face twisted, his eyes red and wet. "Forget about Cootie. You didn't see him. He wasn't there. He had nothing to do with this, all right? You got that straight?"

Gordon nodded.

"You're not as thick as you want me to think, are you, Gloomis?" That slow smile leaked from Neil's mouth. "You want something, don't you. What? What is it? How much?"

"I don't want anything," he said, drawing back.

"Then why the fuck didn't you let it burn?"

He didn't understand men like his brother and Neil, he thought as he walked home. Didn't they know how close to the edge they walked? Couldn't they feel the frenzy, like particles of mad, fatal energy charging the very air they breathed?

The next day, Eddie Chapman was sitting in his truck outside the Market. One of his laborers was with him, a burly young fellow with a thin ponytail halfway down his back.

Probably here to clean the mess out back, Gordon thought as he reached to open the door.

"Hey! Hey, Loomis!" Eddie called, climbing down from the truck. He and the laborer walked toward him.

"How're you doing, Eddie?" He smiled and held the door open for them.

"Shut the door," Eddie said.

"Why? What's wrong?"

"You're through. You're done. You don't need to go in there," Eddie said.

"What do you mean?"

"You're fired, plain and simple."

"I don't understand."

Serena and June watched from their registers, arms folded and tense.

"What's to understand? You don't work here anymore."

"But why? I mean . . . why?"

"Jesus! I gotta spell it out for you? It's like one thing after another."

Gordon opened the door, and Eddie's arm blocked him. "I want to talk to Neil," he said, pushing past. He hurried to the back of the store, past Leo, who continued splitting chicken breasts with his cleaver. With the men right behind, he knocked on the door and Neil opened it, startled to see him.

"What? What're you doing here? What do you want?"

"Why are you firing me, Neil? What did I do?"

"People are nervous. They don't feel safe anymore." Neil peered around him at his brother-in-law.

"Why? What did I do?"

"Jesus Christ!" Eddie growled. "You almost burned the whole fucking place down."

"No! It wasn't me. Neil, you know—"

"All I know is I don't want any trouble. And you don't, either, do you, Gloom? Besides, it's not like I even hired you in the first place. And Eddie, he didn't know, so, What the hell, I said to myself, we'll give it a go, see what happens. But after last night, Christ, I mean, this is a whole new ball game. And it's not just my employees, I got customers to think of here. Public safety, you know? Here. Take it." He stuffed a wad of bills into Gordon's hand. "Tide you over, okay?"

Dullness prevailed. His appetite was gone. Even his vision was off. Everything seemed murky, as if he were peering through a soiled curtain. Sunshine swelled in the windows, but the little house stayed cold and gray inside. Where once he had found peace in this stillness, now there was a constant watery rush in the air. The phone rang unanswered. He opened the front door just wide enough to get the mail. The roses were dropping leaves. Mrs. Jukas went back and forth to appointments in a MediVan. Loose papers and fast-food detritus littered both their lawns. Is that all that would be left? Who in the end would care? His sleep was riddled with distorted faces and frantic prison voices. In last night's dream he sat naked on Mrs. Jukas's porch, masturbating while women and children ran off screaming. Janine Walters was the only one who stayed. She watched with an indulgent smile, then began to pant with him, moaning as he pushed away from her bed, then looked down at her cold, staring eyes and her open mouth's blunted scream.

The phone rang, and once again the machine clicked on. "Gordon! If you're there, will you please pick up?" Delores said, and he cringed. "Please! I'm so worried about you. All right, that's it. I'm coming—"

He picked up the phone and told her he wasn't feeling too well, that was all. She wanted to come right over. She'd stop at the deli for some chicken soup. Was there anything else he wanted or needed? She'd be going right by the drugstore. No, no, he tried to explain. It wasn't that he was sick. He just hadn't felt like going anywhere. Or seeing anyone.

"Oh. Oh, all right," she said quickly.

There was silence, then they both spoke at once.

"I just need—"

"That's okay, I—"

"—to be alone."

"—understand."

Jada came twice to his door, but he would not answer it.

"Gordon!" she called this last time. "Hey, Gordon, you in there? It's me, Jada. I just gotta ask you something, that's all."

He heard her breathing against the door. "Jesus . . ." She sighed and then went away.

His sister-in-law called and left a message, inviting him and Delores out to dinner next Friday night. He called back and said he couldn't on Friday. She was disappointed. It would be their only free weekend for a while. And then Dennis would be away for a week at the International Oral Surgeons' Symposium.

"In Bermuda."

"Bermuda?"

"Yes, it's one of my favorite places," Lisa said. "But this year it's going to be seminars all day long, even some at night, Dennis said, so he doesn't want me to come. He says it'll just be too frustrating if I'm out on the beach while he's stuck in a conference room somewhere."

He hung up feeling even worse. So now Dennis was going on trips with Jilly Cross. He felt guilty in his silence, and weak. He had tried talking to his brother. He couldn't say any more to Jilly Cross without enraging Dennis further. Life was going terribly wrong, but he didn't know how to make it right. The grass below his skeletal rose canes was covered with blighted leaves. Of course his father's roses would die with the son's touch. There had been no place for him then, and still there was not. Even in Fortley he had never felt this helpless. He only had to get through each day there. The rules had been basic, primitive in some respects. His expectations had been foolish. It was far too complex here. And insidious. Nothing was the way it was supposed to be.

That night he lay in bed, unable to sleep. He reached for the phone and set it on his chest. After a few minutes he lifted the receiver and pushed in the glowing numbers, all but the last one. He hung up. A few minutes later he tried again but still could not push the last button of Delores's number. In the morning he woke up startled by the phone looming at eye level, rising and falling with each breath.

CHAPTER 17

"Gordon!" Delores said when he finally opened the door. She had never seen him unshaven. The whiskery stubble made him look old and worn, his eyes faded. "Sorry for all that banging, but I've been so worried. I just stopped by the Market. They said you don't work there anymore."

He nodded. "Neil fired me. A week and a half ago." He shrugged, shaking his head as if unable to say more.

"That selfish, no-good bastard," she blurted over his low voice as he tried to explain how shocked he'd been, too ashamed to tell anyone. Not even his brother. It couldn't have happened at a worse time. As it was, Dennis didn't want anything to do with him.

Now wait, it wasn't the disaster he thought it was, she said, then felt like a hypocrite, remembering her own devastation at being fired. But of course Gordon said nothing. People lost jobs for one reason or another all the time, she continued. He'd find another, probably one that paid a whole lot better than the Market had. He was staring at the floor. "Gordon?"

"I'm sorry. I'm not very good at things like this."

"Things like what?" she asked too quickly, the old dread numbing her heart.

"I don't know." He shrugged. "Everything, I guess."

"What do you mean, everything? Nothing's everything, Gordon. Nothing is."

———

He looked out the side window saying nothing as she drove. Just getting him out of that stale little house had seemed achievement enough, but now, miles from Collerton, her excitement grew. They never went anywhere together. He wouldn't spend the night at her apartment, so she always went to his house. Though he never said as much, it was obvious she was expected to leave after they had made love. He would turn on all the lights, then slip downstairs to wait while she dressed. Their last time together she had pretended to be asleep. He came back up, gently nudged her awake, and said it was getting late to be driving home alone. Yes, she agreed, it was late, and she was too tired to drive, so she'd leave in the morning. No, that wasn't a good idea, he said, then just stood there, holding out her clothes. Embarrassed and hurt, she left quickly, only to feel even more castigated when he didn't call or answer his phone these last ten days. The silent schism had always been Albert's most effective punishment. And the cruelest. Yell, slam doors, swear, but don't just walk away. It made her too desperate, too willing to put up with the next disregard, and the next. But that hadn't been the case at all, she now realized, relief bearing her fears away.

Taking only back roads, she had to keep slowing down. With every turn, she expected him to protest or at least ask where they were going. When she came onto the beach road in Hampton, she rolled down the windows. The tide was low, the warm, boggy marsh smell that filled the car almost obscene with its rich, rank ripeness.

"Isn't that wonderful?" She took a deep breath, but he didn't answer. "You're not mad, are you? I thought you needed a change, that's all. You know, seeing the same thing all the time, the city streets and all the same people."

"Oh no, I just can't believe I forgot this." He strained to see over the white seawall along the curving shoreline road. "I forgot all about the ocean. I always tried to remember things. Things in rooms, rooms in other people's houses, their yards even. Kids' bikes, the way I used to walk to school, where everyone sat in homeroom and all the other classes. And my mother's clothes. I used to try and remember even what dresses she had and the songs my father used to hum to himself when he was working on something. Like something for my mother, he'd go"—here now, Gordon hummed "Here Comes the Bride" so sweetly that she ached for him—"or if it got really complicated and he was having a hard time, he'd always go"—he hummed a frantic rendition of "When Johnny Comes Marching Home Again." "It was like an exercise. A discipline. Because remembering was all I had left, and if I forgot, I'd be losing part of . . . I don't even know what."

Yourself, she thought as his voice trailed off. She pulled into the public parking lot in Rye. The tide was out a great distance, exposing large rocks she didn't remember seeing before. She and Albert used to walk on the beach at night when they first started dating. *Did he take Katie here?* she wondered in a flare of jealousy. But what did it matter? She had never been happier than now, at this very moment. Gordon was the dearest, most honorable man she had ever known. And there was no more beautiful place than this, this beach at dusk. Bands of pink and lavender glowed with the horizon across the wet sand. Behind them, the rose-colored sunset streaked the sky with fiery light. Straggles of people walked and jogged along the beach. Two boys took turns throwing a tennis ball that a bearish black dog chased, crashing time after time into the surf, then galloped back, wet fur flapping. A small yellow plane was flying up the coast. It dipped over the low waves then lifted suddenly, skimming the treetops on Straw's Point before it disappeared.

"I forgot about those, too." Gordon pointed out to the Isles of Shoals, where the first darkness loomed behind the distant islands.

She suggested they get out and walk, and he surprised her by saying yes. She left her shoes in the car, but he kept his on. They were halfway down the beach when the first rim of moonrise appeared over the water. Astonished, Gordon stopped. "Look at that! I never saw that before," he said. All along the way, others paused to watch the bloodred ascent until it was finally full in the pale night sky. They began walking again. She tripped a little and caught his arm. Apologizing, she pulled back. "That's okay," he said quietly.

"I thought I was going to fall."

"Better hold on, then." He lifted his elbow. "There's a lot of holes."

"Kids dig them," she said, easing her hand into the crook of his arm.

He must have been eleven or twelve the last time he saw the ocean, he said. He used to love coming to the beach with his parents. His father's back, that must have been why they stopped. Seeing how stiffly Gordon was walking, she realized he was trying to keep sand from getting in his shoes. "Here." She plucked an egg-shaped white stone from the wet sand and gave it to him.

"What's this?" He seemed genuinely puzzled.

"Just a rock."

"Am I supposed to do something with it?"

"Feel it. See how smooth it is?" He looked at it a moment, agreed it was smooth, then gave it back. As they walked, he kept slapping his hands together to get the sticky sand off. Silly that that should annoy her so, but it did. She reminded herself how artificial his existence had been. Now he was wiping his hands up and down the sides of his pants.

When they reached the long, high wall of riprap, he came to a sudden stop. "I've got sand in my shoes," he said almost accusingly.

"Take them off, then. You'll feel beachier. See!" She gave a quick little jig in the sand.

"I can't," he said with a stricken look.

"Sure you can. Go sit over on one of the rocks there."

"No, I never go barefoot. I have to have something on my feet. I need to." He began trudging back, his gait even stiffer.

"You didn't wear shoes on the beach when you were a kid, did you?" she called, laughing as she tried to keep up, then regretted it when he didn't answer.

In the car he apologized and tried to explain that in prison being barefoot or in any way half-dressed left a man too vulnerable. To make him feel better, she was telling him how painful an experience the beach had been for her as an overweight teenager in a bathing suit. The senior-class picnic had been the worst, an absolute agony, walking around all day wrapped up in the biggest beach towel she'd been able to find. "I spent more time shopping for that beach towel than I did the bathing suit," she called over the wheel. "Then all of a sudden I hear, 'It's Delores the horse!' and Bucky Dean runs by and yanks off my towel and I stood there feeling so exposed and just wanting to die." Funny how those things don't matter anymore, she said. Nothing did, not even his silence, she thought, in such a high state of anticipation that the thirty-five miles back flew by.

She turned off the engine in front of his house and kept the conversation going until he had no choice but to invite her in. She trailed him around the kitchen while he made coffee. His moroseness was back, but she was so determined to keep his spirits up that she found herself giggling at everything, at nothing at all, dropping things, all the while feeling so light that she was almost floating. He poured her coffee, then excused himself to go upstairs for a minute. He had to change his shoes. He thought he was getting a blister from the sand. *He doesn't want me here,* she thought, but continued sipping her coffee. *It's not me he's upset with, but his situation.* She could hear him moving around upstairs. Pipes vibrated as he turned water on and off in the bathroom. Then for a while she heard nothing. "Gordon?" she called from the stairs.

She tiptoed up and saw the light under the bathroom door. He was still in there. Passing his bedroom, she thought of taking off her clothes and slipping into his bed but then knew what a mistake that would be. Sometimes her slightest advance could repel him. It had been the same with Albert, except that his prudery had been a vital part of the relationship, his moral moat against their adultery. As long as she was the one always breaching the barriers, he could be the vanquished, helplessly errant husband. Gordon's reserve was innate, but also self-protective. Maybe all men were like that. Or maybe there was something in her that made them so defensive.

The doorbell was ringing. Opening the door, Delores was shocked by Jada's appearance. Her hollow face was a rash of zits. She looked skinnier, her arms and legs all bone. "Hi!" Jada said, but the old breeziness was forced and weary. Delores asked if she was sick. Jada said she had been, some kind of flu or something, but she was better now. Delores said she looked as if she'd lost a lot of weight. Jada said she'd been too sick to eat very much.

Delores took her into the kitchen and cut a slice from the coffee cake she found in the refrigerator. It was almost gone by the time Gordon came back down.

"What're you doing here?" he demanded from the doorway. His face was flushed.

Jada tried to smile and for a moment seemed almost afraid, stammering how long it had been since she'd seen him and how sick she'd been, but then when she saw Delores's car she'd just run over to say hello. "She gave me some cake." Jada put the last forkful into her mouth and swallowed hard, as desperate to keep talking as Delores was to keep the moment from caving in on itself. "It's good. It's really, really good. Homemade's always the best, don't you think?" Jada's voice weakened under his cold scrutiny. "Did you make it?" she asked him.

"It's Entenmann's," Delores finally answered, and they both regarded her with almost identical expressions of strain and bewilderment.

"I have to do something." He turned as if to go back upstairs.

"Go ahead. I'll keep the coffee warm," Delores said.

He looked at her. "That's okay. It's late. It's too late now for coffee."

Too late for Delores to be here. More than hurt, she was angry with herself for letting the girl in.

"Oh, I don't want coffee," Jada said. "Do you have any milk, though? I'd love some milk. I'm really thirsty."

"There isn't any milk," he said.

"How about juice? You got any juice?" Jada's eyes kept straying to the refrigerator.

"I think you better go," he told her, and Delores didn't know which bothered her more, his icy command or the easy forbearance of Jada's shrug as she rose from the table. Was she so whipped, her threshold for rejection so high, that this one didn't even matter?

"Do you want me to go, too?" she asked the minute the door closed behind the girl.

"No," he said, but she knew he did.

"I'm sorry. I shouldn't have let her in without asking you first."

He rinsed Jada's plate and fork, then scrubbed them with the soapy sponge. Impelled by his silence, she tried to defend Jada, excuse him, and explain herself. She could understand his irritation, but Jada hadn't done anything wrong, at least not intentionally. Deprived of the most basic social skills and manners, she just didn't know any better. Delores had been too startled by her appearance to turn the poor thing away, she tried to explain. "Next time I'll know to ask you first." She touched his arm.

"Well, don't!" He spun around. "Because I don't want her here. Ever!"

"My God, Gordon, she's a poor kid. She was hungry! What's the harm in giving her some food?" His indifference shocked her. Especially after all he'd been through.

"She's not my responsibility."

She looked at him. "Of course she's your responsibility. She's a kid, she's all our responsibility."

"I can't take chances like that."

"Chances? Every morning you get out of bed you're taking a chance!"

"No, it's different with me."

"Why? Because you spent all those years in jail? So you're going to keep living your life like that?" That's exactly what he'd done this past week and a half, locked himself away from everyone.

"You don't understand. I know she's got problems. But I can't get involved. I can't even care."

"You've got to care, Gordon. You've got to reach out. To people." To me, she longed to say. "But especially to a child."

His cold quiet triggered the old fear. She needed to coax him back from the precipice he had backed them both onto. The words came so fast, she felt breathless with their urgency. "We have to help one another. We only get so many chances, Gordon, just so many ways to save ourselves. But then after a while if we keep turning away, then they stop."

"Well, so then they do." He squeezed out the sponge.

"How can you do that?" Her voice rose over the running water.

"How can you shut yourself off like that? I can't imagine living like that. It's like being dead."

He turned off the water and began to clean the place where Jada had sat. Bent over the table and with the light at his back, he appeared to be scrubbing his own shadow.

CHAPTER 18

The lockdown bell is ringing and he can't get up.

His hand shot out and Delores's mirror fell on the floor. The glass was intact, but a lot of the shells had broken off. The phone was ringing.

"Thank goodness," Mrs. Jukas said when he answered. "I was afraid you'd already left for work."

He peered at the clock: 6:10. She was saying she needed a few things from the Market. Her gritty voice buzzed in his ear. Well? If he couldn't do it, he should just say so. She hated insincerity, people pretending they didn't mind when they really did. Even more than that, she hated asking people for help, but she was at that horrible stage in life now where she had little choice. "So do you have a pencil and paper there?"

"Okay." He fumbled in the nightstand drawer for a pen.

"Three medium-size peaches, all ripe. One ripe banana and two green." Was he writing this down? If he got the wrong things, she wouldn't pay for them. Reading it back, he purposely rustled the paper near the phone. "A quart of skim milk," she continued, "and six cans of chicken noodle soup. Low-sodium if they have it." She wasn't sure of the prices, but the Market was such a rip-off, everything cost three times as much now. She'd pay when he came. Oh, and come to the front door. With her leg so swollen and sore, she spent all her time on the couch now.

Before he did anything, he tried to glue the shells back on the narrow mirror frame. Some were broken, others didn't seem to fit; the mirror didn't look the same. He hid it in the drawer. He wished Delores hadn't given it to him. Once again he found himself resenting her generosity and guilty for the poverty of his own.

After his job interview he would walk downtown to the Shop and Save for Mrs. Jukas's groceries. He couldn't tell her he'd been fired. He had a ten o'clock appointment with Treeshrub'nlawn Landscaping. He had circled the want ad for three straight days before working up the courage to call. The company was in the industrial park on the other side of the city. He rode the bus, then walked the dusty few miles past modest one-story homes that seemed part of an unfinished development. When he finally came to the industrial park, his relief quickly faded. Most buildings had company signs, but there were only a few street signs. It was 10:05 before he finally found the right address. It was the last building in the farthest part of the sprawling, treeless complex. Before he went inside, he blotted sweat from his face, neck, and forearms, then folded the handkerchief and put it into his pocket.

"So what's your story?" Bart Pugh asked. He had a red beard, blond hair, and a crushing handshake.

"My story?"

"It's usually kids I get. Illegal aliens, you know, but a guy like you. I mean, what do you want a job like this for?"

"I like working outside. Growing things. Especially roses."

"Yeah, well, mostly we cut grass."

"Sure, I do that," he said eagerly. "I cut the grass at home, my lawn."

"You ever use a commercial rider?"

"No. I use my dad's old mower. It's one of those push mowers. It doesn't have an engine."

"Oh, yeah?" Interest waning, Pugh began to sort through papers piled on his desk. "What was your last job? Where'd you work?"

"The Market. Nash Street. The Nash Street Market."

"Yeah?" Pugh glanced up. "What'd you do there?"

"A lot of different things. Bagging groceries and stocking shelves. Other things."

"What happened?"

"I got fired."

"Oh, I don't usually hear that." Pugh seemed amused. "How come?"

"Well, actually it was a misunderstanding."

"What kind of misunderstanding?"

"I'd rather not go into it. I mean, it involves my boss. And it may well be just speculation on my part. So it really would be best if I didn't say anything. But I can assure you I'm a good worker. And I'm very dependable. I'd never call in sick and leave you in a lurch or anything like that."

"What if you had to? What if you were, like, really sick?"

"No! I'd work anyway. I'd be right here. No matter what."

Pugh put the papers aside. "What kind of license you got?"

"Well, you see, the bus picks me up right around the corner from my street." He pointed back over his shoulder as if it were idling out there now. "And then it's not too far and I really enjoy the—"

"Wait! What? You don't have a car?"

"Uh, no. I don't. I don't have one. Actually, I don't drive."

"Oh. What?" Pugh gave a dismal sigh. "DUI?"

"I don't have a license. I never got one."

"You illegal? An alien? You don't sound like one."

How foolish, how naive, to think he might have avoided this. The reason, he explained, was that he'd been in jail. For many years. Most of his life, as a matter of fact. And with the admission came relief, not that Pugh knew, but that he had been able to say it.

"You're kidding! Usually I can tell. Most of your life! Christ, what the hell'd you do, murder someone?"

"A young woman."

Pugh stared as if something sharp were stuck in his throat. "Jesus Christ," he squealed. "I can't hire you. Half the places you'd be working at there's women and kids. And, I mean, I gotta consider that. You know, security and all."

"Yes. I understand."

"I mean, you seem like a helluva nice guy, but I gotta be careful."

"Yes. I know." He extended his hand, careful to lean back from the gesture. "Thank you for at least interviewing me, though."

Gordon rang the bell. When Mrs. Jukas didn't come, he left the bag of groceries just inside the porch wall so they wouldn't be seen from the street. The phone rang before he had even closed his own door.

"Couldn't you wait? I had to get my purse!" Mrs. Jukas said.

"I thought you might be sleeping."

"Sleep! I never sleep. All I do is lay here. I've got your money. I'd put it out, but that girl, she'd be over here in two seconds. I used to think she was just wild or something, but it's more than that. There's something strange about her. The way her eyes move, the way she only comes out at night. She's always watching your house, you know. She's—"

"Do you want me to come over now?" he interrupted.

"It's up to you."

The exact amount, she said, passing coins and bills through the slightly open doorway. She didn't thank him but seemed pleased he had bought everything at Shop and Save instead of from those crooks, the Nash Street Market, who had been ripping people off for years. He said he'd been going by. Well, next time he did she needed some bleach and a small bottle of Fab.

"Leonardo! Where are you, you stupid dog!" came a shout from across the street.

"Will you look at that." Mrs. Jukas stared past his forearm, for her head came somewhere between his waist and shoulder. "The way she carries on you'd think somebody'd do something."

A cigarette in her mouth, Marvella Fossum stood on her top step in a thin, dingy nightgown that clung to her swelling belly. Coughing, she struck one dead match after another.

"Disgusting, isn't it?" Mrs. Jukas shook her head. "The way they breed. Like rats. She takes men in there. All hours of the night. The landlord, he can't even evict her off his own property, it takes so long in the courts. Everyone's got rights but us. Last week the police came. The Spanish lady, Inez up there, she called them. One night it was three men in there. The girl, she waits outside. Pretty soon, she'll be doing the same as the mother. That night, Inez said it was pouring rain. Two o'clock in the morning and she sees the girl run over here."

"Where?" Had it been raining the night he let Jada in? No, it hadn't been.

"In your garage. She takes the key down."

"Hey! Hey, mister!" Marvella was halfway down the steps. "I need a light. You got a match or lighter or whatever I can use here?"

"No. I don't," he answered quickly, but she kept coming.

"How 'bout you?" she asked Mrs. Jukas, who was already closing the door. In the sunlight she appeared almost naked. "All I need's a match," she whined. "Is that too much to ask?"

"Ma!" Jada was hurrying down the street with a bag in her arms. She stepped quickly between her mother and Gordon.

"Where the hell've you been?" Marvella roared.

"The store. I told you. I said I'd be right back."

"Yeah, well, I hope you're happy, leaving me alone, listening to that fucking dog, when I can't even eat, I'm so sick, I can't keep anything down. Not even crackers." Her little round face twisted into a sour contortion of self-pity and anger.

"It's okay, Ma. Here, I got you some Dew." Jada set the bags down. She twisted off the cap. Her mother cringed as if even the sight of it were repulsive.

"I need matches and nobody'll give me any. That's all I wanted," she whined as if Jada had accused her of something.

"I don't have any," he said. He had yet to look at Jada.

"Yes, you do!" Marvella's beady eyes narrowed in amusement at his discomfort. "You just don't wanna give me any."

"He doesn't smoke, Ma. C'mon, there's some. I'll get 'em for you."

"Yeah, well, you should've told me before," Marvella complained as Jada picked up her bag to take her home. "And then he wouldn'ta got out."

Jada stopped. "You mean Leonardo?"

Marvella nodded with a sob. "I was looking for matches. You must've left the door open. I didn't even see it. And now he's gone."

"Are you sure? Did you look for him?"

"I been out here all this time, what do you think? I been calling and calling. Leonardo!" she wailed suddenly, teetering with the effort. "Leonardo! Leonardo!"

"Did you see him?" Jada asked Gordon.

"No."

"Come on, Ma. Quick, I gotta go look. I gotta find him," she said, almost pulling her mother across the street.

Gordon went right to the garage. He lifted the key from the rusty nail and put it in his pocket. Delores thought he should feel some responsibility toward the girl, but what she provoked most in him was fear. There was no keeping her out. She was like the stinkweed he was always pulling up. It left a terrible smell in his hands, and no matter what he did, vinegar, WeedRout, hacking at the roots, it always came back. Halfway down the driveway he stopped. He could hear whimpering. He looked in his backyard and under his steps, following the sound to the property line. Here the bushes hadn't been cut back from the other side in years, the thickness almost impenetrable, especially for someone his size. Now the whimpering grew frantic. He knelt down and peered in. The dog looked back with an entreating yip. The rope from his collar was so snarled in brambles that he could barely move. Gordon tried to loosen the rope, but it was too tangled. He got his rose pruner from the garage and cut the rope on the first try. "C'mon, boy. C'mon," he coaxed, straining to grab the rope end, but he needn't have worried. The dog wiggled straight out into his hands. He carried him across the street.

"Jada's not here," Marvella called through the open window.

"I found your dog. I have him here," he called back.

"He's not mine. I don't have a dog."

"It's Leonardo," he called, stooping at the window. Seeing her hazy form on the couch, he straightened immediately. Crack. She was trying to light it so she could smoke it through a straw in the side of a soda bottle. "Your daughter's dog. I have him right here."

"Jesus Christ, I don't want him!" She waved him away. "You can have him. He's yours."

"No, I can't. I don't want a dog. I'll just leave him, then. Out here."

The adjacent door opened then and Inez came out onto the porch with her four-year-old granddaughter, who laughed and reached up to let the dog lick her fingers. Her grandmother spoke sharply in Spanish and the girl's hands flew behind her back.

Marvella had opened her door at the same time. She looked at the dog a moment, puzzled, as if she didn't recognize it. "Can't you just take him someplace?" she whined. "Please? Or keep him, I don't care."

"No. I can't. I can't do that," he said, struggling as the dog yipped and strained to get to Marvella.

"He doesn't want your dog," Inez snapped. "He's yours. You want to get rid of him, you go do it."

"Shut up!" Marvella cried. "Just shut the—"

"No!" Inez growled, pointing to the child curled around her legs.

Marvella cringed from the warning. "Oh shit," she said, taking the squealing dog from him. "Like I really need this."

"Thank you," Gordon said when he and Inez and the girl were down on the sidewalk. He explained how the dog had been caught in the bushes.

"You should've left him. Better off there than with that," she spat, then hurried down the street, the child in tow.

Jada was at his door within minutes. She rang the bell, knocked, then tried the back door. She probably wanted to thank him, but that's all it would take, the slightest civility, just a few words, and she would be right back insinuating herself into his life. He stayed upstairs until she finally went away.

When Delores called he was eating a tuna-fish sandwich. He had forgotten all about the band concert in the park. When she had invited him two weeks ago his life had been fine, and now it was a mess. He still hadn't found a job, money was running low, and he had wrenched his back yesterday scraping a patch of peeling paint from the back of the house. Because he didn't have a ladder, he had climbed onto the porch railing, balancing himself quite well until he heard the wood crack. He'd jumped off, landing so awkwardly that something had pulled in his lower back. It especially hurt when he walked any distance, he was trying to tell Delores, but she said he wouldn't have to walk far at all. The parking lot was right there on the edge of the park. It hurt to sit for too long, he said.

"You just don't want to go, right?" she asked.

"No. No, it's not that. I do. It's just my back." He didn't want to go, but he also didn't want to make her mad. He hadn't seen her since their ride to the beach, and he missed her. They had talked on the phone, but she had been distracted, almost cool to him. He was afraid Jada had told her about climbing into his bed.

"All right, I'll pick you up in fifteen minutes, then. Just come out when I toot," she said, and he hobbled around to get ready.

Here he was now, shivering on a low, flimsy beach chair on the Dearborn Common, listening to a four-piece band playing "Sweet Caroline."

It was chilly, but Delores wore a sleeveless blouse. She claimed not to be cold. "All my natural layers," she said, passing him a plate piled with chicken she'd fried, potato salad, beans, and cornbread. The drumstick was still warm and crispy. Delores was a wonderful cook. His mother had hated cooking, so his father had done most of it. Inexplicably, that had changed after Gordon went away. Dennis said she learned to enjoy cooking, but Gordon couldn't help thinking his absence had made it more pleasurable, a less onerous task without her three-hundred-pound oafish son underfoot every minute.

He had eaten practically everything in the picnic basket. Delores had made an apple pie, but it had been too hot to cut and pack, so they would have it afterward at her house. His back ached. He would rather go home when the concert ended, but he didn't want to hurt her feelings, and there was still the pie. Fireflies flickered in the distance while barefoot little girls danced around the musicians, who for some reason sat playing on folding chairs below the bandstand.

Delores kept waving at different people going by. For someone who didn't even live in Dearborn, she knew a lot of people here, he said. Many were customers, she said, and a lot were Collerton people who had made good and moved to Dearborn.

"See her?" Delores said with a nod toward the woman walking by. "That's Dawn Lintz. We went to school with her. She got married the weekend we graduated. Remember? She was so pregnant you could tell even with the graduation robe on."

"Oh," he said. Of course he didn't remember, but once again he let the flow of her voice carry him along through memories that had little to do with him.

"She's been married two times since. Three kids, one with each guy. Her son's an Olympic gymnast. Well, used to be. He's a coach now, I think . . ."

It wasn't so much that he had stopped listening as he was sinking into the comfort of her nearness. Jada couldn't have said anything, he decided. Delores was just the same as always. There seemed less need to keep up his guard every minute. She probably knew more about him than anyone, yet nothing seemed to bother her.

". . . so anyway, that's what I'm thinking. I know everyone in my family's going to have a fit—but you know what?"

"No. I don't. What?" He had no idea what she meant.

"*I don't care!* How's that?" She laughed. "They all have their own families. So why shouldn't I? I mean, all this time I've been thinking I'm a failure because I don't have anyone, because I don't have a family like they all do. And then I was thinking how hard it must be for you. I mean, here you are, coming back here where everyone knows you, but you don't let that get in the way. You just keep plugging along, determined to start over and make a life for yourself. I admire that about you. I look at you and I say to myself, The hell with what everyone thinks, just go for it, girl!" She was rummaging through her satchel-size purse that had somehow gotten mayonnaise smeared into the straw weave. She handed him a grainy photo of a somber Chinese child.

"Mary Catherine," she said when he asked who it was. "Well,

that's what I'd call her. Now her name's May Loo. So what do you think?"

"She's cute. She's pretty, but *who* is she? I mean, why are you changing her name?"

"Because I'm adopting her. That's what I've been telling you. She's almost a year old. She's from the Holy Mother of Christ Mission Orphanage in Kawang. It takes at least six months to go through all the paperwork. And then she'll be mine." She rubbed the picture against her chest and sighed. "I haven't even met her and I love her this much." Her voice broke and she paused a moment. "I can't imagine what it'll be like actually holding this tiny little thing in my arms."

He didn't know what to say. He was confused. She wasn't married. She didn't even have a job. He thought of Jada's pregnant mother, not only unmarried and unemployed, but a drug addict. The world had gone a little more haywire.

"I'm so happy, Gordon." She reached over and squeezed his hand. "I've never been happier in my whole life. About anything. And it's all because of you. Because you're such a good, strong man."

He smiled and for a moment, for just a tick of time, wondered if it might be possible.

He aimed the remote, scanning the channels. Delores's enormous television got ten times as many as his did.

"That's because you're not on cable." She put the two slices of apple pie and ice cream on the coffee table, then sat next to him. "You should get it."

"Why? All I have to do is come over here and watch it," he said, mesmerized by the cascade of fleeting images.

"That's right." For the next few minutes they ate in silence.

"That was delicious," he said, then realized once again he was finished and she was just starting. "You make the best apple pie."

"Thank you, Gordon, but, sad to say, I won't be making another one for a while."

"Why?" He was embarrassed by the alarm in his voice.

"Because! I have to get healthy!" She picked up the girl's picture from the table. "I can't be this big, out-of-shape mother chasing that little bitty thing all over the playground." She held out her arms. "Look, I've already lost ten pounds. The day I made up my mind, that's when I started."

"I thought there was something different," he said, though it wasn't a weight loss, he realized, but the calm that seemed to have settled over her, a resignation.

Delores leaned against him. "Oh Gordon . . ." She sighed and turned, her heavy breasts dragging across his chest as he turned with her. "Is it all right? Do you mind if we're here?" she asked, her mouth at his ear, now his eyes, his mouth. "You can go home. I'll stop if you want. I'll do whatever you want, whatever you say, just tell me. Tell me what to do. . . ."

How could he? His brain boiled with color and heat. Incapable of thought or speech, he could only grunt and nod in assent and pleasure. She had unbuttoned her blouse. She placed his hand on her breast, then gasped and told him not to squeeze. "Just go easy, easy, easy now," she whispered, taking his other hand, stroking herself, guiding him lower. Her face blurred through the blinding waves of desire. When he stood up he was naked. They both were, but he couldn't be sure if he had taken off his clothes or if she had undressed him. Holding her hand, he followed her into her bedroom like a child. Embracing, they fell onto the bed, his entire being lost in longing.

Gordon's first want ad attempt had given him the confidence to try four more. The difficulty was explaining away the twenty-five-year gap without actually telling the truth. Petro, the Athens owner, asked only if he knew how to read and write, then hired him on the spot. The Athens Pizza and Sub shop was across the street from Paramount Shoe Manufacturing. Twice a day, at noon and then again with Paramount's four-thirty shift change, the line stretched out the door. The pizza ovens were manned by Petro, a sweating, bald gentleman whose few English words and phrases shared a common modifier: "Fucking-hot, fucking-ready, fucking-get-out-of-my-way."

Gordon's job was making subs. Chad, a seventeen-year-old Cambodian American who was getting his GED at night, was head sub man. For three days the soft-spoken young man patiently trained, then quizzed Gordon in the various combinations. Each sub's ingredients were listed on the huge sign behind the counter, so Gordon had only to look up if he forgot, but he was constantly on edge. Chad kept assuring him he was a great sub maker, but Gordon's problem was his size. He was always in the way, particularly of Petro and his long-handled wooden paddle sliding pizzas in and out of the huge ovens. Gordon was getting faster on his feet, flattening himself against the wall beyond the reach of the turning paddle. The pay was better than the Market. He was working full eight-hour days and could eat as much as he wanted. On the fourth day he was cutting a meatball sub in half when Petro rushed toward the sink with his paddle afire. As Gordon leaned to get out of the way, the big knife sliced his palm. No amount of toweled ice would stop the bleeding. Chad wanted to drive him to the hospital, but he refused. Even Petro said he should fucking go and get stitches, but he couldn't. Dennis's warnings about not having insurance had come home to roost. One trip to the emergency room could end up costing hundreds, maybe even thousands, of dollars. Chad drove him home. All that night his hand throbbed with pain. The next day, he tried to work with a glove over the bandaged hand, but the bleeding would start with the slightest pressure, filling the rubber fingers with blood. Chad had to drive him home. The next day, Gordon folded a hand towel over the cut, this time binding it with duct tape. He forced on a glove and went to work. The same thing happened. Again, Chad drove him home, but right before Gordon got out of the car, he told him that Petro said not to come in tomorrow. He had hired someone else.

"I'm sorry. It's not fair," the young man said softly.

"No. Well, I know. It's hard, but I understand. He's got a business to run."

"But it was his fault!" Chad said.

"What does that matter?"

"It matters a lot!"

"No, it doesn't. Not really."

"Well, it does. In this country it does," he said with the passionate certainty of hard-earned patriotism.

Delores was horrified. She bound his hand so tightly with gauze and adhesive tape that his fingertips turned blue. "You need stitches." She snipped away the tape and bandaged it again. "It won't cost as much as you think. I'll give you the money."

"No!"

"All right, I'll lend you the money."

"I don't have a job. As it is I'm a month behind on my bills."

"Stop being so damn proud. If I needed money, I wouldn't have any problem asking you."

"The problem would be me not having any."

"But if you had it, you would if I asked. Right?"

"Well, yes. If I had it. And you needed it," he said uneasily, seeing the hurt flicker in her eyes, then vanish as quickly. She was as generous in forgiveness as in everything else. He envied her that, if for no other reason than the actual pain and sense of loss he felt when he had to share or give.

The last time they made love she had told him that she loved him. He didn't know if he loved her, because he didn't know what love was. If it was an ecstasy that stayed with him every minute of every day, then it surely wasn't love. What he felt most with Delores was contentment. He didn't have to consider every word before he spoke. When she called he was glad to hear her voice. Now when the doorbell rang his chest didn't tighten with dread. But when he was alone he hardly ever thought of her. Love, he suspected, was the ache that came with thoughts of Jilly Cross.

"Does Dennis know you cut your hand?"

"No. He doesn't even know I got fired from the Market."

"Gordon!"

"I figured I'd tell him as soon as I found a new job."

"You have to tell him. You can't start keeping things from him."

"Why? He doesn't tell me everything he does," he said, startled by this mix of anger and guilt. Talking about the affair made him feel disloyal to his brother, Lisa, and Jilly, and resentful. He had been drawn into their private lives before he'd had a chance to settle into his own. The affair lay between him and Dennis like an invisible wall. He didn't know what to do but felt sure he should be doing something.

"Dennis just wants to help. He wants to be close to you, Gordon, that's all. Every trip up there he'd always be saying how wonderful it was going to be when you could all finally be a family again."

"Dr. Loomis knows you're here," the receptionist said. "It shouldn't be too much longer. He said to go wait in his office."

"I can wait here," he said before she could get up. "This is fine. I'll just sit here and wait." The last thing he wanted was to disrupt the office routine, but he was desperate. He had to borrow fifty dollars. The electric company's second notice had thrown him into a panic. It was bad enough eating at Delores's almost every night this past week, but it was humiliating to show up empty-handed.

The only job he'd been able to get was with a moving company. Thinking his palm had healed, he had worked two days only to have the cut reopen. Blood dripped onto the white-tiled foyer of a house, horrifying the new home owner. "What if he's got AIDS?" she fumed, pointing down at Gordon. He was on his knees, scrubbing the stained grout and trying to keep paper towels rolled around his hand.

"What about my kids? My baby's crawling now."

The foreman's boot nudged him. "You got AIDS?"

"No."

The foreman gave him cab fare and sent him home until "the damn thing heals."

Determined to get the job back, he did everything with one hand. Twelve fifty an hour was good money, and the men had liked him. There hadn't been anything he couldn't lift. He sniffed at his hand again. It still ached, and this morning there had been a funny odor from the bandage. The surgical tape and gauze were expensive, so he had been changing the dressing only every few days.

"The chairs in the doctor's office are a lot more comfortable than those."

"Oh, I'm comfortable. These chairs are fine." He patted the wooden arms. "They're very good, very comfortable."

"Well . . ." She sighed. "He should be right out." She returned to her keyboard.

He kept glancing over the magazine at her. Maybe Dennis had broken up with Jilly and this was his new girlfriend. Older, she wasn't nearly as pretty as Jilly or as classy. She was chewing gum with her front teeth. Her hair was brassy and ragged, not soft and perfectly neat as Jilly's. An odd pang of jealousy rose in his chest. Why did he feel so agitated? Did he want his brother to still be seeing Jilly? The door opened. An older man arrived and sat across from him. Moments later a nurse led out a gray-haired woman whose mouth was stuffed with bloody gauze packs. The man got up and put his arm around her, asking if she was all right as they left.

"Gordo."

He followed Dennis into his office. The furniture was massive, with dark, burled surfaces inlaid with bands of golden wood. The blinds were closed and the lampshades were black. Gordon had to squint to see his brother on the other side of the desk. Knowing Dennis's pride in possessions, he praised the handsome office, taking particular note of the large gilt-framed oil painting above the credenza. It was a portrait of a white-haired gentleman in a black suit and stand-up shirt collar. "I feel like I know him. He looks so familiar," Gordon said, angling his head for a better perspective.

"Well, he should. That's Clancy Meldrin."

"Who's he?"

"Our great-grandfather. Mom's grandfather."

Gordon was amazed at the resemblance. The man was an elderly version of Dennis. His mother used to brag how Clancy Meldrin had owned hundreds of acres in Ireland until an Englishman cheated him out of it. Gordon asked where he had gotten the painting. It looked old, but he didn't remember ever seeing it around the house. Dennis said he'd had it painted. From what? Gordon asked. An old photo or something?

"From life!" Dennis laughed. "Pretty good, huh?" He had posed, telling the artist to imagine him as an old man a hundred years ago in Ireland, a man of culture and learning despite having lost everything. Gordon's eyes moved between the portrait above and the one below, saddened by the ghostly double image. For the first time in his life, he was embarrassed for his brother.

He abbreviated his reasons for coming. He had lost his job at the Market but had found another one. He held up his bandaged hand with a quick mention of the slicing blade, rush hour, Petro's flaming paddle. Not to worry, though, because he had this other job now, but first the cut had to heal. "They'll take me back. I just have to get it so it won't keep splitting open."

Dennis asked to see it. Gordon peeled back the tape. Recoiling a little, Dennis said it was infected. Yes, Gordon admitted. He'd figured it was, from the redness and the smell these last few days. He needed stitches and antibiotics right away, Dennis said.

But that wasn't even why he was here, Gordon said quickly. He needed fifty dollars to pay his electric bill. A loan, of course. As soon as the moving company sent his check, he'd pay Dennis back.

"Look," Dennis said. He bent over the desk, scribbling angrily. "This is ridiculous. When are you going to start listening to me? What makes you think you have all the answers?"

"I don't think that."

"You don't? You could've fooled me, Gordo." He ripped the check from the pad and slapped it onto the desk.

"I can't cash a check. I had to close out my account. That's not going to work," he said, pointing.

"It's not a check. It's a prescription for that fucking mess of a hand you've got."

"Oh. I'm sorry. When I saw you writing, I just thought . . . I thought it was a check."

Dennis shook his head. "You could've been at Corcopax! I had it all lined up!"

"They weren't going to hire me."

"You don't know that!"

"Yes! They told me. The lady, she—"

"I could get you on at the brewery. One phone call, that's all it'll take. Look, I'm going to call Tom Harrington right now and—"

"No! Don't. I don't want you to do that."

Dennis looked at him. "What do you want? Do you even know? Well, do you?"

"I'm sorry. I don't want to upset you. I—"

"Don't want to upset me?" Dennis threw up his hands and laughed. "You're the most upsetting thing in my life!"

"I am?" His face was burning.

"Here." Dennis said, and stretched back to reach into his pocket. He flipped four one-hundred-dollar bills onto the scrip. "And you *still* don't have to pay me back."

"I only need fifty, and I'll pay you back next week."

"I'll be gone all next week, so here, take it." He held out the money. "And if you don't need it, fine, just bring it back."

Gordon hesitated, then took the money. "Where are you going?" he asked sheepishly.

"Bermuda." Dennis smiled. "Dental conference."

"With Lisa?"

"No, not this time. Too many seminars. She'd hate it."

"You're going with Jilly Cross, aren't you."

"What? What're you talking about?"

"That's where she's going—Bermuda. That day at the post office, that's what she said." He put the money back on the desk. "Why would you do that? What about Lisa and the kids? You've got such a wonderful life, you—"

"Look, you don't know what the hell you're talking about."

"I'm talking about you and Jilly Cross. Going on a trip together. How can you do that?"

Dennis shot out of his chair. "You don't want my help and I don't need yours, okay?" He picked up the bills and flung them into Gordon's face. "So just get the fuck out of here!"

The bus ride seemed to take only minutes, the walk after that even less. He didn't know if she'd be home, and it didn't matter if she wasn't. At least he'd have tried. At least he'd have done something. He couldn't spend his whole life turning his back, not seeing, never doing the honorable thing. It wasn't just Lisa and the children caught in his brother's mess, but an innocent young woman as well.

Jimmy scootered alongside him down the street. "Come on out back and see the treehouse. Me and Dad, we just finished it yesterday."

"Yes. But first I have to talk to your mother." He rang the bell. Jimmy ran up and opened the door.

"Come on!" He gestured Gordon inside. "Mom! Hey, Mom, where are you? Uncle Gordon's here! She's probably working out downstairs." He opened the cellar door. "Mom! Hey, Mom!" he bellowed down.

"What? What is it?" Lisa shouted back, running up the stairs with a look of alarm. "Gordon!" She hugged him. "Oh, Gordon, I'm so thrilled you're here. What a nice surprise." She looked at him. "Is everything all right?"

"I need to talk to you."

"Of course. Yes. Jimmy, you can go back outside now."

"But I told Uncle Gordon I'd show him the treehouse. It'll only take a minute."

"Outside, now." She ushered him to the door. "I'll call you when we're done."

After Jimmy left, she offered him coffee, juice, water. No, nothing, he said, thanking her. Come sit down, then, she said, and he followed her into the kitchen but remained standing.

"What is it, Gordon? Something's wrong, isn't it."

With his nod the color drained from her face. "What happened? Tell me. You can tell me."

He kept looking at her. In all his indignation and anger, he had not planned what to say. "It's all right," she coaxed. "Whatever it is, I'll help you. You know I will. You're like a brother, my own brother." She put both hands on his arms. "I mean that. And I hope you feel that way about me."

"I do."

"Because we're a family, so we have to help one another, right?"

He nodded. Yes. That was it, exactly why he was here, and yet here he was again, paralyzed. He couldn't, couldn't do it, didn't have the guts, courage, strength, whatever it took.

"Do you want me to call Dennis? If he's between patients, he can probably—"

"No, that's why I'm here. It's about Dennis. He's going out with another woman. He has been, and now he's going on a trip with her."

She closed her eyes, for a moment seemed to teeter back and forth. "How do you know? Who told you?" She looked dazed.

"Dennis. And she did too, in a way."

"Dennis told you? He said that? That he's seeing another woman?" She stared at him.

"I saw him with her. And when I asked him he admitted it."

"So all those times he said he was with you he was really with her." Her eyes raced over the room, as if clues were suddenly everywhere. "Do you know her? Who is she?"

"Jilly Cross," he said, handing her the business card with the pretty face in its corner.

After Gordon left, she sat down with the phone in her lap. She was trembling. Trembling with rage and impotence. Her teeth chattered. Even her feet moved up and down, stamping. She doubled up and moaned. Why? Why? Why had he done that? Why had he told her what she'd always known? Now, with no more lies to tell herself, she had no choice. She had to do something, hurt someone, destroy everything important to her.

She dialed the number on the card, then waited through the voice mail message. "Yes. This is Lisa Loomis, Dennis's wife. I just want you to know that I know all about you. I know where you work and I know where you live." Afraid of what she might say next, she slammed down the phone. She called her mother, then hung up before it rang. She couldn't do that to her parents. They loved Dennis too much. He was one of her father's closest friends. It was at times like this she needed a brother or sister. She felt so alone. Her poor children, they deserved a better, stronger mother, one who could hold on to their father for them. What more could she do? She'd tried everything. Better sex. Golf lessons. Being more assertive with him. Being less assertive. Keeping the house perfectly neat, the way he liked it. Letting it be a mess so she didn't have to nag the kids when he was home. Striving to be a better Catholic, her trade-off to God for a better marriage. She burst into tears, wailing in shame and anger—all the PreCana lectures she'd given, all her insipid, shallow, hypocritical exhortations to always be honest with one another, no matter the consequences, when all along she'd known, had carried this worm in her heart, allowing it to feed on her self-confidence and pride until there was nothing left. The one thing she had never done was leave.

She called Father Hensile at the rectory. Mrs. Slane said he had gone into Boston for a meeting. Did she want to leave a message? Her voice was too congested from crying for Mrs. Slane to recognize. No, no message.

It took three trips to the attic to get the luggage downstairs. She packed Annie first, then Jimmy, but left her suitcase empty on the bed. Why, when she didn't matter? Nothing mattered. Not anymore. She had already called the lake ferry. The last boat to the island left at eight tonight. She called her mother and told her she was taking the children to the cottage for a surprise holiday. Delighted to have somebody using the place after all the renovations, her mother offered to call the handyman, Henderson, and have him air the place out. "Tell Dennis to be sure and take Jimmy out in Dad's new Sunfish. Well, Annie, too, of course, if—"

"It'll just be me and the children, Mother."

"Oh. I see. Is everything all right, honey?"

"Yes."

"You sound congested."

"I am. A little," she said with her mother's uneasy breathing in her ear. Fear was in the genes. And cowardice: She didn't want to know, either.

She was loading the suitcases into the car when Dennis pulled into the garage. His face was blotchy and haggard.

"Oh, so she did get my message." She checked her watch. "I called her an hour ago. What did you do, rush over there as soon as she called? What, have you been trying to make her feel better? Did you tell her how harmless I am, how weak and stupid I am?"

"I'm sorry. Please, Lisa. Please listen to me." He couldn't look at her.

"I can't. I have to go. The children are next door. They're waiting for me."

"Wait. Just listen to me. Please. Don't I at least deserve that?"

"No!" She couldn't help laughing. She got into the car and started the engine. He leaned down, clutching the window well. Such beautiful hands; they made his treachery all the more painful. Letting her eyes linger on his for a moment, she pitied him. Always in a hurry, rushing around, quick to laugh, loving too easily but never deeply, always skimming the surface of things, the bright smile, the flashy car, the big showy house, trading his freedom, his happiness, for the Harrington connection, poor Dennis. If Gordon had never grown past eighteen, Dennis was stunted, too, ever the handsome, overreaching teenager, desperate to show the world what a great guy he was, but never forgiving his brother.

"Don't leave me, Lisa, please don't. I'll do anything," he gasped. Tears streamed down his face. "I can't live without you. I don't want to be alone."

"Then move back home with your brother!" she said as she backed out.

CHAPTER 19

Promise seemed to be everywhere this morning as Delores stepped out of The Dearborn Lady on Main Street. She had just been hired by the best dress shop in town and started next week. She had forgotten how busy Dearborn was and yet how tranquil. It was a place where everything worked the way it should. Even the bumper-to-bumper traffic stopped the minute she stepped off the curb. She meandered up one side of the street, then down the other, surprised to see so many gift shops. There wasn't a single one in Collerton. And banks! Banks were everywhere, from imposing institutions of granite and brick to the folksy two-teller branches tucked in next to dry cleaners and barbershops. She tried browsing through a few stores, but the smell of eucalyptus sprays and spices sent her sneezing back into the fresh air. At the corner she paused, surprised that she had come this far. There it was, the stationery store. Well, why not? What would be the harm? Here she was, twelve pounds lighter and all dressed up in her periwinkle pantsuit. She had a good man to love and May Loo's picture in her purse.

The minute she walked through the door she knew things weren't right. Albert was alone. The store seemed understocked and messy. The glass countertop was smudged. A half-emptied carton of computer paper lay on top, as if sales were being made directly from it. Most disturbing, though, was the sunburst of cracks that had been Albert's university mirror on the back wall. He was complaining about the new Staples up on Route 28. *That's* why all his old Dearborn customers had stopped coming into the Collerton store. How many times had she tried to tell him that—she bit her tongue. And now look at the mess he was in, a seven-year lease for five times the old rent, at one-third the business. The worst of it was the unreliable help. He was down to one part-time clerk, a high school girl who turned out to be dyslexic. When he tried to fire her, her father's lawyer wrote him a letter advising him of the girl's rights under the Americans with Disabilities Act. He'd tried to hire someone else, even offering mother's helper's hours, but everyone wanted high-tech jobs and big paychecks. So here he was working sixty- and seventy-hour weeks at a point in his life when he should finally be able "to start smelling the roses." And now, in addition to her tennis league, Cheryl had taken up golf and was always at the club. He'd even had to cancel the annual July Blowout Sale this coming week-end because she had signed him up for the couples tournament, then typically had forgotten to tell him.

Delores wanted to enjoy his misery, but the gloating would only spiral her deeper into guilt and then pity for him. Delores the perpet-ual doormat; she could feel it coming on, this desperate need to be needed. "Where's Katie?" she asked to nick the wound and remem-ber what a bastard he'd been.

"Katie? Oh, gone. It didn't work out."

"That's too bad." She imagined Katie's husband punching the mirror. Or maybe smashing poor Albert's head into it.

"One of the cleaning people broke it," he said, following her gaze.

"That's too bad." She was ashamed of herself for being disap-pointed. Her life had never been better, and poor Albert's was in a tailspin.

"I could pay you more than The Lady," he blurted, face redden-ing. "And here you wouldn't have to train or anything. You could just start right back in."

"Start back in? You mean where we left off?"

"Please, Delores. The minute you walked in everything seemed brighter and better. It was like all at once the cloud lifted. And I real-ized how much I need you. How much a part of my life you are. Everything's a mess without you," he said on her heels to the door. "I should've called, I wanted to, but you were like a crazy woman. I didn't know what you were going to do. Delores!" Of all the things Albert had ever said to her this was the most flattering. He had used and dominated her for years, and she had accepted it.

A surge of raw, womanly power propelled her down the street. And for this she had Gordon to thank. He needed her in a way no man ever had. Instead of her body he had desired her strength, and now in place of visitors' glass he needed her patience between them. The collision between his inscrutable reserve and her natural exuberances continued to leave her drained and bewildered. But she was finally learning to hold back, to walk away when it was time. However, she still couldn't decide whether it was coldness or an almost inhuman self-containment that governed his existence. For a while, his kindness to Jada had seemed the first cracks in that icy reserve. But now he wanted nothing to do with the girl. He had cut her out of his life with no more guilt, concern, or regret than if she had been a withered cane on his rosebushes.

"What's fashion retail?" Gordon asked from the table.

"A dress shop, but that's what she kept calling it," Delores said as she scrubbed the stew pot. "She kept referring to 'the industry.' Like it was some kind of secret society maybe I'd get accepted into if I was really lucky." Her feigned indifference was only to spare his feelings. He was still out of work.

"You're lucky. Every job you've applied for you've gotten."

"Not so surprising, given my vast experience in the various industries." She laughed. Too glum to be happy about anything, Gordon was trying to appear interested, but she could see what an effort it was. He had been like this since his visit to Dennis last week. "Of course, I've been working practically all my life," she added, then turned on the rinse water just as he spoke. "What'd you say?"

"Nothing."

"Yes, you did. What was it?"

"Nothing."

"Gordon, I heard you. You said something about Lisa."

He looked away, and she knew better than to pursue it. Only the prospect of beef stew simmering on the stove had lured him over here. When he agreed to come, she ran out and bought ingredients for the biggest, richest stew that no one in her right mind would want to cook, much less eat, in a ninety-five-degree kitchen. Even Gordon hadn't had much of an appetite.

Poor man. He looked so dejected. She should have insisted he borrow money from her instead of subjecting himself to Dennis's weak-kneed abuse. Whatever Dennis had said that day had devastated him. Every time she tried to get him to talk about it, he'd start looking for the door the way he just had.

Gordon was sponging the table clean. He leaned over to check the surface from all sides to be sure he'd gotten every crumb. The yellow envelope was still in the middle of the table. All through dinner she'd wanted to show him the latest picture that had come with her initial approval and this new set of forms, but he had been too discouraged and she didn't want her happiness and excitement tainted by anything negative. Never had she been more keenly aware than now of the magnetic forces, the powerful energies, surging through the universe. It wasn't just herself she would harness them for, but for him and for this child she wanted him to love.

"What about this envelope? Should I leave it here?" he asked.

"Yes. For now." She suggested they go for a walk. He didn't feel like it. He should probably go home, he said, then sat down and drummed his fingers on the table. She asked if she could change the bandage on his hand before he left. The wound wasn't as red as it had been. Her eyes blurred as she wrapped the gauze around his strong hand. He had never been more trusting or seemed more gentle than at this moment. He had changed his mind, he said, he'd like to go for a walk.

She kept looking at their reflections in the passing storefront windows, pleased with the way she looked and felt. But Gordon was gaining weight. She couldn't help it, but she loved feeding him. To-morrow she had promised him shepherd's pie the way his mother used to make it. She could tell from the picture that May Loo would need some fattening up. She probably wouldn't like American food, and Delores suddenly realized she didn't know how to cook any

Chinese dishes. The Landmark Bookstore was only a couple of blocks ahead. She wanted to see if they had a Chinese cookbook. He asked how long it would take. Fifteen minutes, she said.

"I'm kind of tired," he said with a sigh. "You don't mind, do you?"

It was silly to be this disappointed, but she couldn't help feeling he didn't want to go because it had to do with May Loo. But no, he was obviously distressed. He kept sighing.

"What a beautiful night." She slipped her arm through his as they approached the park. She felt him stiffen. "Gordon, what is it? What's wrong?"

"Nothing. I shouldn't have come. I'm sorry. I just don't feel like walking."

"All right," she said, steering him into the park. "We'll sit down, then." She brushed dust off the nearest bench, then sat down. "Gordon!" she said, alarmed. He just stood there looking down at her. "What's wrong? You've got to tell me. It's about Dennis, isn't it."

"I just want to go back. Can we? Do you mind?"

"Oh, no, of course not."

Trembling with desire, she unlocked her door. He went into the bathroom. The message light was blinking on her answering machine. She hit the play button, then sat down and slipped off her sandals.

"Delores, it's me. Albert. I've got to talk to you. Ever since you left I've been—" She leaped toward the machine and hit erase. Thank God Gordon was still in the bathroom. Suddenly she heard footsteps outside, creaking up the hallway stairs. Then Albert's furtive *tap, tap-tap-tap* on the door. She froze. If she didn't make a sound, maybe he'd go away. *Stay in there, please, please stay in there,* she willed Gordon.

"Delores?" Albert called softly for fear one of her neighbors might recognize him. "It's me. Are you there?"

No. She shook her head.

The key clicked into the lock. She watched the dead bolt latch turn, the knob move, the door open.

"I'm so glad you're here." Albert rushed toward her. "I've been driving around all night waiting for your light to come on."

"Go away." She cringed back as he stood over her, gesturing, weeping, begging her to take him back, to love him again, to forgive him for his stupidity because he had finally learned his lesson. And now he knew what was most important in life. "Loyalty," he gasped, reaching to touch her.

She pushed away his hands and struggled to get up, but he held her there with surprising force. "Stop it, Albert. You have to go."

"No!" he cried. "I'm not going to lose you. I'll do anything. Anything you say. You want me to leave my wife? Well, I am! I have! I will! Tonight! Here, I'll call her right now and tell her." He grabbed the phone. "See? . . . Cheryl? . . . Cheryl?" he kept shouting.

The bathroom door opened. "Is everything all right?" Gordon asked.

"It's Albert," she said weakly.

"Oh, my God! Oh, my God," Albert whimpered in his lunge out the door.

She got up and closed it, locked it again. Neither looked at the other as his footsteps echoed down the stairs.

"I better go," Gordon said.

"No! No, wait. You don't understand," she said, determined to stay between him and the door. "It's not what you think. He was upset. He—"

"He said you want him to leave his wife." He spoke slowly as if to make her understand.

"Well, I don't! Of course I don't!"

"He said he loved you."

"He was upset. He didn't know what he was saying. Everything's falling apart, his whole life. He needs help. He wants me to help him, that's all. That's why he came." She could see he didn't believe her.

"Well, anyway, I better go now." His face was a mask again, uncaring, impenetrable. He reached for the knob.

"Don't do this to me. Don't. Please. Let me explain. At least let me do that," she whispered.

He seemed to be looking at her, though his eyes were fixed and lightless. She wanted him to know the truth, not how quickly the affair had begun or how easily seduced she had been days after Albert's return from Disney World, but how much she had admired Albert's clever business mind and how in trying to be a caring employee and friend, she had become too deeply involved in his stressful life, all the while not only expecting, but insisting that his first responsibility always be to his family. And in this pathetic way she had considered herself part of that family. A most vital part. For she regarded herself as the cog, the one who made all things possible for Albert, his wife and children. She made sure he never went home angry at any of them. She saw to it that his business thrived. Many's the time she had played devil's advocate to get him to see his daughter's or son's side in a squabble. She knew it sounded as if she were making excuses, but she had only herself to blame. Her mistake had been in putting herself last.

"That's always been my trouble. I want to believe in someone so much, I stop believing in myself. Gordon?" Her voice broke. "Tell me you understand. Or if you don't, that you'll think about what I've just said and at least *try* to understand?"

"Yes. Okay." He opened the door. "Well . . . anyway, thank you for dinner."

His face was all their faces, but his was the worst kind of insensitivity. His was willed, worked at, cultivated. He didn't want to care or feel for anyone. Beyond his own suffering, he had no sense of otherness. Everything began and ended with his crime. And always would. *He needs his guilt, feels safe in its suffocating shroud. If he has nothing else, he has that. It gives him heft and substance. It's the only way he knows to feel real and human. It fills the void, fills all that emptiness.* Better to let him go. Without love, his heart had grown too small. And now it was too late. Such a waste, but it didn't have to be. If he would only put the past aside and find the best he can in others, she was saying. "You're so caught up in yourself, I mean, in what happened, that you can't reach out to people. Someone does something wrong and that's it? You're through? You're done? You just turn your back on everyone? Isn't that what's happened with Jada and Dennis, and now me? Gordon, you can't keep walking away from people. We're human. We make mistakes. You have to forgive us." So that you can forgive yourself, she wanted to say but couldn't.

"I have to go now."

"You know something, I've done a lot of things I'm not very proud of, either because I was weak or lonely or stupid, but one thing I've never, ever done, and that's turn my back on somebody who needed my help."

"I'm sorry." His struggle was painful, terrifying to witness. He couldn't look at her, and when he did speak she could barely hear him. "I'm not who you think I am."

"Yes, you are." She reached to touch him, but he moved away. "The problem is you're not who *you* think you are."

CHAPTER 20

A dog was barking in the distance.

"Leonardo! Leonardo! Come on, Leonardo, come on, boy," Jada called from her top step. Head down, Gordon hurried next door, not wanting to see the girl. Or anyone, for that matter. He had alienated the only people he cared about. Dennis blamed him because Lisa had taken the children and left. He hadn't seen Delores in days. But how could he reconcile her affair with a married man while condemning his brother for the same sin? Delores said he didn't know how to forgive because he had never forgiven himself. She didn't understand. Acceptance was the greater struggle. Forgiveness was words, an easy chant to numb the sin, until with time the loss no longer really mattered or deserved its raw place in the heart.

He rang the bell with his good hand. The cut was healed, but the slightest pressure set it throbbing again. He had tried to get his job back, but the moving company had hired someone else. All he had left was thirteen dollars. He couldn't even afford the newspaper, so every afternoon he went to the drugstore and copied the want ads from the classifieds. When Mrs. Jukas finally came to the door, she was all dressed up, cheeks rouged and her lipstick a bright red. Her ride would be here soon, she said. She had a nine o'clock appointment in Burlington with her cardiologist. "I'm out of everything." A sinking feeling came over him when he saw her list. "See there?" She pointed halfway down the page. "Next to the eggs? See what it says? White. Remember that now—white! Last time you got brown."

"I'm sorry."

"Leonardo! Leonardo!" Jada's plaintive call ended again in a piercing whistle. Now two dogs were barking.

"My God, she's making it worse," Mrs. Jukas groaned.

"Her dog's lost," he said. He had been missing for days.

"For good, I hope. Anyway, I should be back before you get out of work. One or two, probably, so I'll pay you then, all right?"

"I need it now," he blurted. "If that's all right," he added quickly. "I don't have much money right now. I'm sorry."

Suspicion narrowed her deep-set eyes; how much did he want? He had no idea. This list was twice the length of the last one, and that had cost twenty-one dollars. Wait, she said, closing the door. She was gone so long that he rang the bell.

"What're you, in some big hurry?" she said out of breath as she opened the door.

"I'm sorry, I thought you forgot."

"I never forget. Ever!" Her malevolent gleam made him squirm. "Here." Stooping close to see, she counted into his hand. "Thirty, forty, fifty. And you'll give me the change back, right?"

"Yes. Of course."

"Gordon!" she called as he came down the walk. "Don't forget now, white eggs. White, not brown."

Across the street, Marvella Fossum huddled on her top step, shivering and smoking a cigarette. He paused to pull a spurt of weeds from the rose bed, but Marvella's thick-tongued rant sent him on his way. "Will you give it up? Will you just give it the hell up?" she yelled at Jada, who wobbled down the street on thick-soled shoes, whipping fences, telephone poles, and now the yellow hydrant with the length of clothesline still noosed to an empty collar.

"Jada!" her mother called from the bedroom. Jada didn't answer. Her mother wanted her to go find Feaster and beg him for a hit. "Jada!"

Jada closed the door softly and slipped onto the porch. She sat on the step, staring down at the car that had just pulled up across the street. A white lady with yellow dreadlocks took a vacuum cleaner from her trunk and hauled it onto the porch. Next she carried up a bucket filled with soap bottles and orange rubber gloves. She wondered if she should go tell her the old bitch had left a while ago in a white van. All dressed up, she had been carrying a small brown canvas bag.

A crash came now from inside the apartment, then her mother's frantic call. "Jada! Jada!" She had been so happy when her mother said she was pregnant. She had wanted a baby brother or sister for as long as she could remember. But if things were bad before, they were a thousand times worse now. Her mother was constantly sick, and they had no money at all. She couldn't even ask Feaster. Ever since the cops had chased her that night, he wouldn't answer their calls or pages. To what her mother owed him, he had added the cost of the crack Jada had thrown away in the park. The cable had been shut off again. Inez had let her watch TV upstairs a couple times. But then she had to go and screw everything up with Inez, just like she'd done with Gordon. On the Thursday night that Inez always baby-sat at her son's house, Jada really wanted to watch MTV, so she climbed up the fire escape and crawled through Inez's kitchen window. She had a lot to eat, but in small portions, a little this, a little that, from all the leftover bowls. She was stretched out on the velour couch with the remote when Inez came home earlier than usual with her son. All hell broke loose. Carlos started to call the cops, but Inez stopped him. As the commotion moved into the hallway, Marvella charged up the stairs. She shoved Inez. Now the whole family hated them. Even Inez's littlest grandchildren yelled and banged on their door when they ran by.

She hadn't found Leonardo yet, but she knew she would. Somebody had probably picked him up and brought him home. The first chance he got he'd come running back, she was sure of it. In her whole life she had never loved anyone the way she loved that little dog. Not even her own mother.

Right after the pregnancy test, her mother had tried really hard. She'd even gone to a doctor for help, but he'd said it had to be her decision. She still couldn't make up her mind. Detox or an abortion. Either way would kill her, she told him. She had been clean for days, then last night Tron came by. When he and Marvella got back at two in the morning, they could barely walk they were so high. Jada stormed out of the house, as if her mother cared or even noticed. She headed for Gordon's garage for another night in the spidery dark, but the key was gone, so she had to go crawling back home.

"I been calling you." Her mother came onto the porch. She leaned against the railing. "My stomach's going whoa, whoa, like on some kind of roller-coaster ride. We got any crackers?"

"No."

"Go ask your buddy, what's-his-name over there, the big guy. Tell him it's for your mother. Say she really needs something in her stomach."

"He left."

"You're mad. You're still mad at me!"

Jada didn't answer.

"I'd just like to know what the fuck I did."

Jada chewed her lip.

"You know how sick I am? You have any idea what I'm going through? I'm tryna do the right thing here, that's all, and you're not helping one damn bit. You don't even care!"

"Yeah, I do. I care."

"No, you don't!"

"I do, Ma. I care a lot. But you—"

"Who's that?" Her mother pointed across the street.

"The cleaning lady."

The woman had gone back to her car for a laundry basket and a sponge mop. Now with everything by the door, she slid her hand up under the mailbox, then took something out. She unlocked the door, put the key back under the mailbox, then brought her supplies inside.

"Where's the old bitch?"

"She left. On a trip, I think."

"How do you know?" her mother asked in a low, anxious tone, all the while watching the house.

"I don't know—she had this, like, suitcase thing."

Her mother went inside, came right back out with a cigarette. "So she's probably gonna be gone for a few days." Every deep, wheezy drag made her cough.

"I don't know, maybe, but, Ma, you shouldn't be smoking like that. That's like the worst thing you can do."

"No! The worst thing's tryna get rid of it. And I'm not gonna go through that shit again." She shuddered. She had almost died trying to abort Jada. Once her mother's cruelest charge, the taunt had come to seem proof of the girl's worth: Nothing and no one could hurt her. And in this indomitability she might also protect her unborn sibling.

"So you made up your mind, then." She tried not to smile.

Coughing and exhaling, her mother stared across the street. When her cigarette burned down to the filter, she flipped it over the railing onto the sidewalk. "I gotta go lay down, so don't leave. Just wait. As soon as she goes, you get me."

Jada had to keep retying the plastic grocery bags over her sweaty hands. Being an intruder in Mrs. Jukas's house filled her with the same tremulous excitement she'd felt in Gordon's and Inez's. It was like her holy feelings when Aunt Sue used to take her to church on Sunday. Scared, she knew she didn't belong but was aware of something beyond herself, a presence that demanded she take notice. But of what, she didn't know. The stillness clung to her from room to room.

Marvella's footsteps moved overhead. Seeing Mrs. Jukas give Gordon money had convinced her mother that the old lady had a lot of cash hidden in the house. Last night Tron had told her about an apartment over on Brand Street, second floor, two bedrooms, just painted, with a screened-in porch. The guy that ran the place owed him a favor, but she'd need first, last, and security, which her mother was sure they'd find stashed away here. She could smell it, she said. Jada tiptoed into the musty dining room. With the shades down and curtains drawn, she could barely see. She felt along the wall, and the minute she flipped the switch the glass cupboard in the corner filled with light. From floor to ceiling every mirrored shelf dazzled with the small painted statues of children, boys carrying pails, girls with flowers, watering cans. She turned the small key that opened the glass door. Oh, she loved this one of a girl and her dog with his head back, barking. She slipped it into her pocket. Strange that an old bitch who hated kids would have all these statues of them. She knelt down and from the back of the bottom shelf took another of a girl in a wind-blown scarf, holding a bucket of flowers. She put it in her other pocket.

Suddenly, there was a crash overhead. She ran up the stairs two at a time. "Are you okay?" A dresser had fallen against the bed. One of the drawers wouldn't open, and her mother had pulled so hard that the whole thing toppled over.

"Look what I found!" Her mother held up a blue velvet Crown Royal bag. She opened the drawstring to show Jada. Stuffed with bills, it had been behind the drawer. "Told you I could smell the bucks," her mother grunted as they pushed the dresser upright.

"We better go," Jada said. The cleaning lady had driven off only minutes ago, but Gordon had left his house long before that. None of his errands ever took more than an hour. Thurman had told her a while ago that he'd gotten fired from the Market.

"There's gotta be more," her mother said from the closet. She'd check the pockets, then toss the suits and dresses back out onto the floor. Mothballs rolled under the bed. Jada kept sneezing. "There's probably thousandsa dollars someplace here," her mother said, straining to see what was on the cluttered shelf above. "Get me something to stand on."

Jada ran into the bathroom for the aluminum stool she'd seen in the bathtub. It was still wet, she said, warning her mother to be careful. Her mother told her to climb onto it; she felt too dizzy. Jada lifted the dusty covers off each box. In the bags her hands were slick with sweat. "Just old shoes. Old men shoes," she called back.

"Shit!" Her mother ran to the window. Outside, a horn honked. The car engine sputtered and backfired.

"We gotta go, Ma. What if it's her? What if she comes up and finds us here?"

"It's not her." Her mother peered through the sheer curtain. "It's

that asshole Carlos. He's carrying boxes out. I wonder if Inez is moving. That's what it looks like."

"Hey, maybe we could move up there, then."

"What're you being, stupid or something?"

"I know, but if we move someplace else and then Leonardo comes
back, he'll never find us." This had been worrying her.

"Jesus Christ, I'm sicka hearing about that dog. Will you just
throw down the boxes?"

Jada tossed them onto the bed, then climbed down.

"See! Look! I told you!" her mother crowed. In the toe of one
shoe were a pair of onyx-and-gold cuff links and a man's tarnished
wristwatch.

"Can we go now?" From the doorway Jada kept glancing down
the dim hallway to the stairs. "I think we should go. Please, Ma."

Her mother was searching through the hallway closet. "Hey, look
at this!" She held up a policeman's uniform. She put the cap on Jada's
head, then burst out laughing. "Oh, Jesus!" She covered her mouth
and staggered back. "You should see yourself. That's the funniest
thing I ever saw." Jada tore off the cap and threw it down, which
made her mother laugh more.

A shadow darkened the lower wall. Jada ran to the top of the
stairs. Someone was on the porch. They'd just passed by the window.

"Who is it?" her mother hissed.

"I don't know!"

The lock clicked.

"Ma!"

Her mother flattened herself in the alcove against the wall, hand at
her mouth, frozen with fear. The door creaked open, then the slow
drag of weary footsteps entering. They stopped at the bottom of the
stairs. "Rosie? It's me. I'm back. How come you're still here? You
must've started late," the old lady muttered as she trudged up the
stairs, breathless with her labored ascent. "Or was the place that—
Oh! Oh no!" The old woman stood in the bedroom doorway, looking in at the disarray.

Jada watched in horror from the opposite wall. Thinking she'd been seen, her mother sprang toward the stairs, trying to get past the old woman, who grabbed her arm in a desperate effort to keep her balance.

"Leave me alone. Let go-a me!" her mother screamed, thrashing and shoving her way free.

There came a sickening crack as Mrs. Jukas fell, landing on her hip. The one grotesquely swollen leg dangled over the steps, stiffly askew as if no longer hers.

As Marvella charged past, the old woman reached out. Whether this angered her mother or frightened her even more, Jada couldn't tell, but Marvella pushed Mrs. Jukas away with both hands. The old woman rolled, hitting each step right behind her mother as if in some last-ditch, desperate attempt to stop her. She seized Marvella's leg. "No! No! No!" the old woman groaned with her mother's kicks. Each blow jerked the old woman's head back.

"Stop it! Stop it!" Jada screamed, suddenly down the stairs so fast that she would afterward think she had jumped. Her mother's fear had flamed into such rabid anger that Jada was afraid to get too close. She covered her face; her muffled cries seemed to incite her mother even more. "She's just an old lady! You're gonna kill her!"

Mrs. Jukas's eyes rolled to whites, then back again, each brief gaze locking fiercely on Jada, a beacon of loathing through the waves of oblivion. Outrage and indignation would sustain her. Even with so little left, she could still breathe, still see as long as she could hate.

The bell rang. The old faded eyes widened, fixed on the door. Her mouth opened, the long wordless, soundless scream like a swarm of angry bees in Jada's brain. Her mother pointed down at the old woman. "Shut up! You just shut up!" she hissed.

Again the doorbell rang. Now the telephone was ringing. Again Marvella pointed. Someone was out there, listening, waiting. Next came three soft raps on the door, apologetic, hesitant, then heavy footsteps moving away. Gordon Loomis's shadow fell across the curtained side lights.

"Ma! C'mon! We gotta go!"

Her mother looked at her uncomprehendingly. She followed Jada into the kitchen, to the back door, where Jada fumbled to open the three locks. "She'll say it was us!" her mother gasped, then ran back into the little front hall. She stood over the old woman, grunting and jerking back and forth as if trying to propel herself into action.

"She's dead, Ma. Look!"

The old woman's eyes struggled to open, her body convulsing with the effort. Jada could look only at her mother, while below her, between them, the horrible effort went on. "I don't know what to do. Tell me, tell me what to do," her mother whimpered as Jada pulled her into the kitchen.

They ran through the old woman's backyard along the route Jada knew well, keeping to the thin strip of weedy woods, not stopping until they had emerged three blocks away. She pulled the bags from her mother's hands and her own and kicked them under a parked car. "It's okay, Ma. It's gonna be okay," Jada kept telling her mother, who limped now, barely able to walk.

Gordon knelt, his cultivator glinting in the sunlight as it clawed out the new weeds. He froze. He couldn't keep jumping up and running, but his cheek had been stung a few minutes ago. He closed his eyes as the buzzing started around his head again. Sweat trickled down his swollen cheek. He rubbed it with his dirty work glove, and the bee flew off.

Craning his neck, he saw the three bags of groceries still by Mrs. Jukas's front door. The milk and orange juice couldn't go much longer without being refrigerated. If she still wasn't home by the time he finished weeding, then he'd bring the bags inside his house. It was a few minutes past three. He was sure she'd said she'd be back by one or two. His phone was ringing. He stuffed the gloves into his pockets and ran inside. Maybe Mrs. Jukas was calling to say she'd been held up at the doctor's. By the time he got there, it stopped. He sat down and waited for it to ring again. Pieces of mulch were stuck to the tops of his shoes. He removed them, carefully placing each bit on a magazine. It must have been a wrong number. The quiet house felt too empty. His hand was sore. It first began to hurt carrying Mrs. Jukas's groceries home. Part of the cut had reopened, and bits of dirt had gotten in. In the kitchen he held his hand under running water. Ronnie Feaster's SUV was parked across the street. Up on the porch Polie was knocking on Jada's door. Three adolescent girls in skimpy tops and shorts stood by the passenger window, talking to Feaster. Gordon leaned over the sink. Across the way, a taxi turned into the driveway, then went down the street. Mrs. Jukas must be home. The taxi must have just dropped her off. He hurried next door to return her change before she called looking for it.

"Yo! Hey! Hey, big man!" Feaster called, and the girls looked back.

Ignoring him, Gordon went up Mrs. Jukas's walk. That was funny; the grocery bags were still there. He rang the bell, then opened the screen door just enough to knock on the inner door. Maybe she had gone upstairs to change before she brought the bags inside. Or maybe she hadn't even seen them. He hated to keep ringing the bell, so he waited a few more minutes, then went around to knock on the back door. She still didn't come; probably afraid to with Feaster out here. He returned to the front porch and pushed her money through the pitted brass mail slot in the door. Sixteen dollars and fifty-five cents. The minute the coins hit the floor inside he wished he'd waited. If any rolled under the furniture, she would think he had shortchanged her. He shook the grit out of his work gloves and put them on as he cut across her yard. He'd putter around out here for a while longer. Feaster had just left, so she'd probably come out now.

"Gordon!" Jilly Cross called from his porch.

"Hello," he said, grinning. Seeing the folder under her arms, he assumed she wanted to tell him about some new properties. Maybe it was her way of putting things back to where they'd been. Her hair was different. Lighter, shorter, almost ragged looking. She was smiling, though her eyes were wary as she came toward him. She seemed younger, more delicate, than he remembered.

"I didn't think you were home."

"I was just at my neighbor's, but she's not home yet. I had to give her her money back. Her change from the groceries. But see, they're still out there." He pointed to the bags, then held up his hands. "I forgot I had these on," he said with a weak laugh as he tugged off the soiled gloves. "I was doing some work out here. Yardwork."

"I need to talk to you," she said so grimly that he knew what it was about.

"Oh. Well, would you like to go in? I've got some Diet Pepsi."

"Do you have any idea what you've done? Do you know? Or do you even care? Dennis and I were business associates, and then the next thing I know his wife's on the phone screaming at me to stay away from her and her family. I told her what you did, that scene in the post office, how you were yelling at me in front of everyone and saying such horrible things. Oh, God," she groaned, blotting her eyes with a balled tissue. "It's all such a mess."

"I didn't yell at you." His mind raced in an assemblage of facts. They had been outside, in front of the post office. He had never raised his voice. No one had been around.

"You might as well have. Attacking me in front of all those people."

"I wasn't attacking you. I wasn't! I was just worried about my brother and his family, and maybe it wasn't my place to, but it was bothering me, and then I saw you and I said what I said, because I thought it was wrong, I mean, you and my brother . . ." His words trailed off. Her face twisted up in anger.

"No! That's not why," she said with a sharp poke at his arm. He stepped back. "And you know it as well as I do. It was this whole weird thing you had about you and me. As if I'd ever be interested in someone like you. That's what bothered you. That's when you turned on me! That's when you started!" This vicious jab knocked the gloves from his hand. Her folder fell, scattering papers down the walk.

He backed onto the steps. "I'm sorry. I'm sorry," he mumbled as he got the door open and stepped inside. Stunned, he watched through the window as she drove off.

Delores had enjoyed her first few days at the store. Small and cozy, The Dearborn Lady was decorated in pale pinks and greens, the ceiling soft blue with fluffy white clouds. That it look more like a lady's boudoir than a dress shop had been Jean Coppersmith's intent when she'd started the business thirty-one years ago. She knew most customers by their first names and kept careful lists of their birthdays, well aware that hers might be the only cards some of her older ladies would receive. Every inch of wall space had been given over to racks. With so little floor space, Delores was constantly bumping into things. Coming out of the storage room now, she had just dislodged a rounder of silk blouses. She could feel Jean's eyes on her as she piled the blouses onto the tapestry-covered armchair. Usually bright and perky, Jean had seemed sad all day. A few minutes ago Delores was sure she'd heard crying in the bathroom. She hung the blouses back up, then turned to see the tiny, silver-haired woman with one hand over her mouth. She asked her if she felt all right. Jean said it had been a difficult day, that was all. Well then, she should go home and take a nice hot bath, Delores suggested, putting her arm around her. She knew how to close up, and if she had any questions, she'd call her. Stiffening away, Jean thanked her and said she'd be fine.

"Well, you don't look too fine."

"No, but I will be." Jean nodded and forced a smile as tears welled in her pale blue eyes. She said she'd been dreading this day for months and now had only a few more hours to go before it was over. A year ago today should have been her wedding day, but it hadn't worked out that way.

"Oh, no," Delores said, trying to hide her surprise. Jean was well into her sixties.

Jean explained that she had stayed single because of a lengthy relationship with someone who finally got a divorce, then died two days before they were to be married in Palm Beach. "We had everything ready. Tickets bought, bags packed, then suddenly it was almost as if he just disappeared into thin air. You know how I found out? I had to read it in the newspaper. His death notice. That's how cruel his family was, how little regard they had for me. His son even asked me not to come to the wake and the funeral. 'Out of respect to the family,' he said. What was I? I said. After almost twenty years, what was I?" Jean said. She stood by the door, staring out at the huge cast-iron urn spilling over with ivy and pink and white petunias. This morning she had showed Delores how to pinch them back for more blooms.

"That's so sad," Delores said.

"You know what he said? The son, when I asked him that? He said, 'I'll tell you what you were. You were a fool. That's all you ever were.'"

"That's terrible!" Delores cried with true indignation. "I mean, you loved him and he obviously loved you."

"Now that I look back, I see that we were always very good friends. If we'd been two men or two women, it would have been so much easier. Really what we did was use each other. Because of me he could stay miserably married all that time, and because of him I didn't have any risks. I didn't have to have any other relationships. I could put all my time and energy into the business. Well!" Jean said, perky smile returning. She began to sort out the credit card receipts. "There you have it, my dirty little secret. Sooner or later, one of my ladies would have told you. They find it quite tragic. Especially the young ones. I can tell by the way they look at me. As if I have nothing. Nothing at all. When the truth is, I have everything I've ever wanted. The problem is, for a long time I wanted what I thought I was supposed to want."

The goose bumps were still on Delores's arms as she stood out on the sidewalk, fighting the urge to beat on the locked door and beg to be told more. More what? About her own life and what she should do about Albert, who was back—two nights in a row now at five forty-five for a drink and a snack, something light before he went home for dinner.

When she got home Albert was already there, laying out his martini ingredients. He was searching through the freezer while news blared from the TV. Frozen peas and frosted blocks of chicken and hamburger patties were stacked on the counter.

"Where's the Grey Goose? I've looked all through here."

"I don't know."

"How could you not know?" he asked with frantic churlishness. "There was at least half a bottle left."

"Maybe someone drank it, I don't know." She opened the closet, put her purse up on the shelf, then stood there a moment. The apartment smelled of his feet. His rolled tie was on the coffee table. His worn shoes lay akimbo by the bathroom door where he'd kicked them off. The bathroom was always his first stop. The water was running in the toilet. She jiggled the handle. Her newspaper was open across the sink where he'd left it propped for easy reading. She shook the air freshener can hard as if it were not just his odor she wished to obliterate, but him.

"What do you mean, maybe someone drank it?" he asked from the doorway.

"Over the weekend, I don't know." She eased past him.

"Don't tell me he was here again, that Loomis character?"

"It was the weekend, so what does it matter who was here?" she said, taking the vodka from the bin, where it had been covered by ice cubes. "Here." She handed it to him.

"No, I know. You're right," he agreed, eyeing the precise measure of vodka and vermouth. "It's just I worry about you, Doe, that's all. A woman alone in the city here, you've got to be careful." He mixed the martini gently, with the sterling-silver stirrer she'd bought him last Christmas. Every year she'd filled his stocking with gifts he'd always leave here. "He may act like a nice guy, but don't forget what he did." He added a jumbo Spanish olive, gave a quick stir, then took a sip.

She refused to discuss Gordon, not just because it hurt so, but because Albert seemed so titillated by the relationship. "Actually, I'll probably be moving in a few months. I need a bigger bedroom. For May Loo. And a yard for her to play in," she said, smiling as always with talk of the child.

"So you're really going to do it, huh? You've thought it all through, the ramifications, I mean, trying to raise her on your own and the whole, you know, different race thing?" he said almost squeamishly.

"Yes, I've thought it all through," she said, bristling. She had forgotten that demeaning tone. And how inferior he could make her feel until she was second-guessing her every move.

"Raising kids, it's not as easy you think, you know," he said with a grunt as he stretched out in front of the television, stocking feet on the hassock. Even the oversize television had been bought to get him to come more often. "You gotta have the right instincts, and some people just don't. They think it's food and shelter and everything else'll just fall into place. . . ."

She went into the bedroom to change. When she came out and went into the kitchen, he was still talking, now about his own parenting skills. He spoke in that hushed tone that came when he felt most profound. One of his biggest complaints about his wife had always been her flightiness. She had no depth, no interest in anyone's opinions about anything, most especially not his. Delores turned the water on low. She was peeling an onion under the faucet when he came into the kitchen, looking irritated. He asked if she'd heard what he'd said. Most of it, she said, quickly turning off the water.

"I was telling Cheryl about you wanting to adopt, and she reminded me of her cousin Sandy and how she got turned down because of her fiancé. I told you about him, the ex-con? Remember? The rape? Statutory, but still. You see where I'm going with this, right? You've gotta be so careful. It's like anything else, like with the business. It's all about presentation. This perfect image you have to create. You can't be having Gordon Loomis hanging around here. I mean, a convicted murderer, how's that look to people? But especially an adoption agency? Is that the message you're trying to send here? I don't think so. Plus, I should think you'd be a little nervous yourself."

"I can't believe you told Cheryl. How could you do that?" She could just picture the two of them with nothing between them, nothing to share but titters about her. And Gordon.

"So I told Cheryl, so what? She could care, so what's the big deal?"

"It's a very big deal. To me." Eyes stinging, she stared, knife in one hand, wet onion in the other. It took all her effort to put them down.

"Aw, come on, Doe. Don't be mad. I'm thinking of you, that's all. And of me too, I'll admit it. I mean, I know how you feel, it's like Cheryl said, 'Tick, tick, tick,' the whole biological-clock thing, so don't be making any foolish, fast moves here, thinking all of a sudden you've gotta go find a job, a guy, move, and get a kid all before next week, before the sun sets, or your ovaries do whatever it is ovaries do. Because that's what's happening here. You're, like, whoa"—he flapped his arms—"all over the place."

He followed her into the living room, her silence inspiring him to new heights of benevolence. "So slow down, because we've got a very good, very solid, very important thing here, Doe. Just you and me, right? The two of us, still together after all these years. That's pretty special," he said with his most indulgent smile. "Don't you think?"

She opened the door and set his smelly shoes and his tie down in the hallway. "You're ridiculous, that's what I think," she said, her burst of laughter flooding her with relief. His whiskery face quivered in peevish confusion, but she couldn't stop. "I'm sorry, but you are. You're so ridiculous!"

CHAPTER 21

A thunderbolt split the night with a savage *crack*. The room glared white. Gordon jumped out of bed, then stood dazed by the jagged edges flashing black-white-black-white, the hot, pulsing negative of nightmarish images slowly taking shape—rumpled bed, closet door, the cowering form in the mirror, his own. It was 3:43 in the morning. Needles of rain pelted the windows. Home. He was home. He sank onto the bed, head in hands. Dennis was right, he shouldn't have come back. *Don't, don't do this,* he told himself, but the dark miseries were already nudging one another for the lead. There were too many distractions. Ever since he'd come home he'd been losing focus.

He went to the window and looked out. The rain was letting up, the thunder stalled in sluggish rumbles like a dead engine someone kept trying to start. He leaned closer. The bags were still on Mrs. Jukas's porch. He grabbed the phone, put it down. He couldn't call her this late. Had she walked right by without noticing them? The milk and juice were probably spoiled by now, the butter melted. Everything else would be all right, but the rain would ruin the sugar and baking soda.

He hurried through the side yards and picked up the wet bags. Somehow this would be his fault. She'd expect him to replace what had gone bad. This couldn't have come at a worse time, no money, job, or friend in the world. He thought of Bernie Samuels in the next cell for the last two years. For Bernie, as often a prisoner as he was a free man, life on the outside was far too complicated. Bills, needy children, hounding women, cars that broke down. Going back in had been almost a relief. Just as criminals are locked up to protect society, so are the imprisoned safe from society's expectations, the nuances of which are like an unfathomable language for some men. Maybe he was one of them, he thought as he toweled dry the last can. Maybe freedom was the worst punishment.

Nine in the morning, three calls, still no answer. Wincing, he tried again, more fainthearted with every ring, dreading her crabby tirade about the constant calls when she was trying to sleep. Relieved, he hung up, then left to get the paper at the drugstore. He'd had to buy it ever since the clerk caught him copying the want ads. He noticed Mrs. Jukas's newspaper wedged between her doors. She always brought it in as soon as it came. He climbed the steps, rang the bell, then gave a few sharp raps on the door before starting off again for the store. He was on his way home when Jada Fossum came around the corner.

"Good morning," he said quietly.

"Morning," she muttered, and hurried on by, hugging herself in the eighty-five-degree heat. Highs in the nineties had been forecast for the next few days. The newscasts were warning people to drink plenty of fluids and stay out of the sun. Especially the elderly.

"Gonna be a hot one," the mailman said as he came down the walk from the old Lang house on the corner.

"Yes," Gordon said with a sudden jolt, remembering the old story of Mr. Petracolli, helpless on his cellar floor for days until a mailman found him.

The mailman slid an envelope into Mrs. Jukas's door slot. He took a roll of magazines from his bag and stuffed them into her mailbox. "Here you go," he said, coming up Gordon's walk with the latest batch of overdue notices.

Gordon thanked him, then asked if Mrs. Jukas had mail in her box. Old mail, he tried to explain. "In her mailbox," he added with an awkward gesture toward it.

"Just a couple catalogs," the mailman said skeptically. "First class she has me put through the slot. Why?"

"I just wondered. I thought maybe she didn't bring it in or something." He shrugged uneasily with the young man's puzzled scrutiny. "Her paper, it's still out there."

"She's there, though, right? I mean, she's not away or anything." He took a notepad from his shirt pocket. "Must be, she's not on my hold list." He flipped it closed. If Gordon was worried, he could call in to his supervisor. They'd get a cop out to check on her.

"Oh no!" Gordon said quickly, knowing how upset she'd be. She was probably just resting, he reassured the mailman. And himself.

Gordon realized he had circled almost every ad in the column when he came to the Harrington Brewery ad. "Warehouse/stock. Excellent benefits. 555-2233." Dennis had wanted him to do this in the first place. If he had, he might not be in this mess. He couldn't very well ask his brother for help now, but doing it on his own might close the breach between them.

The man who answered said he was sorry, the position had already been filled.

"Mr. Harrington? Is that you?" Gordon asked, his throat constricted by such unnatural brashness.

"Uh, no, this is Bill Powers. Did you want Mr. Harrington? I'll put you through."

"No, that's—" Gordon was saying when another voice came on the line.

"Mr. Harrington's office. May I ask who's calling?" said a woman's clipped English accent. When he didn't answer she repeated herself.

"Gordon Loomis," he finally said, then heard a click.

"Gordon," Mr. Harrington answered almost immediately. "What can I do for you?"

"I'd like a job, sir," he said, eyes closed, cringing. "If you have one. Available, that is."

"Certainly, Gordon, but off the top of my head I'm just not sure what's available right now." Had he tried Personnel? Yes, he just had. Mr. Harrington took his number. He'd look into it and get back to him as soon as he could.

The phone rang moments later. "Gordon. Tom Harrington here. I think we have something for you." There had been a new hire, but Personnel said it hadn't been finalized. Harrington asked when he could come in. Now, Gordon said. Right now.

He walked so fast to the bus stop that he was almost running. If they hired him and let him start today, he'd have almost a full week's pay. With health insurance he could get a doctor to look at his aching hand. The slightest pressure caused a foul-smelling yellow fluid to seep out. He'd be able to pay some bills, maybe start putting a little aside every week, a cushion against emergencies. The house had seemed perfect at first, but now he was noticing the hairline cracks in the plaster ceilings and the rattling pipes. The paint on the back of the house was peeling, and the garage roof was starting to rot. With a steady salary he could buy what he needed to do the work himself. As the bus creaked along, he gazed out at the hot streets with growing pleasure. If he did get the job, he'd be Mr. Harrington's best worker. He wondered if he should tell the interviewer he didn't drink. It might be a plus. They'd never have to worry about that being a problem on the job, but on the other hand, maybe some knowledge of the product was required.

The bus passed Delores's building and he peered up at her windows. He wondered if Delores liked her new job. She was probably very good at it given her own flashy sense of style. He had thought of her often in the last few days. With every problem he'd find himself wondering what Delores would say or do. By now she would have given him the inside story on the brewery, who was who and what to look out for. Thinking of her fortified him enough to push open the gleaming dark green doors of the brewery.

"Mr. Loomis!" The receptionist's wide smile greeted him as if her day were complete now that he had arrived. He accompanied her down two flights, then through a series of unmarked steel doors. The familiar *bang! bang! bang! bang!* closing hard behind set him oddly at ease. They continued through a long, winding gray corridor. He'd never find his way back alone but it didn't matter. She was tall and thin, with dark curly hair, a large hooked nose, and a watery trill of a voice. He wondered if she was single, then thought of Delores and felt guilty. "This is such a good place to work," she was saying. "Everyone's always so nice. And at Thanksgiving we all get turkeys. And then Christmas there's a big party downstairs with lobsters and shrimp and every kind of hors d'oeuvre. I think you're going to like it here a lot." She paused at the double steel doors at the end of the corridor.

"Oh, I don't know. I'm just here for the interview."

"No problem. You're in." She opened the door into the bright, cavernous warehouse, where hundreds of green-and-gold cases of Harrington beer rattled along conveyor belts onto pallets, which forklifts moved onto wide ramps into the trailers of waiting trucks. The workers all wore green jumpsuits and weight belts.

"Mr. Loomis!" the barrel-chested supervisor grabbed his hand and shouted through the windowless clamor and stark lights. Gordon grinned. For the first time in weeks a sense of calm, of relief, settled over him.

Jada's feet stuck to the floor as she tiptoed into the hot, airless bedroom. The old lady's statues were still on the dresser. She reached out for one and her mother groaned, struggling to sit up. For the last twenty-four hours she had been drifting in and out of awareness. The old lady's money had bought twenty rocks, and her mother had smoked them all. There was fifteen dollars left. Jada wanted to buy food, but every time she felt under the mattress for the money, her mother would wake up.

Her mother clung to the side of the bed, eyes widening as she swayed back and forth. "Too far down, 's too deep." Her voice slurred with fearful wonder before she sagged back against the wall.

Jada slipped the statues into her pocket. She'd sell one to Bruce over on Alston Street, then go buy groceries. He usually took whatever her mother brought in. He wasn't fussy because he didn't pay much. Jada had already decided to keep the statue of the girl and the dog. Leonardo used to look up at her like that. Yesterday she'd gone by a yard where a black puppy was tied to the clothesline. He squirmed and squealed trying to get to her until a young guy came out of the house and took him inside.

Out on the street, Inez's sons were filling their pickup trucks with the last of her furniture. When they went back upstairs, Jada ran outside. Her eyes locked on the square brown house across the street. Her mother had been on the old lady the minute she came through the door, so maybe she didn't know it was them. Maybe she'd only gotten a few bruises and now she was all right. Probably just too sore to come outside. She could still hear the *thud thud thud* of the old lady's head hitting the steps. Maybe she'd just passed out for a while. Or maybe she was dead.

"Jada! Hey, Jada!" Thurman called from behind.

"Asshole," she muttered, and walked faster. She was sick of him and everyone else in her shitty life. Last night she had called Uncle Bob to tell him about the baby and see if maybe he could talk his sister into rehab. Aunt Sue answered and said he wasn't there. It felt like there was a wall around her, holding her in, stopping her no matter where she went or what she tried to do. She used to be able to take it. Getting in people's faces used to be a rush, but not anymore. Everything sucked. The world felt heavy and slow, like a bad dream she couldn't wake up from.

She'd forgotten what a freak Bruce was. She waited while he finished his call. She stood a head taller than Bruce, whose shiny white skin was like the wet underbelly of a fish. His bright-blue Hawaiian shirt was so much longer than his bicycle shorts that for a moment she'd thought the shirt was all he had on. He paced around the apartment, shouting into his cell phone to someone who had borrowed his car three weeks ago and still hadn't returned it. She realized he was talking to an answering machine when he said, "Fuck!" every time the tape ended and he had to hit redial. If it wasn't back by the end of the day, he was going to call the cops. "You got five hours, that's all. Five fucking hours!" he screamed.

"It's so beautiful here," she said when he finally hung up. Everything was purple—curtains, furniture, the carpet. Even the walls. The television set was as big as a movie screen. When she'd come before, her mother had made her stay in the hallway. So far she had counted six long-haired white cats. Another had just crawled out from under the ruffled sofa skirt to slither its purring body between her legs. She picked up a purple glass clown from one of the tables. "Are these real diamonds?" she asked of the glittering eyes and buttons.

"Put it down! Put it down! Put it down!" Bruce cried, wide-eyed and pointing until she did. "You got something?" He held out his hand. She gave him the statue, and he peered at the base. "Hummel. Five bucks."

"Five bucks! The last guy said . . . twenty-five." Damn, for hesitating. Now the creep was laughing.

"You better go back fast before he changes his mind," he said, handing it back.

"It's too far. My ride, she's gone now. C'mon, twenty." She held it out, but he shook his head. "It's a nice statue, it's worth it."

"Not to me it ain't."

"What, then?"

"Like I said, five."

Her hand closed over the bulge in her pocket. Maybe for two he'd give her fifteen. "All right, fifteen," she pressed, wanting to keep the one she liked.

"No. Get outta here." He waved her off with both hands. "I don't like doing business with kids, especially freaked-out crackheads."

"I'm not a crackhead!"

"Yeah, right. I seen you here before with your friend there, that what's-her-name Marbella rag." He opened the door.

"Marvella. Yeah, well, she's my mother."

"Same difference." He shoved her into the hall and slammed the door.

"Fuck you, you fucking fag!"

———

Jada sat at the last empty table. She told the Cambodian guy behind the counter that she'd order as soon as her friend came. She kept looking out at the street for that figment of her hunger. She wasn't sure exactly what she was going to do, but if she didn't eat something soon, she was going to be sick. Dizzied by the smell and sight of so much food—pizzas, subs, spaghetti and meatballs—she held on to the table to keep from toppling off the chair. Two men came in. She swallowed hard against her churning stomach. The older one had a limp. The younger man's belly squashed over the counter as he placed his order.

"Hey!" the Cambodian called as Jada stared at the stained paper menu. "Hey, you! Girl! They need the table."

"Okay. I'll wait over here, then." She stood by the counter, leaning against the wall to steady her wobbly legs.

"Steak and cheese," the older man said.

"Make that two," his companion said, then they sat at the table.

A few minutes later their subs appeared in the pickup window behind the counter. Jada couldn't take her eyes off them. The Cambodian was writing down a phone order. The two men were talking. She edged closer along the counter. "You sick of waiting for your friend?" the Cambodian asked as he hung up the phone. She nodded.

"So, you gonna order?"

"Yeah, but I don't know." She peered up at the wall menu. "I'm still not sure. But the subs, they're ready." She pointed behind him, and he turned.

"Seventeen," he called, placing them on the counter.

One in each fiercely tight hand, Jada was halfway out the door, running, before he managed to shout, Stop! Stop, as if she would, or could, as if anything mattered beyond the promise of this warm cheesy grease between her fingers.

Thurman was on her front step when she came down the street eating the second sub. Dyed orange hair stuck up from his head like waxed carrot tips. She wolfed down the rest before he could ask for some. She sat beside him and felt sick to her stomach, but not weak the way she had before. He said Polie was looking for her. He needed them to do a drop in Dearborn, a really big one. Polie and Feaster wouldn't look right, but Thurman and Jada would look just like any other kids hanging in the park.

"Yeah, right." The last thing on earth she looked like was some rich Muffy from Dearborn.

He slung his arm over her shoulder. "We'll act like we're on a date or something."

"No fucking way." She pushed him off.

"You have to. Your mother already said."

"Let *her* go, then. Want one?" She gave him one of her mother's cigarettes. Instead of eating, she'd been smoking like a fiend these last few days. She took a long drag, then tossed the burning match onto the dry grass. She watched the circle it burned. JumJum used to do that, even in the house. Her job used to be stamping out his matches. She'd get a buck for every one.

"Twenty each, that's what Polie said."

Two days had passed without a word from Mrs. Jukas. If they had kept her in the hospital, wouldn't she have had someone call him by now? Maybe she was too sick to care about groceries on her porch. He couldn't remember which doctor she was going to see or if she'd even told him. Dennis had her niece's number in Michigan, but he wasn't ready to talk to Dennis yet. At least not until he actually started working next Monday. Again last night the house had been dark, even during all the commotion. Earlier in the evening he had seen Jada and Thurman drive off in Feaster's Navigator. When they returned, it was late. Marvella Fossum ran out and kept trying to climb inside with Polie and Feaster, making so much noise that the police came. One of them was the Jamaican cop Gordon had met his first week home. With the lights spinning on the curtains, he tried to talk himself into going out and telling them he was worried about Mrs. Jukas. But just as suddenly as it had started, Jada led her mother back inside and the police were leaving.

Twenty-five years ago, the biggest ruckus on Clover Street used to be Mr. Shire's weekend binges. When he was especially bad, Mrs. Shire would lock all the doors, triggering Mr. Shire's barrage of rocks banging off the dented aluminum siding until the police would finally come and talk Mrs. Shire into letting him in. Gordon folded the paper towel into a smaller and smaller square. No, the biggest commotion on Clover Street had been the morning the cruisers came for him.

He dialed Dennis's number. No one would be home now. He'd leave a message about Mrs. Jukas. That way Dennis could handle it himself. Lisa answered and he stammered a moment, saying he was surprised, he thought she was at the lake. She had been, but Dennis had asked her to come home, had begged her. Their first appointment with the marriage counselor was tomorrow. Gordon squirmed, almost in real pain. He didn't want to hear or be part of any of this, but Lisa continued. She'd already had one session herself but had been so insulted when the counselor called her an enabler that she almost got up and left. But it was true. She'd ignored the signs and looked the other way for years not because she loved Dennis so much that she was afraid of losing him, but because she didn't love herself enough to do something about it.

"Now that I look back I can see what I was doing, but when you're in the middle of it, it all seems . . . normal. Or at least I convinced myself it was. Every time I think of it, I'm just so disgusted with myself. Everyone must have known." She gave a bitter little snort. "I mean, if you did, so did a lot of other people. But you were the only one who would tell me. The only one with enough courage."

"No, that wasn't it. I was mad."

"Well, thank you, then. I'm glad you were."

"I mean I was mad at Dennis, that's why I told you."

"Having it come from his big brother was a shock, a real wake-up call. He's the one who's always had to put your life back together, and here you are telling him he's doing something wrong."

He knew what she was trying to say, but he couldn't help bristling. "I don't know if you've heard yet or not," he said with bruised dignity, "but I've got a new job, thanks to your father. I start Monday at the brewery. I'll be working full-time."

"Oh, Gordon!" Her voice broke. "I'm so happy for you. For all of us."

As soon as he hung up, he realized he hadn't said anything about Mrs. Jukas. Instead of calling back, he decided to go next door and look around more carefully. He had just gotten outside when his phone began to ring.

"Gordon?"

"Dennis!" He smiled, relieved to hear his brother's voice. "Talk about mental tel—"

"What the fuck are you thinking, going to my father-in-law without asking me? Without even a phone call! What's wrong with you? Don't you get it? Don't you know how things work?"

"I'm sorry. There was an ad. So I went, that's all. Well, first I called."

"You couldn't call me? How 'bout a heads up? How 'bout some goddamn simple consideration for my situation here?"

"That's why I couldn't call you. I didn't want to put you in a tight spot. I figured I'd just call and ask—"

"Yeah, and go right over my head, right? Like Dennis is on everyone's shit list, so forget about him. Don't even consider how he'll feel."

"No! No, Dennis, I swear. It wasn't like that at all. In fact, I didn't even think I'd get a job, much less get put through to Mr. Harrington."

"You know, my whole life I've been living in your shadow. Always embarrassed, always afraid no matter what I said or did, the only thing people'd be thinking was, I wonder if he's like his brother."

"I'm sorry. You don't know how sorry I am."

"No, you're not sorry. You're a fuck-up, a serial fuck-up, and you don't even know it."

Dennis's tirade continued unchallenged. A tide of seething anger rose in Gordon's chest, then ebbed: how naive to think he could work at the brewery. Sooner or later he would offend or frighten someone, and the fallout would be so much worse than if he worked for a stranger. "Don't worry, I'm not going to take it," he managed to interrupt. "I'll call Mr. Harrington—or you can if you want," he added quickly. "You can tell him I don't think I should because of the family connection."

"I can't do that! See? See the corner you've painted me into?" Dennis groaned.

No, he didn't see, he thought, crossing the lawn. His brother was being obstinate. Whatever move Gordon made was bound to be the wrong one. Now more than ever he wished he could talk to Delores. She always understood the complexities of family life, which right now seemed far more trouble than they were worth. For the briefest of moments he regretted the things he'd said to her, then as quickly reminded himself of her terrible duplicity. He wished he were far away from here right now, with no one to think of but himself.

There were two more newspapers on Mrs. Jukas's porch. Her mailbox lid stuck up over the catalogs jammed into it. He rang the bell, knocked on the door, then went around to the back of the house. On the top step the old metal milk crate still held the same three cans that it had for days. The wooden door rattled with his knock, and dust puffed out of the sagging screen. He leaned over the loose railing and looked in the window. Nervous as he was, he strained closer. If she walked into her kitchen right now and saw him, she'd have him arrested; no explanation would suffice. The cupboard doors above the stove were open. Cookies spilled onto the counter from a torn bag. There was a bottle of ginger ale on the table. This was nothing like the destruction in his own kitchen, but it didn't look right, not at all the way the old woman would leave things. As he came down the steps, a glint in the dewy grass caught his eye. A key. He picked it up, then went back up to try it in the lock when he realized how stupid that was.

Instead, he pushed the key through the mail slot. It fell with a clink on the other side of the door. He blew street dust off the newspapers, then forced them through the slot. At least now there were fewer signs of an empty house. Next he slid through the catalogs one by one, then her *Newsweek* magazine. He glanced in the window as he turned to go. What was that? He pressed his face against the grimy glass to see through the curtain. It was a shoe, a black shoe, a woman's foot just barely visible inside the front hall. "Mrs. Jukas! Mrs. Jukas!" he shouted as he banged on the window, then on the door. Wait. What was he doing? If she could get up, she wouldn't be lying there. His hand closed over the doorknob, then pulled back, fearful not of what he might find, but of what might happen if he entered a house without permission. "Mrs. Jukas!" he called, cheek against the glass. "I'll be right back! It's all right! I'm going to get help!"

He ran down her walkway, then stood staring up and down the street. The young woman who lived on the corner was pushing her toddler, who sat huddled in the stroller between bags of groceries. She lowered her gaze and hurried by. "Excuse me. Ma'am!" he called on her heels. Turning, she hissed some Spanish invective warning him away. He ran into his house and grabbed the phone to call his brother. "Is Dennis there?" he gasped. The answering service said the office was closed, but if he wanted to leave—

Before, he'd always had to look up Delores's number, but this time he didn't. Suddenly all things seemed clear, but with a clarity that placed him outside of himself, witness to this blundering, slow-moving, incompetent man. "Please, please, please be there," he squealed, eyes closed, head bobbing with each ring as if trying to reel her in, home from wherever she might be. Her new job. She was probably at work.

"Hello!" She was out of breath.

"Delores! Something's happened. Mrs. Jukas, I think she's hurt. She must be. I saw her foot. It looks like she fell down, and I don't know what to do."

She asked if her door was open. He didn't know, he said. He was afraid to try it. "Call the police, then," she said. "Call 911, they'll come. They'll be there in two minutes. They'll know what to do."

"I can't! I'm afraid. What if they think I did something to her?"

"All right. Look, Gordon, now just calm down. I'll take care of it. I'll call. Wait there. I'll be right over."

———

Jada heard the sirens and knew. The ambulance backed up onto the lawn. Three cruisers had arrived, one parked directly below.

"Are they coming here?" her mother shrieked from the bed.

"No. It's the old lady's house. They're going in."

"What're they doing? What're they doing?" her mother whimpered into her hands, rocking back like a terrified child desperate to soothe herself.

"Nothing yet. They keep going in and out," Jada reported from the front window. The cops kept moving around. Mostly, though, they were talking to each other. The black cop with white hair was the one that had been there last night. He was talking to Gordon. Delores stood beside him, her hand on his shoulder. A small crowd had gathered in front of Gordon's house.

"They're coming out. They got her. They're taking her out," Jada said, her mother screeching with each report. "She's on a stretcher. The doctor, he's holding some kinda thing on her face. An oxygen mask it looks like. They just stopped so he can fix it."

"She's alive?" her mother asked incredulously. She emerged, squinting and cowering, from the dark room into the midday glare.

"I don't know. Maybe. They keep doing things, like, working on her."

"Jesus Christ!" Her mother covered her face and crouched low.

"At least she's not dead." Jada was relieved. For the last few days she'd been convinced the old lady's body was over there swelling up in the heat. Sometimes she even thought she could smell it.

"So now she'll tell, she'll say it was us. Jesus Christ! Jesus Christ! What're they doing now?" Her mother turned in little circles.

"Nothing. They're putting her in the ambulance. They shut the doors. They got the lights on. They're leaving."

Her mother staggered against the wall as she tried to run back into the bedroom. "I gotta go! Quick, we gotta get outta here!"

"No! No, it's too late. They're coming. Two cops, they're coming up the stairs, Ma!"

Her mother wasn't home, she told them. The older cop remembered Jada, but not her name. She told him and he wrote it down.

"How old?"

"Twelve." She was afraid to say thirteen. She wanted to be eleven, ten, nine. The bedroom beyond was silent. She worried that her mother might be crawling out the window onto the shed roof. No, she was way too wasted. The old woman across the street, she was unconscious, the cop was telling her. They weren't sure exactly when, a few days ago, but she'd been viciously beaten. She was in pretty bad shape. Did Jada know anything? No. Had she seen anybody around her house? Anything strange going on over there the last few days? No. What's in that room? A bed. Anybody in it? He reached around the corner and flipped the switch. He stepped inside.

"Marvella!" he called to the blanketed lump in the bed.

"It's okay, Ma," Jada tried to warn her. "They don't care about *that*. The old lady, the one across the street. She got beat up and they just want to know if we saw anybody over there."

Her mother covered her eyes and begged Jada to put out the light.

"Is it okay?" Jada asked the cop. Sweat plastered her T-shirt to her back. Her mother was going to fall apart any minute. She could tell.

The cop said to leave it on. He had to take notes.

Her mother said she didn't feel too good.

"When's the last time you got high?" he asked.

She didn't know. She was trying to quit, doing it herself. Cold turkey. She was pregnant. She had to get clean, she said, and something lurched in Jada's chest. Even in the lie she found hope. If they could just get through this, everything would be all right. Her mother was saying she hadn't left this bed in a week.

"Except for last night," the cop said, and she looked confused. "What was that, Feaster and Polie, what were you tryna get in his truck for?"

"I don't remember. I was mad, but I don't know why." She looked at Jada. "I was mad at you, right?"

"Yeah." She stared at her mother. "The assholes, you didn't want them talking to me. You said to come in and I wouldn't." Actually, she had screwed up the drop in Dearborn. Thurman had shown up so wasted that he could barely talk, and she had to do the deal herself, forty rocks in her crotch, with him in his do-rag and gang pants, slobbering all over her on a park bench in the middle of prepville while people kept walking by, looking at them like they were freaks. The guy that finally came was older. *He* looked like he belonged in Dearborn, but his hands were shaking and he had those jangly crack eyes like her mother's. He said it was too obvious with Thurman there, so they'd go do the deal in his car, just him and her. The minute she got in he took off. He only went around the block, but she was so scared that she riffled through the bills instead of counting and had come up sixty bucks short. As a result, she and Thurman hadn't gotten a penny from Feaster. And when they got back her mother flipped out because Feaster wouldn't give her the rocks he'd promised her if Jada ran for him. Jada had never seen him and Polie as scared as when the cops came.

"Was Feaster here two days ago? He and Polie?" the older cop asked.

"Not that I remember," her mother said.

"Somebody said they were. One of your neighbors, they saw the truck out there."

"Ask them, then, don't ask me," her mother said.

"Feaster doesn't like the old lady, does he?" the cop asked.

Her mother shrugged. Her teeth were chattering. She hugged herself.

"You see anybody over there on Monday? Up on her porch?"

"Yeah," she said, shivering. "That big guy, the one across the street. Gordon. He killed somebody once."

"But all he did was bring groceries!" Jada blurted.

"When?" the younger cop asked. "When'd he bring groceries?"

"I don't know. Sometimes. Whenever she needs them," Jada said.

"Did he bring her any Monday?"

"I don't know. I'm not sure." She could feel the sting of her mother's stare.

"Yeah, he did," her mother said, coughing. They waited for her to stop. The younger cop covered his nose and mouth. "I remember," she wheezed. "He had two or three bags." Her chest rose and fell as she tried to catch her breath.

"But he left them on the porch," Jada told her mother.

"I don't know," her mother groaned, doubling over. "Jesus, I'm gonna be sick again."

The younger cop continued trying to pin Jada down about Gordon and the groceries. She couldn't remember. She wasn't sure. Her own stomach was heaving. She had to go to the bathroom.

Maybe it had to be this way. Besides, Jukas was nothing but a mean old bitch. Even the cops didn't seem to care all that much. So no matter what, life would just go on like always. The cops were gone, leaving behind the sweet, limy scent of their aftershave, the same as Uncle Bob's. The smell reminded her of a long ride to the zoo once with her aunt and uncle. It had been Uncle Bob's first time there, too. When the baby was old enough, she'd take it to the zoo. She'd get a carriage and take it for long walks. Her mother had probably never been to the zoo either. She'd take her, too. There was so much she'd do for them, her mother and the baby both.

Her mother crawled into bed. She couldn't stop crying. Jada stroked her sweaty back. "It's okay, it's okay, Ma."

"I'm scared. I'm so scared, I don't know what to do."

"Don't be scared, Ma. I'm going to take care of you. I promise. Everything's going to be all right."

"He knows," her mother moaned. "I could tell the way he was looking at me."

"No, he was looking at you like, 'Well, it couldn'ta been her, not all sick and pregnant like the way she is.'"

Her mother rose up on one wobbly elbow. "Yeah, that's right. I'm not that strong."

"Yeah, so see, Ma. It's a good thing you're having a baby," she said, her voice racing to the manic pitch her mother hated, but she couldn't help it because this time she knew things were finally going to get better. "So you gotta eat good food cuz you wanna have a healthy baby, right? Right, Ma?"

Her mother sagged back down. She pulled the pillow over her head, begging Jada to leave her alone, but Jada was too happy to care. The choice was simple, her mother and the baby, or the old bitch.

CHAPTER 22

"Why? Why do that to an old lady?" the detective muttered again.

What could Gordon say? What was the motive for any heinous act? He had only known his own, fear and cowardice, and here it was again, tire tracks in the lawn, the confusion of voices, another question while he was still answering the first one. The facts flashed on and off in his brain. The truth was in the details, but they kept twisting the details around. Why hadn't he just gone in the unlocked back door? He'd told them twice, he hadn't known it was unlocked until they told him. If he was so concerned about her, why hadn't he tried the key? Why was his hand bandaged? Why did he put the money through the mail slot? He'd already told them. Here—he gave them the receipt. The time on the slip seemed of most interest to them. Where were the groceries, then? He showed them the bags on his counter. Where's the juice and milk? the detective asked, checking the contents against the receipt. He explained why he'd had to throw them out. A detective in surgical gloves fished the empty containers from his trash. So he had drunk them first. Actually, no, he had poured them down the drain.

So these were his groceries, then. No, they were hers. Why would he make up something like that? Maybe to create a reason for being in her house. But he hadn't, he hadn't gone inside. People had seen him over there. Only because he kept checking to see if she was home yet, but that was all. The detective's apology was abrupt and insincere. It wasn't that he didn't believe Gordon, he said. Tough questions were part of the job. Of course. Yes, he understood. But of course did not. He understood nothing.

In the days that followed, Gordon had little appetite. He could feel his flesh tightening around him. His breath came slower. And as he grew more watchful, quieter, there were moments when his sense of hearing was so acute that the tremble of leaves and branches creaking in the wind was almost painful. A pipe clanged and he jumped. He opened the newspaper and cringed with the rustle. The phone rang and his heart raced. It was Dennis. The detective on the case was Warren Kaminski, a high school classmate of Lisa's. Dennis had just given him Mrs. Jukas's niece's telephone number. She was still comatose. It looked like a house break, the detective said, whether real or staged they weren't sure. The poor old woman probably came home in the middle of it. There were a number of suspects, one in particular, a drug dealer who might have been trying to scare her. Dennis thought it was Feaster. He said he was relieved. Why? Gordon wanted to ask. Did you think it was me? Their conversation was stiff, with no mention of Lisa and none of his new job.

Gordon's first week of work had ended. He enjoyed the brewery's constant racket. In here he was a cog, one more regulated, purposeful, moving part of an orderly world. All he needed was a strong back and an accurate tally of cases skimming off the conveyor belts into the trucks. The wound on his hand was almost healed but still so tender that he wore a heavy-duty glove on the job.

On Friday Delores picked him up after work. She was going to bring him to the bank to open accounts with his first paycheck. As soon as he got into the car, he looked in the envelope. They must have made a mistake, he said, showing her the slip. He watched nervously as she counted under her breath.

"No, that's right. Fifteen dollars an hour. You worked five days. Forty hours times fifteen is six hundred gross." She handed it back.

"A week?" He was stunned.

After they left the bank, he kept touching his pocket to make sure the checkbook and savings book were still there. Delores hadn't stopped talking from the minute he got into her car. These last two weeks of silence had given her so much more to tell him in half the time. He felt himself sinking into her voice the way one surrendered to sleep. As they neared Clover Street, he was disappointed. He wished she'd keep driving.

"That poor thing," she said. They sat in front of his house with the motor running. "Imagine, laying there for two days like that. Remember I said that, how awful something like that would be?"

"Yes, I remember. You did." As long as she kept talking, he didn't have to get out. Her range of topics was like an operatic riff skittering from the tragic to the outrageous, mesmerizing in its confluence. Lifetimes were being fleshed out, each leading into the next tale, on and on in her seamless universe where all things and everyone were not just related, but vitally connected in some ultimately fathomless yet still logical way.

Now she was telling him how much she enjoyed the dress shop. The other day Jean asked her if she might be interested in buying the business. "So I called up my sister, Linda, she's the one, her husband sells bonds, and he goes, 'Oh, no, that would be the worst kind of investment right now with the stock market and everything so uncertain.' I should have known better, he's such a naysayer, but you know what? After I hung up I thought of Mrs. Jukas, that poor old woman. I keep thinking of her laying there like that, helpless, with no control over anything anymore, just waiting and waiting for someone to come along and help her. My God, it must have been so horrible. Can you imagine, every minute, every sound, what it must have been like? And I thought, No! I can't let that happen. I can't be like that. I can't!" she said, smiling.

"No," he said weakly. She patted his arm and he forced himself out of the car. In the late-day shade, the old woman's dark little house seemed to have grown taller, wider. It loomed over the street.

Jada and Thurman sat on the wall in front of the old Collerton Savings and Loan. Empty for years, the cavernous granite building had recently found new life as a furniture store that specialized in massive velour sofas and chairs with a range of custom components, cup holders, footrests, heated seats, vibrators, headphones, and built-in speakers. She and Thurman had been making their voices vibrate as they tried out the massage feature until the salesman told them they had to leave: Thurman's swearing was offending the customers.

Jada kept looking around. She was trying to think of some way to dump him. His cousin Antawan had been his last resort until the cops came around last night trying to find some connection between him and the old lady that got her head bashed in.

"Fucking Polie," he said again, then spat onto the cracked pavement. He was convinced Polie was paying him back for the Dearborn thing. "Like it's all my fault or something."

"Yeah, well, next time give us flashlights or something." The problem had been her eyes as much as the street lamps. If they got any worse, she'd be blind.

"Fucking asshole, know what else he told them?" He passed her his cigarette.

"No, what?" She took a long, dizzying drag. Her stomach was shaky. Now every time her mother threw up, *she* felt nauseated.

"About trashing the big guy's place. So now they're going, 'Oh, okay. That makes sense. The kid, he musta broke in there, too, so then the old lady comes home and he cracks her head open.'"

"Polie, he doesn't know anything about that." She threw the cigarette onto the sidewalk. How could he possibly know that? If he did, then he must know she'd been there, too. Then Gordon would really hate her. Her face was burning. What was she thinking? It was so much worse than that, even. "What about me? He didn't say I was there, did he? I mean, the old lady, he's not saying *that*, is he? That you and me—"

"No! Just me, the fat fucker. You're like the last person he's gonna mess with—'least not until he can get Marvella to get rid of that thing of his."

"What thing?"

"The baby! She's pregnant, right? He's like, 'I can't believe that rag's doing this to me.'"

"It's Polie's? He's the father?"

"Yeah! Where've you been?"

She felt numb. There wasn't any sweet little baby to look forward to, just an ugly little Polie. They had walked on a few blocks when she decided that Thurman was lying. Polie wasn't really the father, which was probably why he couldn't get her mother to get rid of it. Besides, her mother hated Polie. He was just trying to be the *man*, bragging on like that to Thurman, who until now had looked up to Polie.

Thurman hurried out of the liquor store with two cans of Ice jammed into the pockets of his sagging pants. The old guy in there was so worked up trying to show some retard how to fill out his lottery slips that he'd been able to clip the cans. They ran downtown to the common and sat on a concrete bench engulfed by lilac bushes. Thurman popped open his can and guzzled half of it. "I was just thinking, that asshole, that fat bastard, I'm just gonna go tell Feaster. I mean, he told me once, he said, 'Anybody ever give you shit you go straight to me.'"

"Polie's not the father," she said.

"Oh yeah? Well, who is, then?"

"It's a secret. I can't tell you."

"C'mon!"

"I can't. It's private. My mother, she'd like, kill me."

"Why?" He laughed. "What the hell does she care?"

"Fuck you!" She jumped up and sprinted along the dusty path while he hoisted up his pants, trying to keep pace with her long-legged gait.

"I was just kidding! C'mon! Don't be mad," he panted. Easily winded, he kept stopping. "C'mon, tell me!"

"Why? What do you care?" What did anyone? Even she did not. What was the point? She couldn't even think about that pig Polie being the father of the sweet baby she dreamed about nightly now.

With a lunge Thurman caught her around the waist and brought her down. The more she kicked and punched, the harder he laughed. "Let go-a me, you bastard. You no-good son of a bitch," she screamed, jackknifing her knee into his groin. He curled up, groaning. She was halfway down the path when a cruiser pulled onto the wide dirt path on her right. She turned, trying not to run as she hurried back. "Thurman!" He couldn't have gotten very far. She walked around the clump of dusty lilacs and called again.

"Be right out," he said above the spray hitting the dry inner twigs.

Cops, she started to say when the cruiser pulled alongside. The cop at the wheel asked her name. "Izzy Rodriguez," she said. An Anglo cop would remember Fossum sooner than a Latino name. They were looking for a tall kid with spiked orange hair, in jail pants. She see anybody like that? No, how come? What'd he do? Armed robbery. He just held up Crowder's Liquor Store.

"So how much did you get?" she asked as they cut through back alleys.

"Some scratch tickets, that's all." He pulled the strip from his pocket. "I mean, the guy was being such an asshole, I couldn't help it."

"You got a gun?"

"No! Musta been the Ice in my pockets, the cans."

Legs outstretched, she leaned back on his cousin Antawan's steps while Thurman got his head shaved inside. He came out wearing a black shirt and baggy mesh basketball shorts. She'd never seen his legs before. They were hairy and thick as a man's.

"Smooth as a baby's ass." He kept rubbing the back of his head.

She laughed and rubbed it, too. "Smoother even."

They stopped behind the drugstore and took turns scratching off the little metallic squares on the tickets with a quarter. Her heart pounded with each one. She liked this new-looking Thurman, dark eyed and menacing.

"This is it!" he promised, quarter poised over the last one, the million-dollar card. First thing he'd do was buy a red Corvette, then drive someplace where it was hot all the time. "That's a fucking rip!" Eleven cards and no winner, not even a free card.

When they came to the Nash Street Market, Thurman asked again who the father was if it wasn't Polie. She began to tell him about this rich guy from Miami. "He flies his own plane, and when he comes up he's got a condo over in that new place that used to be the old shirt mill. His name's Lenny. Roth," she continued, spotting the Roth bread truck by the Market door. "He's like really handsome and he always wears purple shirts, white silk boxers—"

"White silk boxers!" Thurman howled. "How do you know?"

"Jesus . . ." She sighed and rolled her eyes. "I thought you wanted to hear. The diamond on his pinky finger cost fifty thousand dollars, and right after the baby's born he's taking us on a trip, all four of us."

"Where to?"

"Disney World." Her first ride would be Space Mountain. That was her favorite part of Inez's video.

"Hey! Fucking assholes!" Thurman banged on the Market window. The grimy plate glass rattled, and he hit it again. The cashiers looked back in shock as he pounded the glass with both fists. Jada gave them the finger, and the bitch with the tubes shouted toward the office. The door flew open and Neil Dubbin burst out screaming and swearing at Thurman. They ran through the parking lot, almost blinded by the glitter of smashed bottles, then escaped into the woods behind the store. Neither one spoke as they pushed past spindly branches and wild grapevines that snared the treetops together like an enormous cobweb. Ahead in the clearing was a kind of shelter made from rusting grocery carts that had been covered with flattened cardboard boxes. From inside came a painful whimper. As they crept closer, it grew to a frail bark.

"Leonardo!" She sprang into the clearing. A dog's apricot-colored head rose weakly in the shadows, his hind legs splayed. Each attempt to drag himself forward came with a sharp cry. "Cootie's dog, he can't move!" she gasped, tearing the cardboard roof onto the ground. "Where is he? Where's Cootie?"

"Dead. They found him last week. Downtown, out back of some bar."

"C'mere. C'mere, doggie," she whispered, but every time she came near, the dog bared his pitted yellow fangs and snarled.

"Jesus Christ, it stinks in here." Thurman held his nose. "C'mon, let's go. I gotta get outta here before I puke."

Looking around, she saw nothing but rusted cans and the charred ends of sticks. "He's starving. He doesn't have any food. There's not even any water."

"Yeah? And what're we supposed to do?" Thurman held his nose and backed away.

"Give me a coupla bucks. You said you had money. I'll pay you back, I swear I will. I just wanna go get him some dog food or something."

"Fuck, no! He's almost dead. Look at him." Flies swarmed over the dog's haunches.

"Please, I just wanna get him some dog food, please!"

"Why? So he can stink and shit for a few more hours?"

"No, I know this lady. She'll come and get him. She'll bring him to the animal hospital. They'll know what to do."

"Why bother. I know what to do." Beer bottles and cans clinked as he kicked through the trash-strewn brush. "Same thing," he grunted, picking up a broken cinder block. "Put him out of his misery."

"No!" she screamed, both arms out, afraid if she moved, he'd do it.

"Yes!" He laughed, and the sun glinted on his sweating scalp as he raised the block chest high. The crazed, snarling creature tried to creep back, out from his long shadow, but couldn't.

"Please don't. Please don't, Thurman. Please," she gasped, barely able to speak.

He tossed the block aside. "All right, but now you gotta give me something."

"What?"

He dragged the largest piece of cardboard deeper into the woods. She followed, stopping when he came to a damp, needled patch of ground under three tall, spindly pines. She held on to the cardboard while Thurman knelt and clawed away rocks and sticks. He patted the ground a few times to be sure, then smoothed the pine needles back into place. She handed him the cardboard. He removed his big black sneakers, then lay down with his hands behind his head, looking up at her with an almost embarrassed expression.

"Well?"

"Well, what?"

"You just gonna stand there?"

"I don't know. Maybe."

"C'mon! What're you waiting for?" He held out his arms. "You're scared, aren't you."

"No."

"You ever do it before?"

"Well, yeah." She rolled her eyes.

"So, c'mon. C'mon, bitch," he said softly. "You'll like it. You'll like the way I do it." He sat up, grabbed her hand, yanked her down beside him. "But first you gotta take this off," he grunted, tugging at her shorts.

"No!" she said, crossing her legs. "Not unless we buy him some dog food."

"Not now!"

She kept thinking of Polie and her mother. Polie and the baby. Polie all the time pawing at her. She tried to get up, but Thurman rolled on top of her, forearm hard on her throat. "We had a deal, so now I'm going to fuck you. You know I am, right?"

She glared up at him. He stared back, then burst into laughter and tore at her clothes in a frenzy of giddy, almost weeping passion. When it was over they got up quickly. Neither one spoke. He urinated behind the tree while she dressed. She felt cold. Mosquitoes buzzed at her ears. She wondered if she'd been raped, then decided it couldn't have been that. She had agreed to it at first; then even when she didn't want to, she'd been too afraid to fight very hard. All she could think of was the old woman's twisted face recoiling each time her mother kicked her, so she had clung to him with such desperate anguish that in the end he had to push her away.

"What about the dog food?"

"I don't have any fucking money," he called, trudging on ahead. He was tying his T-shirt around his bare head.

"You had five bucks!"

"Yeah, before. But then I had to give it to Antawan. Sorry." He looked back with a smirk. "Besides, you oughta pay me for the favor.

It'll be a hell of a long time before you get something good as that again."

The rock she picked up was as big as her fist. She threw it hard, then winced when it whacked into the small of his back. He turned, fists clenched and glaring. Scared, she knew better than to run. She kept on walking, safer now on the sharp edge of his cold smile. She could handle this Thurman, the one who didn't want anything more than to hate. When she came to the Dumpster behind the Market, she hoisted herself up and pulled out a crushed loaf of bread.

"What're you, some kinda pig?"

"It's for Cootie's dog," she called back.

He watched her jump down. "What happened to your dog?"

"Leonardo?"

"Yeah, the shitter. That's what Polie called him, anyways."

"I think he got lost, or maybe somebody took him. I don't know. Every day I go out looking for him."

"Yeah, well, don't bother." He laughed.

"Why? You know where he is?" She grinned stupidly, futilely, heart racing with that battered hope that beats its wings faster and faster as it tailspins down from the sky.

"Yeah. He's dead. Polie put him in one of them bin things. He filled it with rocks and threw him in the river."

She dropped the bread bag onto the ground. "No, he didn't." She made herself smile. "You're just saying that." To get back at her and Polie both.

CHAPTER 23

A strand of yellow police tape dangled from the porch railing. The previous night's storm had brought down a large tree limb that covered most of the old woman's backyard. Gordon had just gotten home from work when he saw Detective Kaminski leaving Mrs. Jukas's house. He asked the detective if he thought it would be all right for him to cut up the branches and remove them from her yard so that Mrs. Jukas wouldn't have to come home to such a mess. It wasn't up to him, Detective Kaminski said, and besides, the old woman wasn't any better. Her niece in Michigan wanted the doctors to take her off life support, but without a living will the hospital had refused.

"Thank goodness," Gordon said.

"You're glad?"

"Well, of course. I can't believe her niece would ask that."

"I wouldn't want to be laying there like that, would you, barely alive, hooked up to machines?"

"No, I know what you mean."

"But if the tree's bothering you, I suppose you could always ask the niece."

"It's not bothering me. That's not what I meant."

The detective opened his notebook. "Sheila Brown. She remembers you from years ago when she used to visit here. She said her aunt was always afraid of you."

"She got over that, I think. For the most part, anyway."

The detective flipped a page. "I don't know, according to her lawyer there was some problem about a ladder," he said.

Gordon tried to explain, but the detective kept interrupting: Why had he taken the ladder from her? Where was it now? How long had he been out of work? Had his brother been giving him money? Things must have been getting pretty desperate, then.

"I was behind on my bills, but I wasn't desperate," Gordon said.

"How come you were fired?"

"I'm not sure. Neil Dubbin, I don't know if you know Neil, he's . . . well, he's volatile."

"Volatile?" The detective chuckled. "He said you tried to burn his building down."

A few days passed. As its leaves withered in the heat, the huge limb seemed to be sinking into Mrs. Jukas's yard. Decay was a quicker process when no one cared, eventually a contagion. Every day, Gordon noticed some new deterioration in the neighborhood, in his own house. And it wasn't just things, but people. First Mrs. Jukas, now Inez and her family were gone. They hadn't trusted him, but he had enjoyed watching the comings and goings of their large family. He seldom saw Marvella Fossum. The other night she fell asleep on the top step, smoking a cigarette. Jada tried to wake her up, then gave up and sat next to her. She had still been there when he went to bed, laughing and calling out wisecracks to passersby as if this were a perfectly normal situation in a perfectly normal life. Didn't everyone sit by their stoned-out mother so she wouldn't topple down the porch stairs? Was anyone sitting with Mrs. Jukas? He would ask Kaminski if she could have visitors.

There hadn't been any police activity next door unless they came while he was at work. During the day someone had thrown beer bottles from a car. Gordon went out to pick up the broken glass before his pizza came. There were a few pieces on Mrs. Jukas's front walk, but he was afraid to step onto her property without permission. Her grass hadn't been cut. A drainpipe leaned out from the corner of her house. Across the street the curb was lined with boxes of trash and an old rug that Inez's sons had thrown out at the end of the move. Jada had just come out to look through the boxes. From the corner of his eye, he saw her pull out a bent metal shoe rack, then stash it up on the porch. She pushed the rug away from the telephone pole, then rolled it toward the house. Even from here he could hear her grunting as she tried to drag it up the steps. He started into the house when she began calling his name.

"Hey, Gordon! Gordon!"

He closed the door, then through the curtain watched her struggle to get the rug onto the porch. Every time she got it halfway up, it slipped back down. Now she was trying to push it up, but she was too skinny, the rug too bulky. Watching her shove her bony shoulder up against the coarse, unyielding rug filled him with a terrible anger. He closed his eyes, trying to will away the pain, then shuddered as it tore through him. He would not do this. He could not. He would not feel this. Would not, but there it was, her, all the pain and futility he'd ever steeled himself against, not just loose in the world, but in this place, here, where he'd sought refuge.

A dusty white car was coming down the street, antenna bent, windshield smudged, and, flapping out from under one door, the ruffled red hem of Delores's skirt. "Yes," he said softly, with more longing than he had ever known before. She got out and hurried across the street to help Jada. Together they wrestled the rug onto the porch.

"She didn't want me to come inside," Delores told him when she finally came in. Gordon offered her a bandage, but she kept sucking her bloody knuckle. She'd cut it helping Jada. "She said her mother was sick. But I think Jada's the sick one. She looks awful, don't you think?"

"I don't know," he said as she opened the envelope, getting a little blood on the back of the photograph she was removing. She held it against her chest.

"She said you were just out there."

"I was picking up some trash."

"And you didn't see her?" she said with a bewildered edge to her voice.

"Not really."

"You didn't see her trying to get that big rug up on the porch?"

"Yes, I saw her." He met her gaze.

"And you didn't help her?"

"No. I didn't."

Biting her lip, she looked at him a moment more, as if to comprehend what he'd said. He asked to see the picture, and she handed it to him hesitantly. The agency had sent it. It had just come in the mail, and she wanted to share it with someone. Someone—not her family, but him, he realized.

"She's pretty." He looked closely. May Loo's stern little face intrigued him with its self-containment. "It's almost as if she's trying to send some kind of message or something."

"I thought the same thing! I'll bet they told her to smile, but she wouldn't. It looks like that, doesn't it? As if it's her life and, damn it, she's going to be in charge," she said with tender pride.

"Look at her eyes. How they're staring straight into the camera." His own eyes burned with the press of Delores's arm as she leaned closer.

"I know. It's almost scary, isn't it?"

"Think she'll like it here?"

"What's not to like? Except me, of course," she added with an uneasy laugh, and suddenly the moment had changed again. She was complaining about her family. It wasn't just May Loo they were critical of, but adoption itself. Especially by an unmarried woman not making much money who lived in a tenement in one of the poorest cities in the state. Even her pregnant, twenty-year-old, unmarried-but-engaged niece had weighed in with a warning about single motherhood. "And every single e-mail, that's the bottom line," she continued. Her oldest sister had been bombarding her with stories about adoptions that turned out badly. "The worst one was the boy that stabbed his mother to death while she was playing the piano."

"Maybe it was her playing. Maybe it was that bad." He grinned with Delores's quick laugh.

"That's exactly what I said, too, but Linda, she has no sense of humor."

The doorbell rang and he jumped up. His pizza was here, his third in less than a week. He had worked up the courage to place an order when he saw one being delivered down the street. He usually saved two slices for work the next day. That way he wouldn't have to pack a lunch. "Thank you," he said, giving the delivery boy the exact change.

"Yeah, right." The boy clomped down the steps.

"What's his problem?" Delores said as his car peeled down the street.

"I don't think he likes his job. He was like that last time, too."

"Did you tip him?"

"No!" He was embarrassed. "Should I call and have him come back?"

"Just do it next time. Um, smells good." Delores followed him into the kitchen. "What kind is it?"

"Pepperoni and cheese."

"Oh, I love pepperoni." She leaned over the box and inhaled deeply.

He offered her some, then was annoyed when she accepted. She curled the slice and ate it like a sandwich. Sauce leaked onto her silk shirt, and there was a ridge of cheese under her thumbnail. She wet the corner of a dish towel and scrubbed the stain, spreading it to an orangy smear, then hung the towel back up. He took it down and rinsed it in cold water.

"I can't believe we ate that whole pizza." She stuffed the empty box into the trash.

"I know." He took it out and folded it to take up less room. "I usually save two slices for lunch at work." He hated himself for her crestfallen look.

"Oh. The two slices I just ate. Now I feel guilty."

"No, don't. I'm sorry. I didn't mean it that way. Really."

Yes, you did, her stare said. "I annoy the hell out of you, don't I, Gordon."

"No! Really. I shouldn't have said that. I don't know why I did." He felt horrible.

"Because it was the truth. And that's okay. But what's not is setting me up just to shoot me down." She smiled, but her eyes blistered with tears.

"No! I wasn't doing that. I—"

"That's all right. People have been doing that to me all my life. I guess I'm just one big, easy target." She wiped her eyes, then blew her nose in the greasy napkin, and he forced himself not to look away. "You know what else my sister said? That the agency probably won't even approve me. Then she says the only reason she's telling me is so I wouldn't be absolutely devastated when it happens." She shook her head and closed her eyes. "But I will be. I know I will."

"They'll approve you. Of course they will. Why wouldn't they?"

She still hadn't looked up. "Because of you, she said. Because you're my friend."

"Well, then . . . well, then maybe we shouldn't be friends." Saying it sucked every molecule of oxygen from his lungs. He felt weak.

She nodded. "Maybe not for a while, anyway. At least not until I'm approved. Or maybe I should wait until she's here, you know, with me, and it's all finalized. Do you know what I mean?"

"Yes, I know what you mean. I understand. Yes, of course." But he didn't, instead felt it again, anger so foreign it felt like a growth in his chest. "But it's not just me you should worry about, but Smick, that boss of yours. Being with a married man won't help your cause now, will it?"

Her cheeks flared as red as if they'd been slapped. "That's been over for a while now. And just so you'll know, I'm very ashamed of that."

You should be, he thought as the door closed quietly behind her.

The phone rang moments after he got into bed.

"Hello?"

"Oh, Gordon. Darn, I was just going to hang up. I woke you up, didn't I," Lisa whispered as if he still might be sleeping.

"No, I wasn't asleep." He was disappointed. He'd been sure it was Delores.

"Well, the reason I'm calling so late is that my mom and dad just left. They'd come by for dinner, and all Daddy could talk about was you and what a great job you were doing, and how much your supervisor likes you. He said every single day without fail you do the work of ten men, and I thought to myself, I'll bet no one's told you, and so that's why I'm calling, just to tell you how happy I am and how . . . how proud I am of you."

"Thank you."

"And Dennis is, too, Gordon. But he's having a hard time right now. A really hard time."

"Is he all right? He's not sick or anything, is he?"

"I don't know. He just seems so flat. So distant. He comes home from work, then just sits in the dark listening to music until it's time for bed. And then he only sleeps for an hour or two."

"What do you think is wrong?"

"Us, I think."

He didn't know what to say. The silence roared in his ear.

"Would you come and see him? I think he needs that right now. I think it would help."

He went downstairs and sat on the couch. He remembered the Christmas morning he'd walked in here and found his first bicycle under the tree. His happiness deflated when his mother and father said he was too big for training wheels. He could still feel the terror and the humiliation of those wobbly trips back and forth along the sidewalk with his father running behind while he held on to the back of the seat, trying to keep his huge son balanced. And then his father's disappointment every time he let go and the bike careened out of control. It was eventually easier on them both to just quit. And then one day he looked out the window and saw his younger brother being pushed down the street. His father let go and Dennis kept pedaling triumphantly ahead, ownership his, as always, by achievement.

I'm not a good man, he thought, staring at the sheer, still curtain. *My brother needs help and I know I should care, but I can't. I don't.* He was still trapped, but here there were no guards, no one on the catwalks, and the only locks opened from the inside.

Gordon was scraping patches of peeling paint on the back of the house. His resolve to call Delores and apologize grew with the rhythm of the work. Maybe they couldn't spend time with each other, but they could at least talk on the phone, he would tell her. What would be the harm? The adoption people wouldn't know. And then when she passed all the tests and finally did get May Loo, they could see each other again. He carried the step stool around front, relieved to see more blistered clapboards. Work was his refuge. He began to scrape, working through the layers, not once gouging the wood. He didn't know why he'd lost his temper and spoken to her that way. Maybe he'd never know how to deal with people. How could he be part of a relationship when he didn't even know how to be a friend? Friendships had always been for other people. It had always been easier to not have feelings, to just go through the motions, but he was tired of being alone. Even pain and anger might be better than this. *Climb down now, then, and call her,* he kept telling himself, but he was afraid. He could feel his resolve weakening. He went inside and picked up the phone. What if Delores wanted him to leave her alone but was too kind to say it? Maybe May Loo was her best excuse for getting rid of him. The number he dialed was Dennis's.

"Dennis? Gordon's here."

Lisa slowly opened his study door. His brother's greeting was a dim smile. It was Lisa who told him to sit down, who said Dennis had missed him and was glad to see him. She said she'd be right back with coffee for them. Neither wanting to be left alone with the other, each declined, but she left anyway.

The brilliant July morning seemed worlds away from this stale room dim with closed blinds and Dennis's heavy silence. Gordon was reminded of his father's morose visits to Fortley and the pain of their forced conversations.

He cleared his throat and shuffled his feet. "Lisa says you're not feeling too good. Are you sick?" he asked. Had Dennis nodded? He wasn't sure.

"I'm all right," Dennis finally said in such a low voice, it was a moment before Gordon understood.

"You don't look all right."

Dennis sighed. "I don't, huh?"

"No. You look . . . well, depressed."

"You think so, huh?"

"Are you?" he said quickly, to parry the glint of threat in his brother's tone.

"I said I was all right, didn't I?"

"Well, that's good."

Returning, Lisa set the tray between them on the glass-topped table. Dennis waved off his mug. "Then don't take it," she said. "But Gordon might like some."

"He already said he didn't," Dennis said with such contempt that Gordon couldn't look at her. He squirmed, as unnerved by their strife as he had been by his parents'.

"But this is good," he said with a quick, eager sip. "I'm glad now that I have it. I got up so early to start scraping before the heat that I didn't get a chance to make any."

"Scraping what?" Dennis asked.

"The house. It's coming along good. Yesterday I got the back done. Now I'm starting on the front." His next sip deteriorated into a slurp that sent coffee down his windpipe.

"What the hell're you scraping the house for?"

"So I can paint it," he said, coughing. "Thanks," he wheezed as Lisa handed him a napkin.

"I just had it painted. It cost me two thousand dollars and now you're scraping it all off?"

"It was starting to peel. I did some, so then I figured I might as well keep going."

" 'Keep going'? What do you mean, 'keep going'?"

"The places that peeled, that's all. So I can touch it up like Dad always did."

Dennis stared at him. "Kaminski came by. What's he talking

about, you want to cut up Jukas's tree? What the hell's that all about?"

"No, a branch. A big branch, it—"

"What the hell're you thinking?"

"I just offered. I thought it would help, that's all."

"Help? Help who, you?"

"Mrs. Jukas, of course." He stiffened.

"Don't you get it? Don't you see what's happening here?" Dennis rose from the shadows like a flame to oxygen. "They think you did it! Naturally! Of course they do!"

"They'll find out I didn't." Fury burned in his chest.

"Yeah, and meanwhile they're asking questions all over town about you."

"Dennis," Lisa warned. "What's the point? Gordon knows what's going on. You don't have to make him feel more uncomfortable about it all. So let's just drop it, please. Gordon," she added quickly, "how about coming to dinner next Sunday? I thought we could do something special for Mum and Dad," she was telling Dennis. "The next day they leave for Australia and they'll be gone so long, over a month."

"I don't care. Do what you want. I'll probably be in bed anyway."

"No! No, you won't, Dennis Loomis. I think you can sit down and have dinner with your family at least one night, especially before Mum and Dad's trip."

"That's all right, Lisa. I can't anyway, so—"

"I don't ask much of you, Gordon, do I?" Her tone hardened. "So will you please do this for me and for your brother?"

Stunned, Gordon nodded. She had never spoken to him this way.

"He doesn't want to." Dennis seemed amused. "He wants to be left alone. He doesn't need anybody. He doesn't care about anybody. He never did, never in his whole life, so why the hell should he start now?"

Jada was lonely. She had been looking for Thurman. His cousin Antawan hadn't seen him since he'd shaved his head. His older sister,

Jesenia, on Margin Street, had heard that he'd gone to New York with a couple of gangbangers. "You Jada?" she asked as Jada went down the steps.

"Yeah!" she said, turning with a smile.

"If you're smart, you'll stay away from him."

"Thurm's cool. He's good. He's my friend."

"He's saying things about you. Bad things."

She shrugged and continued on her way. She went into the drug-store and looked at the pictures in *People* until the Indian at the counter said buy it or leave, he wasn't running any library here. She walked by the Market, slowing down just enough to flip the bird at the bitch with the tubes. She turned in to the parking lot, then pushed her way through spindly trees and trash-blown brush. Twigs snapped underfoot. Maybe Cootie's dog was still alive. She should have gone back that day and given him something to eat. No sound came as she neared the cardboard lean-to, not a cry, nothing. Not wanting to look, she ran by. When she came to the flattened box on the ground, she sat down and hugged herself. If only someone would hold her like this, be close to her the way Thurman had. She closed her eyes to meditate the way she'd seen once on television. *Sink into the dark, into the deep, deep, deep, deep,* she tried to will herself. Instead, she thought about the baby and how much she already loved it, even if Polie was the father. Her mother was still on crack. She had prom-ised Polie she was getting an abortion. Twice now he'd come to bring her into Boston, but she'd start throwing up and saying she was sick. Jada knew she was just too scared. Scared of everything and everyone. Yesterday a sheriff banged on the door. Her mother locked herself in the bathroom, shaking and sobbing that it wasn't her, that the old lady was lying, but all the sheriff did was slide another evic-tion notice under the door. Jada almost hoped they did get evicted. Because that's what her mother needed right now, a jolt to get her back on her feet and thinking straight. Yesterday when Delores helped her carry the rug up the steps, she had almost told her how bad things were.

She was cutting through backyards when she heard barking. "Hey, c'mere, boy," she called softly. The black-and-white puppy ran toward the fence, wiggling all over, the way Leonardo used to. His little snout stuck out through the chain link. She touched the wet pink nose and laughed. "What's your name, pretty boy?" She hurried to the gate with the dog squealing and yipping alongside the fence, his stubby tail wagging. "Yipper, huh? That's a good name, you little yipper." The puppy jumped against the fence and squealed even more. "Shh. Shh. What's the matter? You don't like it in there, do you. Jesus Christ, I don't blame you."

The rusty gate creaked as she forced it open. A tattered trampoline took up most of the tiny yard, leaving little room for the puppy to roam. A scum of leaf bits and dead midges floated in his water bowl. "Wanna come with me? Wanna go for a walk? Yeah, you need some exercise." The minute she touched his warm, fuzzy head, the puppy grew quiet and she knew how desperate he was for love. Nobody was ever out here with him. He was always tied up. They probably only came out to give him a kick when he barked. "Good boy, that's a good boy, now," she whispered as she untied the rope from the red leash. "Here we go!" she cried, snatching him up and running as fast as she could, four, five, six blocks. Three more and she'd be home. Safe. She put him down on the sidewalk and pulled on the leash, expecting him to strain back the way Leonardo used to. Instead, he trotted alongside. His jaunty bounce made her laugh.

When Gordon finished priming the scraped clapboards, he washed his brush and then went back out to spray the roses. All his care was finally paying off. There were only a few black spots on the leaves, and each bush had new blooms. He cut off three full-flowering stems. They were for Lisa. Her dinner was tonight, and he was dreading it. He wished he could call Delores and ask her to go with him. It seemed so strange that just when he realized how much he needed her in his life, she had to step away. A plastic grocery bag and newspaper pages had blown up against Mrs. Jukas's steps, but there was nothing he could do.

"Hey, look at my new dog," Jada called, crossing the street. The puppy wiggled toward him. "Sit down! Sit!" she said, and he did.

"Good boy!" she said, and the puppy leaped at Gordon. "Sit!" she ordered, and once again he obeyed, however reluctantly.

Gordon laughed. He knelt down and petted his back. The puppy sprang, jumping and squealing. She told him to sit again, but Gordon said it was all right, that he was a very nice puppy. "A very good little puppy," he said now as he rubbed his head. "What's his name?"

"Yipper."

"How long have you had him?"

"Not too long."

"He's pretty well-trained."

"Yeah, well, we been working on it, haven't we, Yipper?" She knelt down, too, and stroked her hand along his back to the tip of his tail. "I told him, You gotta have manners. You can't be jumping and barking and pissing on people all the time."

"Well," he said, standing up. She did, too. "I'd better get my things put away here."

"Yeah, I been watching you. You been working out here a lot, huh? How come?" she asked as he reached down for his spray bottle. She picked up his pruner and handed it to him. With the puppy happily alongside, she followed him toward the garage. "You gonna sell it? That's what my uncle Bob used to say, 'Time to fix 'er up and sell.' He does that every place he lives to get a better house, and now you should see his house, the one he lives in now. It's like this wicked nice place with marble floors and all kinds of beautiful paintings," she called into the hot, musty garage as he hung the pruner on its nail. Her ragged, run-on voice filled the bright doorway. "I was just there last week and my aunt Sue, she wanted me to stay a couple days and help her with this big party—she's always having parties—but I couldn't. My mother," she said as he stepped out past her. "She's gonna have a baby, did I tell you that? Yeah, I'm really excited. I can't wait, but anyway, she's got, like, that morning sickness, 'cept for her morning's all day long. So I have to stay home, you know, to help her and stuff," she said, so close on his heels that he almost tripped on the puppy. He picked up the cut roses. "Oh, my God, they're so beautiful." She leaned close to smell one. "They for Delores?"

"No, my sister-in-law."

"Oh yeah, the one with the kids, a boy and a girl, right?"

"Yes, well, I better go in and get ready." He started toward the house.

"Get ready for what? She having a party or something?"

"No, just dinner."

She picked up the puppy and climbed the steps after him. "You should get a dog. I'll bet you'd like that. It's nice to hold them, and the way they love you and stuff," she said as the puppy licked her chin.

"It wouldn't be fair to the dog, having to be alone all day."

"Oh, yeah, where you working now? I see you leave early, but you don't get home till after six usually."

"Yes. It's a new job."

"Where?"

"You probably never heard of it." He put his hand on the knob. "Well, I'd better get busy. I've got quite a few things to do in here." If he opened the door, she'd be right in after him.

"Too bad about the old . . . about Mrs. Jukas, huh?"

"Yes. It's a terrible thing. Poor woman."

"Well, don't feel too bad. She hated you almost as much as me and my mother."

"She didn't hate me," he said quickly.

"Well, she was a bitch—to me, anyway. Like I'm some piece of . . . crap. Like I don't have feelings or something." She looked up at him, and for a moment he was afraid she might cry.

"I better go get ready."

"You're still mad at me! I told you, I was scared, that's all. That's what happened that time." She gestured up toward the second floor.

"Yes. Well. I understand."

"No, you don't. You think I'm some kinda little slut or something. Well, I'm not! I'm a good person. I am!"

"Yes. Of course. I know you are."

"Then how come we're not friends anymore? Ever since that night you won't even talk to me."

"We're friends." He cringed. *That night.* Even the way she said it was an indictment. "See? Here, take this. It's for you." He handed her one of the roses.

"Thanks," she said, grinning.

Once inside, he hurried upstairs. He was supposed to be at Dennis's at six for dinner, and it was four forty-five. He was unbuttoning his shirt when loud voices rose from the street. He looked out the window and saw two young men, shouting and running toward Jada. The shorter man, burly and bald, grabbed her while the other tried to pull the dog from her. Jada kicked and shrieked for them to let her go. The burly man was behind her with his hairy forearm across her throat. Yelping, the dog ran in circles while the second man tried to grab his leash.

"What are you doing?" Gordon demanded as he ran into the street.

"She took my dog! This is my dog!" The second man had finally gotten the leash.

"Leave her alone!" Gordon ordered. The man still gripped Jada's neck.

"She's a fucking thief," the man shouted as if to justify his hold on the skinny girl. "She came and took him right outta the yard."

"I don't care what the hell she did. Let go of her," Gordon growled, advancing on him.

He released her, and Jada rubbed her neck with both hands. Up on the porch, Marvella Fossum peered down from the doorway.

"It's not his dog!" Jada cried. She grabbed for the dog, and the man pushed her back.

"What are you, nuts? It's my dog!" he said, lifting his chin from the puppy's lapping tongue.

"Jada." Gordon moved closer until he was between her and the men. "He says it's his. Is it?"

"No! It's mine!"

"She says it's hers."

"Hey, look, I ain't got time for this. It's my dog," the man said, backing off, the exuberant puppy in his arms. "And if you got a problem with that, then you do something about it. You hear what I'm saying?"

"It's not your dog, you fucking asshole!" Jada screamed, and now the burly man charged toward her.

"Watch your mouth, you crazy spook, or whatever the hell you are."

"Jada!" Gordon grabbed her as she lunged forward, trying to get at the man. "Stop it! Stop that now," he said. The man laughed as she screamed obscenities at him.

"It's not your dog," Gordon told her. "You know it's not, so stop it! Stop it! Why are you doing this?" Even with both arms around her, she struggled and screamed.

"Why?" He turned her to face him. "Why?"

"I found him." She sank against him, sobbing. "I didn't steal him, I swear I didn't. I found him. And I wanted to keep him. That's all, I was just tryna help him, that's all I was doing."

"Go home, Jada. Go on inside." He stepped away now that the men were gone. "Go on. Go ahead now."

She picked up the rose from the sidewalk. "You don't believe me, do you."

He nodded. "I believe you." Believed that she'd take whatever she needed to get by. Believed that for her there was no other choice.

CHAPTER 24

fter drinks in the great room, Lisa had eased her guests into the dining room. It was a casual affair, the women in slacks, the men in open-necked shirts, place mats instead of linen. Up and down the table, small votive candles floated in bowls of water above iridescent glass chips, reflecting ripples of light off everyone's faces. Lisa looked especially pretty tonight, radiant, Gordon thought as she sat beside her mother. His initial panic at seeing so many people here had subsided into a careful busyness with his utensils and his food. He was pleased to see his roses in the middle of the table, however spindly they were compared to the profuse arrangement they had replaced, pink and orange dahlias spiked with pink and white astilbe. The brighter bouquet sat on the sideboard, but it was the fragrance of roses that graced the room. He was grateful for the anonymity he felt as conversations cross-fired around him. They were all vigorous talkers, each as anxious to be heard as he was to be ignored. Twice now from his end of the table, Mr. Harrington had tried to include him. Gordon's responses were brief. His pallor ashen, Dennis sat at the other end. Above the untouched food on his plate, his fixed smile made him look bored and distracted. Across from Gordon was Father Hensile. Next to the priest sat Luke, the new youth minister. A delicate young man with thinning hair, he seemed only a shade less nervous than Gordon, and his fair cheeks smarted with any attention. Farther down the table were Marty and Becca Brock, Mitzi and Tom Harrington's very best friends. Tom and Marty had been roommates at Dartmouth. In fact, it had been Marty's sister who had introduced

Lisa's parents. Well into her seventies, Becca Brock was a petite, startling-looking woman with heavily made-up eyes and long, inky-black hair. Busily opinionated, she was able to tune in to three or four conversations at once. She had just asked Jennifer, the teenage girl hired to help with dinner, to get her another fork, her tines were bent. Dennis stared at her.

"And that was the last we ever saw of him." Tom had been telling Father Hensile about a man he and Marty Brock fondly recalled as Mossie. Lisa looked up quickly and asked her father if he'd like more wine. It was obviously a story she'd heard too many times before. The way both men told it, Mossie, heir to a steel company, got up one day in his parents' Pittsburgh manor, had a robust breakfast with his father, "steak, home fries, eggs, put on his snowshoes, then went three miles into the woods out back—"

"Oh, five or six, anyway," Marty interjected. "They owned half the county."

"He dug a little hollow in the snow, sat down against a tree, and put the gun in his mouth—"

"Tom!" Mitzi said with a pained smile. "Lisa wants you to try the new Merlot. Here, dear, let me." Mother and daughter exchanged looks as Lisa passed the bottle.

The teenage girl had returned with a new fork. The men continued to wonder why Mossie would choose to end such a charmed life. "Looks, brains, bucks, dames, the kid had it all!" Marty sighed as he cut his veal.

"Amazing," Tom agreed, as if suicide had been just another of Mossie's accomplishments.

Gordon thought of Jerry Cox. He had killed only what was already dead. His suicide had been the ultimate pretense, an empty contrition, the coward's last opportunity to inflict more pain on good people.

"Would you pass the sauce, please," said John Stanley from Gordon's right. John Stanley was a reedy, droopy-faced man whose crisp British accent Gordon found unnerving. Its authority announced itself like the running *tap tap tap* of a guard's baton along the bars, demanding attention, respect, obedience. Gordon couldn't see any sauce.

"Gravy. Right there." With John Stanley's sharp nod, Gordon seized the boat too quickly by its handle, splashing gravy into a candled bowl. "May I have its dish, please?" Stanley held the gravy boat over his own plate to catch the dribbles. "It's right there."

"Oh, yes, here. I'm sorry." Gordon handed him the dish.

Like a slow-turning beacon, Dennis's dull gaze caught him.

"You are just the most fabulous cook!" Becca Brock called across to Lisa, who had gotten up to fill her father's wineglass, though he had already said he didn't want any. She leaned close and squeezed his shoulder.

"So, Gordon, I hear you're painting the house," he said with the cue.

"Yes, sir. Well, touching it up."

"Well, you ever need any help now you be sure and call"—he peered over his glasses—"your brother here."

"I don't know, Dennis is pretty busy."

"He could use the exercise."

"He gets plenty of that, sir," Gordon said, and everyone laughed—with some relief now that Gordon had spoken and seemed normal enough.

"I did some work with the Samaritans," Rena Stanley was telling Marty Brock.

"Suicide should be a person's right," Becca Brock declared. "I mean, we control everything else in our lives, why not that?"

"For God's sake," Dennis said under his breath.

What's wrong with him? Gordon thought, looking between his brother and sister-in-law. In the watery candlelight her olive skin glowed. *Doesn't he know what he has here? Two beautiful, healthy children downstairs watching videos with the Stanley children. Friends, a brother who loves him.* Or was that it? Did Dennis really think he had no feelings? That he didn't care about him? That he never had? Gordon's chest felt heavy, watching him.

Dennis gave another sigh, sprawled back in his chair, bored with the too familiar repartee, irritated and making no effort to hide it.

Mitzi launched the roll basket and meat platter around the table again. "So tell us, Gordon," she said. "What kind of a boss is Tom?"

"Very good." He looked to make sure there'd be enough for everyone, then took a few slices. "He's a very good boss."

The teenage girl returned to say the children wanted to watch another video. Lisa said they could. Becca Brock and Rena Stanley were still on the subject of suicide. Luke (Gordon hadn't caught his last name) was telling them that his brother was a fireman. Last week he had rescued a woman threatening to jump from the roof of her apartment building. Her husband had just left her with three small children to support and—

"Luke," Father Hensile interrupted, "tell us about your sister. She's a caseworker, isn't she?"

"Yes, for an adoption agency," Luke said. "Most of the babies she places are from China."

"My friend's trying to do that," Gordon blurted, surprising himself as well as everyone else.

". . . which is my whole point, a personal, moral issue," came tatters of Becca Brock's voice into the hush. "If I want to die, I should be able to do it when I want and how I want."

"As well you should, Becca," Dennis sighed to uneasy laughter.

Lisa smiled and leaned toward Gordon. "Trying to do what?"

"Adopt a baby. Well, a little girl. She's Chinese. May Loo's her name." The regurgitation of words piled on the table in front of him.

"Who? Your friend?" Lisa asked.

"No, that's the little girl's name. She's pretty. Delores showed me her picture," he said miserably.

"Delores? She's adopting a baby? Oh, that's so wonderful!" Lisa cried, eyes bright in the flickering light. "She'll be such a wonderful mother. Oh, thank you, Gordon. You've made my night. That's the best news I've heard in ages."

Shocked by what he'd done, he looked down, his brow slick with sweat.

"You know Delores, Mum."

"Oh, yes, of course. Delores Dufault," Mitzi told Rena Stanley. "She's quite a character. One of those flamboyant, larger-than-life women, she's . . ."

Larger than his own stunted life, Gordon thought. He had told her secret, exposing her to strangers. Now Becca Brock had taken on foreign adoptions, a farce when there were so many needy children in this country. "It's just another kind of racism."

"I wouldn't say that," Father Hensile said. "Foreign adoptions are just speedier, that's all."

"So why aren't people trying to adopt African babies, then?" Becca Brock asked.

"Excuse me. . . . Excuse me," Gordon repeated a little louder, dredging the words from the pit of his stomach. "I just thought, I shouldn't have said what I did."

"Oh, no, Gordon." Tom Harrington was quick to come to his aid. "Nothing like a little more fuel on Becca's fire."

"I resent that," Becca Brock huffed with coy indignation.

They sensed his misery. Only his brother looked at him. "What I mean is, Delores hasn't told anyone. I shouldn't have betrayed her confidence." Again lowered his eyes. Dennis seemed only more amused.

"Well, *we* won't say anything, will we?" Lisa asked around the table.

"Well, no."

"Of course not."

"Absolutely not."

"Besides not knowing the person," John Stanley said, "I've quite forgotten the name."

"That's all right," Rena Stanley assured Gordon. "You were just so excited for your friend."

Now he felt worse. And foolish. The conversation quickly turned to golf. The teenage girl brought out more warm rolls. He was the only one who took one. Dennis pushed away his untouched dinner plate, a signal, Gordon realized, that everyone else was done. He set down his fork. If only Delores were here. She would have been in the thick of it by now, allowing him to fade into her presence.

"They're very beautiful," Father Hensile said. "The roses, they're from your garden, aren't they?"

"From my yard." He had been staring at them. "They were my father's. He planted them a long time ago."

"Is gardening as relaxing as everyone says it is?"

"Yes. It is. It's very relaxing."

The doorbell rang. Lisa slipped out to answer it.

"I wonder why," the priest continued. "It's pretty hard work, right?"

"Not really."

Roses are so beautiful and yet so hazardous, the priest said as he poured more wine. *Hazardous.* Gordon glanced up. An odd word to use.

"Did you ever wonder why roses have thorns?" the priest asked. "I can see why blackberry and raspberry bushes do—to keep birds and animals away from the fruit, but why roses?"

"Maybe for the same reason, but to keep people away. Until they're ready. The roses, I mean," he added nervously.

Lisa entered the dining room. Her mother's expectant smile faded as Lisa leaned over and whispered in Dennis's ear. He stood up at once. He said something. She nodded, went to touch her face, and her hand shook. She laid it on her shoulder and watched him leave.

"What is it, dear?" her mother asked.

"Emergency root canal?" her father called down the table, and she stared back, face frozen in placidity.

"Can you imagine," Becca Brock sniffed. "The nerve of some people just showing up on your doorstep like that. My uncle was a doctor and, I'll tell you, nobody ever did that!"

"He was a plastic surgeon, for goodness' sake," Marty crowed.

"Dennis shouldn't have his number listed," Mrs. Harrington said. "And it's not very safe, either, dear," she told her daughter, who had folded her napkin and now was lining up her water goblet and wine-glass, side by side. "That's how they do it, they call first to see if you're home."

"Even the thieves are high-tech."

"You mean lazy!"

"They don't want to confront you, just like you don't want to confront them."

"Well, Lisa and Dennis have a wonderful security system," Mr. Harrington said. "Top of the line. Care-Guard. Same one as you, Marty."

Lisa was looking at Gordon. She seemed exhausted, utterly exhausted, by the talk of violence, of breaking into someone's home. *She feels bad for me,* he thought, and then, seeing the horror in her eyes, understood. *No. She's just now realizing who I am, what I did, how freakish I am compared to these normal people.*

"Well, I know what I'd do," Rena Stanley said.

"What? Hide in a closet and call 911?" Becca Brock scoffed.

"No, shoot them!"

Everyone laughed, except for Lisa, who looked around her table as if she had no idea who anyone was.

Jennifer returned and said something that Gordon missed over the melee of voices. "I said, 'Are you all done?'"

"Here he is!" Mr. Harrington called with a big grin. "My favorite son-in-law!"

Dennis stayed in the dining-room doorway. "Gordon, I need you out here for a minute."

There was silence as Gordon stood. The bitterness in his brother's voice had not gone unnoticed. Lisa started to get up, then sat back stiffly as if weighted there.

"Probably Jimmy," Mrs. Harrington said quickly. "He told me he couldn't wait to show Uncle Gordon his new video game. What's it called again, dear? He told us."

"Duke Nukem!" Mr. Harrington laughed. "God, I wish that were my name."

Halfway down the hall, Dennis nudged Gordon, then veered suddenly into his study. "There's four cops in the foyer. They've got a warrant, but I wouldn't let them go in. I told them I'd bring you out."

"A warrant. Why? For what?" The two men, their little dog, the girl, he couldn't even think of her name. No, it was Mrs. Jukas—they did, they thought *he* had beaten her.

"So they can arrest you."

"For what?"

"Mrs. Jukas's murder. She died this afternoon."

"Oh, my God! No! You've got to believe me, Dennis. I didn't do that. I wouldn't. All I ever did was try to help her. I swear to you."

"Come on." Dennis put his hand on Gordon's arm to lead him from the study.

"No!" Gordon pushed him away.

"Don't do this to me!" Dennis's coarse, close whisper hit his face like acid, stripping the flesh. "Don't you dare. Not in front of everyone. Not with *my* children downstairs! Do you understand? You better go out there. Right now. Don't just stand there looking at me. Jesus Christ, do you hear what I'm saying?"

"I didn't do anything! I swear I didn't. Please believe me! Please, Dennis! Tell me you believe me and I'll go. I swear, I'll go right out."

Dennis grabbed the front of his shirt. "What was it, another accident? She got in your way and you just beat her into a fucking coma?"

He walked the rest of the way over the black and white marble tiles, alone. Dennis followed slowly. Of the four men, only two were uniformed. The two in short-sleeved shirts and chinos might have been dinner guests down the hall. Detective Kaminski stepped forward. "Gordon Loomis?"

"Yes, sir."

This arrest was made quickly, without anger or loathing. The deaths of pretty Janine Walters and baby Kevin had happened too long ago for them to despise him. His victim this time was an irritable old woman who had already lived her long life. The policemen seemed ill at ease, embarrassed to be here, even Kaminski as he cuffed him. The other detective was telling Dennis they had come in unmarked cars, as if that might make him feel better. "Here. Just till we get to the car." He grabbed Jimmy's blue windbreaker from the settee and wrapped it over Gordon's bound wrists.

"I'm sorry, Dr. Loomis." Detective Kaminski opened the front door.

Dennis sighed and shook his head.

"Soon's he's in, I'll run the jacket back up," the second detective called back.

"That's all right. Don't bother," Dennis said, but he meant, Keep it. Throw it away, I don't care.

It was after midnight and he had just dozed off in the cell when the guard unlocked the door. His brother was downstairs. The chief said he could go down, but just for a few minutes.

"All night I've been calling Miridici, at home, his office, but he doesn't even have an answering service, just a fucking machine. I must've left fifty messages so far."

Miridici had represented Gordon during the parole process. Gordon hadn't been particularly impressed, but Dennis considered him the best criminal lawyer in the state.

"Anyway," Dennis continued, "that's why I came. To make sure you're careful. I don't want you talking to anybody. I don't want you even asking a cop for a glass of water until I can get Miridici in here."

"I already did. But mostly it was stuff they already knew," he added quickly, seeing the shock on Dennis's face.

"Stuff? What do you mean, stuff?"

"Details. The facts." He repeated what he'd told Kaminski, the weather that day, the taxi he'd thought had dropped off Mrs. Jukas about three o'clock. He had been able to remember everything he'd bought for her that morning, even though he didn't have her list. He'd thrown that out. When he heard how grave her condition was, he'd realized he was stuck with the groceries.

"You said that? You said *stuck*?" Dennis stared in disbelief.

"Well, that I'd have to keep them, that's what I meant."

"But is that what you said?"

"Yes." He nodded. He must have, wasn't sure, didn't remember, couldn't believe any of this was happening. This strange calm was like a glass wall through which reality could be viewed but not felt.

"Gordon! Gordo, look at me. Every word counts, do you understand? Everything you say, they'll use it against you. This time do it right. Don't be telling them every goddamn thing you can think of!"

This time? *This* murder. He had only told them the truth. They had been most interested in the exact time he'd bought the groceries, which showed on the register slip. They knew when the cleaning lady had left and when Mrs. Jukas had been dropped off. That put the time of attack between 12:25 and 1:10. Dennis asked why 1:10.

That's when the clinic had called to change the date of her next appointment, but Mrs. Jukas hadn't answered her phone. Gordon said he'd told them that must have been the same time he was on her porch with the groceries. He'd heard the phone ring inside. It rang for a long time.

"You told them that?"

"Yes. That's what happened. I heard it."

"Jesus Christ, what're you doing telling them things like that?" Dennis looked toward the corridor. The guard was pacing back and forth.

"I'm not going to lie. That's worse," Gordon said in a low voice.

"You didn't lie last time, either." Dennis's whisper came as a hiss.

"Last time . . . ," he started to say, then closed his eyes. Last time, the cell was dark, with bars on all four sides. This was a brand-new jail, bright with recessed lighting. He still had no belt or shoelaces. The inventory of confiscated possessions included his wallet, comb, and pen. Signing it had seemed a mark of hope. Last time, they hadn't given him such a document to sign. Last time, he had also told them the truth. "Dennis, I didn't touch Mrs. Jukas. I swear. I didn't hit her. I didn't even see her. She never came to the door."

Glancing over his shoulder, Dennis dug his knee into Gordon's, then huddled close and whispered, "They don't know it, but there's a witness. Jilly Cross. She saw you."

"Yes, she did, that's right. Is she going to tell them? Will you ask her to?" He couldn't help smiling.

"Jesus Christ, she saw you, that exact same time, coming out of Jukas's."

"No! That's not true!"

"She said you were upset, that you were angry. She said all she did was ask why you were over there and you grabbed her."

"No. I didn't. I didn't grab her." Gordon shook his head, so agitated that he was panting. "It wasn't like that at all."

"She told me that two weeks ago," Dennis whispered. "The very day she heard about it she called me at the office. She said it was you, she was sure of it, it had to be, but if I didn't want her to, she wouldn't go to the police. She keeps calling and wanting to know what she should do. What *we* should do. And I don't know what to tell her. It's like I'm being sucked into this whirlpool and I can't get out."

"I'm sorry." There was nothing more to say. His brother would help but didn't believe him.

"I'm meeting her right after this." Dennis checked his watch, then leaned close, whispering more softly. "I think she'll cooperate. But from now on you shut up. The only one you should be talking to is Miridici."

Dennis had snapped out of his malaise. It was either the imminence of meeting Jilly Cross or the prospect of getting his brother out of his life. Or maybe it was just being in charge again. "Your brother is always such a help," his mother used to write. "We seem to rely on him more and more. Aunt Gert says a teenager shouldn't be making such important family decisions, but with your dad so low all the time, Denny has to, and besides, he always does such a good job."

"Do you want me to call Delores?"

"No."

"She'll want to know."

"She won't."

CHAPTER 25

Only the stem was left. Jada picked up the last few rose petals. She added more water to the soda bottle, then put it back on the sill. If roots grew, she would plant it and have her own rosebush. She looked out the window: all that food going to waste over there in Gordon's refrigerator. By the time he got out, it would probably be spoiled. Poor guy. Why couldn't the old lady have just stayed in a coma and not bothered anyone ever again? His yard was starting to look like hers, littered with papers, twigs, and pieces of the yellow crime tape. The grass needed to be cut. A new telephone book had been thrown on his top step. Its pages were swollen and curled from last night's downpour. A man was jogging down the street with his German shepherd. Twice yesterday she had run outside thinking she heard Leonardo barking. She didn't believe Thurman. Polie might be mean, but he was too lazy to tie his own shoes, much less go to all the trouble of killing her dog. No, Leonardo was out there somewhere, and one of these days he'd make his way back here. She wished she knew a real prayer to say. All she remembered was Aunt Sue telling her to close her eyes and tell Jesus what was in her heart. She closed her eyes and held her breath, but no prayer came, only an ache like a voice begging, *Help me. Please. Will somebody please, please help me.*

She tiptoed into the bedroom. Her mother slept on her side, curled and unmoving, in the exact same position for the last hour. Jada leaned close, relieved to hear the watery rasp of breath. All she did between hits now was sleep. When she did get up to go to the bathroom, her legs were so shaky she could barely walk. The more she slept, the less crack she smoked and the more pregnant she got. Soon she'd be too far along for an abortion. Jada didn't know how long they could last like this. Her only hope was getting her mother into rehab. She had gone down there a couple days ago, but she didn't have an appointment, so she was supposed to go back tomorrow at one-thirty.

Jada locked the door, then hurried across the street onto Gordon's porch. She propped the sodden telephone book against the railing to dry. His door was locked. So were the windows. She tried the back door and windows, the cellar windows. Everything was locked up tight, even the garage. She came around the side of the house, then reached into the bush to break off a stem of three new roses. "Motherfucker!" she yelled as the thorns scratched her arm. Angry now, she kicked the dirt, then squatted down, looking for a rock to smash the back-door glass the way Thurman had.

A silver car pulled into the driveway and the doors opened, one right into the bushes as a tall, dark-haired woman got out. "Hey! What're you doing?" Gordon's brother called over the roof of the car.

"Just picking stuff up." She dropped the rock and held up an empty popcorn bag, a plastic water bottle. "And the new telephone book, it got all wet, so I moved it over by the door there."

"Well, thank you. That's very nice of you," the woman said as the man went up the steps two at a time. Jada watched to see if he took a key from a hiding place, but he used his own to get inside.

"Yeah, well, Gordon, he never likes crap around, you know, so that's why." She walked across the lawn with the woman. "I'm Jada. I live over there." She pointed.

The woman held out her hand, introducing herself as Lisa, Gordon's sister-in-law.

"Oh, yeah, you've got two kids, right? A boy and a girl. I seen you here before."

"You've got a very good memory."

"Yeah, phonographic, that's what my teachers all say." She grinned. "But then hardly anybody ever comes here. A priest did once. And Delores. You know her?"

The woman said she did. Opening the door, she said she'd better go give her husband a hand.

"Need any help?" Jada stepped closer.

They didn't, but Lisa Loomis thanked her. They'd come to check the house and pick up a few things for Gordon. She slipped inside.

"How's he doing?" Jada asked, face at the screen. "Probably not too good, huh?"

"He's all right. Gordon's a very strong man. He'll be fine. I know he will."

"Lisa!" her husband called from the stairs. "I can't find any slippers!"

"Yeah, it's like, how can they do that?" she said as Lisa Loomis stepped away. "How can they arrest him? He'd never do something like that. And he didn't. I know for a fact he didn't."

She came back to the door. "What do you mean? How do you know that he didn't?"

Her husband rushed up to say he didn't have much time. His next appointment was in forty-five minutes.

"Because," Jada said. "Because I know he wouldn't hurt anybody. Especially an old lady, even though she was a bitch."

"You shouldn't say that. That's terrible," Lisa Loomis said.

"Will you come on?" her husband snapped.

"Well, it's true. She treated him like crap, and now look, just because he was nice, they blame him. It sucks. It really does!" she called at the closing door.

She sat on the step, waiting. "Hey!" She jumped up when the door opened. The brother came out carrying a green canvas bag. "I just wanted to ask you," she said, following them to the car. "Would you tell Gordon I said hi?"

"Yes, I will. That's very nice of you," Lisa Loomis said.

"Watch out, them prickers, they really hurt," Jada warned as Lisa Loomis opened the car door. "And tell him I'm watching the house for him. I'll keep the freaks away," she said at Lisa's window as the car backed out of the driveway. "I won't let the place get all crappy looking. I'll keep it nice!" she called as Lisa waved. "Fucking snob, can't even talk to me," she muttered.

———

The office was freezing. Jada stuffed the paper into her pocket, then folded her arms and tried to stop shivering.

"Sorry for that," Mr. Crowley said when he returned.

Mr. Crowley didn't look like a mister in his jeans and black T-shirt. He was a young guy with a bony face and closely set eyes that narrowed with doubt whenever she spoke. It was the second time he'd been called out to see someone. The place was a zoo, junkies lined up, waiting outside a door marked MEDS and the waiting room filled with even more of them.

"We're a little shorthanded today. Now let's see, you were telling me about . . ." He looked for the paper he had been writing on. He shuffled through the stack to his right, then pushed back in his chair to look down at the floor. "It was right here. Well, anyway." He ripped a new sheet from the pad. "I remember most of it. Your name is Jana and your mother is addicted to crack and she needs to be placed in one of our programs." He raised his eyebrows: Was that right so far?

"It's my aunt. I said mother, but she's, like, really kind of my aunt." She had to be careful. What if he'd gone out both times to call Social Services or the cops?

"What's your last name, Jana?"

"Brown."

He wrote it down. "And your age?"

"Seventeen."

He looked at her. "Seventeen?"

"In a couple months."

He didn't believe her. "Your address?"

"Why, what's that matter? It's not me, I'm not tryna get in rehab. Is that what you think?" He did. She could tell, he thought it was her.

"No, I know. It's just for our records. Standard procedure, that's all."

Yeah, standard procedure; next thing she knew, some social work-er'd be banging down the door. "Look, all I wanna do is to get my aunt in. She's too sick to come down. I told her I'd do this. She has to get on a list, right?" She pointed to his papers. "A waiting list or something?"

"Yes, and right now ours is very long, but—"

"How long?"

"Three months, anyway."

"Jesus Christ!" She felt as if she'd been punched in the stomach. What would three more months of drugs do to the baby? And to her? "She can't wait that long! She'll be dead!" Having actually said it, she was limp with the certainty. Sometimes in the night she woke up afraid to move, afraid to feel a corpse at her back. "There must be some other places," she said weakly. "Someplace she can get in faster."

"Well, yes, private centers, hospitals, but she'd have to pay. We're state funded, so here it's—"

"Can't you just put her name high up on the list? I wouldn't tell anyone, I swear."

"I'm sorry, I can't do that. It wouldn't be fair."

"Fuck fair! They're all out there getting their fucking shit and she's not gonna make it! She's not!"

"I'm sorry, Jana, now you just calm down. You have to understand that those people also had to wait. It's just the way things are."

She couldn't believe that, couldn't quit, couldn't just give up and say, I'm nothing because no one cares, and that's just the way things are. She closed her eyes. "Please? Will you please help her?"

"That's the other thing, Jana. You'd have to bring her in here. It's got to be voluntary. She has to want the help. It's the only way this works."

"She does, but she can't. She's too sick." She looked at him. "She's pregnant."

"Or it could be mandated by the courts."

"How does that work?" she asked, stiffening with his answer: If her aunt were arrested, then she could be ordered into treatment. She nodded dully as he handed her brochures and a list of hot-line numbers, some for emergencies, others informational.

"Jana?" He patted her hand and tried to make eye contact. "Sometimes we have to hurt people before we can help them."

She grabbed his hand and leaned over the desk. "Whatever you want, I don't care, I'll do it, anything. I'm really good! Anything you want," she said, feeling her face break into a thousand pieces as she tried to smile. "Just move her up the list, that's all."

"No." He shook his head with a futile sadness. "No, that's not what I meant."

She dropped the brochures onto the desk and left.

Feaster waited in the Navigator while Polie came to the door. She had to do a deal down by the canal. It was a guy and a girl. They were on their way there right now in a gray Volvo, so she had to hurry. No, she said. She didn't feel like it. She was too tired. She started to close the door, and he pulled it open.

"This is big and Feaster don't wanna lose it. They're down from Portland."

"Yeah." She laughed. "Like I care, right?" Her mother had been up all night, crying and saying she was so sick she just wanted to die. Jada didn't dare leave her alone for fear she'd take off and be gone again for days. Little by little her mother was getting clean. But it was taking its toll, leaving her weak from all the vomiting. A little while ago she'd been burning up with a fever.

"Come on!" he said with a glance at the Navigator. "Now! There's ten other places they can go." He sounded frantic.

"No. Not unless you tell me where Leonardo is."

"Leonardo?" he said in a high voice. "Who the fuck's Leonardo?"

"My dog. You took him, didn't you."

"Jada?" her mother called from inside. "Who's that? Who's out there?"

"Just a minute, Ma!"

"Is that Polie? I gotta see Polie."

"Don't fuck with me. I don't want her out here. Not now." He glanced down. Feaster waved for him to hurry. "Come on!"

"Then pay me. In cash," she whispered back, seizing on his desperation. "We need money bad. There's no food here, and she's really sick."

"You know he won't. She already owes him too much."

"Too bad, then. I'm not doing it."

"Take the rocks, the extra, what you get for her, and sell 'em."

"Oh, yeah. And then I'll be a big fucking dealer like you, Polie."

She laughed. "I don't think so! Hey, you better go. Feaster's got his door open."

"Here." He handed her a ten-dollar bill.

"That's not enough."

He gave her another ten. "That's all I got."

She ran inside, but her mother had fallen asleep or passed out, one or the other, same difference; at least she'd be all right alone for a while.

"Come on!" he said when she came to the door. He grabbed her arm, and she jerked back.

"What'd you do to Leonardo? You drowned him, didn't you."

"Jesus Christ."

"Tell me and I'll go."

"Yeah." He nodded. "All right?"

"Fuck you!" she cried. So Thurman hadn't lied.

He grabbed her and steered her down the stairs.

"Why? Why'd you do that?" Her voice broke as she struggled to hit him. "He was just a little dog, a puppy."

"Shut up! Just shut up!" He pushed her into the Navigator.

Feaster turned up the music. He bobbed his head to the beat and twirled his straggly chin hairs. His silky blue shirt clung to his knobby shoulders. The back of Polie's neck glistened with sweat. He kept glancing at her through the mirror. The Volvo was parked in the weeds by the canal. Feaster turned down the music. They drove by to be sure.

"Maine. It's them." Polie gestured at the license plate.

"So where'd you take him?" Jada leaned forward between the seats, then repeated the question when he didn't answer.

"Someplace. I don't know. The river." Polie glared at her.

"Take who?" Feaster asked.

"My little dog, Leonardo. The asshole drowned him."

"What the fuck did you do that for?" Feaster looked at him in disbelief.

"Marvella, she said to. She hated that dog. And the smell, it was making her sick."

Jada sat back. Her mother had done this, had killed the one thing she loved. They could do whatever they wanted, and nothing would ever stop them. A deadness came over her, but it felt good. Walls went up, windows slammed shut, doors closed. Nothing was ever going to work out, and knowing that with such absolute certainty was almost a relief. There was nothing in her heart, no ache or prayer to say. The sunstruck brick of the mills kept flashing by in this wild orbit, 'round and 'round in the purple rocket, no cops, the right car, crazy the way they even stopped for red lights, but they were alive and she was not.

"Here." Polie shoved back a plastic bag. "Take out five rocks. Fifty's theirs." He parked by a weedy lot on the corner and told her they'd be giving her five hundred dollars. This time count it first, Feaster instructed.

Her hand felt numb as she removed the five rocks and put them in her pocket. "How come only five?" she asked, struggling to care as she shoved the bag inside her underpants. Pride was all she had left, but it was burning up the last of her energy.

"Jesus!" Feaster groaned. "Tell her, will ya tell her?"

"After that last fuck-up," Polie said, smirking at her in the mirror, "you're lucky you're getting—"

"She's not getting rid of it," she interrupted, smiling. "She won't. I know she won't."

Feaster spun around. What was she waiting for, cops? Get out! Now! he told her.

She walked slowly, kicking stones as she went. She looked back and waved. Actually, cops would be perfect right now. Arrest Polie and then her mother would be too far along to get rid of it. "Bastard, no-good bastard," she muttered, approaching the car. A baby was screaming. The driver rolled down the window. It smelled inside: dirty diapers and sour milk.

"Hey!" the driver said. He was older than she'd expected. Thin gray hair, gray mustache. The woman was young and skinny. Her eyes settled on Jada's with a glassy vacuity. She tried to smile, but her mouth only hung open, drooling. In back, a little girl sobbed, her pale, sweaty head turned against the car seat. "Shut up!" the driver screamed at the frantic child, making her cry louder. "Whatcha got?" he asked Jada, checking the street in his mirror.

"I don't know. What do you got?"

"Here." He handed her a wad of new bills folded in half. "Jesus, do something, will you?" he snapped at the woman.

"What?" the woman shrieked with a hounded look. "Do what?"

"Sounds like she's sick. She's got a fever or something," Jada said as she tried to count. The piercing cries seared like a hot knife through Jada's numbness. *Desperate, crackhead assholes, bringing their baby. What if the cops come? Don't they care?* No, this was all they cared about, the shit between her legs. That's all her mother cared about.

Reaching back, the driver kept trying to force a pacifier into the child's mouth. "Shut the fuck up!" he screamed. Again the young woman struggled to smile, looking longingly at Jada, the bearer of all happiness, all that she desired. Flailing her arms, the child kicked the back of the seat. The driver began to slap her legs, only to have her howl louder in outrage and helplessness.

"Leave her alone!" Jada yelled, but he kept hitting her. "She's not doing anything wrong. She's a baby, that's all. It's not her fault."

She pulled out the bag and threw it into the car, spilling the glistening rocks onto the front seat and floor. The man and the woman were picking them up. The child's screams followed Jada through the hot afternoon as she walked alongside the still, black water of the canal. The Navigator slipped up beside her. "Here." She held out the money. Polie passed it to Feaster and told her to get in. She ignored him and kept walking.

On her way home, she tried to figure out which of these houses was Delores's. They all looked the same. She was pretty sure it was Lowell Street. She asked a few people if they knew Delores, but no one did, and Jada didn't see her car anywhere. Her mother was probably climbing the walls by now. She knew she should go home, but for the first time in weeks she didn't care. Just like Leonardo and the old bitch, that poor baby didn't have a chance. One way or another she'd kill it, too. Hurt and disappointment, that's all she was good at, the only things Jada had ever been able to count on her for. That little girl just now screaming from buy to buy, sick and hungry in her dirty diapers, that's the kind of life it would have, if it was lucky, because this time there wouldn't be any Uncle Bob and Aunt Sue, nobody but her to pick up the pieces, or some foster home that probably wouldn't even let Jada come and visit.

When she came to the projects, she leaned against the chain-link fence and watched some guys playing basketball. "Hey, Jada," a voice called from the shade of the bleachers. It was Thurman.

Jada sat next to him. He was eating a sub. His hair had sprouted to a black fuzz. He needed a shave. He had a job nights now at the pizza place, so his grandmother had let him back in. For a few minutes they sat in silence, watching the sweaty game while he ate.

"I went back there, you know," she said.

"Where?"

"The woods. But Cootie's dog, he was gone."

Thurman wiped his mouth with his hand. "Oh yeah?" He grinned. "Wanna go find him?" He stood up and flipped a heel of bread into her lap. "You can give him that!" He grabbed her hand and pulled her up. "C'mon," he said, rubbing her belly as she leaned into him. "Let's go."

"Oh, I don't know," she said, stroking his fuzzy head. "I should go home first. My mother, she's sick in bed."

"She's down by the tracks. I saw her. She was with some creep. One of them bums from under the bridge. Scary guy with no teeth."

Jada ran down to the railroad tracks, but no one was around. When she finally got home her mother was on the couch, holding a bloody towel to her nose. It wouldn't stop bleeding. The blood was running down her throat, she said, gagging. Not knowing what else to do, Jada ran into the kitchen for a glass of water. Her mother's hands shook so much that the water spilled all over her. Jada held the glass to her mouth. Her mother tried to take a sip, but she choked and blood gushed down her chin. Jada pressed the towel against her nose. She'd looked everywhere for a rock, she gasped through the towel, but couldn't find any. She'd even gone out looking for Polie, but no one would tell her where he was. All she could get was shit some junkie shot her up with, some poison that was killing her. "I think I'm dying. That's what it feels like." Her skin was sweaty and greasy gray. Her eyes bulged out of her head.

"All right. All right," Jada said in a panic. "That's why you gotta quit, Ma. For you and the baby." She wished she had the brochures. Her head felt woozy.

"I don't wanna baby," she groaned. "I just wanna life, that's all, a normal fucking life like everybody else has."

"You will, Ma." Jada ached to put her arms around her, but was afraid.

"No, I won't. I never will." She doubled over, gagging and holding her belly. "Oh God, I'm so sick. I'm gonna die. I wish I could. I wish I could just die." She was trembling so violently that her teeth banged together. "Get me something. Help me, baby. Help me," she grunted, looking out in terror past Jada.

"Okay, Ma. Okay, I'll get you some. See?" she said, fumbling a rock from her pocket. "Just this one, okay? I'll get it ready, then to-morrow we'll go down to rehab and get you all signed up, okay? Where's the pipe, the bottle?" she asked, lifting her mother's arms, feeling down between the cushions.

She ran into the bedroom and ripped the blanket off the bed, and the Mountain Dew bottle rolled onto the floor. She stuck the straw back in the side as she ran around, looking for a lighter. Matches. Any-thing. "Jesus Christ! Jesus Christ! Just wait!" she panted, and dumped out her mother's pocketbook on the couch. The first match hissed out. She struck another one and held the trembling flame to the rock.

"Here, here it is, Ma." She put the straw in her mother's mouth. Her mother's eyes widened, glaring with such rage that Jada jerked back and held the bottle at arm's length. "Inhale, Ma! C'mon! Try! You have to!"

With that her mother's body shuddered. Head back, spine arched, she stiffened, seized by a groan from deep in her bowels, from a foul and wrenching darkness. Her eyes rolled back and her mouth hung open. She sagged forward and her chin hit her chest.

"Ma? Ma?" Jada cried, trying to pinch the slack lips around the straw. "Ma! Don't! Don't do this!" she screamed, throwing herself at her.

CHAPTER 26

The minute the guard opened the door, she changed her mind about showing Gordon the new picture of May Loo. Stiffly erect, he seemed as immovable as the metal table and chairs bolted to the floor. His face under the wire-caged ceiling lights was haggard and gray. Days after his arrest, the papers had been filled with stories of the first murder. She'd vowed not to read them, then spent hours poring over every word, looking for some portentous fact that had eluded her the first time. The details had evoked a new horror in her. She had been too young then. It had barely seemed real: the boy on trial, the murderer in the papers, was not the same Gordon Loomis she had known. But this man, this murderer, was someone she loved, which made her part of the ugliness and her life even more pathetic. As much as she wanted to comfort him, the new, strong voice in her head warned, *Keep your distance. You have your own future to think of. And May Loo's.* She couldn't even be sure of his innocence anymore. The impenetrable calm thickened around him like ice. She couldn't tell if his was the inertia of shock or disinterest now with his forced half-smile. Her monologue felt like a flimsy boat she could barely cling to as they drifted further apart. Soon it would be over, and they both knew it.

She had just told him how the drug dealers were out in force again, back on the streets. "And here you sit, but I guess the police think that's okay," she said, wanting to agitate him, the guard, someone—or maybe just herself. Anything would be better than his funereal composure. How could he just sit there and let this happen all over again?

"It's been cool these last few days, thank goodness. I've been painting the spare room." She didn't dare call it May Loo's room. "Yellow walls, with the cutest border—these little ballet dancers. Now I'm going to do the bureau. It's unfinished." She had to take a deep breath. "You've done a lot of painting. How many coats do you think I should do?"

He blinked, trying to refocus. "I don't know. I didn't paint furniture."

She glanced at her watch. This was a waste of time and a day's pay. Her home visit was next week. She'd lose another day then.

"You should go," he said, and she felt guilty in her relief, then sad with the loss of an old hope. When she used to visit him at Fortley, she'd be so giddily nervous that the words would just spill out, then all the way home she'd cringe, remembering every inane thing she'd said, prattling on about people he didn't even know, places he'd never been to, and never once would he tell her anything about himself. She'd always felt the need to entertain him, as if she might entice him to freedom with the wonders of ordinary living. Or had she just been trying to convince herself each time that it was worth it, that thirty-day span between visits a perilous footbridge made bearable because every experience, no matter how dull or painful, could be reworked, refashioned, polished, and cut for his diversion? And what pleasure the anticipation and telling gave her compared to the flatness she would feel afterward, this same emptiness. Freedom had been a disappointment for both of them.

She asked if he needed anything. No, he said. Dennis and Lisa had brought a few things from home. She stood up. Could she check on the house for him? No. She couldn't get in anyway: Dennis had locked everything up, he said too defensively, irritating her again. Could she water the lawn, then? It hadn't rained all week. Things were getting awfully dry. *How cruel and sadistic to goad him like this, to pick at his scabs.* What about his roses? *His precious roses, that's all he cares about.* The roses . . . He thought a moment. No, he answered hesitantly, they should be all right. She could water them, she said. Every day on her way home from work, she could swing by. *Free as she was in her car out there in the world, where living things still needed care.* Just tell her what to do—should she spray them with the hose—

"No!" he interrupted, as if it were painful to hear. If she wanted to, if she didn't mind, that is, then she should fill the watering can and water only the base of the bush. For about a minute—he usually counted slowly to sixty. Anything else? Well, if she had time, there was a special mixture he'd made. The bottle was on the back steps, and if she could spray the whole bush once a week, he'd really appreciate it. She asked if that was the fertilizer. No, the fertilizer was in a tall can in the garage; measure out an eighth of a cup into the cap and spread the granules around the base.

"Just pour them out? That's all I do?"

"Actually, I use the hand cultivator. It's on a nail in the garage, and I just kind of scratch it around." Demonstrating, he clawed the table-top with his fingertips. "Just work the granules in a little, then water. And be sure and take some roses. The pruner's in the garage, right next to the cultivator. The key's under the bottom step."

"I don't want to cut your roses, Gordon. You worked so hard on them."

"No, the more you cut, the more they grow. It makes them stronger." He smiled.

"Does that work for people, too?"

"Maybe. For some people."

"But not for you, though, right?"

"I don't know." He stiffened.

"Why? Why don't you know?" *Are you that numb, that dead inside?*

"Because I don't think like that. I can't. I never have. I wouldn't dare."

"So in other words, this is fine. It's just the way things are, and you don't have a damn thing to say about it!" She didn't want to cry.

He leaned forward and gripped the sides of the table, trembling, as if to wrench it up from the floor. "What can I do? There's nothing I can do. Nothing. Nothing but wait."

"You could talk to me! You could tell me what you're thinking! What you're feeling. Something, goddamn it!"

He stared, bitterly, as if she had demanded something vile of him.

"They never should have let me out, all right, that's what I keep thinking. That I should have stayed. At least then they'd be looking for the one that did it. I let her down both ways. First by not helping her and now by being here. You want to know how I feel? I feel like this loose gear that just kind of rattles around in space, and every now and again I crash down into someone's world and ruin everything."

"Gordon." She closed her eyes.

"It's true. I just don't want to mess yours up any more than I already have."

"You haven't messed anything up for me, Gordon—far from it."

"Like the adoption. May Loo. You shouldn't even be here. Think how this looks."

"Things like that don't matter to me. I know they should, but they don't. I'll do everything I'm supposed to, and if it works out, then great! But if it doesn't because of you, Gordon, because you're in my life, then that's too bad. That's just the way it goes, you know? Here," she said, fumbling open her purse. She handed him the color photograph. "I wanted to show you. I just got it."

"She's smiling!" He almost smiled himself.

"I know. Isn't she cute?"

He nodded.

"No, tell me. Tell me what you're thinking right now as you look at it."

"I . . ." He looked up in panic.

"Tell me. Say it. Please."

He held it closer, studying it. "I'm thinking . . . I'm thinking how lucky this little girl is because pretty soon she's going to have you with her every day for the rest of her life."

For a moment neither one spoke or looked at the other. "Thank you," she finally said.

He nodded and held out the picture.

"No, that's yours to keep. I have another one," she lied.

After work she drove straight to his house. The watering can wasn't on the back steps or in the garage. *Probably stolen,* she thought, trying to keep the hose low while she counted to sixty, though it was too late. Her first explosive aim had already drenched the bush. Next, she sprayed the leaves with Gordon's soapy mixture. He hadn't told her how much to use, probably the whole bottle if it was weekly. By the time she was done, bubbles floated everywhere, fat and shimmering on the wet leaves, across the weedy yards, down the street. Working the fertilizer into the soil was quick but messy. She stood up, knees, hands, and feet muddied, her cloth sandals probably ruined. She should have changed first. Using the pruner, she cut the fullest blooms. She rinsed her scratched, stinging hands under the hose, then gathered up the cut flowers. What was the pleasure in that? she wondered, slamming the trunk shut. She glanced back at the twisted hose. Why coil it back up on the hanger when she'd just have to take it down again? She patted her arms dry with a tissue. The scratches stung, but it was a good hurt.

The next time she came, she tried not to wet the leaves, but somehow they were soaked again. What difference could it possibly make? They'd get a lot wetter when it rained. She turned off the water. She had to get home and sand the dresser before the second coat.

"Hi," said a voice from behind.

"Oh!" she gasped. "Jada, you scared me." The girl just stood there with her hands in her pockets. "So what's going on?" Delores said as she yanked the muddy hose into a pile. "How've you been? I haven't seen you in a while."

"I saw you. You were out here the other day, too." Jada's eyes shone flat, the way light hits a mirror.

"Yeah, I told Gordon I'd do this, but it's not my thing. Look at my hands, look what his roses did. They attacked me," she said, trying to laugh.

"He's still in jail, huh?" Jada asked, following her to the car.

"Yes, I'm afraid so." Delores got in.

"You think he did it?" Jada asked through the window.

"No. Of course not."

"Well, he didn't," the girl said as if she hadn't heard her.

"Do you know who did?"

Jada shook her head.

"How do you know it wasn't him, then?"

"Because. Because I just know. Gordon, he wouldn't do that. He'd get mad, but he'd never, like, do anything."

"Yeah, like the night I let you in, why'd he get so mad? What was that all about?"

The girl's answer was a weary shrug. She asked Delores where she was going. An appointment, Delores lied. She could tell Jada wanted something. "Well, I better get going." She started the engine, but Jada moved closer to the window.

"You live on Lowell Street, right?"

"Yes, why?"

"Remember you said I could come there sometime?"

"Yes, uh-huh." What if she showed up during the home study interview?

"Well, I was over there, near your house, I think, but I didn't know which one it was, what number."

"Well, we'll have to do that. I'll come get you sometime." She shifted into gear and started slowly ahead. "See you!" She waved out the window but stared straight ahead so she wouldn't have to see Jada still watching her drive away. At the corner she glanced back. Jada was crossing the street. *Sometimes you just have to keep going,* the voice assured her. *You have to help yourself first. She's not your responsibility. The world is filled with girls like her. Nobody else is breaking their neck to help her so why should you?*

She pulled into her parking space and turned off the engine but couldn't get out of the car, didn't have will enough or strength. Why did there have to be such pain in the world? "Why? Why?" Her fist made a dull thud on the wheel. Why, when she was so close to fulfillment, was there this emptiness, this loss, as if the child had been already plucked from her arms? The rusty fire escape on her building spanned four stories but ended on the second floor. In a fire, the only way down to the street would be to jump. "Unsafe emergency egress," the home study worker would surely note in the report. It wasn't just adultery and a convicted killer in her life, but knives in the kitchen, scalding water in faucets, loose treads on the stairs, trucks that tipped over, tornadoes in the night, rabid bats in the attic, stray bullets, toxins in the water, in the air, and all the invisible hazards of loving too much, trying too hard, and never knowing what was enough or when to stop.

Jada opened a Coke and lit another joint. Nothing hurt this way, not even hunger or fear. But here she was safe between the two doors as long as she could keep them closed, one leading into the street, the other into that silence where the mound under the sheets was her whole life. At first she kept checking in the hope it was another drug-deep stupor and when it wore off her mother would begin to stir. Except for last night's buy, Jada had spent most of the last few days sleeping on the couch. Every time she tried to think about walking to Uncle Bob's, she got exhausted and fell back to sleep.

She crawled back onto the couch. Pretty soon she'd have to tell someone. Delores had taken off too fast, as if she knew and didn't want to be told. There was enough food for a couple more days. She wondered how much a bus ticket to Florida cost. She could always sell the extra crack. She figured she had sixty dollars' worth, anyway. She had packed some clothes in an old suitcase Inez had thrown out. But leaving took more energy than she had right now, even though she knew she had to get far away before Social Services got here.

Someone was banging on the door. Polie. Last night she had almost told him, but then she'd been afraid of what he might do to her, so she went downtown like nothing was wrong and passed some rocks for them. She opened the window instead of the door. "What is it?" She leaned dizzily on the sill.

"You gotta come. Ronnie just got a call." He gestured back at the idling Navigator.

"I can't."

"Twenty-five bucks he says he'll give you."

"Where?"

"The South Common."

"Forget it." She closed the window and locked it. She'd almost been arrested there last time. That's how little she was worth. Better her than their other runners. He was banging on the window. A long, white car pulled up behind the Navigator. Polie was yelling for her to come out, there wasn't much time. Delores came up the steps behind him. He spun around. Jada pressed her ear to the door.

"What's wrong?" Delores demanded in a high tone.

"What the hell do you care?"

"I'm a friend of Jada's," Delores said, and Jada's grin felt as if part of her face were leaking down the door. "Is she in there?"

"Look, just get outta here, will ya?"

"Are you serious?" Delores laughed.

"I gotta talk to her about something important."

"Well, so do I!"

"Look, I don't think you understand. I don't have much time here, and I gotta see her, so get the fuck outta here before something happens."

Delores took another step, hands raised as if to ready herself for whatever came next. "Are you threatening me?"

"No. I'm fucking telling you," he said, coming toward her.

She put her cell phone to her ear. "Nine, one, one," she yelled, still dialing as he grabbed it and smashed it onto the porch floor. He ran down the steps.

"Delores!" Jada opened the door as Polie got into the Navigator and drove off. She hurried out, picked up the cracked phone, and listened, afraid a voice in her ear would demand to know what the problem was and where. When she came back, Delores stood just inside the doorway, trying to catch her breath. "It doesn't work." Jada held it out. She kept glancing past Delores, as if at any moment the bedroom door would swing open.

"The battery's dead," Delores gasped, hand at her heaving chest. "What was that all about? What did he want? What was so important?"

"I don't know. He's just an asshole, that's all."

"Was it about your mother? Is she home?"

She saw the sweaty woman's shrewd eyes move between the closed doors. Like her, Delores had that extra sense, she just knew things, things beyond the telling. "He had a buy he wanted me to do. But I said no and he got mad."

"A buy. You mean drugs?"

"Yeah."

"Are you hungry, Jada?" Delores asked, hugging herself.

"I think so. I don't know, I forget." She slipped the statues into her pockets.

Jada had eaten half her French fries before they pulled out of the McDonald's lot. Delores hadn't ordered anything. She felt sick to her stomach. The girl's head kept nodding back and forth, her rabbity cunning distorted by this glassy-eyed euphoria. She was high, but there was something else, something that had filled Delores with dread the minute she had stepped over the threshold. It clung to her still, like grease on her skin. She shouldn't have gone back. Now that she had, she barely knew what to say, much less what to do with the girl. "Do you need anything while we're out?"

Instead of answering, Jada chuckled softly, like a hunched cat purring as it ate.

"Anything from the drugstore?" She pointed ahead. "I have to get shampoo."

"Sure."

Delores was done, but she continued to move slowly up and down the aisles, so that Jada wouldn't think she was being rushed back home. Yet she had the feeling that they were both killing time, going through the motions, each waiting for the other to strike. Jada was still at the front of the store. Delores watched her pick magazines from the rack, stare at the covers, then put them back.

"Want one?" Delores asked, coming down the aisle, her basket filled with shampoo, a yellow plastic duck for the tub, coloring books and crayons for May Loo.

"Sure," Jada said, then just stood there.

"How about this one?" She handed her a *Seventeen* magazine. Jada opened it and, squinting, brought it close to her face, then held it out at arm's length.

"Here." Delores grabbed a pair of reading glasses from the display next to them. "Put these on. Now look at the page."

"Whoa!" Jada drew her head back. "It's, like, a magnifying glass. I can even see eyebrows. All kindsa shit." She laughed and turned the pages.

"Try reading words now." Delores had her try three more pair with increasingly stronger lenses.

Jada read like a child, emphasizing each syllable. " 'Ever since she was a little girl, Marka Stanley has been wearing . . . ' " She pointed.

" 'Haute couture,' " Delores read. "It's French for high fashion."

"Jesus, you can even read French with these." Jada looked around to see what else might be possible.

Delores had the clerk snip off the price tags. Jada put them back on when they got outside. "Jesus, how come everything's so friggin' blurry?" She grabbed Delores's arm as she tripped on the sidewalk. Delores told her to take them off; they were just for reading. "Well, what about everything else?" she asked with a sweep of her arm. As they got into the car, Delores explained that distance required other lenses, which would have to come from an eye doctor. If Jada wanted, Delores could make an appointment for her. "If it's all right with your mother, that is."

Jada held the glasses in her lap and stared out the side window. Delores asked if there was anything else she needed before she brought her home. Annoyed with her silence, she asked again.

"I don't want to go home."

"Where do you want to go? It's got to be quick, though. I've got tons of stuff to do at home," she said, but Jada only grunted. "Well? You gonna tell me?" She slowed down. "We're almost there." Delores kept glancing over at her. Sweat ran down the girl's face, and she grunted again. "What? What're you saying?" She turned onto Clover Street.

"No. Don't. Don't bring me home. I can't. I can't go in there. No, don't stop!"

Delores drove past the house. "Why? What's wrong? Why can't you go home?"

Jada wouldn't answer. At first Delores thought she was trying not to cry, but now Jada seemed to be gagging. Was her mother mad at her? Was her mother okay? Was she there? Or had she taken off again?

"She's dead."

Delores listened as Jada described the terror of these last few days, not knowing what to do, afraid to tell anyone. She had considered running away but couldn't bear the thought of leaving her mother alone like that, because even if Polie or Feaster found her, they wouldn't do anything. They'd just leave her, too.

"Oh, Jada, honey." She reached out for her arm, but the girl cringed back. "You've had such an awful time. I'm so sorry for you. I am. I really am. And I'm going to help you. I promise. I swear I will. I'll talk to people. We'll find you a good home, a place where you—"

"I want to live with you."

"Oh, no. I can't. It wouldn't work."

"Why? I could, like, clean and help with the cooking and stuff. And I'd go to school, I would. Like, I've even got these, the glasses, now." She put them on, and they were as crooked as her smile. She hugged herself, shivering.

"Honey, look, I can't. But I'll make sure you're with really good people."

"Yeah, in some home again for a few months until they say, 'Pack up. It's not working out,' or I don't fit in, or the foster mother's gonna have a baby and they need my room, or the foster father goes and tells his wife I'm, like, tryna come on to him or something, when all the hell I'm tryna do is make him like me. That's all, that's all I ever try to do," she said, teeth chattering. "And you, you like me. You already do, right?"

"Yes, I know, hon, but you see, I've got a little girl coming and—"

"Well, when she leaves, then."

"No, she's going to live with me. She's coming from China. She's going to be my child, my daughter."

"But you don't even know her. You already know me, and what if you don't like her, then what?"

"I'll like her."

"What if she doesn't like you? You can't, like, just send her back, like you could me."

"Jada."

"It'd be a lot easier with me. The whole thing. You just call the caseworker. Sometimes they come right out, a couple hours, even, if it was real bad, if you wanted me out fast."

"Look, Jada, this isn't even the time for that. We've got to take care of other things first, your mother."

"No! I gotta know about me first. You don't fucking get it, do you? I'm all alone now. You know what that fucking feels like?"

"Yes, I do."

"No, you don't. No. I know you don't." Jada's mouth twitched as if to suppress a smile. "I know who killed that old lady."

"Who?"

"Let me with live with you, please."

"Tell me who, Jada. Please." Barely able to breathe, she eked out the words. "If it would help Gordon . . . oh, my God, that poor man, if you know something, please. I'll do anything, please, I promise, just tell me."

"I got proof."

"What kind of proof?"

"These." She held out two small statues.

"Hummels?" Her hands were slick on the wheel. Gordon had told her about Mrs. Jukas's collection.

"They're from her house."

"Who gave them to you?" she asked, then suddenly understood, saw it as clearly as if she were there watching it happen. "It was him, wasn't it? That guy Polie, the one on the porch. That's what he wanted. That's why he was so upset. No wonder you wouldn't go out, you must've been so scared. And your mother, he gave her those drugs, didn't he, the ones that—Oh, my God, no wonder he grabbed my phone. But it's over, Jada. All of it, from now on. You don't have to live like that anymore, with people letting you down and taking advantage of you."

Delores kept talking as she drove slowly, erratically, braking, accelerating, coming in right angles, as always, spiraling into the center, gradually, directly, but as unobtrusively as possible without alarming the wild-eyed girl, all the while telling her how good life was going to be from this moment on. She could have pets and friends and a nice place to live, and all she had to do was want it badly enough.

Jada seemed almost amused. "Yeah? Well, if it's that easy, then I should have the best life of anyone in this whole fucked-up world by now."

"It's not a fucked-up world." Delores eased around the corner. "Believe me, it's not." The car was still moving when Jada opened her door and jumped out. Delores slammed on the brakes. The police station was three buildings ahead.

"Liar!" she screamed, heaving one Hummel and then the other off the side of the car. "You fat, fucking liar, you!"

She got out, talking all the while she advanced on the frantic girl. "All right, so maybe I'm fat, but I'm not a liar. I'm not like everyone else in your life. And you know I'm not, right? Because I don't quit, I don't give up ever, on anyone."

Jada stood waiting, watching her come.

CHAPTER 27

L ast night's snow wouldn't last long. The noonday streets were gray with slush. Dennis was parked in front of the house, doors locked, motor running. Gordon had called earlier to say this was the only time Delores could take him driving. He might be late, so if Dennis wanted to cancel, that was fine, they'd meet again next week. Dennis said he'd wait. He looked out the window. He was committed to this, didn't want to break the streak. As long as he kept up his end, carried his share of the load, then maybe everything would be all right.

There was a new FOR SALE sign on Mrs. Jukas's lawn. They kept getting knocked down or taken. Kids, Gordon said. Covered with snow, the little house didn't look half-bad. Maybe someone would come along desperate enough to overlook what had happened there—and who lived next door. The tenement across the street was being fixed up, new windows and siding. The purple Navigator was gone. It had been five months since the driver was charged with Mrs. Jukas's murder and the dealer with being an accessory. He shook his head. Gordon had been lucky. This time, anyway. Next time there might not be a witness. And Kaminski had even admitted it, privately, of course: There'd always be some cop somewhere thinking he never should have been let out in the first place.

Delores's car pulled into the driveway, slowly, as if in two sections, the hood and then long tail end rising and sinking. He didn't know which irritated him more, the ridiculous berm or seeing Gordon behind the wheel of that junk. Delores hurried over to say she hoped he hadn't been waiting too long; some of the roads hadn't been very well plowed. Gordon was apologizing. The back door of Delores's car opened and a tall, skinny girl climbed out.

"We made it!" she cried as she pretended to stagger toward them. "All in one piece!"

"Dennis, this is Jada Fossum," Delores said. "And Jada, this is Dr. Loomis, Gordon's brother."

"Yeah, I seen you before." Her smile was alarming.

"But it's nice to meet him, isn't it?" Delores said.

Wincing, she held out her hand. Her fingernails were yellow and black, tiger-striped like Delores's. "Yeah, that's right. It is. Very nice to meet you. I'm sure," she added with that almost threatening grin.

Even the touch of her hand was unsettling. A child who'd never been a child, she knew too much and wanted it known, especially by men. "Very nice to meet you, too, Jada. I've heard a lot about you," he added to make something clear, though he couldn't have said what.

"Only good stuff, right?" The edge in her voice was as sharp as her stare.

"Of course." He smiled, then looked at Delores. "So how're the lessons going?"

"Pretty good," Jada answered. "Long as you got a couple hours." She laughed.

"It's not that bad, is it?" Gordon checked his watch.

"Actually, he's doing great." Delores patted Gordon's shoulder, a gesture Dennis found oddly repulsive. Those two big bodies, he thought, all that flesh, one against the other.

"Every time, he just gets better and better," she was saying.

"She says I'm too cautious." Gordon smiled at her.

Dennis dug his boot into the snowy rim of the sidewalk.

"Yeah, he's always riding the brake," the girl interjected, hands up, swaying from side to side. "Like, whoa, watch out! Any minute now we're gonna crash!"

"Jada." Delores touched her arm.

"Hey, I'm the backseat driver, right?" the girl said, but to Dennis, still trying to make him laugh.

"I don't think so," Delores said quietly.

Ignoring the girl, Dennis asked Delores how the dress shop was going. He knew she was either going to buy it or already had. Gordon was always so vague, it was hard to remember what he said, the little he did. Business was good, she said. She was bringing in a few new lines. Aiming for a younger, more hip clientele. *Jesus,* he thought with a glance at her red-velvet-and-fur bomber jacket. Her black-checked pants ended inches above her ankles. Lisa had come in the other day, she was saying. She'd bought a silk sweater for her mother, a birthday present.

"Hey, Thurm!" the girl shouted, then darted across the street toward a tall slouch of a boy shuffling by. Except for his orange knit cap, he was dressed in baggy black, hands deep in low-riding pockets. They stood on the corner. The girl's arms flew as she talked.

"Who's that?" Delores asked.

"Thurman Dominguez," Gordon said, staring. It was a look Dennis hadn't seen before, menacing and cold.

"Jada!" Delores called. She waited a minute, then called again to say they had to go. Ignoring her, the girl bounced with excitement and kept talking.

"Now what do I do?" Delores said under her breath.

"Get in the car," Gordon said.

"I can't just leave her."

"She'll come."

She opened the door and the girl ran across the street and climbed in beside her.

They were led to the back booth of the bright little restaurant. As soon as they sat down, Gordon began to study the menu. Dennis asked if he was in that much of a rush.

"I'm sorry." Gordon closed the menu. "I just wanted to see what they have. I really like Italian food."

Maybe he liked it too much, Dennis said, laughing.

"I know." Gordon patted his belly. "I've gotta do something about this."

They talked for a few minutes about dieting. Dennis suggested he sign up at a gym. There was a Gold's Gym near the plant. "It's within walking distance. You could go after work, you know, an hour or so. Lift a little, put a couple miles in on the treadmill. Maybe even go early, before work. That's really the best time. I don't even think straight in the morning unless I've run a couple miles. . . ."

He has that look again, Dennis thought, *that childlike courtesy. I can talk myself hoarse and those flat eyes just keep on looking at me. That big, implacable face, never disagreeing, for fear of what, an argument? A stir in the air? The energy it might take?* These Saturday lunches were far more effort than they were worth. And boring as hell. Thankfully, today's would have to be short. The receptionist was coming in for a while this afternoon to go over the new phone system. She was attracted to him. He could tell. Nothing like Jilly, of course. This one was older and married with a couple kids, two in college, not the type to have any illusions. No desperate need for a family. If anything, just the opposite: her husband bullied her, and the older son had what sounded like one hell of a drug problem. He had missed Jilly terribly at first, still did in a way, though the therapist said what he really missed was the excitement of being with someone who barely knew him, someone he could be a good person for, a confidante, someone he could help without being permanently committed to.

"Same with Lisa," he added quickly, brightly, to bring himself around. "She's running five miles a day now."

"How's she doing?" Gordon asked.

"Good. She's deep into Father Hank's youth thing, the new center, so she's happy. Well, busy, anyway."

Gordon seemed about to say something, but just then the waitress brought their meals. He ate with a fixed intensity Dennis could not watch. There was so much his brother needed. *It's more than food. Poor bastard, he's never gotten any breaks, just the short end of the stick. Second best, far behind, it's the only way he's ever known.* "Hey, Gord. Something's been bothering the hell outta me ever since that night at the house—the police, and what I said. I'm sorry. I was way outta line."

Gordon looked up, surprised and still chewing. "No. You weren't.

You weren't at all. Of course you'd think that." He gave that imploring little shrug. "Who wouldn't?"

Anger flashed through Dennis at once again having his feelings, his efforts, so trivialized. There was no getting through the thickness. Ever. "And that's okay? That's all right?"

"I didn't say that."

"No, but that's the way it is."

Gordon pushed back his plate. "Why do we keep doing this?" He spoke urgently, yet so softly that Dennis had to lean over the table to hear him. "What's the point? You always end up mad at me. It can't be very pleasant for you. So why bother?"

"Because we're brothers!" Truly it was that simple, but for some reason that was the part Gordon least understood. They stared at each other a moment. "Jesus Christ," Dennis said, shaking his head. "You really think this is a bother? Seeing you once a week? Calling you, checking to see how things're going? See if you need anything? Or maybe it's a bother to you. Maybe that's it." Yes. That's exactly what it was.

"Of course not. It's not a bother. I like to hear from you." Gordon paused. "I enjoy your company," he said so stiltedly, so formally and falsely earnest, that Dennis felt as if he'd just been punched in the chest.

For the first time he felt the vastness of the chasm between them. "No, you don't. You never call. You're not the least bit interested in me or my kids. There's no feeling there. There never was. Even as a kid you were like that. You never got it. You still don't. I mean, who've you got in your life if you don't have family? Delores? That, that trampy kid, that what's-her-name?"

"Jada."

"Yeah, and what the hell's she doing in a car with you? Are you nuts? Someone like that? She's a lost cause, a quick trip to disaster! Jesus Christ, don't you ever think things through? All right, so Delores is a flake, she's a little light on top, but that doesn't mean you—"

Gordon seized his wrist, squeezing so hard that it stung. "Shut up! Shut up, Dennis. For once, just shut up and listen."

All the while his brother talked, Dennis smiled thinly, because it was all he knew to do, keep his chin up and smile, hang tough through the hard times, the grimness, the shame and helplessness.

"Leave Delores out of this. She's a good person. She deserves better than me and Jada Fossum and everyone else she tries to help, but the thing is with Delores, she doesn't know that. She thinks she's lucky that people like us need her. She thinks that's what life is all about. She really believes that, that people can be better. Me! And a kid like Jada, that we can be just like everybody else. You know? She does. She really does," he added with a rueful chuckle.

"Same as me, Gordo." His voice cracked. He rapped on the table a few times, then continued. "That's all I'm trying to do, give you a fighting chance here, that's all."

Gordon looked down, then finally back, struggling to meet Dennis's gaze. "Then trust me. Please?"

It was a raw, windy day, spring now after the long, stormy winter. The little stone house they passed was not a house at all, he realized when he saw the wide double doors in back. It was the repository where caskets were stored when the frozen ground couldn't be dug. Their footsteps over the crushed white stone seemed all the noise on earth as he followed her down the hill. She knew exactly where it was, she said, clutching the gold-foiled pot of red and yellow tulips. There, there it is, she called with orange pollen on her chin.

Her grave was on the lower slope, in the shade of a tall tree just beginning to leaf. There were two dates under Janine Walters's name, under the baby's only one. The stone of polished gray granite was smaller than he had expected. Modest, like those around it, no hint of the violence, no image or engraved lament of the terrible wrong that had been done. *There should be something,* he thought, looking around, *something more than this.* What, though? Why did it bother him so? What awful arrogance had made him assume she in any way belonged to him? Life was commemorated here. And at least in this she had communion with all these others, he thought, not with relief or solace, but with a painful, humbling submission.